4/10/91

To Jim Robinson

Hoping that you enjoy it.

Jim Ernst

Coincidence

Jim Ernst

VANTAGE PRESS
New York

To Anna Mae—
the love of my life for thirty-seven years

Webster's New Collegiate Dictionary (1961) states as follows:

coincidence . . . 1. Condition, fact, or instance of coinciding; correspondence. 2. A group of concurrent events or circumstances, or one of them, remarkable from lack of apparent causal connection.

What happens when fate decrees that a continuing series of connecting happenings occur, so far out of proportion as to boggle the mind, and make one ask, "What the hell is happening in my life? Have I offended God in some way? Am I being punished?"

If you were Mike Burke, you are ready to bet that you are. . . . But why?

CONTENTS

PROLOGUE

The weather seemed unable to decide if it really was in the last stages of fall or if it was letting us in on a touch of early winter. Rain, almost icy in consistency, pelted the windshield, and the wipers performed dutifully in steady monotony with a cadence that seemed to match the pulse that beat in his temple.

Only a few more minutes and the area known to the local residents of this small upstate town on Route 304 as "New Car Alley" came into view. He thought that it seemed funny and not at all correct to call it an alley since most of the dealerships were on the right-hand side of the road. Set back quite a bit from this main thoroughfare, on the left side of the road, were many homes, most of them built within the last ten years. They were interspersed among many older homes which had been refurbished to much of their former grandeur.

A quick glance at the expensive digital watch, and a confirming glance at the digital on the dash: both of them indicated 5:15 P.M. on Sunday two days after Halloween. It would seem that the very hot summer, which provided much of the East coast with record temperature days that exceeded ninety degrees, was starting to be paid for by a bone-chilling late fall and an early winter. This was the order of nature, to provide a balance for another year by maintaining the mean temperature the same as it has been for the past fifty years.

Turning to the right to the far end of the street and parking to the left just behind a large metal shed, he reached his destination. Time to get to work, he mused; and although he disliked his work with a passion of utter disgust, he was after all a professional. He knew he was the very best that money could buy. He had long since reasoned to himself that it was only a job, and that somebody had to do it, so why not him. But deep inside the human instincts boiled at his ever active brain that wouldn't allow him to get more than a few hours' total sleep each night. As such, the disgust he felt had to share itself within him with the pride that he took in the meticulous planning and perfection he put into every operation he would take on as an assignment.

As anticipated, the dogs, two mean, lean, and angry Dobermans, were already loose on the property, having been set free of their chains within the confines of the fenced area. They sure as heck were there to give anyone a wet feeling around their anus with their ferocious white teeth, and a growl that preceded their bark, just prior to their lunging for the jugular of anyone who even came close to the fence. They banged against it hard, trying to get at you through the heavy duty chain link fence that towered over the entire perimeter of the luxury automobile dealership. He had prepared for this night well in advance by arriving each evening at exactly the same time. Now, once again after slipping the black hood over his head, he put on the heavy duty black latex gloves. Slipping out of the car, whose light switch was adjusted so that the inside lights would not go on whenever the door was opened, he approached the fence where the dogs had met him with a barking frenzy for ten nights in a row. Just about everyone in the neighborhood had heard and felt that the excitement and noise created by the dogs, which then quickly died down, was just one of the quirks that these dogs had developed over time.

He slipped his "dog goodies" in between one of the diamond-shaped openings in the fence—just two large pieces of beef that had been laced with enough knockout tranquilizers to keep these two black beauties of terror out for an estimated one- to one-and-one-half hours. This should be more than enough time for him to finish his task. And if they woke up a little early, he was prepared to handle that situation as well. They took the bait (one would think that they had become addicted to the same dosage for ten straight nights) and were rendered unconscious just as they finished swallowing the measured piece of beef.

He took the ten-foot high fence in stride and laid a black leather two-foot wide towel over the barbed wire at the top. He slid over the top and pulled the leather with him to the ground, so that the piece of black leather would not stand out against the background of the twilight night. The most time-consuming part of this operation was the locating of the car. This was the one that he had identified as belonging to the target when he visited the manufacturing plant in Michigan and after reading the manifest of the cars to be delivered to this particular dealership. Once delivery was made he knew that the car had to be made ready by cleaning and prepping it prior to customer pickup. The car prep operation had to be stopped until his activity had been completed, as he could not take any chances that the new owner would pick up his car. This was an extremely large dealership, and thirty-six new cars had been shipped in on Friday.

It was now Monday evening and two of the three people who prepped the cars had all fallen ill after eating a pizza during lunch hour. These three guys had always ordered a pizza from the local Domino's every first workday of the week. The owner was pissed because not one single car had finished being prepped when two of the men started to have the runs and severe stomach cramps at about 1:15 in the afternoon. The dealership owner had only one option left to him. He started calling his customers to advise them that their new cars would not be ready for them to pick up until sometime later in the week. He got a few irate remarks from the customers, but for the most part everyone understood the problem.

Earlier research done by him had identified that a similar stomach and bowel disorder had started about four months back. The result had devasted the dealership's entire operation over a three-day period. At that time, the doctor who ended up treating most of the employees and the owner had advised him the best way to stop a virus from passing from one employee to another was to immediately separate the employees in close contact with each other. As he had planned in the event his crew would ever start to show the same signs of a flu-type illness, the owner decreed that everyone had to go home for the rest of the day. The last auto prep specialist and the rest of the crew of five mechanics would not be allowed to be exposed to the "twenty-four-hour virus." The owner and his son stayed on for the rest of the day, feeling somewhat assured that by tomorrow they would have everyone back at work. Besides, they closed at 4:30 P.M. on Mondays anyway. The owner had chuckled to himself that this gratuitous giving of time off to his employees didn't cost him a cent, since there were only two cars in the shop for repair, mostly because of the weather, and now he could get a few of his mechanics in on Saturday at straight time for three hours while he billed his customers for overtime work.

He thought to himself, No one even suspected the pizza as the cause of the problem because only two of the three prep specialists got sick. It was simply the chemical sprinkled over the top of the pizza in combination with the chemical in only two of the three containers of soda. Just another of the planning touches that brought perfection to the operation . . . just like in every previous operation that had been accepted by the "Specialist-Assassin," who also is most times called by his trade name "THOR."

In about fifteen minutes he located the car. It was already in the prep area and, from the looks of it, another two hours was all that was needed to get it ready for delivery. Apparently it was one of the first to be put through the makeready process. He carried everything he needed attached to his utility belt. It took him another thirty minutes, first working under the hood, then under the front of the car, then inside the car in the front seat, and back under the hood to finish up and slam the hood shut. He checked the area to be sure that he left no telltale sign and retreated out the open window that he entered, pulling it closed behind him. He carefully walked only on the stone outside the window to the cement walkway and made his way to the point of entry at the fence.

The dogs were still out, but they were stirring a bit since they would come out of their induced sleep earlier each day as their bodies became more used to the drug. But, he thought, it was still well within his planned safety factor.

Again he scaled the fence and used the leather towel to protect himself from the tearing effect of barbed wire. He remembered back when it had ripped his both arms their full length and he almost bled to death. He shuddered and thought about that time in the past. "Never again," he muttered to himself.

He had to wait another half-hour for the dogs to regain consciousness and just start to growl a bit before he could leave the scene. He remembered waiting for the same thing to happen each and every one of the ten earlier nights he had gone through this ritual. But his car was safely out of sight of the road and hidden behind the shed. At the car he stripped the mask and the latex gloves off and placed them into the trunk. The light was also rigged in the trunk not to go on when opened. He backed out from behind the shed, put it into forward gear, and pulled down the street. As he moved away from the shed, he was greeted by the glaring revolving lights on top of the police squad car and an officer of the law pointing to him to move the car to the side and to get out of his car.

"What the hell do you think you were doing back there, buster?" questioned the police officer.

"Sorry, officer, but I just had to take a leak, and I didn't think I should take one out there in the open. So I turned in down this road where it was dark and took care of my problem. I just flew into La Guardia about three hours ago, and I'm on my way to this hotel in Spring Valley to meet with my boss tomorrow morning early. This is a rented car. I'm not familiar with the area, nothing seemed open, and I did not feel I could wait until I got to my hotel."

The officer checked his driver's license, reviewed the Hertz rental contract and told him to get the hell out of there.

"Can't you hear the noise those dogs are making back there because you went and disturbed them? Next time you got to take a leak, do it in another town," he said with a grin as he handed him back his driver's license and the rental agreement.

By now the dogs had quieted down somewhat. He drove off as any normal law-abiding citizen would . . . albeit with a smirk of satisfaction on his face. He had his canned story down pat, just in case he was stopped. And if the cop had pressed him further . . . the poor bugger didn't know how close he had just come to being another one of those officers killed on the job and in the line of duty. But that never came to pass and, he thought, just as well.

Another job well done, or should I say well started, he thought to himself. All he had to do was wait. Everything had been all figured out. So what else was new?

BOOK 1

CHAPTER 1

It was 11:00 A.M. on Friday, the day before what most people felt was the big Memorial Day weekend. Because the holiday fell on Monday, the top brass in Personnel were giving everyone a two-plus hour jump into the weekend. Instead of having to work until the usual 4:45, this work day was to end at 2:30. Of course, that was if your work load was kept up to date. Mike was swamped, but he just had to get out of there as soon as he could. He was really up-tight. No way could he be up to date after being back only ten days since his three-month stay in the hospital and another two months recuperating at home with his daughter hovering over him like a mother hen; he was not back to his old self. His body was weary even though he had been building up his stamina each night by power walking for an hour in the morning and then again at night. More importantly he felt that his mind just refused to function with any measure of deliberation. The accident that put him into the hospital, with only the narrow miss on taking his life, kept coming back into focus over and over.

Why? Why? Why? Why didn't my life end in the same way as death took Kathleen? He was told she never felt a thing. But this tragic accident was sure playing havoc with his life. Very happily married for twenty-four years to his childhood sweetheart; three children, twin boys and a beautiful daughter; and the whole thing went up in smoke when a truck broadsided the damn little car after the driver never even stopped for the light. The miserable drunk SOB didn't get as much as a scratch. Knowing he was sentenced to ten years in jail was no consolation at all for the devastation he had caused the family. And then, that god-damned little car. Why did the big car have to break down and have to be put in the shop? He never used that little shit of a foreign car for anything other than to get him to and from the

9

train station. He drove it down to New York City to take in a show only this once.

He tried to focus on the piles of work which had accumulated on his desk, but his mind kept drifting back again and again to that one miserable night. He said out loud to himself, "I've got to shake this thing and get on with my life. Kathleen would want me to." It didn't help. Bob Jacobsen just then popped his head into the office.

"Hey Mike, Sally would kill me if I didn't get to see you today. Are you going to make it to our house tonight with the rest of the gang when we kick off the start of the season for another year?

"Look, I know that it can't be easy on you to face a party without her, but you know that you've got to start living your life again. The pain just is not going to go away for a long time, no matter what you do. So why not at least drop in for a drink, say hello to the gang, and then just bug out whenever you feel like it."

"Bob, I'll really give it some thought, but don't count on me. Okay! I really mean it. You know I don't have a damn thing to do, and I really appreciate the offer. But just in case I don't make it, give my best to Sally. I'll try and make the next one."

Bob shrugged, and then ducked back out of Mike's office. Mike and Kathleen had been to many of Bob and Sally's parties in the past. Bob headed up the Data Processing Department of the company and was forced to spend so much of his life on the job that he and Sally just jumped at any opportunity to throw a party. Mike thought it must cost Bob a bundle each time, as nobody was ever asked to bring anything but themselves. Most people brought along a bottle of what they liked to drink anyway.

They were really good sports, the Jacobsens, and he and Kathleen had reciprocated their hospitality many times with dinner back in their home. They were the best friends they had, and Bob had taken care of the burial arrangements for Kathleen while Mike was in the hospital. Bob also took care of tracking down and notifying the two boys. And then he brought the doctor in to sedate Jennifer after he had the unpleasant task of telling her that her mother was killed in the crash and that her father's life was hanging on by a thread. Yes, he was a real good friend who seemed pained when Mike gave him the very soft "maybe."

10

Mike looked at his watch and it was fast approaching 2:00 P.M. His assistant, George With, had done a great job in keeping the Investigation Department for the Hinton Amalgamated Group, Limited, a not-so-small casualty insurance company with its home office in Brighton, England, smoothly running while Mike was out for the previous twenty-two weeks. His current and most pressing chore now was that he had to review all the cases that were closed by George during his absence and prepare a summary of the savings versus cost his department had produced during the last six months. He had to make a presentation to the head office honcho who was coming to town on Wednesday of next week. And to compound the problem, this presentation was the basis for approving the rather large budget additions that he was asking for in the next year to set up the new special department.

George came into the office and told Mike that since he had not been sure if Mike would be able to return to work in time, he had gone ahead and prepared the summary and presentation material. All Mike had to do was to brief himself on what George had pulled together, and he was as ready as he could be. Mike jumped up from behind his desk, came around to the front of the desk where George was starting to back away when he saw Mike charging at him, and he grabbed George in a friendly bear hug.

"Thanks, you're one hell of a backup and a real good buddy," Mike said. He immediately began to throw his stacks of paper into the file cabinet, not gracefully at all, and breathed a sigh of relief. "I don't know what I would have done without you. I'm getting the hell out of here now, and not midnight, thanks to you. Why don't you pack it in yourself and get a good start on the weekend."

"Sure. I'll see you at the party tonight, won't I?" replied George.

"Yeah, you bet." Then he thought what an asshole he had just made of himself. Now he really better show up for the party after all. The least he could do was have a drink with George and "what's her name." Oh, well!

It was just 2:30 P.M. when he got out of the elevator and headed for the revolving doors. He thought he could probably make the 3:15 out of Hoboken if he didn't get hung up at PATH.

11

He started with a hustling walk towards the World Trade Center where he caught the "tubes" to go to the New Jersey train station. Funny, he thought, I still call the commuter underground by that damned name. He didn't even know where he picked it up from, but it did seem to fit.

At the entrance to PATH he went down the long escalator, still wondering why everyone who was in such a hurry in the Big Apple didn't run down the escalator to save some more time. He looked at his watch again. It had taken him twelve minutes to walk to the WTC; and if he could get on the 2:45 PATH (the trains left every fifteen minutes), he should be able to make his commuter train. I'll be damned, he thought as he just got into the car before the doors closed, no newspaper; but I can always get one in Hoboken; should be enough time.

As the PATH train pulled into Hoboken, he had exactly two minutes to get on board the 3:15. The train had creaked and moaned every step of the way, and the usual fifteen-minute ride had taken twenty-three of his precious minutes. He was first out of the car and immediately inhaled the sour smell of dampness that lingered all the time at this station. What a terrible smell, he thought, how tough it must be on the people who have to work here all the time. Maybe they get used to it and don't even notice it anymore.

He saw that the previous train that had unloaded passengers still had the doors open on both sides. He really thought that he could make up a few steps by shortcutting through the empty car, and made it through the first opening of the doors, but just as he was about to go through the other side, the doors closed in front of him. He had no alternative but to cut back through the doorway that he had just entered, and then to make his way to the proper train platform. He got to his platform, without his newspaper of course, just in time to see his early train start to roll out of the station. It apparently had filled up early due to the holiday, and would you believe, it actually left one minute early.

At this point Mike burst out laughing, while everyone around thought he was nuts. He mentally cussed himself out for being such a stupid shit, and vowed to himself not to get too serious about anything as silly as missing a train. It just wasn't worth it. He also realized that this was the first time he had laughed in so long, even if it was at himself, that he felt he must be on the way back to living his life again. So he walked back to the newsstand, picked up the evening edition a bit early, found out that all the final stock closings were not in it yet, and looked at the headline. It seemed that a "Special Prosecutor" was really getting into the ways of the Mob and some indictments were expected early next week. Wouldn't want to be in his shoes, he thought. Those guys play rough, and they were not about to just sit back and let their dirty business go down the drain. Well, good luck to him. As the cliche says, "Somebody has to do it." Better him than me, he thought.

He got onto the next train that was scheduled to leave at 4:00 P.M. and settled down in the bar car. The bar car was also a smoking car and he wondered if the smoke would bother him. Why not, it was the only way that he could get a drink on the train. He picked up a beer and a plastic glass from the porter at the entrance to the car and settled down deep into his newspaper. The car was filled with a very boisterous crowd, getting into the swing of the weekend, along with the usual assortment of bridge and pinochle players.

Just across from him sat the most attractive blond that he had seen in a long time. To him she looked a lot like Marilyn Monroe, and he sure liked that type of female. He felt a little quivering in his loins, and chuckled to himself as he tried to think of the last time he made love to Kathleen. And then that morbid feeling grabbed at him again, so he tried to shake the feeling out of his mind and took a big gulp of beer.

He then fantasized how he could break the ice and start up a discussion with the good-looking chick. He noticed a wedding band on her finger, but what the heck? He only wanted to talk to someone, and he knew that he needed some intelligent female conversation, if only to not let his mind wander back to that terrible event. He started reading his paper in earnest, and then his mind wandered again to the early days when he met Kathleen.

He was only fifteen when he noticed that his best friend, the girl that lived next door to him in the quiet Ohio town known as "Best Days," was a girl. He was playing catch with her one day when he threw the ball too fast and hit her in the chest. The ball had knocked her down when it hit her and he rushed over to her,

13

saw where she was hurting, and then started rubbing her chest. The only problem was that it wasn't a chest he was rubbing, but a breast. It only dawned on him after he stopped that it was a bit softer then he thought it should be; maybe, he thought, it had started to swell after being hit by the ball.

As she picked herself up she laughed in her usual funny way, as she could see the embarrassment rising on his brightly glowing face; it was getting very, very red indeed. She also noticed the growing bulge in his pants, and she said, "Leave me alone, I'm okay now. It was just an accident and I should have caught the darn ball and not be such a sissy and miss it. And by the way, I'm glad that it took this little freak accident to get you to at least make an attempt to touch my breast. You know, we may be the best of friends, but after all, I'm a year older than you and if you don't know that I've got the hots for you then you're just a little kid. I don't know how long I was supposed to wait around for you to notice me."

"I'm sorry," he said, "but my dad talked to me about sex when he caught me leering at you. He cautioned me about what I'm not allowed to do until I grow up some more. Damn it, I want you so bad, and I didn't know if I could ever talk to you about it. I think I love you, and the problem is I'm not even sure what love really is."

And this was the start of the most beautiful thing in their entire lives. They saw even more of each other and had some very intimate moments while they were growing up. Nothing ever had to be said between them, they just knew they would marry someday. In time they both attended Pennsylvania State University, and they were married. They had both of their families' blessing to do so during the summer break after she was in school for three years and he had just finished his sophomore year.

And so Michael Burke married Kathleen Hanna O'Rourke in a grand wedding held in "Best Days" during June, and she bore him a set of twin boys nine months later on March 30. It happened to be his birthday, too. The boys, as expected with their Irish heritage, were named Sean Peter and Thomas Henry. They weighed an even seven pounds each. Lo and behold, Kathleen also bore him a daughter exactly one year to the day later, and she also weighed seven pounds. At the time everybody thought and said, "What a coincidence!" Little did they know. They named their daughter Jennifer Theresa. The five of them lived sometimes from hand to mouth for the next year until Kathleen finally graduated and was able to get a full-time job in the university library. Of course they had a little help from the family to make ends meet.

But then Mike's mother passed away suddenly from pneumonia, and only two weeks later Mike's father died from complications caused by injuries from an earlier accident. This particular accident had left him with a broken left arm, a compound fracture of the right leg that resulted in his walking with a limp, and internal injuries with broken ribs puncturing one of his lungs.

Yes, there was a lot wrong physically with his father, but Mike knew that he had lost his will to live after losing his wife. He was only forty-one years old, and they had a great loving life together, at least for the part of his life that Mike was around to see. After his mom's funeral his father told him about the family's finances. He also told him the story about how he was hurt before they moved to Ohio, and a real surprise story about how he got his name. Mike found out that he wasn't pure Irish at all, but that his father was Jewish. Kathleen and Mike discussed what they should do. They decided to sell his family's house back in Ohio and buy a small house off campus while Mike went to graduate school for a masters in investigative studies. This was after he had graduated cum laude with a bachelor's in business administration. The O'Rourke family was pretty much upset with this decision. Mike was thinking about going on for a doctorate, another three years of study, when the offer came in to become an investigator for a premier insurance company in New York City. They both thought it to be a chance of a lifetime.

He then took his exam in New York State and became a licensed private investigator. He even had a gun, a .38 caliber revolver, with which he became an excellent shot at the target practice range. But he never carried or used it after he had qualified. He chose to stick it in a locked drawer so that the children could not get at it. Besides, he really didn't need a gun while tracking down mostly white-collar fraud.

When they first came to New York City, they moved into a

three-bedroom third-floor walk-up in Queens in a not-so-nice neighborhood. It was not the best place to raise children, but the boys, now nine going on ten, became pretty tough in this neighborhood, as they had to be.

Kathleen and Mike had their dream come true when they purchased a previously owned home in the upstate New York community of New City. They stayed in their first house only three years, before having their custom dream home built to their specifications. They now could easily afford the new home as Mike was advancing rapidly at work, and had gone the route of Supervisor, Assistant Manager, Manager, and finally to Director and Head of the Investigation Department. His salary was fast approaching six figures, when the tragedy of a lifetime was sprung upon him.

The train lurched as it started up and pulled out of the station. He heard a soft voice ask him for a match, and he looked up to see a pair of beautiful blue eyes. He had stopped smoking as a result of the accident and had no intention of ever starting up that miserable habit again. He set his beer on the floor, instinctively reached into the pocket of his jacket, and was surprised when he found a book of matches that he had been carrying before the accident.

He remarked, "Left over from the old days," as he struck the match and held up the light to her cigarette.

She puffed to get it lit, inhaled deeply, let the smoke out of her mouth and her nose slowly, and said, "Thanks."

Fate, he thought, as she said, "I'm Martha Grant. I don't remember ever seeing you on this train before."

He told her his name and went on to relate the events that led up to him catching this train.

They had a laugh over it, and continued with a lot of small talk for about another thirty-five minutes, when the conductor called out "Nanuet," the station nearest to his home. During their discussion, he found out that she worked as a schoolteacher in one of the best high schools in New York City. It was not a problem school, as many city schools were. This one had high academic standards. He told her his name and when she asked if he was married, he told her he was a widower and did not elaborate any further. They found out that they each liked to have a single martini to start off each weekend, and a lot of other little things.

He got off the train after saying that he had really enjoyed the conversation and that he hoped to meet her again sometime. She smiled at him when he left the train. That was a nice chance meeting. It felt good. He thought to himself, What a coincidence. What if I never missed that early train? The train departed the station bound for its next stop.

"Only one more stop to go until the end of the line for that train," he said out loud to himself, while many people stared at him to see whom he was talking to. "She can't live too far away. Maybe I will see her again."

CHAPTER 2

While Mike looked around the train station for Jennifer who would pick him up he only then realized that he never called her to tell her that he was going to catch an early train. It's a good thing that he did not make the call, as he never did make the 3:15 and was only able to get on the 4:15 which put him in Nanuet at 5:10. So here he was fifty minutes early; then he heard the familiar voice of his daughter. He looked in the direction of the call and there was Jennifer, her red hair blowing a bit in a light breeze.

"I thought that you may get home a little early because of the holiday. So I took a chance and came to the station. How's that for hitting it on the head," she said.

It was just what her mother would have done. She had the same instincts and vibes about things like this, and he had always thought that Kathleen could read his mind. Now he was sure that Jennifer had picked up the same trait. Jennifer was almost twenty-three and was finishing up her master's degree in education. She had dropped out of her full-time job to return to school, after saving up her money. Boy, was she a tightwad with a buck. She had an agreement with her sweetheart, Charlie. She was going to concentrate on this last leg of her studies while he spent a year in the Peace Corps. He had rationalized giving back to life something of what had been given to him. Mike thought he was a wee bit wacky, and he told them both so before Charlie left. They told him they had both discussed it in depth, and she felt as he did and thought that the sacrifice of the year separation was something that had to be done. Their love was seemingly only interrupted by time and space, and had grown deeper. At least that's what she told Mike the last time they had a discussion on the subject.

"Got another letter from Charlie today," she said in her usu-

18

al bubbly manner. "He is coming home from Uganda on July 13, and damned if he still doesn't want to marry me. We've set the date of the wedding for October 17."

She thought that he wasn't paying any attention to her chatter, so she said, "Do you think he wants to marry me only to get into my pants? At least that's what he said in his previous letter."

She paused for effect and said, "Dad, am I going to have a sex maniac on my hands when he gets home? At least I sure hope so."

And then she put on her cute tricky smile.

"Well, I think you can count on it," he said. "So make the best of it while you're young, but don't be too foolish now, you hear. You hot-blooded kids got to get your rocks off someway, but you had better be careful."

She blushed, as she didn't expect him to reply to her in that matter-of-fact way. She was counting on his being shocked by her boldness. That will teach her, he thought. They both giggled, and that was the end of that conversation. Dad 1, Daughter 0. He never won too many with her, and he knew he could gloat about this one.

She turned into the driveway of their two-story colonial home and let him out at the driveway to get the mail, while she parked her car in the garage. He looked up the driveway and saw his late model Buick LeSabre Limited in the garage. Well, tonight he will be using the big buggy again to go to the party. He had not driven a car at all during his long rehabilitation, but tonight's the night. He thought of another old cliche that seemed appropriate to his thoughts: "Today is the first day of the rest of your life." Yes! That sure was appropriate, he mused.

He put on his walking shoes and his lightweight jogging outfit and took off for his usual evening walk. He told Jennifer that he would be back in about an hour to eat the terrific smelling supper that she was preparing. Her good cooking and tender loving care were some of the reasons that his recuperation had gone so well. But now he knew that he only had her to complain to about all her mothering for only a few more short months. Gad, how lonely he was going to be without anyone around the house, he thought.

While on the walk, which was now up to three and a half miles in fifty-five minutes, he started to think about the wedding that he was going to give for Jennifer and Charlie. He was going to make it the best that everyone would remember. After all, that's what Kathleen would have wanted for her only daughter. Damn it, he thought, I'm doing this for me, I want to do it, not just because Kathleen would have wanted it. He came back after only three miles, because he really pressed it and did it in forty-one minutes. He was really tired. He showered, came down to dinner in his dressing robe, and promptly ate like there was no tomorrow. There was certainly nothing wrong with his appetite. Now he was ready to make his excuses about being too tired to go out this evening when Jennifer told him that the female members of the bridal party were coming over at 8:30 P.M. She told her dear old dad to quit his bellyaching and to get lost for the evening while they made a lot of girl talk. Once again this brat of a child had read his mind. Once again she had preempted an excuse. So he would be going to the party at the Jacobsens' after all.

He got dressed in his light blue slacks, striped long-sleeved sport shirt, and dark blue blazer. He put on the same old black shoes, because he was going to be comfortable if he had to stand around most of the night making words with everyone who felt sorry for him.

Oh well, he had to get this over with sometime, and tonight was as good as any. When he went downstairs, Jennifer gave him the once-over and her stamp of approval with a big kiss. She also gave him a reminder that he was just getting back into the groove and not to push it. Boy, she really was a mother hen; he wondered if Charlie knew what he was getting himself into.

He went into the garage, pressed the automatic garage door opener, and sat in the driver's seat. He started the car without any problem, and then made a mental note to thank his neighbor who took the time to take the Buick to his gas station where he had his mechanic give it a tune-up. It had been put into the garage by his son who had picked it up from the Buick service department while he was in the hospital.

Mike went down through town, and then followed Route 304 into New Jersey. The digital clock, still working after all this time that the car was idle, indicated 8:35. As he pulled onto Kinderkamack Road with its many stop lights and twists and turns, he paced himself to be able to get to the Jacobsens' house no earlier than 9:00 P.M. He hit it on the button and had to park seven houses away. Bob Jacobson had found a way to weather the storm of protests by the neighbors about all the noise and disturbance that a party would cause. He simply invited the entire neighborhood, and most of them always came. He gave good parties.

The party was already humming with about seventy-five people. No problem for Bob as he had finished another of his large basement game rooms. This was about the third one. He said he needed the therapy of hitting something, and that was why he liked finishing basements. This one was long with an *L* at the end and a built-in bar. A bartender who was hired by Bob was busy making drinks to order. Would you believe it? Mike had left his bottle of cream sherry that he knew Sally liked, back on the kitchen table at home. He felt like a cheapskate. Moving up to the bar he ordered a white wine and turned to look at the crowd to see if he saw anyone that he knew. He took a quick glance at the back of a blond wearing a dress cut low in the back, did a double take, and walked around to look at the front of her. She was standing with a mixed group of couples and when he recognized her he just started to leer in her direction.

She excused herself from her group and walked over to him. She was beautiful, and she was very shapely as well in the deep-cut dress. He thought she was gorgeous, not just a look-alike of Marilyn Monroe, but even more striking.

She said, "Hello again, Mike, it really is a small world after all, isn't it? Look, do me a favor and stop undressing me with your eyes, and I'll let you get me one of those martinis that we talked about. You know, the kind we both like to start the weekend."

He broke into the famous Mike Burke smile, didn't say a word, and retreated toward the bar to get her the drink. All the time he was thinking of the stupid schmuck that he had just made of himself. He got the drink, turned to give it to her, and found that they were now joined by another person.

"This is my husband, Steve Grant. Steve, this is the guy that I made a pass at on the train this afternoon that I told you about. His name is Mike Burke, and I can tell already that he likes me because I just caught him staring at me," and then she winked at them both.

They shook hands in a robust manner. Steve was a very good-looking guy, had wavy black hair, stood about six feet four, and was on the thin side.

I hate him already, Mike thought to himself.

"Do me a favor would you, Mike? I'm glad that Martha found someone that she knows here. I've got to make some political hay with a couple of guys that are here. You seem to be alone, so would you mind staying with my wife and introducing her to some people that you know? Thanks!"

Steve didn't even wait for Mike to reply, and Mike stood there positively stunned. This guy just gave his wife away to him on a silver platter. Not that he was not grateful, just very surprised. Martha immediately explained to Mike.

"Look, I better tell you what's going on here before you get the wrong idea. Steve and I were married during our first year in college. We had a great few early years together, we've got a nice house in Spring Valley. About two years ago we had a frank talk and we both agreed that there was no love left in our marriage. It happens, you know! We just grew apart over time and each of us got interested in different things. I've got my teaching, I play tennis three times a week and golf on the weekends. I like to ski and ice skate and swim and dance; I guess I'm what they call a 'jock,' or a 'jockess' or something. Oh yes, I've also got a plane and I have my pilot's license. Would you believe, I travel every chance that I get; one of the benefits of being a schoolteacher with lots of time off.

"Now Steve has got his job! He eats it, lives it, sleeps it, and dreams about it twenty-four hours a day. It has become his lover, as well as his best friend and confidant. He is not gay or bisexual, or anything like that. He is just so engrossed with his job that he has no time for anything else, which includes no time for me, not for sex or anything." A tear formed on the corner of her eye that she wiped away.

"So you see, Mike, we are only staying together until one of us decides to file for the divorce. Of course, it will be congenial and uncontested; we already decided to split things down the middle.

"You know, he really did give me away to you. He wants me to find someone special and to get on with my life. So tag, you're it; that is, if you want me for this evening."

Another tear formed and Mike handed her his handkerchief. Then he handed her the drink. They were just finishing up on this strange conversation when Bob and Sally spotted them. They both told him how glad they were that he could make it tonight, and introductions were made all around. George With and his Cuban wife, Nina, came into the group, and more introductions ensued. Thank God he finally remembered her name! She was a cute little thing, stood only about five-feet tall. She had a bright smile and, of course, a great tan. George and Nina went well together. They were in love for more than fifteen years, she had made him five daughters, and finished off their child making with a son.

A crowd was now forming around Steve, and he seemed to be becoming the center of attention. Martha volunteered that it always happened lately since he was getting all the publicity about sending members of the Mob away to do hard time. So he was the "Special Prosecutor" that Mike read about in the paper. Martha and Mike spent the rest of the evening sitting in the corner of the room telling about their pasts and their backgrounds.

He told her about his two redheaded twin boys, and his beautiful red-haired daughter, who was now making plans to marry. Thomas Henry was by far the brightest. He had an IQ of 198, and had accelerated and finished college at age 19 as a straight A student. He joined the Marines for three years and came out a captain. He was now a private investigator of sorts, but he never did tell his father exactly what he did. He had to make a lot of money though, as he drove around in a Jaguar. Now Sean Peter was more average. He worked hard and finished college at age twenty-two and immediately entered law school. He was now twenty-four and expected to take his bar exams around December.

Martha still had her father living, her mother died during childbirth, and her father had remarried. Martha was thirty-eight, never had a baby, never even became pregnant. She did tell him that she thought she would always love Steve, and she felt that Steve also loved her, in his own way. She had to feel that way just to keep her sanity. You can't live with someone for over nineteen years and not feel something for that person. But, she did insist that their marriage was over.

Steve sought them out and asked Martha if she was ready to

go home. It was 11:30 by Mike's watch. He was able to get Martha's telephone number before they parted company, with a hearty handshake between Steve and Mike. Mike thought to himself, What a stupid shit this guy is to give up on such a personable gal like Martha. He said his good-byes to the host and hostess along with a little small talk, said good-bye to some of his other friends from work and their wives, and headed out the door.

As Mike was getting into his car, he saw down the street that Steve and Martha were boxed in by another car and had to wait for the owner to move it. He tooted as he passed them by, they waved at him, and he headed for Kinderkamack Road. He was on the weaving, winding road about six miles from the New York State Line, when his Buick coughed, sputtered, and died. He was able to get it to coast to the side of the road with the help from the last sputter. He believed that it was a piece of dirt in the carburetor when he was unable to start the engine. This seemed like the same problem that had put the car in for servicing on that fateful day. Best to lock it up and get a tow truck tomorrow during the daytime hours. It may be a problem because of the holiday, but that's why he belonged to AAA. He went to the side of the road and stuck up his thumb for a lift when he first saw approaching headlights.

A Lincoln Town Car pulled over to the side of the road. He hopped in behind the driver's seat, looking up with a "thank you" on his lips, and saw a grinning Steve and Martha in the front seat. He gave them the sad tale about what happened, along with his diagnosis of the problem. He told Steve where he lived, and Steve replied, "No problem; it's on our way." They got to talking about big cars versus small cars. Mike was very emphatic about the need for safety as his major priority. Steve liked comfort, and explained that he did so much driving, what with going down to Washington every Sunday and not returning until about midnight on Tuesday. Then he also drove back and forth to New York City each day that he was not in D.C. That round trip added another seventy-eight miles a day.

"Now look at this," he said, "I just picked up this car on November 6 last year, and I'm going to crack ten thousand miles already."

Mike pulled himself up from the deep comfortable rear seat,

perched himself in the middle of the car, and peered over at the speedometer.

The number hit exactly ten thousand, at which time a violent explosion pushed the steering mechanism back towards the driver's head.

During Mike's last conscious moment, he saw Steve's head being separated from his body as the steering wheel acted as a guillotine. The car went out of control and headed directly toward a large maple tree. The tree brought the car to an abrupt stop. There was no movement from within the car.

Newspaper headlines in the early Saturday edition reported only sketchy details about the accident.

The afternoon edition carried the story as follows:

SPECIAL PROSECUTOR HIT PUT ON BY MOB

Special Prosecutor for the Justice Department Steve Grant met a violent death last night. An explosion coming from within the car decapitated him and mangled his body. This incident occurred just a week short of major indictments being made ready against top Mafia kingpins.

A break-in was reported at Grant's home in Spring Valley, NY, while his wife remains in guarded condition at General Hospital. It was further reported the burglary netted the intruders with working copies of the detailed evidence Mr. Grant had been accumulating over the last ten months.

A subsequent break-in was also reported at Grant's office in the Federal Building in Washington, D.C. Reports from a spokesman at this office indicate that the original copies of the evidence being stored there are also missing. "No indictments are forthcoming at this time" is the authorized report being issued by the Justice Department. Officials there have gathered for a high-level emergency meeting to discuss what to do, and to set a new course of action.

A passenger in the car, Mike Burke, an insurance executive working for the Hinton Amalgamated Group, Ltd., who is believed to be a longtime friend of the Grants, remains unconscious with a severe concussion and other internal injuries. Doctors have stated that he is expected to live, but were unable to project when he will regain consciousness.

Authorities are anxious to question Mr. Burke to see if he can supply them with any additional information. There are some early indications that this may be the work of the master assassin known by the name of THOR.

CHAPTER 3

It was four days that Mike remained unconscious and oblivious to everything around. He started to emerge from this blackness of mind when he realized he could hear voices nearby. He tried to open his eyes, tried to move any part of his body all to no avail. He didn't even know where he was, but his brain was alert enough to let him believe that he was still alive. The voices that he heard were not talking to him, but it seemed to be about him.

Dr. Aaron Roth had been the physician on this case since Mike Burke and Martha Grant were brought into General Hospital at exactly thirty-five minutes after midnight on Saturday morning of the Memorial Day weekend. When the ambulance arrived, Dr. Roth had already been on duty for twelve and a half hours and was forced to stay on duty until relieved. Working on a holiday weekend was nothing new to him. He had lost his wife of forty years to cancer, and working long and hard was his only way to try and forget. He was now sixty-six years old, and all the younger doctors were only too happy to have him fill in for them any time that he wanted. The administrative staff wanted him to retire, but he had convinced them to let him work until the end of the year. He had a reputation for being a very thorough doctor.

He examined the woman first. She was conscious and in a great deal of pain. She had a four-inch long laceration right in the middle of her forehead. There were many other superficial assorted bruises and contusions, none that he thought too serious. He made arrangements to have the resident on duty, a young Asian woman by the name of Dr. Ah Leh who had been on duty longer than he had in the past twenty-four hours, do the stitches on her face. He cautioned her about taking the time to make sure that she did not leave too much of a scar that could not be cleared up with a small amount of cosmetic surgery at a later date. Dr.

Ah Leh was well aware of how a scar could affect a person, having been the recipient of a bayonet slash across her right cheek when she and her family were on a boat getting out of Vietnam.

He then turned his attention to the man. He had been told by the ambulance driver that there had been a pulse, but that he had lost it during transit to the hospital. Because of this early prognosis he thought that the patient was DOA when they brought him in, and all he had to do was examine him and write out the Death Certificate. Mike was moved, not too gently, onto the examination table. The good doctor took his pulse and was unable to come up with one. He checked for the pulse at various points, always with the same results: nothing. One final check, and he rubbed his tired eyes to clear them; then he lifted Mike's eyelid and used the special instrument to peer deeply into the back of the patient's head. He could see activity in the eye cavity.

"This guy is still alive, but he is in such a deep state of unconsciousness that most of his vital signs are almost non-existent. He's got to have one hell of a concussion. Must have been very near to the point of the blast."

The police officer who arrived with the ambulance had briefed him as to a blast being the cause of the accident. Dr. Roth told the duty nurse who was assisting him to get twenty cc's of adrenaline, stat, and then reached for the syringe. In a single fluid motion he plunged it into Mike's heart and drove the fluid home. He put his stethoscope into Mike's heart once again, and breathed a sigh of relief when he was able to detect a heartbeat. He ordered X-rays and a full work-up on the patient, as he had done for the other patient. He told the nurse that he thought that there may be some other internal injuries that needed prompt attention. She was to alert him immediately when the test results were available. In the meantime, he said that he was going to sack out in the Doctors Lounge. When he left the Emergency Room on the way to the lounge, he had the strangest feeling that he knew this man whose life he had just saved. He got off the elevator, made a quick pass at the toilet just inside the door to the lounge to relieve himself, and entering into the doctors' quarters, fell exhausted onto the bed.

It seemed like only minutes of sleep had passed when the duty nurse shook him back to consciousness. It was now 4:15 A.M.

28

and she reported that the X rays indicated the patient had four broken ribs on the right side, and another one broken on the left side. However, his blood work-ups indicated no other internal bleeding. Dr. Johnson, Dr. Roth's backup, had come on board and was picking up all turnover activity.

Sensing that Dr. Roth knew the patient, the nurse related that he was identified as Mike Burke and he was holding his own. "Thanks to you and your experience, I might add," said the nurse as she pulled a lightweight cover over Dr. Roth. He couldn't fall off to sleep right away and he kept thinking, I know this man, but his name, that can't be right. He finally drifted off into a deep sleep.

Dr. Roth was talking to the head nurse on duty. Mike's ear picked up most of the words, but they were talking very softly, and about him. Dr. Roth was telling the nurse that the patient was lucky to be alive and that he was being spared the extreme pain of the five broken ribs because he remained in a state of unconsciousness. Funny, Mike thought, I can't feel any pain. But then he couldn't even move a finger or a toe. I must be unconscious, he thought, but then how can I hear them? He felt as if he had closed his eyes, but they were already closed. He mentally came to grips with the fact that he really was unconscious, at least in the part of his brain that controlled all body movement and function, but the thinking part of his subconscious brain was already starting to function. So he just lay there, feeling nothing and unable to move. From time to time he heard voices. They were familiar, at least most of them. And they were talking about him, but most of the time they were talking at him. They were saying things that were comforting and reassuring. One of them spoke to him so softly and tenderly, but he was unable to place who it was. His brain actually went to sleep at what seemed like regular intervals. In between these mentally conscious intervals, his brain activity roamed from one thing to another. It fastened onto his father talking to him shortly after his mother's death and the story that he was told in all of its exquisite detail. His mind focused on this story, and he reviewed it over and over in his semiconscious brain.

Mike's father's father and mother, Mike's grandparents, were born in Hamburg, Germany, both of fine old Jewish heritage.

Their names were Jacob and Sara Berkewitz. It was an arranged marriage as was normal in those times, but the two of them grew to love each other dearly. The elder Jacob made a good living by operating his own tailor shop. He was quite good at it. His son, Mike's father, was named Joseph, and he had dreams of becoming a doctor of medicine.

Hitler had just come into power and the family had saved enough money to send Joseph to college to pursue becoming a doctor. They took everything they had, even sold precious personal articles, and bought him a round-trip ticket to Ireland. At the last minute, the total wealth of his family was converted into gold and inserted in a money belt that was wrapped around Joseph's waist. Joseph, only eighteen years old at the time, made the trip over land and by boat during a four-day period. He was dead tired from carrying all that weight, plus a large cardboard valise with a big belt wrapped around it which contained all of his clothes. Arrangements were made to stay at the home of Meyer Rothstein, an old family friend who had immigrated to Ireland many years earlier. The details of these arrangements were that the gold was to be used to enroll Joseph and Mr. Rothstein's son Aaron, who was also eighteen and had just finished secondary school, into medical school. Joseph was to board in the Rothsteins' home while he pursued his medical studies. Meyer kept his part of the bargain. However, one day after receiving a letter from the homeland he asked Joseph to come into his parlor for a talk. He did all of the talking and was saddened deeply by what he had to tell Joseph.

"Your mother and father were executed by German soldiers when they were caught escaping from a train that was taking them to a concentration camp. You can, of course, live here and continue with your education. Your uncle, who just sent me this letter, advises that you should not plan to return to Germany. He feels that it will never be safe again for a Jew to walk the streets as a free man in his homeland. He said to tell you to find yourself another country to live in.

"He even suggests you go to America, after you complete your education." Again he warned, "Don't ever plan to return to Germany."

Joseph cried softly at the news. He retreated to his room to be alone with his thoughts, and came out the next morning vowing to make something of his life and planning to extend his Berkewitz bloodline for all time. It seems that he had been secretly seeing a beautiful redheaded Irish lass by the name of Margaret McGee. Everybody called her Maggie, and she was as full of life as anyone seventeen years of age, with her whole life before her. Even though Joseph was one of the brightest students at the college, Maggie's family discouraged her from seeing her Jewish boyfriend. Aaron and Joseph had become fast friends during the year that they were in school together. Joseph had given help to Aaron with his studies to get him past that first year, and Aaron looked upon him as a brother. When Joseph told Aaron that he had just gotten Maggie pregnant, they schemed about what to do. It was a shotgun wedding and Maggie's father had to be restrained from striking Joseph at least two times during the ceremony, which was hastily arranged and performed by the local parish priest. As a wedding present the family of the bride paid for two one-way steerage tickets on a steamer headed for New York Harbor. Hard to figure out how they got their visas, but it was wartime then, and with the excitement generated by the USA getting into the war, they made it to the United States without any trouble.

Aaron had gotten his father to release some of Joseph's funds, which amounted to only about a hundred dollars, to get him started in the new world. The return-trip ticket to Germany wasn't worth the paper it was printed on. When Aaron gave Joseph the money, Aaron embraced him and thanked him for all his help in getting him through that first tough year. Things were going better for Aaron now that he had gotten into the swing of it at school.

He said to his friend of only less than two years, "If not for you and the money your family sent, I would not be getting a medical education. Now you're leaving, and I don't know if I'll ever see you again. You are my lifetime friend, and I only hope that in time I can find some way to repay you for all that you have done for me."

Things were not easy for the young couple in their new strange land. They settled in a fourth floor walk-up on the Lower East Side of New York. At this time they decided to Americanize their name and so they used the short form of Berkewitz and called themselves Berke. There was a tailor shop on the ground floor of the tenement, and Joseph got himself a job as a tailor's apprentice working for Mr. Alphonse Gatto. He wasn't a bad sort of a guy, and immediately recognized the talent for tailoring that Joseph possessed. But he never offered Joseph any extra money for all of the professional work which he consistently turned out. But Joseph had a job and they settled down while the baby developed inside of Maggie's womb. They celebrated with a bottle of wine on the day they first felt the baby move within her. And they fell more and more in love with every passing day. While out shopping one day, Maggie had made friends with a large jolly black lady by the name of Jessie. She had three children by three separate husbands, each of whom died of stomach disorders. They laughed every time that she told them that she was looking for another husband, but was having trouble finding one.

In Mike's delirium he thought it funny how every single word that his father had told him came back so very clearly.

On the day when Maggie was due to give birth, Jessie was with her. The Berkes lived only three short blocks from the Downtown Memorial Hospital, where arrangements were made to deliver the baby. Joseph was in the tailor shop working, when he reacted to a lot of noise coming from the front of the shop. Mr. Gatto had just left to purchase a bottle of wine for his evening dinner, and as usual he left Joseph in charge. Joseph came face-to-face with a large burly man with a barrel chest and biceps bulging under a black sweatshirt. The man told Joseph that his name was Tony, and he had been sent to collect the protection money. Joseph had seen the payoff being made many times before, but he never got involved. And this was a new guy making the collection. Joseph told Tony that he had to come back when the owner was there, and the man flew into a rage and started to break up the place.

Joseph tried to reason with him and he spewed out a barrage of offensive language.

"No fucking Jew bastard is going to stop me from getting the money I'm supposed to pick up." He reached into the cash register and scooped up the money from the cash drawer, about thirteen dollars in all. "I'm supposed to get fifteen dollars this time around."

Joseph reached into his own pocket, took out five singles that he had, and gave Tony two. Tony then snatched the other three dollars from Joseph and said, "I think I'll teach you a lesson." And he promptly started hammering away at Joseph with his fists.

Joseph spit out two of his teeth and tried to fight back. This only intensified the giant of a man, and he beat Joseph into a state of semiconsciousness. Tony wasn't satisfied and when he had Joseph on the floor, he broke his left arm with a twist while holding down his shoulder with his foot. Then he reached down and broke his right leg, pulling at it with such a violent tug that the bone broke through the skin. Still not satisfied, Tony kicked at Joseph's chest a few more times trying to inflict some more damage. Joseph was still not fully unconscious when he heard Tony say, "So long Jew boy, see you around sometime and we'll do this again."

Maggie went into labor and Jessie went downstairs to fetch Joseph. The lights were out and she peered into the storefront. She was unable to see Joseph lying in a pool of blood at the back of the store where Tony had dragged him. So she did the next best thing and helped get Maggie to the hospital. By the time they reached the hospital entrance, Maggie's water had already broken, and she was rushed into the delivery room. Jessie was left to fill out the entry record, but she was hardly literate. She asked someone to help her fill out the card and told the nurse who was helping her that the name of the person they had just admitted was Margaret Berke and that she called her Maggie. The nurse, an Irish gal by the name of Millie O'Hanrahan, looked up and smiled, and spelled it Burke.

The new baby boy with the bright red hair was laid in his mother's arms right after she had given birth. She was then asked to give the baby a name. She told them that she and her husband had decided to carry on a bit of the old heritage, and they were going to name their boy child "Micah," as in the Old Testament of the Bible.

The duty nurse wrote it down as Maggie had spelled it, but the old biddy who recorded the name thought that someone had spelled the name wrong, never asked anyone, and changed it to Mike. Then she thought, Better not leave it as a nickname; and changed it to Michael.

A detective visited Joseph as he lay in his hospital bed. The man was a sloppy fat slob and reeked from both booze and perspiration. He stated that he was there to question Joseph about the attack. He never even offered Joseph his name, and seemed to know already that it was a guy named Tony who had beat him up.

He did most of the talking, and went on telling Joseph about Tony's background. He said that Tony was a product of an incestuous rape of his mother by a brother, and that his mother had died in childbirth. He was eighteen now and had just been released from reform school. He moved in with his uncle who was believed to be in the rackets. This punk's name was Anthony Calese, and his nickname on the street was "Mean Tony," because he had the reputation that he liked to hurt people.

Joseph asked the detective, "How did he know that I was Jewish?"

And he replied, "That's easy, your boss, Alphonse Gatto, was bragging all over the street that he had this dumb Jew working for him and doing quality work for peanuts. Also the word was out that collections had been falling off and that it was time to make an example of someone. You were chosen by Tony who wanted to make a big name for himself."

He bent over and confided to Joseph, "You know, if I were you I would forget about pressing charges against this guy, or you may not be so lucky the next time. The judge will just throw the case out of court anyway because there were no witnesses." He finished that sentence with a wink.

He never even asked Joseph a question. As he turned to leave the hospital room, he took out a handkerchief to wipe his brow, and Joseph saw a crisp new twenty dollar bill float to the floor. The detective picked it up, put it in his jacket pocket, and patted the pocket with a smile on his face.

Maggie found out from Jessie when she visited her that Joseph was in the same hospital. Maggie was not aware of the physical damage that had been done to her husband. When she entered the room and saw his badly broken and beaten body, she was shaken. She told him that he had a beautiful seven-pound boy. They cried together, some of it happy and some of it sad, and they made up their minds to leave the city. Joseph instructed her to take all the money they had saved out of the bank and to use seventy-five percent of it to purchase a car. She was out of the hospital three weeks before he was, and gave all of her meager furniture to Jessie. She picked Joseph up at the hospital with the car she had purchased, while leaving Micah in the backseat on the floor. She also picked up Micah's Birth Certificate at the hospital. They started driving due west out of New York City, but had to stop at some cottages for the night somewhere in Pennsylvania, as Joseph was in a great deal of pain. His casts were a constant source of irritation, and he was still spitting up some blood from the broken rib that had punctured his lung. But he was happy to be alive and to have a brand new healthy baby boy to carry on his bloodline. It was in the cottage that they rented that night that they looked closely at the Birth Certificate dated March 30, and found out that it was for a Michael Burke, and the parents' names were listed as Margaret and Joseph Burke. They thought that was an omen from God and kept the names as their own from that point in time. That miserable person who had beaten Joseph could never find them.

The car broke down in the small Ohio town called "Best Days." And it turned out that they were the best days in their lives. They sold the broken car to get enough money to live on while Joseph healed from his wounds. He was able to get a job in the local steel mill, and they bought a house four years later. They became very good friends with their next-door neighbors the O'Rourkes, who had been told the story of their flight from New York. They helped to conceal the Burkes' true identity and introduced them into the Irish community as old friends from back in Ireland. The O'Rourkes also were their sponsors when they received their American citizenship.

Mike stirred, felt pain over his entire body, especially in his chest. He opened his eyes, and the pain in his head became unbearable. He saw his daughter Jennifer, who was crying, and a beautiful blond who looked exactly like Marilyn Monroe. He caught a glimpse of his two redheaded sons standing in the back. He saw a doctor in a white coat leaning over him and beaming with a wide smile, and a nurse, who was now busy injecting a needle into the tube that was attached to his arm.

He heard the doctor say, "Welcome back to the world of the living. We're giving you something now for the pain, as it is going to hit you pretty hard as your body starts to resume normal function. So lie back and enjoy all the fuss we're going to make over you during the next few weeks.

"You have been through a hell of an ordeal, and your family is all here with you. I'm not going to let them talk to you right now, but when you wake up tomorrow morning I'm going to let you have visitors. You have been unconscious now for nine days. Oh yes, and there is a government investigator from the Justice Department in Washington who wants to talk to you, too."

Mike didn't have any idea what this man was talking about, as his conscious brain was very groggy. He tried to say, Where am I; but he knew, he knew too well.

The sedative was starting to take effect, and the pain eased as he drifted off into sleep. The last thing he could remember was him saying to himself, I'm still alive . . . I'm still alive.

CHAPTER 4

Mike awakened with a start. The pain was intense in his chest, and every move brought another shot of pain. A soft voice spoke to him and he looked up to see a cheerful brown face. He recognized it as belonging to Nina With, the wife of his friend and business associate. She said that George had asked her to stay with him at night when he first came out of his comatose state.

"You know that I've been a nurse for eighteen years now, and I've been doing this night work from time to time, while George stays at home with the children. I'm only too glad to help out, especially after all you've done for George.

"I've looked over your chart, and Dr. Roth has left authorization to keep you out of pain with morphine. As a friend, I want to tell you to take as little of that drug as possible, as it's too easy to get hooked. I know it hurts you badly, but I'm also allowed to give you some hospital strength Ibuprofen, and that will help a great deal. It's much stronger than you can buy over the counter."

She went on to say, "My kid brother back in Cuba became an addict as the result of being hurt in a construction accident, so I know what I'm talking about. Take as much of the pain that you can handle. Use the pain to sharpen your concentration. It's an old trick that people who were being tortured used back in the old days, and they say that it really works. Try to home in on the things that are important to you, and think them out in detail."

He knew she was right and told her to fetch him the pills rather than the shot. She told him that it was about four in the morning, and that she came on board at 10:00 P.M. and would be going off duty at about 6:00 A.M.

"Got to get the kids off to school, as they only have two more weeks to go before summer vacation."

She helped him hold his head up to swallow the pills, saw him

37

wince with pain every time he moved, and then fetched him the bedpan. She saw embarrassment creeping up on his face, and she told him he was only an inanimate object to her, so he was to just go ahead and do his business. He was just going to have to get over the fact that he was reliant on someone to help him at this time of his life, and he remembered doing the same thing only less than three months ago. He felt that she was a regular "Florence Nightingale," and he was happy to have such a good friend looking after him during the ever so tough nights. She also told him that she had made plans to be with him every night for a week, and he thanked her and blew her a weak kiss. He wasn't even able to raise his arm to throw it to her. He also thanked her for the good advice about the drugs, and then winced in pain as he tried to turn over on his side. He never made it. Morning came and they brought him in some goppy-looking yellow stuff that the day nurse had to feed to Mike. But he knew better, and when she told him that it was a soft-boiled egg he told her that she lied, as she was in cahoots with the cook who wasn't allowed to use the real thing. How about that, getting sassy already, he thought quietly to himself.

The pain was coming on very strong again, and he asked the nurse for something. She started making an injection ready, when he stopped her and asked for the nonnarcotic. She frowned and said, "Why anybody would want to keep himself in pain is beyond me," and left the room to get some pills. Dr. Roth came into the room and introduced himself to Mike. He was pleased that Mike had rejected using the morphine, and told him that he thought that he did the right thing. Mike asked Dr. Roth to give him his prognosis as the nurse entered the room and gave him his pills with a glass of water. This time the doctor helped him by raising the bed with the button that controlled it. Dr. Roth told Mike about the concussion that had kept him in a virtual coma for nine days, and about the broken ribs. Once the pain from the ribs had subsided, he wanted Mike to use the time in the hospital to build up his strength with therapy. Mike was only too eager.

Dr. Roth also relayed to Mike that the driver of the car was killed, but Mike already knew that. He told him that the other passenger in the car, the wife of the driver, Martha Grant, was cut up and bruised a bit, but that she was recovering nicely. She had been released from the hospital after only three days, and had since maintained a vigil at his bedside, along with his lovely daughter. "What a pretty lady," Dr. Roth commented, and Mike mumbled that she looked like Marilyn Monroe. Dr. Roth said he didn't see a resemblance at all, but then everybody sees only what they want to anyway.

"By the way," said Dr. Roth, "but I get the strangest feeling that I know you." And he let it drop. "Your visitors are waiting to get at you, but don't get into it too much the first day. You've got to get your rest."

The doctor left the room and Mike heard him talking outside to someone. It sounded like he was cautioning them.

The first one through the door was Jennifer, all bright-eyed but no longer with tears in her eyes. She kissed him gently on the cheek.

Thomas Henry was behind her, and he embraced his father so tightly, until he saw him grimace. This is not like Tom at all, Mike thought. Tom had always been a bit distant and only seemed to show affection to Kathleen's parents, whom he loved dearly, and they also seemed to favor him over the other two children. Oh well.

Sean came in and was his usual quiet self, and he looked a bit pale around the gills when he saw all the tubes that were still sticking in his father's arms. But one thing Mike knew for sure, the clan had gathered, and all of them were going to get the feeling after this visit that their dad was going to come out of this none the worse for wear. He even believed it himself.

The last one to enter the room was Martha Grant. She had a big bandage on her forehead, and her cheek was still showing the signs of a bruise. Otherwise she looked pretty good. As a matter of fact he thought that she looked just great. Mike wanted to throw his arms around her and kiss her as soon as he saw her, but he could hardly move in the bed without feeling pain. When she came over to the bed and asked him how he was feeling, he saw both a brightness and a deep sadness in her face. He told her that he was sorry about Steve, and she nodded with an acceptance of her misfortune to have lost her husband. But then, they both knew that it was over a long time ago. She had already met his family while they had all performed the waiting vigil. They all seemed to like her, and this pleased Mike. The nurse came in the door and announced that visiting hours were over and that from this time on they would have to limit it to only two visitors in the room at one time. They said their good-byes to him, and one by one they all shuffled out of the door. Martha was the last to leave, and she bent over and kissed him on the lips. She didn't say anything else, but their eyes said much to each other.

The nurse announced that a Mr. Smith from the Justice Department was here to ask Mike some questions about the explosion and the accident. He told him all that he could remember, which wasn't very much at all. He really didn't tell them anything else that Smith didn't already know. Mr. Smith told Mike that they were sure that this bombing was the work of a specialized Mafia hit man they called THOR. Mike filed this information away in a pocket of his brain as Mr. Smith left the room. I wonder if his name really is Smith, he thought to himself.

The week went slowly, but each day that passed he started to feel better. Dr. Roth visited with him each morning and night. Mike could see more of the life draining out of the doctor every passing day. One of the nurses had told Mike that Dr. Roth had been working fourteen hours each day. She also told Mike that she thought that it was his way of forgetting the past. The doctor did seem to be very happy with the progress that Mike was making, and had the needles and tubes that were hooked up to him taken off on the second day out of his coma. For that Mike was grateful. Both of his sons visited with him each morning before he had his breakfast. They too were pleased that he was recovering as fast as he was. But Tom Henry continued being his unusual self with his father. He got so emotional at one time, that Sean told him to cool it. The boys told Mike that they could not keep this up during the week, as they both had business to attend to. Therefore, they could call him during the day and visit only on weekends. This was fine by Mike.

Each afternoon Mike was visited after lunch by the two women in his life. His daughter and Martha both came in together, and after an hour of visiting and fussing over him, Jennifer left for the day. She was aware of the bond that seemed to be growing between Martha and her father, and wanted to give them some time alone together. They talked about everything and anything, and sometimes just sat holding each other's hands. They just knew that they were going to make it together. Martha then said something very forthright to Mike, and without batting an eye. She said it so sincerely that Mike just registered the comment, and it really did not seem out of place.

. "I can't wait to get you home so that I can make love to you. I think it has been too long for both of us."

With that, Mike felt the first excitement in his loins that he had in too long a time. He actually got an erection, and chuckled to himself that he was really on the mend. He did not have to answer Martha, she knew the effect she was having on Mike. And she knew that she wanted to make good her boast as soon as possible. When she left him later that day, she was telling him about all the places that she was going to fly them, and all the things they were going to do together. She was happy and he was, too.

At the end of the week Nina told him, when she went off duty at 6:00 A.M., that she was not going to be his nocturnal nurse anymore. She hugged him, and he thanked her for all her care from the bottom of his heart.

Nina told him that George was coming in that evening to see him. She gave him her prognosis, and she thought that he was dong very well indeed. He was scheduled to be getting out of bed this morning, despite any pain that he may be enduring. She was right though, through his pain he was seeing everything more clearly. Her trick was working, and he was able to focus in on anything with a great deal of intensity, and he planned on using it as a major tool in his mental deliberations from now on.

That evening George came in as Nina had promised. Mike was now sitting up in a chair, after he had been helped around the room a few times by Dr. Roth and the nurse. He told Mike that the presentation he had made in Mike's behalf to the guy from the home office was being given serious consideration. Mike thanked him for sending Nina in to help him over the bad times, and offered to pay for her time. George would have none of it; Mike thought that he may have hurt his feelings, and immediately backed off.

No sooner had George left when Bob and Sally Jacobsen came to see him. Bob reported that he had been talking with Jennifer, and she seemed to have everything under control at home. That was good news that really put him at ease.

Dr. Roth came back in to see him that evening, just looking terrible. He asked Mike if he had a relative by the name of Joseph, and by chance could this Irishman by the name of Burke have any Jewish blood in him. Mike told him his father's story, and then Dr. Roth told Mike a story of his own.

It seems that Dr. Roth had come over to America after the war with his Irish wife. He had tried to contact his old-time friend at the address that he had from the only three letters which he had received. He was unable to track down Mike's father. He picked up a bit of information from a tailor who told him that no one had seen his father in the neighborhood after he was taken to the hospital after the beating. Dr. Roth further told Mike that, at his wife's insistence, he, too, had Americanized his name from Rothstein to Roth. And now, after all these years, he had come across the son of his best friend. He was delighted that he was the doctor who was able to help Mike. Dr. Roth went on to tell Mike a lot of things about his father from the short year and a half that they were friends. Dr. Roth seemed to pick up strength from his talk with Mike.

At the next afternoon visit by Martha, she was edgy and disturbed. When Mike asked her what was the matter, she gave him a two-inch thick folder. She told him that she found it in the basement of her home, behind some cans of paint.

She said, "I hope I'm doing the right thing by giving this to you."

She didn't stay very late that afternoon, and it was quite obvious she had read the folder, and the contents had upset her. She told Mike that she just didn't know what to do with this material. She thought that this was responsible for taking Steve's life.

The nurse came in right after Martha left the room and told Mike that he was to start therapy immediately on Dr. Roth's orders. He stashed the folder in the drawer of his night table.

Boy, it was tough going, that first round of therapy, and yet Mike hardly did anything but perform some basic calisthenics. In between going to therapy twice a day, he started reading the

material in the folder. Everything that he read seemed more un-
believable. Steve had broken down each crime type into categories.
There were fifteen different types of illegal activity, from simple
prostitution, which netted the Mob $32 million per year even in
a bad year, to dope smuggling and jewelry robberies, which were
only fraud since the jeweler was in on the theft. There were more
details of dishonest fur merchants and other types of businessmen
who had sold out to the Mob for greed and more dollars in their
pockets. The list of crime categories went on and on.

With each crime group listed were the name or names of the
Mafia head who had the specific responsibility. There were names
of the so-called honest businessmen who were in on the crime.
Some of these characters were listed as deceased. The causes of
death varied widely, but more than just a few were listed with
death by natural causes. Out of everything that Mike read, one
thing stood out like a sore thumb. There was never any documented proof to be able to put any single member of the Mob on
trial and be able to get a conviction.

So it was all a farce; Steve had built up these elaborate fact
sheets, but every time he had homed in on an indictment, somebody who could be a witness for the prosecution had died in some
convenient manner. Thus, Steve's bluff had cost him his life. The
most important item in the folder, which caused Mike's heart to
beat faster, was the identification—again, no proof was available—of the top boss of all the rackets combined. His name was
Tony Calese, also known as "Mean Tony." He and his son Tony
Jr., were making a mob profit of $.5 billion per year from all the
illegal activity combined. The address of their home—or should
he say stronghold—was located in Westchester County, in the
beautiful town of Fox Hollow.

Mike read the name over and over. Tony Calese had somehow
climbed up the crime ladder and became the kingpin, the overlord
of a gigantic crime empire. Mike made a little vow to himself that
he would bring them down, not just to avenge the act of brutality
done to his father, but because vermin like that had no right to
exist in anybody's world.

Martha was soon back to her old self and asked Mike to be
present when her doctor removed the bandages from her fore-

head. Dr. Ah Leh agreed to let Mike sit in on the unveiling of Martha's face, which had taken fourteen stitches to close. Dr. Roth was also present. When Dr. Ah Leh took the bandage off, she handed a mirror to Martha. Martha looked at herself and gasped a sigh of relief. "Thank God," she exclaimed and turned to show Mike her face. It was a little red where the cut was stitched, but no trace of a scar. She hugged Dr. Ah Leh, she hugged Dr. Roth, and she really hugged Mike. Dr. Roth said, "Well done, young woman," as he shook Dr. Ah Leh's hand vigorously.

Mike continued his therapy and pushed himself harder to build his body back to what it was, not to a forty-five-year-old moderately healthy individual, but as he had envisioned, a hardened rock of a man who was determined. He knew that he would have to work even harder at home to bring about this self-inflicted metamorphosis, but he was driven by very visual memories of the beating inflicted on his father so many years ago. Mike believed that the beating was what had shortened his father's life.

The day finally came for Mike to leave the hospital. It was agreed that Jennifer would sign him out and pick him up. Martha would meet them at his home. He had been in the hospital thirty-two days, but it seemed like a lifetime. He clutched the folder that Martha had brought to him to his chest as he got into the wheelchair to make the final pass down the hallway to the exit. Dr. Roth, as tired as he was, pushed the wheelchair to the exit. Mike stood up and shook Dr. Roth's hand, and he grabbed him in an embrace. They said their good-byes, and Mike headed for the car. They both said that they would keep in touch.

Dr. Roth retired to the Doctors Lounge to get himself a cup of coffee, happy with the fact that he had been granted the privilege of saving the life of the son of the man to whom he owed so much. He felt, at last, he had paid a debt.

Mike had just arrived at the house when Martha handed him the telephone. She said it was Nina With. Nina told him that they just found Dr. Roth in the Doctors Lounge. He had died. They did not have a cause of death, but everyone at the hospital would say that he died of a broken heart. She also told Mike that Dr. Roth seemed to have a smile of satisfaction on his face.

Mike told the sad news to Martha and Jennifer. He was visibly shaken up, and they tried to coax him to take a nap. But he wanted to get right down to start working in the gym that he had ordered to be installed in his basement.

He did exactly what he wanted to do . . . there was no stopping him.

.

CHAPTER 5

Mike started on a bodybuilding routine that left him exhausted by the end of the day, but he always had time to have a quiet lunch with Martha. She came to his house and chatted with Jennifer before his daughter went to school, and then made Mike's lunch which always started with salad, and then filled in his appetite with either soup or a sandwich. Then back to his daily routine. Jennifer always had something to do that couldn't wait each evening, and Mike and Martha went out to eat at about 7:30, each time to a different neighborhood restaurant. They always shared a bottle of wine. On Friday night, they always had a martini before dinner.

He started to build up his stamina with the daily routine, which he interrupted only on the weekends. He set his alarm and awoke at 5:45 A.M., and was on his way to a power walk by 6:00 A.M. He walked for about an hour, and was doing about four and a half miles. Back to the house to shower, he then had a light breakfast and went to his judo and karate lesson at 8:30 A.M. The lesson lasted until 10:00 A.M., and he was back in his house by 10:30 A.M. Then he headed for his gym in the basement and put in another hour and a half, using all the muscle toning equipment that came with the gym. He showered again just before having lunch with Martha. They just sat and talked until 2:00 P.M., never tiring or finding nothing to talk about—just a gentle rambling of words that told each other how they felt about each other. At 2:00 P.M., he took a nap while Martha watched the soaps. Then back to the gym for another workout, finishing up in the late afternoon with another power walk. After two weeks of this routine, the aches from the broken ribs ceased to bother him anymore. His body fat was slowly being replaced by muscle. He actually gained weight, yet his waist size dropped by two full inches. He was pressing to put his body into top physical shape, knowing that he had to get back to work soon. He could then kiss good-bye the free time that he needed to pursue his strength-building routine. Martha drove herself home to her house each night. They had never slept together because it was quite obvious that Mike had other priorities, at least for the time being.

After almost three full weeks of recuperation, Mike received a call from his boss, Wellington Fernrock III, on the Friday before he was due back to work. Mike was instructed to go straight to the boss's office upon his return, rather than to his own. He thought they were ready to lower the boom on him, and he really couldn't blame them. For all practical purposes he had missed all but two weeks of work in the last seven months.

On Monday morning, a somewhat edgy Mike went to the office of his boss as instructed. He was greeted with a warm hand-shake, and after all the little niceties had been put behind them, they got down to business. The home office had agreed to fund his Special Investigation Department. They wanted him to sepa-rate himself from all of his current activities. This would be easy, he thought, since George had been handling the entire depart-ment's work load anyway for all the time that I was out on sick leave. It got even better. Mike was told that five insurance com-panies had been hit by excessive losses in all areas of their casualty business because of all the robberies and fraud which had been occurring due to Mob activity. It was because of this that they had banded together to fund this "Special Investigation Group." They called themselves the "Insurance Consortium."

Mike was the unanimous choice to head up this group, as he was well regarded in the industry. He was given a first-year budget of not $175,000 as he had asked for in the proposal to his man-agement, but twice the amount. He was offered a contract for one year at a salary rounded up from his current salary to an even $100,000. Of course he knew that if he failed to put a stop to these losses in a year, he would be out on the street. But best thing yet about this assignment was that he was to work out of his home. He would have access to the large computers of any one of these five major casualty insurance companies. The extra money that was budgeted to him was to cover benefits for himself and for a secretary that he was supposed to hire, as well as the expected large travel expenses that they were sure he would incur.

Naturally he accepted. There was one small caveat that was required of him. He was to prepare a confidential report once a month on his activities, and on any progress to date he had made. He was instructed to submit only three copies of this report, one to his boss who would use it to make confidential briefings to the other assigned members of the Insurance Consortium who were sponsoring his efforts. The second copy was to go directly to George With, who would now be promoted to Director of Mike's old department. Lastly, he was to go to Washington, D.C., on a monthly basis and provide an in-person briefing and leave a copy of his report at the Justice Department. His contact there was a man by the name of John Smith, who was recently appointed as Special Prosecutor to replace Steve Grant.

Mike then was given the privilege and honor to tell George about his promotion in a special meeting called by his boss. Bob Jacobsen was also asked to attend, as he was made liaison to Mike in support of any computer assistance required in his new assignment. When Mike left the office after having lunch with his friends, he could not believe his good fortune.

Jennifer was home when he arrived, and she was bubbling over with joy. Her Charlie had just arrived home from his stint in the Peace Corps. Life for her was about to take the high road. Charlie came to the house and Mike shook his hand in congratulations for their engagement and to welcome him back to the States. Charlie remarked later to Jennifer that he did not expect to see her father in such fine form after all the time he had spent in hospitals and in convalescence. Charlie told her that her dad damn near broke his hand with his handshake, and she said, "That's my dad." Mike got on the telephone to Martha and asked her for directions to her home; he never even knew where it was that she lived. He said he was coming over to pick her up for dinner, and he had so much to tell her he could hardly wait.

She only lived five miles away in Spring Valley, and he drove up the driveway of her lovely colonial home. He sized it up as a four-bedroom house, and he couldn't help but wonder why they needed so much room for just the two of them. He looked at his watch, and it was only a quarter to three. But he just had to see

Martha now. She greeted him at the door, and as he stepped inside they drew to each other in an embrace and a deep loving kiss.

After that kiss, it was quite apparent to both of them. All the animal instincts for sex that had been pent up in each of them for so long a time were about to explode. Without a word she led him up to her bedroom. While both were very eager, there was no rushing. They undressed each other in between short kisses and tender touches. When they were both completely naked, they stepped back to look at each other's bodies. He was a fine figure of a man, stood six-feet tall and was very muscular. His bright red hair, with only the slightest tinge of a few gray hairs at his temples, made him look to her like an Olympic god. His manhood had sprouted and was as ready as could be.

She was so lovely, with breasts so supple and perfect in size for her build. Her curves leading to her smooth hips and down the sides of her perfectly proportioned legs, which were brown from the sun, and the whiteness of the part of her skin covered by a bathing suit was so soft looking. Yet her entire body was firm. Mike also noted that she was a natural blonde.

They lay in the bed together, and their bodies coupled in a slow rhythmic movement bringing pleasure to them both. This was not a quickly climaxed lovemaking, even though they had both been without sex for so long. He whispered, "I love you"; and she replied, "I love you, too," and then gave a groan of pure ecstasy. They made love all the rest of the afternoon, and finally got up and took a shower, together of course. They went out about seven for dinner at the best restaurant in the area. He still had not told her about his good news. The only thing he told her was that he was tired, and she remarked that she couldn't understand why, and then chuckled. They went back to her house after dinner, where he called his home and left a message for his daughter, telling her he would not be home.

Morning came, and they were at it again. It was still the gentlest of lovemaking, and both of them said it was the only way for them. While she was busy making breakfast and he was setting up the coffee pot, it finally dawned on her.

"When do you have to go to work?" she asked. "You're not still on sick leave, are you?"

He replied, "I'm on special assignment," and promptly told her the whole story. She was aghast.

"I've already lost my husband, albeit not a man I still loved, but he was still my husband, and I cared for him. Now I meet the man of my dreams, and he tells me that he is going to track down mob figures and their scheming associates. And you're going to see them put behind bars where they belong. My God, man, do you have a death wish?"

He let her vent her anger. She went on and on for the next fifteen minutes, and when she finished her tirade, she started to weep. Mike told her the complete story about his father and how during his recent bouts with death on two separate occasions, he felt deeply that he just had to dedicate himself to destroying this enemy of all that he held to be important in his life. She told him she understood, but she really did not. She wanted him to stop, but knew deep down inside herself he would not. She did not want to lose him, and so she did the next best thing. She asked to join him in this cockamamie plan he was fabricating.

She told him that she would not plan to return to teaching in September, and she was going to take a one-year sabbatical from the high school. They could not deny her this privilege as she was tenured. She was supposed to take on a learning experience with the sabbatical, and she sure wouldn't have any problem looking someone square in the eye and telling them she was learning something new. Since Mike was authorized to hire a secretary, she could fill that bill. She had acquired typing and speed-writing skills in college. And she had the plane, which could be used to get them to any location in the shortest possible time.

Now it was Mike's turn to get excited. He feared for her life, should he become effective, and then what if somebody associated the two of them together? But she persevered and argued her case with him, having a clear and concise answer as to why she should be the one to help him for every barrier he laid in her path. In the end, it was he who acquiesced.

She took him for a tour of her home. He had only seen her bedroom and the downstairs area. She led him down the hall to a good-sized room which contained the latest and most powerful personal home computer made by IBM. She told him Steve had it equipped with all types of available software and that this computer had a dial-up communications link that could put him in communication with any other computer, just as long as he had the proper access code and an authorized password. Martha told him this was Steve's pride and joy, and that he spent many evenings working at the keyboard, and she added bitterly, "When he could have been in bed with his wife."

The next room was Steve's bedroom, and it had an adjoining bath. Martha explained that they had lived this way since they had moved into the house, almost three years ago. The last room was a private study with an entryway from Steve's bedroom, as well as from the hallway.

They next went down into the basement. It was a mess, with boxes and assorted junk that one accumulates over time. She showed him where she found the folder. He looked down and thought he saw something else behind another can of opened paint. He bent down and picked it up. It looked to be an address book. It was, and a quick examination by Mike indicated it was broken down into sections of types of crime categories, the same as in the folder. The books listed the names and addresses, even the telephone numbers, of every single person who had a connection to a particular crime grouping.

"This is a find of monumental proportions, especially when coupled with the details contained in the folder," he told Martha. "We won't let Steve's work be wasted after all. Steve was closer to putting the wrap on some of these hoods than anyone ever knew, but time ran out on him."

They schemed the rest of the morning on exactly what they were going to do. Martha asked Mike to move in with her. He asked what the neighbors would think, and Martha responded not very ladylike with, "Fuck 'em!" "My, my," said Mike, and they both burst into laughter. They worked it out that Mike would indeed move in with her, and he would power walk the five miles each day back to his house, take his car to and from the judo and karate lesson, and use his gym set. He would power walk the five miles back to her house, which he now considered "home base." He still had to keep up his vigorous bodybuilding routine, as he just knew that some day he would need all his strength when push came to shove.

In the afternoons they would review all the material that they

51

had and plan an attack, or work out a plan to gather more evidence.

Mike decided he would rent his home to his daughter and Charlie, after they got married of course, at any price they thought they could pay. He was just going to bank the rent money anyway and give it all back to her sometime in the future. With his pay now at six figures, and the possibility of a bonus if he was successful, he needed the tax write-off from the house. They jointly told Jennifer of their decision, and while they believed she would take it as any young adult should in this day and age, she wanted to know immediately when they were going to get married. She told them she did not like the fact that her father was going to be living in sin. When they explained to her they were only waiting a little while because they had both lost spouses within the last year, she told them she loved them both and she wouldn't stand in their way. Martha and Mike didn't laugh, even though they thought they had cause. Mike just looked Jennifer straight in the eye and said he knew she would understand. She told him that it was okay to tell the boys, but not to tell Kathleen's family, the O'Rourkes, not yet at least.

Jennifer liked the idea of her and Charlie having a house all to themselves and ran to the phone to tell him the news. Mike and Martha slipped out of the house and went to the supermarket. They were going to play house together. How about that!

The next morning Mike started his new half-day physical regimen. During the walk he set his mind on exactly what steps he would take to insure Martha's and his safety. When he arrived at his home he unlocked the drawer and took out his .38 revolver. Before he came home from his martial arts lesson he made a stop at the gun store and purchased a new .45 caliber, a new 9-millimeter pistol, and a very small single-shot derringer, along with assorted ammunition for all these different pieces. He used his Private Investigator License to get permits for all the weapons. He told the proprietor of the store that he was starting a new gun collection and that seemed to quiet down the man's inquisitiveness. He stopped at an army surplus store and bought two specialty knives. He thought to himself what a risky game he was about to play, and he felt he had to have the right armament at his disposal and know-how, and be ready to use it. His quest was the top man, the boss, "Mean Tony" Calese, and then, in his thoughts, he added the man's son as well. He would bring them down, by first cutting away all the backup and support they had. As they stood alone unprotected, he would make his move on them.

He was late on his walk back to Martha's, as he was carrying a bag with all of his new acquisitions. He held nothing back from Martha, and she was appalled at seeing all the guns and knives. He calmed her down and reminded her that she had agreed to all this yesterday. He told her that it was a must that she also learn to use all the weapons.

And she meekly agreed once again to help him to do this thing which he called "justice," but she thought of only as "revenge." He then called his contact at the Justice Department at the number he was given by his boss. He was told by a mechanical sounding voice to leave his number and he would be called back shortly, and not to leave the area by the telephone. After he gave the number he found himself about to talk further to the machine, caught himself, and then hung up. In one minute flat the phone rang and John Smith was on the other end returning his call.

The first question to John Smith, "Is that really your name?" was answered with an emphatic, "Yes!"

"Now let's cut the shit and get on with the business at hand, if you don't mind," he said rather curtly. "Can you be in Washington on Friday morning, at let's say 10:00 A.M.? I am prepared to brief you upon where we stand in our operation that we have code-named 'Mousetrap.' If no one has told you already, you have been supplied to us by the private sector to obtain the cheese. You know what I mean, don't you?" The conversation was ended abruptly.

Mike told Martha of his summons to Washington, and she said that she would make plans to fly him there. They went to bed that evening after a late supper that Martha had prepared. They were both troubled, each in their own way. They didn't make love, but spent the entire night wrapped in each other's arms. When they awoke in the morning, they were—as one could best describe—full of piss and vinegar.

Mike hit his routine as planned in the morning, arriving back at the home base of operations (he liked the way that sounded), in the early afternoon. Martha reported that the plane was all gassed and ready for flight and that she had filed her flight plans for the next day. They set out that afternoon to determine who and what crime they should concentrate on by using the information collected by Steve, which he had hidden away so carefully, in of all places, out in the open. It was as if Steve had left a legacy to Martha, and his spirit was guiding them. At 8:00 P.M. they had agreed that they would concentrate on the stolen car ring that cut up cars for their parts, and then fenced the parts through legitimate parts suppliers. The hood responsible for this operation was Pete Russo. His fence was a bachelor by the name of William Jennings, and he was believed to be gay.

The meeting at the Justice Department Friday morning lasted only an hour. Martha waited at the airport while Mike took a cab into Washington proper. John Smith was really quite happy to have Mike on the team, and the curtness of their telephone conversation was never evident. Apparently Mike had hit a sore spot with John when he asked him about his very common sounding name. The subject never came up again. John told him the Justice Department was about to issue a warrant for the arrest of Mark Russo, brother of Pete, on charges of murder of a prostitute who was being run by one of Mark's pimps. They had a witness under protective custody who could fix Mark Russo at the murder scene, who actually saw him with a bloodied knife in his hand standing over the victim. They also had the suit that was taken by him to the cleaner's, and it had the dead girl's blood on it. This looked to be an open-and-shut case, but they had learned all too often in a criminal case not to count on anything until they had a guilty verdict, one that they were sure could not be overturned.

Mike told Smith about the work that he and his new secretary were doing in the pursuit of evidence against Pete Russo. John encouraged him to follow up on the subject, and gave him a copy of a file on Pete Russo collected and documented by an around-the-clock surveillance team. Mike felt sure it would be of help in nailing Pete Russo. Then John asked him to tell him about his secretary, whom Mike had mentioned earlier. He was more than a little surprised to find out it was Steve Grant's wife whom Mike had enlisted. And didn't he think bringing her in on it was a bit risky, for both of them? Mike never answered the question, and John never asked it again. Another sore point put to the past. He volunteered and said he thought she was a beautiful woman; he had first seen her about to go into Mike's room back at the hospital. Mike asked if John thought she resembled Marilyn Monroe. He said he didn't think so, and Mike just shook his head and shrugged as he left the office.

In the plane going back to the Ramapo Airport, which was located near Spring Valley, he told Martha that he thought she bore a strong resemblance to Marilyn Monroe.

"Well, I really don't think that I do, but for your information, my maiden name was Monroe."

"Well, I'll be damned," replied Mike.

The return trip was uneventful, but only if you can think of heavy fog, quite a bit of static on the radio when the tower was giving landing instructions, and an instrument landing because you couldn't see your hand in front of your face, as being normal and everyday occurrences. Through it all Martha was cool and completely under control. In fact she kept telling Mike not to worry, as she had to make a landing in soup many times before. Between his being scared half to death and watching the professional piloting being performed by Martha, Mike didn't know what to think. Worse yet, there was no way he could even help, so he just prayed. But when the six-passenger light plane had landed he was sure of two things. One, more than ever he was sure that Martha possessed an inner strength to see this thing through and he was glad she had talked him into letting her help him. And two, he had better get to the bathroom . . . quickly.

CHAPTER 6

The fog which had settled in early on Friday afternoon in July was now being washed away by a terrible rainstorm. The rain was driving down so hard, and with the wind blowing at about forty miles per hour, it was traveling sideways. When Mike and Martha got back to home base, they went directly into the study to review the report on Pete Russo. Not only did it confirm his seeing Jennings at least twice a week, but he was seen speaking to a pair of young punks outside a suspected chop shop in Queens. The surveillance team took remarkably clear telephoto pictures of Pete handing money to these creeps. The two were identified as Vito Zirro and Jesus Rameriz, both with arrest records for stolen cars on multiple occasions, but no convictions, as they always had some big-time lawyer get them off on technicalities. Just a little benefit of being in the employ of the Mob.

They now had more names to add to those found in Steve's address book and in the folder. It was quite obvious to Mike they could be overwhelmed with all of the information and have a tough time in trying to tie it all together. He called Bob Jacobsen in New York and told him he had a big personal computer at his new home base, and wanted to put a lot of information into a database which could provide him with quick direct access and be able to tie different files together. He needed help to write the programs that would allow him to do this. Bob told Mike to hang on for a minute and put him on hold. He was back on in just about a minute and asked for the address and directions for someone traveling from Brooklyn. Bob's best PC specialist would be up to see Mike by 9:00 A.M. on Friday. His name was Bo Denville. Mike was to tell him what he wanted, and then leave him alone with the computer for a while.

"Oh, and one other thing," Bob said. "Have two six packs of

the cheapest beer you can buy on hand, and leave it warm. And another thing, don't be at all surprised at how he dresses. Just remember, he's the best I've got, and he will deliver."

The weather and the early morning trip to Washington put the stops on any physical activity for the day. And what with waiting for the PC specialist scheduled to arrive early in the morning, this activity would have to be put off again. There was no other option, so Mike had Martha drive him over to his house where he loaded the gym set into his car for the trip back to Martha's. It was good that Charlie was there to help him get the heavy equipment out of the basement.

Mike dragged Charlie back with him to Martha's to help him unload as well. He had to make two trips to get it all, but that gave him an excellent time to get to know Charlie. He got to like this young man, and he told him so when he drove him back to his house where Jennifer was waiting with a frown on her face. He found out that Charlie had received an offer for a job as a Management Trainee in Group Insurance Sales for Met Life right in Rockland County. He also found out his last name—Russell—as it never dawned on him to ask before. But now that Charlie was going to be Mike's son-in-law, that was different. By the time he got back to home base, he was getting the where-were-you-so-long from Martha. John Smith had called and said it was important. He went through the call routine again, and John called him back.

"Bad news I'm afraid," he told Mike. "Just got the word from the safe house where we were holding our star witness against Mark Russo. It seems our little prostitute who saw the murder needed to keep current with her birth control pills, and was about to run out of them. She complained she needed them to provide herself with protection when she got back to the street. So in order to keep her happy, we had the doctor call in a prescription to the local pharmacy. It was six days ago when they arrived, and she took one pill faithfully each day after breakfast. They found her this morning in the bathroom right after breakfast, dead from cyanide poisoning. This has the look of a hit by this THOR character; it's his style.

"There's more. Even though it would seem that the Mob paid to have the witness against Mark removed, I received word that they found Mark Russo's body in the trunk of his car. They took him out because he had committed a cardinal sin by getting himself involved with the prostitute he killed. It seems he fell in love with her, and she didn't want to quit the street. She told him she liked the variety, and he went berserk and killed her. So the Mob closed all avenues of exposure back to the top man. The word is out on the street already that a new crime group leader was named by 'Mean Tony.' His name is John Porter, and they call him 'Big John,' as he is six feet eight, and weighs 300 pounds.

"Look, Mike, the lead you're working on with Pete Russo and this Jennings guy is all that we currently have going for us. Stay with it, and for God's sake, call me if you need help. And be careful, these guys are playing hardball, and they will take you out fast if they think you're on to them."

He hung up before Mike could say a word. Mike told Martha what had happened, and she winced, but never said another word. She made dinner and they ate quietly without speaking.

At exactly 9:00 A.M. Friday morning a Volkswagen Beetle, vintage 1950 painted with several bright colors, pulled into the driveway. The driver wore a black raincoat that was down to his ankles, and a plastic lady's weather cap that was tied under his chin. He also wore what best could be described as sneakers, at least that's what they looked somewhat like. He had long curly hair tied in a ponytail, and a full scraggly beard.

Martha let him in and he introduced himself as Beauregard Denville, but his friends called him "Bo." "Where's the computer?" he questioned, and they pointed him to the stairs. He found the room at the top of the stairs, and asked them to give him a little time to see what was already loaded into memory and what kind of software was available. Mike used the time to run to the store for the beer. After about thirty minutes of fiddling with the keyboard and humming to himself, Bo asked them what they wanted the computer to do. They described their requirements to him.

He asked for a beer, and when he popped it open, he said, "That stuff you want is already in here. The programming is a little sloppy which makes it cumbersome and inefficient as hell, but it's here. I can clean this up for you in a hurry, and then I'll teach you how to use it. Okay?"

They told him to go ahead and to call them when he was ready. Before they left, he asked for another beer. Martha gave

58

him both six packs, and he rolled his eyes around in his head, and said, "Thank you, ma'am!"

Mike went to the basement to set up and use the gym equipment for a while. Martha busied herself in the kitchen with some sandwiches. She made eight of them from all the cold cuts in the house. Somehow she just knew. At 12:30 Bo told them he was ready.

They asked him to take a break and have a bite. He brought the last two remaining beers with him to the feast, and asked if there was any more. Mike and Martha shared a sandwich, and Bo devoured the other seven, and his two beers. Mike excused himself to go down to the store for more beer, while Bo went to the bathroom. Martha thought to herself, "Thank goodness."

After Mike returned, Bo ran them through what was already in the system. It was the entire contents of the folder, and it was accessible by just keying in the "Crime Group Name," or could be brought to the screen sequentially just by pressing a control key. Or you could key in the last name or a nickname and the associated crime group information was also readily available with the press of a button.

Everything was cross-referenced, and any one thing could get you into another, just by asking the computer to "get assoc data." Bo pointed out the latest update to the file was May 22. They both winced. It was the day of the accident, the day Steve was killed. It was all there, except for the two new additions and the other information contained in the file John Smith had given to Mike.

Bo showed them how to update the file and, most important, how to make a backup copy on a small floppy disk. Mike asked to try it out and sat down at the keyboard. He entered the words "Find, Mean Tony" and pressed the enter button. Almost immediately the reply was visible on the screen.

Anthony Calese, alias Mean Tony, age 64 at last birthday, son Anthony Jr. Home: 16 Winding Way, Fox Hollow, NY 10898 Telephone: (914) 648-2276 Occupation: Reputed czar of underworld Calese Family, with Mafia approved control of entire Eastern Seaboard States, Pennsylvania, and Ohio. Sits in Council with five other top mafiosi at annual meeting. Next meeting planned at home of Calese, now scheduled for Thanksgiving weekend. Health: Known to be in midstages of syphilis infection. Prognosis: 3 to 5 years to live. Backup: Anthony Calese Jr., who is already reported to be giving the orders to support their crime family.

Mike typed the word "more" and hit enter. The screen filled again with a profile of each of the men who reported directly to Tony, their particulars followed for each. Again he entered "more." A list of the men identified on the previous screens appeared, and next to each was a list of the times they were arrested, and the dispositions of their individual cases. In Tony's list, there were arrests only when he was young, with a few minor convictions. He once was sentenced to two years for grand theft, and released on good behavior after serving only six months. He had never been arrested after his twenty-fifth birthday.

Mike typed "get assoc data" and hit enter. The next twenty-two pages of data scrolled on and then off the screen rapidly. Bo showed Mike how to stop at each page, and to go to the next page when he wanted it to. It was a composite list of every crime group, and within each group was the specific crime listed, with dates and location which were tied back someway to Tony. Following each crime was the word "Evidence." There was not a single item listed. It was most disheartening not to see anything concrete to date to be able to put him away.

Bo stayed another hour and showed both of them how to connect up with the main computers of the five insurance companies who were Mike's sponsors. He gave them the proper access codes for each, and he assigned a password that he would be prompted to change every thirty days. He showed them how to transmit data to another computer, and went through a routine with them which they could use to gain access to the Justice Department computer in Washington, D.C., once they had the proper codes. It was quite obvious Bo had been cleared and briefed by Bob on the assignment Mike had been given.

Bo left at about 7:00 P.M., and gave them his home and office telephone numbers in the event either of them had any questions. He finished his last beer, that made twenty-four in all, hit the bathroom once again, and went out the door humming. They thanked him profusely, and he commented, "All in a day's work. Gosh, how I love this job."

They went to bed early that Friday night. There was so much to do that Mike had to start to use up the weekend free time to get it all in. Neither could sleep, and Martha sat up in bed and said to Mike, "You know that the only way to put both Tony and his son out of operation in our lifetime is for you to take them out, permanently. Are you prepared and capable to go that far?"

"Yes, I sure am!" replied Mike. "Somehow I always thought that was how it had to be. Yes, you're right, it is the only way."

They both had a troubled sleep, and Mike thought he heard soft sobs every so often during the night. The alarm went off at 5:45 A.M. and Mike was out of bed in a moment. He told Martha to catch up on some sleep, that he was going for a five-mile power walk that should only take an hour. She gratefully accepted the offer, and as usual Mike did some planning on his walk. He would go to New York City on Monday to the office of William Jennings. He was going to pressure him using knowledge that was in the folder. He was also going to pay a visit to the two young hoods identified by the surveillance team.

When he returned to home base, Martha was already in the shower. He took the .38 revolver from the dresser, leaving the other guns and the knives for another time. He cleaned the gun, loaded it, and stored it away in a night table drawer. He called in to Martha that he was going to work out for a half-hour in the basement gym, and she should plan to go out for breakfast. He finished his workout, showered, and then they went to the diner, where he devoured a three-egg omelet, home fries, and three cups of coffee. Martha had a bagel and coffee, and ate only half. She was not hungry.

Back at the house Mike took Martha to bed and made love to her. He told her that he knew how badly she was feeling, but that they had to go on. He told her about his plans for Monday. He wanted her to continue the review of the information which was now available to them on the computer and to make a detailed list of what in her opinion were the next five crime group activities she thought had most of the evidence in hand. She had a lot of reading to do and she had to document her findings.

The doorbell rang. Martha looked out of the upstairs window and could see Bo's car. Mike put on a robe and answered the door. Bo said that he had forgotten his raincoat and that while he was in the neighborhood he thought he would bring them a printer. How else would they be able to print out selected pages of information they had generated? He also brought them a shredder to destroy anything confidential they had printed. He went right up to the upstairs computer room, installed the equipment, and called them up to show them how to use it.

Then he sprung a surprise on them. He had worked up a little program on his own that he just loaded in the system. He started the program running and it took all the deceased people that were in their various crime groups and loaded in the computer as just old associated information, and created another cross-referenced file. Then he used the list of the deceased parties to inquire against the entire documented file and identify names of crime group bosses where ties to the dead people existed.

It was amazing, but it showed clearly that it was a member of a different crime group that set up the hit on a person identified as a problem in another crime group. For example, if a witness against a drug crime group required an action, another crime group head arranged the hit. This is why they always had a perfect alibi while the crime was set up, and never were involved when the execution took place. Someone had to coordinate all those hits which benefited the boss, none other than the top man, the one who had the most to gain by the removal of witnesses. Here was the link to the top. All Mike needed was some document or some connection which would give them all the proof they would need to indict.

Again they thanked Bo and apologized for not having any beer for him. He told them he was unable to sleep and it only took him ten hours on his computer to write and test the program at home. He needed the live data to really see it work, but he was not surprised at all. It dawned on them that he had been working on this ever since he left yesterday. He left again to go home and get some much-needed sleep, and forgot his raincoat again. The phone rang and Martha answered. It was one of her neighbors who had seen the strange-looking car in her driveway, and noted the weird looking character that went into her house two days in a row.

"Is anything wrong? Who was that horrid-looking man anyway?"

"Oh, I'm planning to marry again, and he is a personal friend of my fiancé. I think we're going to ask him to be best man."

The neighbor hung up after saying that she didn't mean to pry and was only trying to be helpful. Mike heard the conversation and told Martha he thought it was a great idea. If he was able to bring Tony Calese and son to justice, he would indeed ask Bo to be best man. They laughed at their little joke, but they both knew that they had talked about getting married in two separate and remote conversations. This seemed to have pleased them both.

On Sunday they both slept late, and Martha joined Mike in the first ten minutes of his power walk, but had to give it up as she could not keep up with him. She did join him later in a workout on the gym equipment. Mike found out that she was in pretty good condition. Martha told him that before she met Mike she worked out at the Lady Beautiful Health Spa four times per week. You bet she was no slouch when it came to physical fitness. For the most part, they relaxed most of the day and had a great dinner at home.

Monday came and Mike drove to the city and went to the office of William Jennings. He represented himself as from the insurance company that was responsible to pay the exorbitant charges for spare parts, and made a lot of noise by shouting about an investigation into overcharging that was going to nail Jennings's company to the wall. He made enough noise and was finally given a chance to speak to Jennings himself. When Mike got into his office and once the door was closed, he pounced on Jennings, grabbed him at the throat, and shoved him back against the wall. He took out his revolver and stuck the barrel of the gun up Jennings's nostril.

While Mike had Jennings scared shitless, he went on to name names, identify places, and spouted out other material information he remembered from the folder. He told Jennings he had proof positive on him already, and was only waiting for some final evidence before he would indict him along with Pete Russo, and that the feds were holding him up. However, if Jennings would confess and turn state's evidence against Russo, he could personally guarantee Jennings would never spend a day in jail. What's more, he would be allowed to keep all the money in his bank accounts, and he would be put into a witness protection program.

Mike lied, of course. He had no authority to offer anything. But he had to get down to Jennings's level, and if it meant lying to get a point across, then so be it. He told him about the two punk kids, Vito Zirro and Jesus Rameriz, who were indirectly working for him by getting him car parts from Russo's chop shop operation, and he was going to lower the boom on them. To finish it off, he told him he was coming to his home tonight to get him to sign a confession and to tape it with a video recorder. He dropped him into the chair, and it started to smell in the office. "I guess I didn't scare him shitless after all," Mike said to himself as he left the office.

Next stop was Queens, where with a few dollars in the hands of the right guys, he was able to track Vito and Jesus to a pool room. There was no one in there except the two of them and the owner. He gave the owner a fifty dollar bill and told him to get lost for fifteen minutes.

"Don't worry; if I break anything, I'll pay for it."

The owner grabbed the fifty and left. He said, "You don't have to pay for any heads you break. Those two back there beat me up pretty bad a month ago. Help yourself."

Mike went to the back of the room primed for action. He told the two of them he was making a citizen's arrest, that he had seen them breaking into his car and stealing it.

"Says who, man," replied Vito as he reversed the cue stick in his hands so that the large part of it could be used as a weapon. Jesus started to circle around the pool table to his right. Vito lunged at Mike swinging the cue stick, and missed as Mike ducked below the swing. Mike threw the heel of his hand up against the nose of Vito, breaking it, but not killing him as he had been taught by his karate instructor. In the same forward motion as he came up he grabbed Vito's hand and jerked upward. He heard Vito's arm break in the socket, and he continued the flip of the body backwards and landed him on his back between the tables.

Almost in the same fluid motion, he shot his left foot backward into the solar plexus of Jesus who was coming at him. All the air left him in a whoosh! He came around with his left arm in a strike motion that landed on the collarbone of Jesus. Jesus dropped unconscious to the floor, and his body started to quiver and shake. But he, too, was still alive. A lesson had been taught. Mike was sure it would get back to the right people.

Besides, he had single-handedly put the car thieves who were stealing his company blind out of action for a long time. Almost better than an indictment which would probably be thrown out of court anyway, he thought to himself. He left the pool room with human debris on the floor. Oh well, someone will be along to clean up that garbage soon.

The adrenaline was really going now. He headed toward the very fine apartment house of William Jennings on Park Avenue and Sixtieth Street. This particular apartment house catered to males only, and you had to be of a certain persuasion to be allowed to live there. He started with a hundred dollar bribe to the guard on duty at the door to this fine establishment. By the time he finished peeling off bills, he had given him five hundred dollars to get into the elevator. He thought it was worth it. He carried a small video recorder that one of the boys had given him for Christmas. He rang the doorbell, and when Jennings answered the door and opened it with the chain on, Mike pushed the barrel of the revolver into his face. He convinced Jennings to open the door, even though Mike had to take the gun back out so that he could close the door and remove the chain. Mike told him that he would shoot through the door, and this frightened Jennings enough to give Mike access. Mike got him to make a full confession in front of the camera without any trouble. Mike had to answer questions, made by Jennings, about the witness protection program and Mike made up the answers as he went along. He knew the evidence that he was obtaining under duress wasn't worth a damn. But he also knew that the Mob would go crazy when they saw a copy of the tape. He left the apartment with Jennings believing that he had just bought his freedom. Mike was betting that the poor bastard had really just bought himself a visit from THOR. He left the building and said most politely to the guard when he left, "Good evening." He checked his revolver before he got into his car and noticed that he never loaded a bullet into the chamber to be able to make it fire. He made a mental note not to be so careless again. He drove over the George Washington Bridge just after the rush hour was finished, and pulled into the driveway at 7:45 P.M. Martha

65

met him at the door with a hug and a kiss, and asked him how his day went.

"Just another average day at the office, dear," he said. They closed the door and he told her all the details and, to his surprise, she was enthused.

CHAPTER 7

That evening Martha gave Mike a printout of her assigned task for the day. The list was sequenced by Martha, based on her judgment of the criteria outlined by Mike.

Crime Group	Headman	Mob Associates	Business Associates
Fur Robbery	Ben Meyer	Ralph Ascot	Nancy Preston–Pres.
		Joe Baker	National Fur Retail Group, Inc.
Liquor Truck Hijacking	Pete Roget	Bill Jackson	Wayne Thompson—Mgr.
		Al Scraggle	FTW Fast Freight
		Al Dimpson	
		Jay Wish	
Perfume-Smuggling	Norm Cotter		Nelson Bidder—Pres.
			Exquisite Aroma, Inc.
Protection	Harry Cotter	Phil Cotter	
		Warren Sennaca	
		Mario Parisi	
		Noble Garcia	
Gambling	Antonio Kim	James Hsiung	
		Shin Lee	
		Matt Morrow	

Each of the above Crime Groups are further broken down on separate attached fact support sheets, which provide all particulars. Status of evidence collected, and opportunity areas for new evidence is included.

Originally believed Narcotics to be a best area for early prosecution. This is not supported by the facts gathered to date, and thus have elected to exclude from the initial high opportunity list. Note that wherever business associates are required to support the crime category, opportunity for prosecution is highest.

Prepared by Martha Grant

Mike reviewed the list that Martha had prepared, and he was pleased. Martha told him that while she got deeply into her assignment today, she built up a deep hatred for the people she was reading about. She now agreed with Mike that something drastic had to be done to stop them. She said she couldn't help herself, but she had built up a hatred for these people and all they stood for.

"Does this make me as bad a person as they are?" she asked Mike.

"Don't you believe it," was his reply.

Martha had made plans to go to her school on Tuesday so she could make arrangements for her leave. Mike needed to stay home and get on with some of the other things in his plans. He told her that he would tell her more about these activities when she returned home.

Next morning, after they both did a workout on the gym equipment, Martha left for the city. Mike took out the guns and knives he had purchased, and did some measuring with a ruler. He went to a local store where he purchased some sheets of thin leather, some leather sewing needles, nylon twine, and some large heavy duty rubber bands.

Back at the house after he cleaned and oiled each gun carefully as best as he could without firing the guns, he checked the firing mechanisms.

Mike's mind drifted back in time to when he learned all about these things. He was given the choice of enlisting in the National Guard, the Army Reserve, or waiting around to be drafted and not have any choice about what he wanted to do or where he wanted to go. He opted for the Reserve, as he only had to spend one weekend per month away from Kathleen and the children. He also had to spend two weeks each year away at camp. He felt he could handle four years of the reserve, as opposed to spending a two-year hitch away from his family with the regulars. The reason he chose the Reserve over the Guard was because he would be assigned to a newly formed Special Forces Unit. He learned all about the use of guns and knives, and a great deal about hand-to-hand combat. He was taught how to use automatic weapons and an assortment of other military killing implements.

Mike actually saw combat when his outfit was nationalized for a two-week hush-hush special assignment. They used the normally scheduled annual two-week training period so as not to call any attention to their activity. The mission was kept out of the papers, but he was dropped by parachute at night into North Korea, where a small group of American soldiers were still imprisoned. They were never repatriated, as was agreed with the signing of the Peace Accords at Panmunjom located on the 38th Parallel. A twelve-man Ranger Assault Team freed nine still-captured Americans. They killed the entire garrison of the captors, eighteen North Koreans. These renegade North Korean soldiers were still keeping eleven American flyers who had been shot down far inside North Korean territory near the end of the hostilities. It seems the Koreans were dissatisfied with the negotiations and the arrangements that were made for the peace, and decided to keep the Americans as virtual slaves. US intelligence picked this up almost ten years after the agreement was signed. But by the time the rescue attempt was finally made, two of the American flyers had already died. North Korea never could say anything about the attack, as they weren't supposed to have any prisoners. Inquiries through the United Nations as to the disposition of the flyers fell on deaf ears. The North Koreans never had any intention of returning our MIAs. And of course, the US couldn't say anything because of all the damage done when the men were freed. It was what they call "a political standoff" and was best forgotten by both sides. Mike went back to work at the insurance company a week after the incident and was sworn to secrecy.

His mind refocused on the business at hand. He crafted holsters for each of the guns from the leather he had purchased. He stitched the leather to hold the cut pieces together. The .45 was to be stored in a shoulder holster. The .38 was put into a holster to be attached to the belt in the small of the back. Another holster for the 9-millimeter pistol was attached to the left leg. He then fashioned scabbards for each of the knives. They were power driven from their holders by the large stretched rubber bands. One knife was to work off his left arm, and slip into his hand when he rapped his arm hard against the side of his ribs.

The other knife was placed into another rubber band spring unit on his right leg. The trigger for release was a lever on the inside of his knee. It would take quite a bit of practice to get the hang of fast access to all of his weapons. But he had no choice, he had started the attack on the Mob and they sure as shit were coming after him. He had to be ready, for both their sakes.

69

Now he concentrated on Martha's weapon, one that he had carefully selected as a defensive tool only. He took one of her brassieres and sewed a pocket to the outside and just under the left cup. He now had another reason to be thankful that Martha had generous-sized breasts. Just like he was going to have to master both wearing his weapons and using them, Martha was going to have to put up with the uncomfortable single shot derringer next to her breast.

This activity had taken him all day. He was busy putting in a call to John Smith when Martha came home grinning from ear to ear. They waited for the return call from John and the telephone rang before they had a chance to say anything to each other. John told Mike about information he had received about "Big John" Porter. He had come up the ladder in the Mob along with Tony's son, and they didn't get along. However, Tony himself had requested that Big John be brought in from his Chicago assignment with prostitution to replace Mark Russo in the East. John didn't have anything else to report.

Mike called for a meeting with John, and told him to be at the Washington National Airport on Wednesday morning at 10:00 A.M. They would talk securely at ten thousand feet. Mike got the nod from Martha that tomorrow was okay. He should have asked first, and he whispered to her that he was sorry. John wanted to know why they couldn't talk over the phone.

"What do you mean? This line is clean," he said. Mike told him to please wait until tomorrow. John then asked if the plane Martha was flying could handle another person. Mike asked Martha and returned a yes answer. The meeting was set.

Martha had brought in the mail when she returned home. There was a big envelope, about an inch thick, that was addressed to Mike. The sender was Bo Denville from HAG Ltd. The envelope contained detailed written procedures for them to use. The procedures covered everything Bo had instructed them in while he was at their house. He included a note.

Thought you folks might make use of this. I threw a lot of technical stuff at both of you in a short amount of time, so I thought it best to write it down for you to reference. Regards to you both, Bo.

70

* * *

Didn't this guy ever sleep? they thought. Mike and Martha went up to the computer room, and Mike used the procedures furnished by Bo to access each of the five insurance companies' casualty loss files.

Mike requested a listing be compiled of all losses and the amounts, regardless of the cause, for the last two years. One by one he made the requests and received and printed out the lists. When he had them all, after about two hours, he scanned them and crossed out some that just could not be tied to a conspiracy. He added up the totals that remained. The insurance companies had paid out $1.5 billion in the last two years. Allowing for a margin of error in his thinking of fifty percent, the number was still staggering.

He said to Martha, "Enough for tonight. By the way, how did you make out today." Before she answered, he said, "Wait until you see what I've got for you." He swooped her into his arms and headed for the bedroom.

He dumped her on the bed not too gracefully, gave her a big kiss. Just when she thought he was going to become amorous, he hopped out of the bed and went to her dresser. He took out her brassiere, tossed it to her, and said, "Put this on, I made it just for you."

She felt the weight of the bra as she caught it, and knew the feel of the gun through the material.

"You've got to be kidding."

From the look in his eye, she knew he wasn't. As she stripped down to put it on, he looked again at her beautiful body. She saw him looking and said, "Don't give me any of this Marilyn Monroe crap now," as she slipped the bra on.

He then said, "Doesn't look like there is too much of a bulge showing. It looks like I got it right." She adjusted herself, and found she had to agree with him. "Now I've got to teach you how to use it."

"No you don't. I was a member of the shooting team, and a crack shot on the pistol range back in college. I've had to handle much more than this peashooter you just gave me."

He never ceased to be amazed at this woman, and once again found himself thinking how lucky he was to have her with him.

71

He told her to keep it on, and to get used to wearing it all the time. She sassed him by saying she was going to keep it on in bed, too. They laughed, and he started strapping on all of his armament. She remarked that she thought it was a lot, and then he started to show her how different and functional each weapon really was. Tomorrow they would start wearing the weapons whenever they were coming out of the house. But tonight he had the hots for Martha and was contemplating a romp in the bed. After they had made love and were lying there nose to nose, she told him how she felt so comforted and quiet after having sex with him, but he was asleep already.

Mike awoke before the alarm went off, and went for a walk. He was prepared to tell John Smith everything he had done, which included setting himself up as the cheese for "Operation Mousetrap."

When he got home, he started to make a backup copy of all the data stored in the computer. It took three disks to get it all. Then he copied the disks and popped them in a mail container. He sent them to Bob Jacobsen with a note asking him to keep them available as backup for him. He put the disks into an attaché case along with the original address book he had found in the basement and the folder Martha had given him in the hospital. He then added Martha's analysis report, and took along the operating procedures which were prepared by Bo.

Martha was awake and he told her what he had gathered up to give to John Smith. She thought it was a good idea, but reminded him to take the copy of the videotape of Jennings's confession that he had made the evening he brought it home. He went into the study and added it to the contents of the attaché case. They got dressed in casual clothes, and both wore their armor. It was a shame they did not have time to practice getting it out of the storage positions on their bodies and into their hands, but that would come with time.

They really did have an uneventful flight to Washington, and it was a clear late July sky. John was waiting at the airport as agreed, and he had a tall black man of medium build waiting with him, who was introduced to them as Special Agent Jesse Garrison. He was assigned to the case by Justice, and if they didn't mind, he would be returning with them to New York to set up a Protection Alert Screen. Yes, he was going to protect them both.

John was rather silent until they were gassed and into the air. They had flight plans to North Carolina, where they would stop for a bite, gas up again, and drop John off back in Washington; then they would continue their trip home with their passenger. Mike asked John for the codes that allowed him access to the government's computer. Mike was given them without question.

A visibly angry John then said to Mike, "What the hell do you think you're doing? Damn it man, you have set yourself up as the cheese, what with all that macho shit with those two creeps. Sure, you took them out, but you may pay the price for that little shot at them and your few moments of glory.

"And what's all this about my phone line not being clean enough to hold a conversation?"

Before Mike could get in a word, John wanted to know what he had in the attaché case. Mike spelled it out for John and the new man. When he told him about the contents of the tape, John officially didn't want to know. But you bet he did. Somebody had just made an inroad into the Mob, and it wasn't even legal. Oh the joy of it all, kept running through John's brain. A surveillance team would be immediately assigned to the Jennings character, and an anonymous tape would find its way to the estate of Tony Calese. Then Mike briefed them on the folder and the address book, and turned them over to them. Mike said he assumed all along that Justice had copies of the same information.

John told him about the theft from the Washington office on the morning after the accident, when Mike's life was touch and go in the hospital. But even John was unaware of the existence of the address book which Steve Grant had secretly compiled. Now Mike brought out the analysis that Martha prepared on the computer, and he went on to relate what the special programs created by Bo Denville told them about how they cover up Mob hits. It was all there in the attaché case, including the disk representing the files on Mike's computer. He was loaning John a copy of the procedures to make a copy for himself.

"But I need them back in a hurry," Mike stated.

"I sure could use a guy like this Bo Denville character," said John.

73

Both Martha and Mike looked at each other at the use of the word "character" by John. Mike told them he was now packing, meaning he was now carrying a gun.

As the plane was landing in Greensboro, North Carolina, they had completely discussed the approach they would use to get more evidence on the crime groups outlined in Martha's printout. John could smell some success in the wind for the first time since he took the job. He told them he was Steve's assistant, and he felt that he had let him down. Now it was his turn to run with the ball.

"Thanks to you two, we are finally starting to move," John declared.

On the flight back, they talked about the suspected leak coming from somewhere in the Justice Department. Mike argued the point that how else would the Mob get knowledge that you had a witness in the first place. And how would they know where you squirreled her away and that she had asked for birth control pills, etc. Mike made a believer out of John, and from then on they would hold their meetings in the air. John was determined to plug the leak.

They dropped John off, and Martha advised she had more than enough gas to fly them back. Mike found out from Jesse that he had been born on the Lower East Side, was forty-four years old, and had a master's from Fordham. He said that his mother, also called Jessie, but spelled differently, had put his three sisters and himself, all from different fathers, through college by scrubbing floors in office buildings at night.

Mike couldn't believe what he was hearing. He told Jesse about the story his father had told him shortly before his death. Yes, it was the same Jessie who was his mother's friend and helped her get to the hospital on the night she gave birth to him. He asked how she was, and he was told she lived in St. Albans in Queens with her youngest daughter. She was constantly complaining about all that white trash that had moved in nearby and were ruining the neighborhood. Oh yes, she was fine indeed, and Jesse would be most happy to tell her that Mike grew up just fine.

Mike thought to himself, Life is funny; here is the son of the woman who helped my mother, and he is now assigned to help me; no, not just help, but protect my life and the life of the woman I love.

When they landed at Ramapo Airport, Jesse shook their hands and assured them that either he personally or one of his men were always going to be close by. He was picked up by an official-looking limo. That was a comforting feeling, thought Mike, not just for myself, but for Martha and the difficult time that lies ahead.

Back at home base Martha used the word processor in the computer, while Mike dictated his first report for the Insurance Consortium. He was sure they would be satisfied with the progress he had made. Three copies went into the mail that night. They would be on their way by early morning.

Mike and Martha spent the rest of the afternoon by practicing getting their weapons into their hands fast. By the end of the evening, Martha could get at her piece in a flash. She was busy sewing the pocket into her other bras. Mike was concentrating on getting at the knives. He was getting pretty fast himself. He called and made arrangements for another two-hour judo and karate class tomorrow. Martha was going to this class with him.

In bed that night she got around to telling Mike about her application for the sabbatical. She laughed and told Mike she had been propositioned by the dean, who wanted to run off with her for a year and just shack up. She shocked him when she told him she was already shacked up with someone, and he seemed so dejected. Oh yes, she had her leave approved.

The phone rang.

It was Bob Jacobsen, and he wanted to know if Mike knew why he just was told to send Bo Denville to Washington.

Mike told him he thought they wanted to offer Bo a job. Bob sounded shocked, and hung up.

CHAPTER 8

He woke up with a start and in a cold sweat. A quick glance at the digital indicated it was 3:15 A.M. The same dream preceded his awakening as it had so many times before. He was back in the interrogation center, and the so-called doctor had been working on his body with those long thin needles again. He was strapped to the table, and a single light overhead shone directly into his eyes. There was no protection from that terrible light, as his eyelids were kept open by adhesive strips.

The pain was excruciating. It was never the sweet excess of pain which left a numbing in the body, not that at all. The large Arab with the beard and the breath of a sick camel, at least he thought it smelled that way, hovered over him and told him once again that he did not tell him everything. This pig of a man knew he had, but he had called the doctor back in to inflict more pain because he liked to see men suffer. The long thin needles were inserted directly into the thigh this time, until they touched the bone, then backed off just a bit. The needle itself never hurt, but then the Chinese mercenary doctor would, on direction by the Arab, start a slow rotation against the bone. The pain was always extreme and never stopped, even after the needle was withdrawn. He had undergone this interrogation each day for six consecutive days since he was kidnapped from the American University in Lebanon. They had put him through this ordeal as many as six times in a single day. It started almost as soon as he became awake. He then endured what they did to him until once again he was able to fall back into that beautiful state of unconsciousness. He had told them everything, as there was no way a human being could hold back any information under the relentless physical torture. Very early in the first day they had gotten him to admit that he was in fact an operative of the CIA on assignment at the university as a military liaison. He told them who he reported to and any other secrets that he knew. But they continued with his pain-inflicting interrogation anyway.

The pain from bone scraping at all different parts of his body never let up in any conscious moment, and he knew this type of internal damage, while it showed no outward physical marks, would be with him for a lifetime. He wanted to die, and each time he slipped into an unconscious state, he thought he had made it to the promised land. He remembered his family, his mother and father, his brother and sister, his grandparents who he knew loved him so dearly. And he would have sold them all into slavery if it would help him get away from this terrible pain that racked his body.

He remembered awakening in his cell and looking up at the Arab, and he felt the pain again starting up within him. This time, the Arab was alone with him, he was telling him that he was now going to cut his throat, and he wanted to see the fear in the eyes of the infidel. As the Arab neared his throat with the knife, he lunged up at the Arab with all his remaining strength. Somehow, between the surprise attack he had made on his captor and the next few moments when he found the knife in his hand, he had managed to overcome the Arab. He relished the feeling of the warm blood of the Arab gushing over his hands as he cut his throat, almost decapitating him.

He struggled to his feet, and leaned against the wall to steady himself. The noise made in subduing his captor apparently went unheard. He knew that all the training he had received prior to his assignment would now have to be put to use. Pray that he would be able to still use these killing skills after all of his days of deprivation and torment. The pain gnawed at his body in so many different places, but his adrenaline had also started to flow. His instinct for survival had prevailed, but he still didn't know if he would have been better off dead. He knew the pain would be with him for his lifetime.

He opened the door to his cell and peered down the corridor where a light was shining dimly. He could make out the form of a man sitting in a chair, leaning back against the wall. There was a sound of a repeating snore that he could distinguish.

The dirt on the floor masked the sound of his movement, as

he traversed slowly down towards the light with his back against the wall. He saw there was a clearing of about ten by ten feet, and a floor to ceiling set of bars with a hinged doorway. There was a lock on the doorway. He also saw the guard had a key attached to his belt, and he prepared his assault on him.

As he cupped his hand over the mouth of the guard, he could see the fear rise in his face. He was only a boy, seventeen years old or younger. "Go to Allah," he said, as he plunged the knife deep into the heart and twisted as he had been taught. There was no cry, only a swift death for the young disciple of terrorism. As he eased the body to the floor, he took the key from the guard's belt. He let himself out into another corridor, and at the end of it he could see a stairway. Since there were no windows in his cell, he believed he was in some sort of an underground cavern all along. Now this seemed to confirm these thoughts. He heard the shuffle of footsteps. He could not wait until this new person came down the corridor and saw the dead guard.

He pressed himself back into a doorway near the stairs, and the Chinese doctor came into full view. Hatred and rage once again boiled within him. Revenge was all he could think about, and he threw a karate chop at the doctor's neck as he came past him. He took the unconscious man back to where the guard was, and tied him to the chair with the belt from the dead guard. He used the man's own kerchief to stuff into his mouth, and secured it with his belt.

He found a pouch the doctor was carrying, and upon examination he saw it contained his assortment of needles. While he was no expert in their use, he was still able to bring pain to the so-called doctor. He could see it in the man's eyes, as he inserted needles into five different parts of his body until they touched the bone. He saved the last two needles for his eyes, and as he punctured them, the eye fluids joined the blood on his hands. He had his revenge on the doctor, who was gagged and unable to even scream, and he was still alive and squirming in agony when he went up the stairs.

Somehow his actions were having a soothing effect on his continued pain. He came up to a small vestibule, and for the first time in a week he could smell fresh air and not the dampness that had permeated his nostrils. He looked out of the door and saw a fence about fifty yards straight ahead. There was no one around, and he dashed to the fence. It was only about ten-foot high, and he started to climb. His hand caught on the barbed wire at the top, at the same time he heard voices moving in his direction. He pulled himself over the fence, and the barbed wire tore at his inner arms as he slid to the ground. He heard a commotion, and it sounded to him that they must have just found the bodies. Mustering all of his remaining strength, he pulled himself to his feet, and he started to run toward a lighted area he could see in the distance. He was running toward the light and stumbled. He picked himself up and again started to run, only to stumble again.

By some superhuman effort, he had run almost a quarter of a mile. He fell again, and the pain was mounting in his body. He lay there with his whole body shaking in sheer agony. That was the last thing he remembered . . . and then he awoke. He looked around the room and the sweat made his underwear stick to his body. His mind began to focus on only one thing. The pain, ever so present, was starting to once again increase in intensity. He switched the light on at the night table and reached into the drawer for his salvation. He fumbled to fill the syringe, and like so many times before, stuck himself with the point of the needle because he was shaking so violently. Where to put it, where to put it, he questioned himself. I can't let anyone see these needle marks. He pulled up his foot and stuck the needle under the toenail of his big toe, pushing the fluid into his body. He dropped the syringe on the bed, and let his own body fall back on the bed. In only a minute his rapidly beating heart slowed to normal, and that terrible pain retreated back into the inner part of his body. He lay there until morning, while he reviewed in his mind how he got hooked on the morphine that eased the pain, but which also consumed his body. He had gone through this mental review every time as an anticlimax to his dream.

He was found unconscious in the early morning in the center of the street bazaar, as the vendors prepared to open their booths. His pursuers had given up the chase as he ran into the populated area that was patrolled by Syrian troops.

He was taken to the military hospital barely alive. The doctors were aware of his terrible pain, but outside of the tears on his arms from the barbed wire which they used fifty-two stitches to close, they were unaware as to the cause of his unnaturally severe pain. When he was conscious and able to tell them about the needles on the bone, they immediately gave him morphine. They wanted to keep him out of pain, and so they overcompensated, and gave him morphine any time he requested it.

He was sent back to a hospital in the States, and they continued to feed his growing habit. He needed a shot every third day. Every doctor who examined his record saw the report of what he had been through, and authorized him a continual supply of morphine to allow him to function. He was fully debriefed by his superiors in the service, as well as in the CIA, and they seemed unhappy with all he had told his captors. After all, he was supposed to have been trained to be able to resist interrogation. He received a medical discharge and a legitimate supplier of his required morphine for life. At least that is what he was told. He was by now a hopeless addict and out on the street. But he thought at least he had a supplier for his needs at the VA Hospital. That is until they abruptly cut him off when a new administration was voted into office. The doctor who took charge over at the Veterans Hospital where he was being treated as an outpatient issued the order, "No more outpatient drugs."

He roamed the streets and the bars and was able to make a buy a few times. But by now he was getting desperate. His money was running short and he knew he would do anything for a fix. Then he met an old buddy from the same outfit where he had trained, and he took him into his apartment and bought him more morphine. This guy had a few friends back in New York, and he was told they could always use a man who could do rough things and keep his mouth shut. And through it all, somehow he became "THE Specialty Hit Man for the Mob."

He had taken on the trade name of THOR, because deep down inside of him, for the sake of his sanity, he felt he had to keep some of his identity. He never liked his job and took no pleasure in taking human life. He never planned a hit where the victim would not be taken out as quickly as possible. He did not want his victims to suffer pain for any prolonged length of time. He only wanted that to happen one time in his life, and he was never sorry for what he did to the doctor. He conned himself into believing that he was really compassionate by not prolonging pain for his victims, but deep down inside he knew better than to believe his own con story.

But successful he was, and he took pride in the planning that he put into every hit. His price had grown to where he was the highest paid for the job he did, yet the Mob believed he was worth it. He had set a price list for the types of murders he would perform. For a quick hit, in which they didn't care if someone knew it was mob-sponsored, he would charge $75,000. He really didn't like these, as they usually wanted it to happen right away, and this cut deeply into the time that he wanted to plan the murder properly. He had a quirk, and it was that the amount he charged was specifically only for his services. When he sent his bill to them after a job, he always included his expenses as an extra charge. For example, he would bill them for the bullets he used and the rental car he needed to make his getaway from the scene of the crime.

When they wanted someone put away and it had to look as if they died by natural causes, he charged his highest fee, $200,000. On this type of job he could not be rushed, and it could take months to set it up. In one instance he put a special poison about a quarter of an inch deep into the man's soap, and when he finally washed the soap bar down far enough, the victim washed the poison into his pores. The remnants of the poison would also wash down the drain, and the man would simply drop dead on a street corner while waiting for a bus. This particular type of poison made death look like a heart attack. On this one he billed the Mob his fee and expenses of $3,000 for the poison, and even $2.50 for the special soap the man used. He was a perfectionist.

However, his usual price for a hit was $150,000. This was for a contract where he was able to take all the time he needed to plan it out properly and allow him to be far away from the scene of the actual death of the victim when it happened. It was to be an obvious mob hit, and no one, not even himself, would know exactly when it would occur.

His home was exquisitely furnished and had a beautiful view of the New York City skyline and the George Washington Bridge. He went to a wall safe in his penthouse apartment in the New Jersey Palisades. He extracted a beautifully bound black leather book with a single large gold engraved word on the cover,

"RETRIBUTION." He opened the book and examined the pages where he had written, ever so carefully, all the details about every single hit he had made for the Mob. He knew someday all of his deeds would require payment in some way. He knew the viciousness of the men who hired him and the terrible ways they earned their money. In his own irrational mind, when he went, the contents of this book would take them down shortly after he was gone.

Each hit was listed on a separate page. It recorded who made the contract, the date and time of the meeting when the identity of the victim was disclosed to him. It described the plans he made in all their gory detail. It also identified the amount he received, and most importantly who paid the money for the execution. Lastly, at the bottom of the page, he kept a running total on the cumulative amount he had earned from the Mob over the last two years. There were seventeen pages of entries in the book, and the total on the last page had reached an astounding $1,925,000. He smiled, closed the book, and returned it to the safe.

He thought to himself, I've got to get this book into a position to make a delivery to the authorities in the event something happens to me. He put it out of his mind until another time.

He went to the phone and punched the keypad with the number of his date for the night. She was at work in the hospital when he reached her.

"Hi, babe, just want to make sure you were coming off duty at six tonight. Yes, I'll pick you up at 7:30 sharp. Let's have dinner at Brandy's tonight, and after dinner we'll go to my place and play a little. No, you can't stay over. I told you before I have problems sleeping at night with my condition, and I don't want to put you through a bad time. Yes, of course I love you. Oh, and don't forget to bring the package. I have a nice surprise for you, too, picked it up at the jeweler's yesterday. Can't wait to see you, too."

He hung up the phone and smiled. He had three other nurses, each one worked at a different major hospital in the area. He used them as his suppliers of morphine, and they also provided him with their sexual talents as well. They were all beautiful, and he was engaged to each. Also, each one brought him a small amount of morphine whenever he saw them, and none of them were aware of the depth of his addiction. He reminded himself to be careful, as he had called one of the girls by another's name one time while they were making love. Yes, he had better be careful.

He then showered, dressed, and went out. He was to meet with Harry Cotter, who had just called on his private line. Harry was in protection, so you could bet that this hit had nothing to do with protection. He went to the meeting to find out who was his next assignment. The Mob had him very active lately, but he could always use the extra money to live more lavishly than he already did. He knew very well that it couldn't last forever, but he may as well enjoy it while he could. Something must be going on after he made the hit on that Special Prosecutor.

"Boy, oh boy," he said out loud, talking to himself, "that hit almost took out my father, as well as the guy's wife. Maybe I had put a little too much explosive into that charge. I'm sure glad my father survived. He has been through so much lately, what with my mother's death and everything. And now Sis tells me that he is shacking up with the wife of the guy I killed. Never thought of my father as a ladies' man. I guess I'll get to see this babe again when we get together at my sister's wedding in October. As I remember from the hospital, she was a pretty thing."

He rode down the elevator to the basement of the building where he garaged his Jaguar, and gave a ten-dollar tip to the attendant as he pulled out. Why not, he thought, I can afford it. And now he was going to get some more. Yes, he was going to make this a very special hit. Harry had told him that the guy he was going to hit was a queer.

He mused to himself as he pulled on the ramp entrance to the GW Bridge, not a bad code name he came up with. THOR—he made it up from his own name and that of his grandparents. It was an acronym and stood for *T*homas *H*enry *O'R*ourke. After all, it is his grandparents on his mother's side who really love him, so why not use their name. He felt like an O'Rourke and not a Burke, especially after his father told him that his grandfather gave him that tall tale about his being part Jewish. He was not Jewish, no way! He was Irish, through and through.

CHAPTER 9

The next morning Mike had his walk and came home to a waiting breakfast. They both ate lightly and went to the basement for a workout on the gym equipment. Mike told Martha he was taking her with him to his martial arts lesson, and Martha's eyes brightened.

"Now don't tell me you're into judo and karate, too," he said, as he noticed the glisten in her eyes.

"You bet I am. My father started me with lessons when I was thirteen and just starting to bud, you know, my breasts were starting to show. I had a close call with a few boys at school and was lucky to get away from them with my virtue still intact."

And then she added with a smile, "One of those creeps is still having trouble with his testicles, and the other guy still walks with a limp because I broke his foot when I stamped on it. Dad didn't want to take any chances, and I took lessons all the way up to a brown belt in karate."

Mike got tired saying he never ceased to be amazed at that woman, and that was the truth.

They spent the two hours with the instructor going over the moves and countermoves. Martha was a bit rusty, but came back to it real fast. When they left at noon, their instructor told them he was pleased and suggested they come in about once a week in order to keep themselves tuned. So they scheduled the next five Fridays.

Back at home base, they reviewed the list of most probable candidates and focused in on getting evidence on Ben Meyer, the head of the fur robbery crime group. They had the name of Nancy Preston who was setting up robberies of her own fur vaults where she stored already purchased furs and of truck shipments of newly crafted furs. They thought a sting operation might work.

Using the computer, they decided to look up the insured shipments scheduled for delivery in the files of the insurance companies. There were seven scheduled shipments in all, and a value was put on the first fur shipment of $3.5 million. Nancy had always notified her mob contact about the shipments she wanted to be hijacked. In this way she could spend some extra effort to see that they were lightly guarded and not prone to problems when the actual heist was made. From the file information of Steve's, now available to them on their computer, they had found out that she always notified Ralph Ascot at a special telephone number. It was obvious to them both to have Martha make the call. Martha said she had a sore throat when Ralph answered after the second set of five rings as was the established code listed in Steve's notes. He accepted her excuse. He also told her on the phone that he had a little tickle in the back of his throat as well. Ralph let it be known he was very glad to hear of another easy shipment going on the road. After the call was completed, they called John Smith in Washington. He went to a local telephone booth to return their call. The trap was set. They were ready to apprehend the thieves when they stopped the truck.

Two days later they received a call from Jesse that they got the thieves. A fellow by the name of Joe Baker was killed during the robbery attempt. They were told they could get more information about the specifics of the foiled robbery attempt on the evening news.

Next day the newspapers carried the full story of the foiled robbery. The newspaper also carried the story about Ms. Nancy Preston, President, National Fur Retail Group, Inc. She was singing praises about the excellent police work which foiled another hijacking of her company's products.

It worked once, so they decided, why not try again. They repeated the notification procedure to Ralph Ascot, and Martha pretended to be Nancy Preston once again over the phone. She told him about one of her vaults that was bulging with prime furs and they had to be taken before the owners started to withdraw them for the current season. However, this time when Martha was speaking to Ralph he was wary of the information he was given. But he never said anything about her voice sounding different. He just wanted assurances that this was solid information and the furs were an easy target and not going to be protected.

He told Martha, "You know, my friend Joe Baker got wasted on the last job. This better not happen again. Ben Meyer is having a shit fit, and he's pissed off at me. He's getting pressure from the top, you know."

Martha, sounding just as cool as a cucumber, said in a most irritated street sounding voice, "I can't be responsible when you fuckin' guys blow a job. You know I don't make any money when you don't get the merchandise either."

Martha's rough conversation must have done the trick, because Ralph sounded as if he was satisfied. They made another score against the Mob, and it was reported that Ralph Ascot was taken into custody at the site of the trap at the fur vault. He was not talking. He only wanted to see his lawyer. In order to keep up her facade, Ms. Preston continued with her story about all the fine police work in order to keep up her image of respectability. But by now Tony was the guy really having the shit fit. He told younger Tony to immediately contact THOR and to have him do a job on this Nancy Preston.

He ranted, "He'll teach that little bitch a thing or two, cross him will she, not on her life. She is going to be gone real fast."

His son authorized the contract for the hit, and made the call to THOR's private number himself.

In between all the bodybuilding, martial arts lessons, and the assault on the Mob that was being so successfully planned and executed, they had to find time to make arrangements for Jennifer and Charlie's wedding. The couple had set a date of Saturday, October 17, and had already made arrangements with the church. Jennifer asked the matron of honor and Charlie lined up his best man to stand up for them along with two bridesmaids, both Charlie's sisters. Jennifer then finagled that her twin brothers would be the ushers. They just forgot to get a restaurant or a catering hall booked for the big occasion. And so Mike got an urgent call from Jennifer telling him that as father of the bride he had a chore to perform. After all, he was going to pay the bill and she and Charlie had agreed that he should select the place where the celebration would take place. She knew her little con would be read loud and clear by her father, and she also knew she could count on him to do the impossible.

At the end of her conversation she said to him, "I really blew it, Daddy, and I need your help. Thank you, Daddy," sounding just like the little girl that she was.

Once again, Mike enlisted Martha's help. She was on the phone about an hour when he heard her say, "Thanks a lot," and hang up. She had a big smile on her face like the cat that ate the canary. She was just in contact with an ex-teacher friend of hers who had quit teaching to open his own catering firm. He had his cook lined up and was able to cater the entire affair for up to 150 guests. He had used the Elk's Hall in nearby Montvale, N.J. before, and it was available on this particular Saturday.

Mike was really pleased with the way Martha had moved into his life so completely. She was really filling a void that he thought would never be filled after he had lost Kathleen. He got to thinking that they were starting to function as a normal family. And then he got to thinking again, nothing is normal when your main goal in life is to go after the Mob. He had to shrug off the thoughts. They were depressing him.

THOR, using a fictitious name, rented an apartment in the building where William Jennings lived. As a matter of fact, he rented the apartment right next door to Jennings. It was furnished quite lavishly by its owner. He had just left for a one-year tour of Europe with his boyfriend, at least that is what the letter to the building superintendant stated. The letter contained instructions that the super was to rent it out to someone who, after he had checked his credentials, he felt was the right kind of person to take up residence in the building. The rent was to be $2,000 per month, with $5,000 security deposit required, and for a minimum lease rental period of six months. The super was to take $1,000 of the security money for himself, and he was authorized to subtract fifteen percent of the rent money to keep for himself. The super thought this deal was just great, and then a nice-looking young man arrived looking for a rental apartment. He said he was in town from San Francisco on an assignment that would take seven months to complete in the Big Apple.

He arrived quietly at the super's door the day following his receipt of the letter. It was quite obvious that the prospective tenant had the proper credentials, since he made a pass at the super himself. Also, he paid in cash $7,000 up front without a quibble.

No one noticed on the back page of the papers that a body without any identification was washed up on Atlantic Beach in Long Island, and no one came forth to claim the body. He was apparently garroted with a thin piece of wire.

Jennings had not come out of his apartment for two weeks following Mike's visit to him. He was still scared silly, but his sex drive had to be filled. He called down to the super to have him find him someone, preferably a young boy with muscles, yes he had to have big muscles. The super told him about the new tenant living right next door to him, and he was so well built and looked to be about twenty-four or twenty-five years old. Jennings had seen him in the hallway a few times over the last week, but thought he was taken. He thanked the super for all the good information and told him that he would be sending him a little something for his help. After he hung up, Jennings placed a fifty-dollar bill in an envelope, sealed it, and addressed it to the super. He bathed in his finest bath oils, got dressed in his best silk dressing robe. He put a bottle of his best champagne on ice in his freezer. Then he put a stamp on the envelope, and went to the mail slot in the hallway where he deposited the letter.

Once he had completed these basic chores, he then meandered to the door of his neighbor. Fixing his ascot scarf, he held his breath as he rang the bell. It was important to make the right kind of impression, because after all, he needed someone desperately to make love to him. He knocked, and a disguised THOR came to answer the door. In a most neighborly manner, Jennings introduced himself and found out that his new neighbor's name was Ronald. He thought he was just beautiful. He had blonde hair and a dark mustache. Oh, what a lover he could be. He invited him back to his apartment for a drink. Ronald accepted, and fluttered his eyes in such a manner that he really turned Jennings on.

Four days later another neighbor complained of a terrible odor coming from Jennings's apartment. Police were summoned to accompany the super when he used his passkey to obtain entry into the apartment. As he opened the door, the smell permeated the entire floor. The officers held their handkerchiefs over their mouths and started to search through the apartment. They just followed the smell and found the body in the bedroom. He was naked and was propped up on the end of the bed with pillows stuffed under his stomach. His backside was high in the air, held there by rigor mortis, as if he was prepared to receive his lover. An empty champagne bottle had been shoved up his rectum, and his face was grotesque in death. There were two empty fluted glasses on the night table. He had been garroted by a thin wire which had severed his windpipe.

Mike felt bad that Jennings had died in so horrible a manner. They had just watched the details of the murder being explained over television in a most careful manner so as not to offend anyone. He knew he was the one who had caused Jennings's death. He rationalized to himself, that if not him, then someone else. But it had to be another killing by THOR. At least this time they would have a chance to identify THOR. After the copy of the tape was sent to Tony in the unmarked package, they had set up a surveillance team, headed up by Jesse Garrison. It was part of their job to take pictures of everyone who had entered or left Jennings's building. They had to have a picture of that bastard THOR, they just had to.

The telephone rang and Mike answered. It was Bob Jacobsen, and he was pissing and moaning that the feds had just recruited the best programmer specialist that he ever had. He needed someone to complain to, and Mike let him rant on for about fifteen minutes before he tried to say a word. Bob kept saying that the government would never stand for the likes of a guy like Bo around for too long of a time, and he was sure he would get him back. He ended the conversation with the comment that the boss liked Mike's first report. And if he didn't mind, would he increase the frequency to every three weeks.

Mike got Martha to take his dictation and enter it directly into the word processor on the computer again. As he clearly outlined the details and results of their efforts over the last three weeks, he sadly thought of what he had set Nancy Preston up for. He shuddered at the thought. She was a human being after all, and he surely had put her squarely onto THOR's agenda. An agenda he was sure would only bring her to her death.

He put it out of his mind and concentrated on the next crime group identified on Martha's list. It seemed that Wayne Thompson, the manager at FTW Fast Freight, performed a very simple function for the Mob. He called Pete Roget, the head of this crime group, every time a liquor truck with only high-priced specialty liquor was being shipped. He always used what he thought was a safe phone to make his calls. He went to the phone outside of the FTW Fast Freight office where he worked.

John Smith got a Federal Wiretap Authorization from a judge who was damn tired of seeing these gangsters flaunt the police. They never thought they would need the recorded information, as they were only interested when an alert was given to the Mob. They knew from the files that the Mob never went after every truckload. And one other important fact came to light. They found out another liquor company never got hit at all. With a little more investigation, they determined this company was the one that fenced the stolen liquor. An elaborate trap was set, one designed to allow the hijacking to take place. The planned apprehension of the criminals would occur as they unloaded the truck at the location of the company used to fence the booze.

The bust was a huge success. They nailed Pete Roget, and his underlings, Bill Jackson, Al Scraggle, Al Dimpson, and Jay Wish. Unfortunately, there was a shoot-out. Jackson and Wish were wounded, as was one federal marshal. The hoods were in an ambulance which became involved in an accident on the way to the hospital, and they were both killed. The federal marshal only had a flesh wound and was reported doing fine. In reality, the two hoods were in protective custody in a safe house somewhere in Pennsylvania. Their wounds were not serious and both were singing like canaries. They had agreed to turn state's evidence if granted immunity from prosecution. "Why not?" John Smith had said. These two guys were only little fish in the pond, and he wanted the top man. A side benefit was obtained with this particular bust. They were able to get a warrant to serve on the president of the company who was fencing the stolen liquor. And he, too, was looking for immunity. He told Jesse he had received payoffs directly from none other than Tony Calese Jr.

Mike went to be fitted for his tuxedo, and Martha went along with him. They noticed someone was always in the background and out of direct sight whenever they left the house. When they came face-to-face with him as they made an abrupt unplanned change in direction, he just smiled at them and moved back into the shadows. Jesse was keeping his promise.

That night they made a call to John Smith, and it was unusual because they had to wait more than three hours for him to return the call. As soon as Mike picked up the phone, John told him his ten-year-old daughter was hit by a car while riding a bicycle near her home. The driver never stopped. Before they could ask, he told them that she was in intensive care, and it was only a fifty-fifty chance as to whether she would live or die. He was at the hospital now. He wanted most urgently to set up a meeting with them as soon as possible. They scheduled it for Thursday following Labor Day. Same airport, same time. John hung up before Mike got a chance to tell him how sorry he was. Mike was visibly shaken by the news.

After the conversation with John, Mike told Martha about John's little girl and her fight for her life. He told Martha that he was not sorry for anything that would happen to the people they had set up. These people had sealed their own fate when they got greedy and took dirty money. In his mind, they were as guilty as Tony Calese. Martha and Mike went to bed and clung to each other all night.

Tony himself made the call to THOR. He ordered an immediate hit on Mike Burke, and while he was at it he should also take out the broad Mike was living with. He would pay twice the amount for the double hit.

CHAPTER 10

The Labor Day weekend came and went. They had a barbecue with the kids, and all of them had gathered at his home in New City. There was the usual light talk going on, mostly joking to Charlie about the wedding. Tom pulled his father aside to talk privately.

"Hey Dad, what have you been doing with yourself lately? You know, since you got out of the hospital. Jenny tells me that you and Martha seem to have a thing going. I can understand that, but I just spoke to Mom and Pop O'Rourke, and they don't know a thing about you two. Is there any reason why you're keeping them in the dark? They are our family, too, and they have a right to know."

"Look, Tom, I plan on telling them about me and Martha at your sister's wedding. I haven't said anything to them as yet simply because I don't want to hurt their feelings. Your mother is only dead less than a year, and older folk, especially the parents of the deceased, may feel a long period of mourning is in order. I can tell you truthfully, your mother would not be hurt by my getting it on with Martha. I get the feeling that somehow she pulled some strings up there and got Martha sent to me someway. You may as well know that we plan to get married just as soon as I finish up on a little job I'm doing for the insurance company. They have been real good to me, you know. As I said before, I plan to tell your grandparents at Jennifer's wedding, so let's just leave it sit."

"Just what are you doing, Dad? I'm in the private eye business, too, and the word is out on the street that you've taken on the big guys, you know, the Mob. Is that what's going on with you?"

"Tom, let me tell you something that only a few other living people know about. This tough guy I'm supposed to be afraid of, this character called 'Mean Tony' Calese, he's the guy that put my father, your grandfather, into his early grave. I've told both of you boys the story about what happened to him, just over in this country a short time, trying to make a decent living for himself and Grandma. That man Tony is a vicious animal, and I'm the guy that is going to bring about his downfall. Now I've told you more than I should. Let's get back to the others and try to have a good time. Believe me, I can take care of myself."

Mike did not see the look on Tom's face. Once he accepted the fact that he was not going to be stopped, short of killing him, he made a vow to himself to help him nail "Mean Tony."

Tom was now sorry he had just finished up with Nancy Preston last night. Once again he had done the dirty work of the Mob, but he had made his last hit on the innocent, and the not-so-innocent. They had identified his targets for him in the past, now he would select the targets. He was going to reverse the course of events. Since the only thing he could do well was to kill, he may just as well kill members of the mob. So he wouldn't get paid, so what. He had saved more than $750,000 in a local savings account and that should help him hold his own until his retribution would come along. For the first time in a long time he felt good about himself, and he knew he did not have too long in this world. He joined the rest of the gang at the picnic and had a great time with his family.

Mike took Martha aside and told her he may have blabbed a bit too much to his son that day. Martha told him not to worry so much about it, as after all, he was his son.

On the way home in his car, THOR reviewed his last job for the Mob in his mind. He really had outdone himself with this one.

Nancy was a fairly good-looking woman who had just turned thirty-five, but she didn't look it at all. She looked more like twenty-five, as she had firm rounded breasts, great legs, and a terrific-looking body overall. He had followed Nancy Preston around to all of her haunts. She had a label on her on the street that she just loved to ball young guys, and that she was a nymphomaniac. The word was that she also went in for any kind of sex, you name it, and she had already done it with someone. But she was terrified that she would get AIDS. No one was allowed to get near her without using a condom. He watched her, night after night, pick up a young stud and go back to her apartment for a night of "good clean fun." He followed her and her selected lover for the evening, every evening, and it was the same routine. The young lover would never stay the entire night. She wore them out after about three hours. Many tired-looking young men were seen leaving her apartment at between two and three in the morning. And on more than one night they could hardly walk.

THOR knew it was just a matter of time before she would notice him and set her sights on him. He took off one night to set up his proper love scene that he planned to have with her. He couldn't wait to make it with this fabulous woman. His plan was a simple one, but it required that he make a stop at his local friend at the pharmacy, the guy who was able to get him the exotic poisons. He had just the thing, a slow-reacting poison, which after actually entering the bloodstream, would then bring paralysis quickly to the body. It had a delayed action that triggered the release into the bloodstream all at once in just about three hours flat. Now that should give him some decent amount of time to flee the scene. The poison was a derivative of curare, the drug South American Indians used on the tip of their darts to kill their enemies. The victim would seem to die from respiratory problems.

But the big difference with this poison was that it took all those precious getaway hours before it would produce its lethal effect. It did not happen immediately as when the pygmies used it to kill their enemies. The fee for the poison was his usual $3,000, which THOR paid for in cash. Before he left the pharmacist's drugstore he picked up two dozen condoms, one package with reservoir ends and the other with plain ends. They were the best money could buy and were guaranteed not to break. Nothing would be too good for his future date.

He spent some time that night slipping one condom into the other, and then rolling it up so it looked like it had never been used. He had first inserted the poison into a very small gelatin capsule. Then he put the capsule into the reservoir end, before he put the other condom into it. He was almost ready. All he needed was a warm body, but a hot one would do even better.

On Friday morning he ate four eggs, believing he needed all the protein his body could handle. For lunch, he went to a local oyster bar and polished off two dozen raw ones. He capped it off with a large bowl of "New England Homemade Clam Chowder," the specialty of the house. During the early afternoon he took a long nap. He needed all of his energy.

When he awoke again, he was back in a cold sweat after having his special dream again. He gave himself a fix, and noted it was less than eighteen hours since the last one. His body was becoming less tolerant and was requiring more and more morphine.

The longer he tried to put it off, the more pain he had to endure. He knew time was not on his side any longer.

On that very night, it was the Friday night beginning the Labor Day weekend, the bars were only lightly filled. Most of the regular crowd had joined the exodus from the city. As soon as he entered the bar, she spotted him and sat next to where he was at the bar. He had just ordered another dozen raw oysters.

"Missed seeing you around last night, honey," she said with a very sultry voice.

She then reached over and scooped up one of his oysters as soon as they were put in front of him. He told her he was busy getting ready for the big holiday weekend, but now he was as free as a bird for the weekend, and hers, that is if she wanted him. Within the hour, they left for her apartment.

At about 10:30 P.M. they arrived at her apartment complex. The doorman was surprised to see her home this early, but he just shrugged it off as her being very hot in the pants this particular evening. He was right. She was very excited! They had a few drinks to warm them up, but she didn't need any warming up. She was all over him, and they were both stripped down and ready for the lovemaking. She told him that he had better put on a rubber and that she had a supply in the bathroom. He told her he had brought his own, and she hastened him to get it on. She cried to him to hurry up and start to fuck her.

She couldn't wait for it any longer. He did her once, and when she aroused him a second time, he got out of bed and put on another fresh condom. This went on another three times, and she kept bringing back his erection. What a woman! This time he put on the special condom. When his back was to her, he put a pinhole in the reservoir end. He mounted her again. It was a long slow lay this time, as even he was fast running out of steam. He never ejaculated, he couldn't anymore. He was completely satiated, and he crawled out of her bed. Not her, she still wanted more. He heard her saying, "Just one more time." He told her that he had given her all he had. She told him he was a sissy, and she had expected much more sex variations with him. Was he some sort of a prude, or something?

He went into the bathroom and looked down at his spent organ. There was seepage coming from the end of the condom. The gelatin had melted with the heat of the body, and the time bomb was planted deep inside of her. Now it was just a matter of time. He carefully slipped off the condom, taking real care not to let any of the poison touch any part of his skin. He flushed it down the toilet. Since he would not come back into bed with her, despite all of her coaxing, she told him to let himself out. He showered and dressed, taking his time and singing softly to himself, and he left her apartment. The shower had washed most of the dark coloring out of his hair, and he hoped the doorman wouldn't notice.

He left the building. It was 5:00 A.M., and it was a different doorman on duty. He remarked when he was leaving, "My, my but you must have real stamina to be able to keep up with her so long." They all knew the lady's habits.

She awoke from her pleasant sleep of exhaustion at 5:45 A.M. And she was feeling very horny again. Her thoughts went back to earlier in the evening when the lastest of her conquests had provided her sexual appetite with an extended period of pleasure. She made a mental note to look up that chap again for another go around. She hoped she hadn't hurt his feelings when she told him to leave. She reached her fingers into her vagina and started to masturbate as she always did each morning.

Her body froze, she found it harder and harder to breathe, the neck muscles constricted. The paralyzing effects of the poison had entered her bloodstream. Her legs and arms contorted in every direction on the bed. THOR's time bomb had gone off on schedule. She was dead in less than fifteen seconds.

The Tuesday morning papers had the story about her sister finding her dead on Monday evening. She had failed to answer any phone calls, and so the sister let herself into her apartment. It didn't say exactly how she died, as the medical examiner had not performed the autopsy as yet. But only he, THOR, knew how she died, and chances were the ME would never discover the real cause of death. She went to her maker the way she wanted to. She had literally been fucked to death.

After returning from his walk, Mike read the story in the morning papers and told Martha what had happened to Nancy Preston. His only comment was that he hoped they had plenty of pictures of the people going in and out of her apartment house. He was determined to nail THOR. He muttered to himself that the surveillance team had better have been on their toes this past Labor Day weekend. He no longer cared about the people on the list that he had set up. All he could think about was John's little girl, lying in the hospital and hanging on to her life. He had called the hospital over the weekend, and the report was that she was still in deep coma. He didn't care a damn about those other people.

They went down the basement for their morning workout. Mike had mastered getting the knives into his hand, and now he was working hard on being able to get at, and be ready to fire, any one of his three concealed guns. Martha tried to be a little light with him, and called him "Quick Draw McGraw." He never cracked a smile and just kept on practicing.

After lunch they went into a strategy session. Next on Martha's list was the perfume-smuggling operation that was headed up by Norm Cotter. On the surface, it would seem to anyone that Norm Cotter ran a legitimate business. He had a factory operation where chemists had analyzed all the ingredients in the expensive perfumes. In his factory his workers mixed and prepared copies of perfume smelling exactly like the originals.

This wasn't illegal, as he bottled it and sold it as copies. He even called his bottled products by his own trade name, "Copy Cats." The imitation perfume did smell exactly like the more expensive originals, but they simply did not last as long when put on the body. Not only that, but the original manufacturers had each put a special inert ingredient in their expensive perfumes. In this way, chemical analysis would be able to tell the expensive originals from any copy fragrances. The market had been recently flooded with bogus perfume. The bottles used were look-alikes to the genuine perfume bottles.

Norm Cotter did not need any other mob associates to help him with his illegal bottling operation. He used illegal aliens supplied by one of his brother crime groups. They came from Viet-

97

nam, Cambodia, Laos, Mexico, Haiti, and all countries of the Caribbean. They worked for him only a week or two at most, before they moved them further inland and away from the federal immigration marshals. This work was part of the price they had to pay to be smuggled into the country. They came here looking for the land of plenty, and ended up as virtual slaves. Score another one for the Mob.

Martha had just asked Mike, "Now what would be the best way to gather evidence on Norm Cotter?" when the phone rang.

It was John Smith, and he advised them, "The legal beagles at Justice called and told me they had enough concrete evidence in hand to put Pete Roget away for twenty years. Those two hoods of his were singing so loud that it was making music to their ears. An indictment will be coming down today, and an immediate warrant will be issued for his arrest. Nothing more is needed as evidence to put him away. The case is that tight already. Also, it turns out this Nancy Preston was done in by none other than THOR. We've now got that tied down as a definite fact."

"What happened to the fence? Do we have enough to nail Tony with this guy's affidavit?"

"No way, Mike, the legal guys say his evidence won't hold up by itself. It will take corroboration, and we don't have it. But this will go into the file as another nail in Tony's coffin. If we get enough of this type of evidence, the combined package will really do a job on him."

"How is your daughter doing?"

"Still holding her own, the prognosis by the doctor is good. My wife is down at the hospital now, and she is praying an awful lot.

"By the way, this guy Bo Denville is now on board. He is tearing up the old book on computer search for evidence and is writing a new one. You should have warned me about what to expect. We had a few hurdles to get over before we could bring him on board. But we got him, and he did agree to some changes.

"Got to go now, have a meeting over at Justice."

Mike said to Martha, "Finally got some good news, and I wonder what's all this about changes by Bo?" He put the phone back on the cradle. "Now let's set up a strategy to nail this Cotter guy." His voice had a definite upbeat to it, Martha could tell.

It was quite obvious that to nail Cotter they would need proof he was manufacturing illegal bottles. He also had to have a printer to make the bogus labels.

"I'll go after evidence on the manufacture of the glass. There can't be too many places around where they can bring up the heat necessary to form glass. In the meantime, see if you can get me a list of all the print shops capable of making those exotic-looking labels. You know, Martha, it's not going to be as easy as with the other guys getting necessary evidence to stand up in court. We can't use anything circumstantial."

Mike drove up to the Corning Glass Center in upstate New York early the next morning. He had a friend working up there who was going to take some time out with Mike and give him a quick education on what it takes to make a perfume bottle. Actually, he found out it takes all different types of equipment to make so many specialty glass bottles. He came away with a lot of good information from his friend. The most important information was that these bottles had to be made somewhere other than the USA. As he started on his trip back home, he turned on the radio and he heard the following report.

Main story making the news for this evening was that the bodies of three Orientals, and one Caucasian were found in a known gambling establishment. The Orientals all had long needles protruding from their eye sockets. However, the autopsies indicate that the cause of death was a needle that pierced the brain. The needles used were of the type used by doctors who practice acupuncture. The one Caucasian found dead had a dumdum bullet, one that flares out when it hits its target, fired through his ear. It tore the other side of his head to shreds. The police think it could be mob-related violence, but the utter savagery of the crime leaves them baffled. It could be possible that some heavy gambling loser went crazy.

This radio station suggests that we may have a madman loose in the city. One thing is for certain. The gambling syndicate in this town is out of commission, let's hope for a long time.

The dead men were identified as Antonio Kim, Korean, reputed to be the East Coast Crime Boss for all gambling; Shin Lee, also Korean; James Hsiung, Chinese; and Matt Morrow, nationality unknown. The latter three all worked in the employ of Mr. Kim and were known to be strong-arm collectors of overdue gambling debts.

When Mike got home, Martha had already heard the news. Jesse had called, telling her to turn on the TV as they were showing the crime scene. Martha reported to Mike what she saw on the TV.

"It was a mass of destruction and blood all over the place. None of the cash that was lying around looked as if it had even been noticed by the killer, or killers. There was just no obvious motive."

Mike crossed that crime group off Martha's list. Someone out there who had to be a little bit on the crazy side had just made all their lives a little easier.

Mike said to Martha, "Three down on your list, and two to go before we start another list. I wonder how that sicko Tony is taking the news?"

Tony wasn't happy at all. He blamed it on that insurance guy Mike Burke, and his broad, the wife of that guy he took out a few months back. He put in an urgent call to THOR's private number. He received a call back from THOR in about ten minutes.

"I told you to take out that insurance private eye and his broad. I'm paying enough, and I want results now."

THOR answered, "I just finished up with the hit on that Preston woman. You know I can't be in two places at once. I need more time to set this guy Burke up for a hit. It's got to be done carefully so that I don't get caught. If you can't wait until I can do the job like the professional I am and not expose myself to getting caught, then do it yourself." He hung up on Tony.

Tony was fuming. "Nobody hangs up on me, Tony Calese. I'll teach this guy. I'll get the job done now by a few of my own men, and I'll save myself a bundle, too. Who needs him anyway?"

Tony called in four of his most trusted men and assigned them the task of hitting this Mike Burke character, and his woman. One of the hoods was sent to Washington to bring some grief to that new federal prosecutor.

As soon as he hung up on Tony, Tom called his dad's home. Jennifer answered and reminded her brother where their father was now living, and gave him the phone number and address and asked him to write it down. Tom dialed the other number. Mike answered.

"Dad, got the word from one of my private sources that you and Martha have been fingered for a hit. Can't give you my source, nor can I tell you when it will happen. Be careful, I love you."

After he hung up, he realized that he never told his father that he loved him ever before, not even when he was a little boy. The pain in his body began to torment him again. He had to give himself another fix. He got to thinking out loud.

"That afternoon workout with that bunch of Chinks reminded me of that Chinese doctor and that other fat slob of a man. It took a lot out of me. I'll have to pace myself. From now on, unless absolutely necessary, no more than one at a time. I'll have to plan each one ever so carefully. After all, I am a professional."

CHAPTER 11

It was Thursday morning, and Tom's warning to his father did not go unheeded. Before he went out for his morning walk, Mike gave Martha strict instructions not to leave the house unless she went out with him. Martha was more than a bit perturbed by the restriction Mike had placed on her, and she told him so in no uncertain terms. But she did honor his request, that is, until she would have a chance to discuss it with him when he was a little more rational.

The weather had changed quite considerably, with cool September mornings replacing the hot and muggy days of August. This worked out well for Mike. When he only wore shorts and a lightweight pullover short-sleeved shirt, he was then only able to carry the .38 in the holster fashioned for the small of the back. Now he put on his martial arts clothes, which had wide bottom pants legs where he was able to mount both a knife and the 9-millimeter revolver. He was also able to wear the .45 in the shoulder holster, and he was able to mount the spring loaded knife device up his left sleeve.

He felt that he had to start wearing all of his armor all the time, as if it were part of his body. The morning walk was uneventful. After breakfast, during their workout, Martha really let him have it. The end of the discussion occurred when Mike reluctantly agreed that Martha had to be able to do her own thing. Mike told her of the warning he had received from Tom. Martha pledged to him that she would be extremely careful whenever she ventured out of the house alone.

They spent the afternoon floundering as to how to go about finding glass bottle imports into the United States, when it dawned on them simultaneously, why not use the computer. They had received the procedure book prepared by Bo Denville back from

John Smith in the mail just the other day. He had added the routine and codes which allowed them to access any of the large government computers. Mike was aware the United States Customs Service requires all shipments of anything coming into the country to be put onto an approved declaration document in order to support the bill of lading. There would be no need to try to smuggle glass bottles into the country, so why run the risk of lying on the shipment documents. They set up a computer search of all incoming shipments of small glass bottles, four-ounce size or less, made during the last six months.

Everything seemed to be started okay, and about an hour into their search they received a call from Bo Denville from Washington.

Bo was monitoring a big search job that was submitted to the main computer, and realized they had been the ones who submitted it. When they explained what they were looking for, Bo advised them it would take about sixteen hours to complete this task. The amount of information which required comparison to their specifications was immense. He told them to leave their computer on all day and through the night. Each time it would find a match to their criteria, a transmission would be dispatched to their printer. They would be able to assemble a list of all the shipments, dates of shipments, where they were produced, and a company name and an address of where they were shipped. Oh well, and they always thought computers were fast. This seemed like an awful long time to get such a small amount of information. But Bo always knew what he was talking about, so they just had to wait.

Next morning, long before they were to go to the airport to fly to Washington to the scheduled meeting with John, they checked their printout. It was nine pages long, and contained 237 separate shipments. They had a starting point, and set the list aside until they returned to home base. Mike still had time for his walk, and he carefully attached and slipped on his guns and knives, and all was covered with the flowing martial arts outfit. Martha said she planned to make a visit to the all-night supermarket while Mike was out. When he came home, they would grab a bite before they left for the airport. About twenty minutes into his walk, he heard the sound of footsteps running in his direction.

The joggers and the runners were always passing the walkers, as all types of exercising men and women generally used the same paths. He looked back and spotted a runner quickly closing the gap between them. This guy was dressed in the standard running uniform, a sleeveless undershirt with a number thirteen on the front and the usual pair of shorts.

Mike noticed his shoelace had become loose, and just as he was about to be passed by the runner, he stopped his walk and bent over to tie his shoelace. He felt a grazing slice at his right shoulder. He looked and saw blood. It was his! His survival instincts flared immediately, and the adrenaline surged within his body. His left arm slapped hard against his ribs, and the knife slipped into the open fingers of his awaiting left hand. He quickly rolled to his left, and at the same time glanced past where he had been when he had taken the first onslaught by the assailant. The man was about six-feet tall and weighed about 210. He was now coming straight at him with a full head of steam and had a knife in his hand. He did not see the knife in Mike's hand as he lunged forward to Mike's heart. He still did not know how he had missed his target when he first came upon him, but now he was intent to finish the job he started. Mike stepped aside the lunge, and his foot went into his assailant's stomach with a thud. He lost some of the air in his lungs, but apparently not enough to really slow his forward motion. He turned, and they stood face-to-face, about ten feet apart.

Now he saw the knife in Mike's hand, and he winced as it dawned on him that the odds were more even than he had first thought. Mike told him to drop the knife, that he was being covered by others. He paid no heed to the warning and lunged again. He was an expert with a knife and just missed the flesh of Mike's arm, this time cutting through his flapping shirt sleeve. Mike went on the offense, stepped to one side, and put an elbow into his back as he went past him with a lunge once again. The assailant fell onto his face, and Mike immediately jumped on his back, grabbed him by the hair and yanked at it hard extending his neck. Mike placed his knife under his assailant's chin. This time he followed Mike's command and immediately dropped his knife. Even though it seemed minutes had passed, the entire action had taken only a total of thirteen seconds.

Both of them heard the report of two gunshots close by, and Mike could see Jesse's man heading toward them. Jesse's man introduced himself as Greg Peters as he charged up to them. He pulled the assailant's hands behind his back and placed handcuffs on him. Jesse came on the scene and told Mike he had taken out the backup hit man another forty yards down the path. He related that this guy was not so lucky, as Jesse had to put two slugs into his back to stop him from firing the high-powered rifle he had aimed at Mike's head. Mike looked at his shoulder, it was bleeding only slightly.

Then it dawned on him, and Mike shouted out loud, "O my God, they're going to be after Martha, too!"

Martha had made the trip to the supermarket as she had told Mike she would. The daytime shift of clerks had already started their daily routine. Shelves emptied during the long evening hours were already being restocked. She just checked out and was carrying her two small shopping bags, one in each arm. Her car was parked on the side of the building, and she turned the corner of the building.

She was in the process of placing her grocery packages into the trunk of the car, when the assailant made his attack on her. She first heard a set of soft footsteps approaching her from the right side. Remembering Mike's warning, she set herself firmly in place and was ready to fend off a blow. Instinct and timing came into play. She moved to the left while turning her body. An arm with a heavy blackjack-type instrument in its grasp spent itself in a whooshing sound, just about four inches off her right shoulder.

He was a big man, by anyone's standards, and he now was off-balance after missing his target so completely. Martha stepped on his instep as hard as she could, and grabbed at his left arm while pulling it forward to keep his forward motion traveling in the direction of the raised trunk of the car. The edge of the trunk caught him right on the bridge of the nose. Martha then hit him on the back of the neck with a chop, and it hurt her hand. He dropped to his knees. She placed two more chops to the back of his neck, and her hand hurt even more.

He crumbled into a heap at her feet. Her "Guardian Angel," the guy Jesse had assigned to watch over Martha and she had nicknamed him accordingly, arrived as she was placing her final chop to the assailant's neck. He came upon her so quickly that Martha first thought another attacker was coming at her.

She whirled to face him, while positioning her arms in the defensive stance she had been taught by their instructor. He put both hands up in front of her and said, "Whoa!" in a loud voice. "I'm a good guy." Martha relaxed when she saw who it was, and she breathed a sigh of relief. Then she felt faint and got very weak in her knees. He helped to steady her.

She got into her car, and her hands were shaking as she placed them on the wheel. She took a moment to calm herself and proceeded to drive herself home. In the rearview mirror, she could see her "Guardian Angel" pulling her assailant to his feet. She drove off after she watched him fasten handcuffs on him with his hands behind his back. He was also speaking over his handheld transmitter/receiver. No doubt he was calling in a report to Jesse. He was, in fact, doing just that!

Mike heard the report as it was received over Jesse's handheld communication device, and was relieved to hear the good news. Both he and Martha arrived back at home base at the same time. They embraced on the front steps of the house. There were no words, only the embrace that comforted each of them. They went into the house, and Mike came back out quickly to fetch the groceries.

In less than fifteen minutes, they were back in the car and on their way to Ramapo Airport. They still had a job to do, and they both knew it was the toughest job that either of them had ever taken on in their lives. They were both unusually quiet on the trip to the airport.

After they arrived and parked the car, Martha went to the airport office to file her next flight plan. She also had to check to see if the plane had been serviced. Mike took the opportunity to call Jesse's office while Martha attended to her chores. He wanted to know if they had found out anything after interrogating the prisoners.

"Good thing you called in," said Jesse when he answered the phone. "Just heard from John Smith. He said to tell you he will be about a half-hour late, so don't be in too great of a hurry to get there. He also has something to tell you, and it had best come from him.

"Oh yes, he also says to tell you that he will have two passengers today, as well as some luggage. He will tell you everything when he meets with you.

"As for those hoods who attacked you and Martha. The one I shot died on the way to the hospital. The guy you brought to bay has clammed up, except for his first saying that you attacked him without provocation while he was out doing his morning exercise. He wants his lawyer and says his constitutional rights have been violated.

"We're keeping him under wraps for a while. Maybe we can get him to sing a bit. As for the guy Martha took out, he has a concussion from striking the bridge of his nose on the open trunk lid. He keeps passing out on us and still doesn't know what happened to him. Tell Martha that he has the most beautiful set of black eyes, courtesy of our gal. She really was able to defend herself in a fine manner, you know. If that guy had hit her with that sap he was carrying, it's Martha who would be in the hospital, or even dead. My guy was close, but not close enough at the time to be able to stop him from getting at her. So be extra careful you two. Do you hear me loud and clear?"

When he ended the conversation Mike thought he detected something in Jesse's voice, like something he seemed to be holding back. Yes, he was sure of it. Martha and Mike boarded the plane and taxied to the end of the runway to her takeoff position. Once in the air, and after she had brought them up to ten thousand feet, she set the compass heading for Washington National Airport and set the autopilot. Her right hand was starting to swell some, and she put a first aid ice pack on it. Mike thought she may have broken a bone in her hand, what with having to give three rapid chop blows. Russ, their teacher, had showed her just the other day how to use the weight and direction of an attacker to act in her favor. He also gave her some preliminary instruction on how to hold one's hand to administer a chop. They also remembered being told to build up the hand over time by striking harder and harder objects.

She had gone from one lesson on how to, and found herself using what she had been taught in a real life-and-death encounter.

Their luck was still holding out, and they seemed to always be one step out in front.

"Thank God for small favors," Martha said.

Mike told her of his conversation with Jesse. Then he told her that they didn't have to rush, and she throttled back on her speed in order to conserve gas. She told him that he should have told her earlier, as she was rushing to get to the meeting place. That little encounter they both had earlier in the morning had thrown off their timing by about three quarters of an hour. It was good that John had delayed the meeting.

They landed at their destination at 11:10 A.M., just a little later than the revised meeting time. They looked around, and John was nowhere to be seen. Perhaps he was being slowed down by his mystery passengers.

A small van moved toward their plane waiting at the end of the tarmac. Mike tensed when he saw it, and then smiled when he saw that it was John who was driving. John got out of the van and walked over to the plane, poked his head into the cockpit, and just stared. He was drawn-looking, and his skin was both white and tight against his face. His clothes seemed disheveled, and his eyes were sad and red.

"Those bastards couldn't get at me, so they went after my little girl again, this time in the hospital. You know, the doctors said she was doing fine and they expected her to come out of her coma anytime now. But she did need the life-support system to help her breathe. First they went into the basement of the hospital and disconnected the battery backup for life-support systems for the entire hospital. Then they cut the electric power to her floor. It took only seven minutes to get the master switch for the floor turned on again. But it wasn't fast enough. Without the machine to breathe for her during her deep comatose state, she was dead in three minutes. My little baby, those bastards killed my little baby. She was only ten years old."

Martha and Mike were aghast at the news. They gave John a few minutes to compose himself.

Then John asked them, "Look, I know I'm imposing on you two but I've got to get my wife and son to a safe place, and fast. Can you fly us to her mother's farm deep in the western part of Virginia? There is a landing strip used by the planes that do crop-dusting in the area, right close by the farm where her mother lives."

Martha chimed in, "No problem. I already have a flight plan filed to take us to Greensboro in North Carolina. It is only a short distance by air away, and it's in the same general direction. I won't change the plan. If anyone has seen you getting on this plane, they will think you were taken to Greensboro. After we drop your family off, we'll just continue on to Greensboro. So we get there a little late, who would notice?"

Mike put in his two cents. "And after we leave Greensboro we'll go back to Washington so that John can pack a bag. We'll wait for you at the airport. It shouldn't take more than a few hours for you to get your things, John. We're taking you back with us. We have a room for you back at our home base. It's Steve's old room. We'll have your daughter's body taken to the mortuary. Arrangements can be made to give her a decent funeral later, when you and your family can be there together."

John meekly accepted their offer. They went to the van to meet his wife and four-year-old son. She was weeping softly, the kind of weeping that only a mother does for a child that was lost. Martha helped her and she carried the child into the plane. He was sleeping in her arms. Mike and John loaded the luggage. It was only two large suitcases, and Martha requested instructions from the tower for takeoff.

They arrived at the western tip of Virginia, and Martha had no problem landing on the small dirt field. There had been no words spoken by anyone during the entire fifty-five-minute flight, other than some radio contact by Martha. There was nothing to be said, and sadness permeated the entire trip.

Martha had called ahead to the local sheriff, and requested he pick up Mrs. Smith and her son, and take them to her mother's home. He was waiting when they landed, and Mike explained the situation and asked him to keep a watch over them. He was only too happy to oblige. John and his wife said their good-byes, and as he kissed his child who was now wide-awake and squirming, you could see a tear surface. He hopped into the cockpit and said, "Let's get going, we have lots to do."

And both Martha and Mike knew what he meant by that statement. On the short flight to Greenboro, which had to be made to keep the real location of John's family secret, they reviewed the attacks made on Martha and Mike. They all agreed that Tony was losing his cool and was well aware of the inroads being made into his crime organization. They were not only going to keep up the pressure, but they were going to accelerate it.

By the time they made the return trip to Washington, waited for John to pack a bag, then to Ramapo Airport, the entire day was shot. They arrived at home base and put John into Steve's old bedroom, with the adjacent private bath. He didn't seem to be surprised to see that they shared a bedroom. It was none of his business. Calls were to be placed. First one to Jesse to let him know about the new living arrangements. This allowed him to pull his men from Washington and relocate them to Rockland County. The second call was to arrange for another special clean telephone to be installed in order for John to speak to his wife. An installation crew from the telephone company was installing the special circuit, one that could not be tapped, bugged, or traced by any known device, within one hour after the initial call was made by John. John closed the door to his room as he made the first of twice daily calls to his family in Virginia.

The next morning John heard the sound of Mike's alarm going off. He got up and told Mike he was joining him on his walk. Martha was in the bathroom, and John watched Mike strapping on his armor under his flowing martial arts suit. He had to throw out the top of the old one as it was cut and bloodied from his little run-in with his attacker. He gave the trousers portion to John, and he also gave John his leg knife. John already had his own sweatshirt and knew exactly how to fasten the knife to his leg. He then took his own .38 revolver and stuck it into the small of his back. They were off for their early morning walk, just two friends who meet every morning for a little exercise before getting ready for work.

Back at the house Mike placed a call to George With at the office. Even though it was a Saturday he was always in early and had a cup of coffee at his desk. He told Mike that the boss was pleased with the results that he had already reported, but he wanted to know why Mike was not just concentrating on only insurance-related crime. Before Mike could get out a steamy comment, George said that he told the boss that he, Mike, was proceeding down all avenues of crime as he had to, so that the top man would be nailed. George told Mike that had seemed to put his boss on hold. He advised Mike from now on to only include in his reports information relating to insurance. Mike thanked him for his frank advice and hung up the phone.

"Those chicken shit freaks back at the Insurance Consortium are only interested in nailing crooks that put their fingers into the insurance companies' pockets. What small-minded people they are," he told Martha and John.

Mike was still boiling when Jesse called to tell them about a new casualty in the war on Tony Calese. Jesse asked to be put on the speaker phone so that both Martha and John could hear as well.

"It seems that one of Tony's closest friends, his buddy from the early days when they broke heads for the crime bosses back on the Lower East Side, has just been executed. This guy called 'Fat Howie' Goodring, who never made it to the top ranks of the mob empire simply because he was stupid, was blown up in his bathroom. He was still a head breaker, and got the name 'Fat Howie' because his weight had grown to 350 pounds. It seems that someone had planted a pretty good-sized charge of plastic explosive under his toilet seat. The device that set it off was recovered by the demolition team who were called in to determine how by the local police. The trigger was a special switch which would not make contact with the battery point to set off the charge unless weight of more than 300 pounds was applied. They checked around and, to the best count they could get, eleven people used the bathroom. Of course not all of them sat when they did their thing, but none of them even weighed as much as 200 pounds. If I didn't know better, you would think that this job was engineered by our old enemy THOR.

"And there's more. They had to pry his body out of the skylight fourteen feet above the toilet bowl. It was wedged in very tight, and it was reported that it took them four hours to extricate the body."

As soon as Jesse broke the connection, Mike was at the computer making an inquiry. He got Tony Calese's phone number and punched in the digits.

"Mr. Calese's residence," the butler answered. "Whom shall I say is calling?"

"Tell him it's his insurance man, Mike Burke." When Tony placed the phone to his ear, Mike said, "Listen up carefully, Mr. Big Shit. Your whole world is going to come apart, and I'm the one who is doing it. Just thought you would like to know that I hired THOR to do a job on you folks. Oh, I know you will claim that it's illegal, but what the hell, you can't fight fire without a little fire of your own. So long, Tony. We'll have you in jail soon enough, creep." He hung up before Tony had a chance to answer.

Martha and John sat there with their jaws dropped. Mike told them that he may just as well take the credit for lining up THOR to hit on Tony's people, as not. He wanted to strike while the iron was hot and to force Tony into making more mistakes. That night while he lay in bed he thought to himself, What if it really is this guy THOR who did those grotesque murders? Could it be he has switched sides?

CHAPTER 12

They took John along with them to a special Saturday session with their martial arts instructor. On the way they stopped off at the hospital to have an X ray taken of Martha's hand. She was told she would have to wait about two hours before the X-ray technician would be back in the lab to read them, so she opted to come back later for the results. They introduced John Smith to their instructor, Russ. Then they went on to tell him how their training had paid off for both of them. He looked at Martha's hand, and saw and felt the swelling. He said he thought it was not broken, and took her into his office. There he wrapped her hand in some awful-smelling damp weeds. Martha sat out the training session and watched the two of them throw each other all over the mats. Two hours later, when the guys were showering, Russ unwrapped her hand. It felt almost back to normal, and the swelling had almost gone. They went back to the hospital as a formality, only to have the nurse in charge report that the hand was not broken. However, the doctor did leave her with a prescription for the severe pain he was sure she was experiencing. She tore it up on the way out of the hospital.

"Let's get back to work," she said to the guys as she got into the car. "I hope you two were able to work off some of your feelings. I haven't had that luxury, and I'm most anxious to get even with those bastards."

The strategy for the day, and for the weeks to come, was for each of them to pursue obtaining evidence on a different crime group. They would all meet daily after supper to report on the success or failure of the day, and to offer each other advice as to how to go about the next step. Martha was going to follow up a new lead that had emerged from their investigation of the perfume smuggling, or bootlegging, of bogus perfumes. She was going to attempt to identify and collect evidence on the illegal alien activity, which it turned out was used to some degree to provide slave labor in the making and bottling of the spurious perfume.

She had remembered her conversation with her doctor at the time she was in the hospital immediately following the explosion that took Steve's life. The doctor herself was from Vietnam and was in the process of bringing her family to the States, one by one. She had told Martha back then about paying a large sum of money to some group who guaranteed that her brother would be brought safely into this country.

Then she had received notification of a snag, and was being asked to come up with another $3,000 on top of the $4,500 she had already paid. Martha called Dr. Ah Leh and made an appointment to meet with her at the hospital.

Her "Guardian Angel," she still did not know his real name and he wasn't offering it to her either, came with her. After the attack on her in the supermarket parking lot, Jesse was not taking any chances with any of them. He had his people staying real close.

Mike had the list of 237 shipments into the United States from the computer printout to review. It was still like trying to find a needle in a haystack to be able to identify which company receiving small bottles on consignment from overseas sources actually was importing them to fill with copies of the original high-priced perfumes. They had all agreed, in one of their evening strategy sessions, not to pursue the label-making process. They theorized a small printing machine being used by a knowledgeable person, could easily duplicate any label wanted, and it could be done in a small area adjacent to the bottling process. So Mike started in on his chore.

John busied himself at the computer and with the placement of many calls around the country to other Justice Department officials, using only the safe telephone line. He had Bo back in Washington making all sorts of computer runs and analysis reports. They were sent to him by computer communications transfer, and the printer always seemed to be active. With John joining them at home base, the house had been transformed into an office

114

environment, and in effect it was an arm of the Justice Department.

Jesse was responsible for all security, as well as their safety. He had by this time transferred in fifteen more personnel, plus himself. Yet Jesse always worked out of his own New York City office.

THOR had read the newspapers which described the takeout of "Fat Howie" Goodring in all of its gory detail. He was pleased with all the coverage he was getting in the press and on television. His only problem was it did nothing to soothe the pain racking his body with more and more frequency each day. One of his girlfriends had broken off their so-called engagement, and this abruptly reduced his supply of morphine. All this was happening just when he needed more each day. He didn't have the time or the patience to cultivate another nurse. He had to focus on making a big score, one that could last him for the rest of his life. He held no delusions that this would be more then a couple of months at the most.

Phone calls had been coming into his private nontraceble number at a rate of two to three times a day, especially after the "Fat Howie" hit. Was it possible that Tony was on to him already? He called back and answered the first couple of these calls by telling them he was sick with the flu bug and had a fever and all that. It only worked for a while, and they knew damn well that it was THOR who had hit their gambling people. He was sure they would identify him as the one who hit that miserable punk Howie.

His next planned attack would bring him in 2,500 plastic ampoules of morphine for his personal use, fifteen kilos of cocaine and eight kilos of pure uncut heroin. Total street value was estimated at $47 million. He had found out from his sources that the shipment was to arrive at Pier 96 on the Hudson River. It was located in a large containerized unit, and the drugs had been packed in with down feathers taken from geese raised in New Zealand. The feathers were compacted tightly into bales that weighed forty-three pounds each. In the center of each bale was some portion of the drug shipment. Each bale was marked with a unique-smelling perfume which denoted what type of narcotic it stored. The morphine was stored in bales smelling like Chanel No. 5.

The strong odors emanating from the container were able to drive the narcotic-smelling dogs damn near crazy. As planned, the Mob then left the container on the pier for thirty-three days without anyone going near it. The Mob had arranged to pick up the contents using a legitimate unclaimed freight dealer. They had in fact, already hired and paid to have the pickup made on September 15 at 2:30 P.M. THOR made a call to the unclaimed freight vendor and changed the pickup to the same time, but one day earlier.

The pickup from the pier went off without a hitch, and the employees of the unclaimed freight company transferred the entire contents of the container into two large tractor trailers. They arrived back at their warehouse, where the trailers were transferred to tractor rigs driven by men hired by THOR.

Payment was made to the owners of the pickup tractor trucks, with a $1,000 bonus to each of the two owners for the fine job they had done in adjusting their schedule at the last moment. The new drivers took the trailers to a holding location identified by THOR and disconnected their tractor rigs. They were paid as agreed, and they departed.

THOR entered the trailers and extracted three of the morphine-loaded bales and broke them open and took his morphine. He now had 500 ampoules, enough to last him eight months at two shots per day. Even he thought it was a little excessive, as he knew he would not live that long.

To complete his flair for the dramatic, he wired each of the trailers with incendiary and plastic explosive devices which he decided he would set off by remote control. He called the head of the crime group responsible for narcotics smuggling and told him where he could pick up his load of narcotics. The guy was totally unaware that someone had already beaten them to the pickup point on the pier, which was only scheduled to take place that afternoon. Reluctantly he took three of his henchmen with him to the location where he was directed to by THOR. When the men arrived on the scene, THOR waited until they entered the trailers to check out what was loaded in them. From a distance when he saw them enter the trailers he pressed the detonator in his hand. The explosion and the flames were the biggest bang anyone in that immediate area of two miles had ever heard.

Before the fire engines were even on the scene, THOR made an anonymous call to the Drug Enforcement Agency. He told them about the contents of the trailers that just went up in smoke. Of course he didn't mention that he had removed 500 ampoules of morphine before he set off the big bang. He wanted to make sure that the media gave him proper credit for his single-handed assault on the drug dealers and the filthy products they deal to the public.

The newspapers and television had a field day with this one. They seemed to be making him out as some sort of a Robin Hood or something. When all of a sudden it dawned on them that they were making this cold-blooded killer out to be a hero of sorts. Clearer heads then prevailed, and the media folk began to correctly portray this THOR character as a psychopathic killer of men in the most violent way. They reported that his scorecard over the last few weeks contained three men murdered with needles in their brains, and one had his head practically blown off with a bullet. Then there was the one who suffered an inglorious ending when he was blown up while sitting on a toilet bowl. And now, four more men died in an inferno of dope and feathers. Yes, the authorities had better get their hands on this man before he murdered again. It did not make any difference to the reporting media that all these men were outside of the law. It was the law alone that had the authority to punish them.

Martha, John, and Mike all watched the evening news together. They had each become hardened to the violence that surrounded them and they all expressed the same thoughts.

"Good riddance, you sons of bitches," said Mike.

"You deserve everything you got, and more," said John.

Martha just nodded her approval of what was said. Each of them were deep down ashamed at what they had thought and expressed, and they made a pledge to each other to someday become normal people again and clear their minds of the hatred they had built up.

That is, as soon as they put Tony Calese and his cohorts behind bars. Mike couldn't resist the opportunity; he called Tony's telephone number again, and lo and behold, this time Tony himself picked up.

"Just wanted you to know that I was not bluffing and that I really do have THOR working for me now," and he hung up again before Tony could reply.

The phone rang to break the utter silence that had prevailed in the room. Mike answered; it was his daughter.

"Dad, I need a list of the people you want to invite to the wedding. We have to get the invitations into the mail this week, as the wedding is only four weeks off. Oh, and Dad, don't forget that you have to pick up your tuxedo and be sure that it fits on October 15th, that is a Thursday. And also you have to be present the night of the rehearsal on Friday, October 16. It's at the Church of Our Savior at 6:00 P.M.

"After that we are all having a dinner at The Chop House. Don't worry, Charlie's father is paying for the rehearsal dinner; it's the right thing to do, you know."

"Okay, honey, I'll make out the list tonight and Martha and I will drop it off to you about 10:00 P.M. See you then."

Mike and Martha put their heads together on the list. First off, he put down Martha's name. They then put down the Jacobsens, the Withs, Martha's dad George Monroe and his third wife. Martha's mother was dead. They decided it was a good time for Mike to meet his prospective father-in-law so that he could see for himself what a nice family Martha was going to marry into, and vice versa. They listed John Smith, and he reluctantly agreed, and of course Jesse and his men, all fifteen of them. John told them to only give Jesse six open invitations, as some of the bodyguards had to be off duty and sleeping at some time. But Martha prevailed and one of the invitations was to be made out to "G. Angel." They all chuckled at that one. And then Mike added Bo Denville to the list. There was a look of shock on Martha's face when John chimed in, "He is okay now; I guarantee you he won't embarrass anyone."

So it was agreed the list would contain fifteen names. They went to Mike's house at 10:00 P.M. as promised and gave the list to Jennifer. Charlie was still there with her. Mike used the opportunity and told them that his wedding gift to them was a first-class round-trip and two weeks of fully paid hotel and meal expenses any place in the world.

Charlie blurted out, "That's just great, Mr. Burke. Jennifer and I wanted to go to Alaska, and we just didn't know how we could be able to afford it. You really saved the day for us."

"Isn't Alaska kind of cold in October?" he asked, and both he and Martha looked at them quizzically.

"Oh no, not at all," claimed Jennifer. "Charlie doesn't like the hot weather anymore, not after his one-year assignment in Uganda."

They left the house shortly thereafter, and Jennifer and Charlie were bubbling with enthusiasm. As they went out the front door, Mike was asking Martha, "Alaska, why Alaska is already having winter weather that time of the year, don't they?"

His question never got answered. He picked up the reflection of a revolver across the street. It came from the hand of a person at his neighbors' house. Only he knew his neighbors hadn't been home for more than six months. He pushed Martha to the side of the steps as he jumped off the porch in another direction. Martha actually fell into the shrubbery. A series of quiet thuds were then heard striking the solid front door of his home. So the assailant had a silencer on his gun. Mike had already drawn his .45 and had rolled to a position on the lawn. He was holding his gun in both hands in front of him and taking aim. He saw another flash of light from the gunman across the street, and just as he was about to fire, the assailant fell quietly to the ground.

"Guardian Angel" had taken him down with his own silencer-equipped weapon. He dragged the man to his car, and in doing so he left a trail of the man's blood. The car drove off with not a word from their protector. As they drove back to home base, Mike said to Martha that if he had used his .45, the whole neighborhood would have been woken up, and there would have been hell to pay. When they arrived at home base, they told John about the latest encounter. He moved methodically. First off, he called and arranged to have around-the-clock protection for the members of Mike's family. This thing was coming to a head and he could not afford to risk anyone's life. Then he called Tony's number this time. He left a message on his answering machine telling Tony that his latest attempt had failed and that the assailant was talking to them loud and clear. He finished his words to Tony with his sweetest sounding Southern voice, "Have a nice evening now, you hear!"

Martha had agreed to fly John down periodically to visit with his wife and child in Virginia. She made out flight plans for Greensboro, and added an hour to her planned arrival time in order to make the stopoff in Virginia. She reversed the flight plan for the trip home. Mike always joined the flight to keep her company. They gave as much time as they could to John, and they spent as much time in the Greensboro general area as they could before they made the trip back to pick up John.

They ate early dinners in some of the best restaurants down there, and as time went on they fell more and more in love with each other. They did this every two weeks on Friday for the benefit of John. They knew it pained him not to have been able to bury his child, but the body was already embalmed and had been stored away in a cold vault. Each of them were all making some sort of progress on their crime group assignments. Life for them was becoming very routine, mind you not normal, just routine. Mike dictated his next report to the Insurance Consortium. He had nothing to report, other than that he was busy pursuing and gathering information on the bogus perfume that was flooding the market and inundating the insurance company with claims of bad products being distributed on the street. The legitimate producers were paying large premiums to the insurance companies to pay off on these claims, so as not to lose the image of their products. It was really a convoluted way of supporting the people who were trafficking in the bogus perfume. The whole thing didn't make any sense.

Martha reported to them one evening on her meeting with Dr. Ah Leh. Her earlier scheduled meeting was put off several times due to emergency situations that called Dr. Leh away at the last moment. So the meeting finally took place two weeks after originally planned. Dr. Leh told Martha that after she had paid the additional $3,000 dollars to get her brother into the country she never heard anything from them.

By now she was well aware that she had broken the law, but at the time she was so concerned with the plight of her brother. He had made the trip by boat from Vietnam, and through some

120

twist of fate he ended up in the Caribbean country of the Dominican Republic. From there he had contacted his sister at the hospital, and she had tried all legal means at her disposal to get him a visa. As a last resort, she was introduced to this Latino-type, a man with a greasy head of black hair, by the name of Vica Porofundo. He told her he could have her brother in the States within two weeks. She gave him $4,500 he said he needed to bribe the proper gringos and to get her brother a valid workers' visa.

She had not heard from her brother for more than three months, when she received a letter from him. He said in the letter that he entered into the country hidden in a new gasoline tank that was being shipped into the country, along with five other aliens. One of the others was an Asian, the other four were Hispanic, and so conversation was limited. They never came out of the tank until four days later and had existed on some dried meat and rotten fruit and a single quart of water per person for the entire four-day trip. The smell of the human excrement and urine was horrible. All of them were sick for more than three days after they got here. It was reported that one of the Hispanics died shortly after they arrived in this country. They never heard another thing about him.

Shortly after they got out of the tank and off of the ship, they were given two days to get over the effects of the trip. Then they were made to work in a factory putting perfume into bottles for another three weeks. They were told that it was part of their training for a job that would assure permanent status on their visas. His letter said he was able to look out of the window and see two bridges in the distance. The letter was postmarked Arkansas, where he said he had been working as a field hand picking vegetables. He said that he did not receive any pay at all for his labor, but they were feeding him pretty regularly. He got this letter into the mail by a friendly farmer who gave him a drink of water. He had heard word that they were taking him and another fifteen of them to California to work on the tomato fields. He would write again when he got a chance. The part of the letter that broke her heart was that he was sure that he would soon complete paying for his fare over here. Then he would come to live with her.

Martha reported that Dr. Ah Leh was heartbroken. She was

willing to take any consequences as a result of her illegal action, if it would help to stop these men who prey on human needs. No one should be able to make slaves out of these people who wanted to make a new life for themselves.

Upon hearing the information, John said he would dispatch someone to visit with Dr. Ah Leh and get her to sign an affidavit. She would be required at some time in the future to make a court appearance, when and if they could nail this guy Porofundo.

John would see to it that she would receive immunity from prosecution, of course.

Mike picked up a lead from her story as well. So her brother had reported being able to see two bridges from the window of the factory where they bottled the perfume. He took out a map of New York City. The only place where you could see two bridges was either from someplace in Brooklyn near the East River, or from across the way on the Lower East Side. He checked over his computer-generated listings. If he was correct, he had the bottling operation pinned down to any one of only five locations. Yes sir, things were getting a little brighter. He also had his work cut out for him tomorrow. Martha was just sitting there and smiling at them both. She felt good about what she had found out.

The Cotter brothers lived in a two-bedroom condominium apartment complex near the East River. It was a posh neighborhood, and these apartments cost over $.5 million to purchase in today's market. They had lived in the seven-story building since it first opened five and a half years ago. They were able to purchase it then for $185,000. It was a drop in the bucket compared to the profits they were taking in from their protection racket. Tony was letting them keep twenty-five percent of what they collected, and their collections now were netting them $1 million per month.

One of the apartments in their building had just been put up for sale, and they saw the chance to launder some money in a legitimate way. They purchased the apartment for $735,000. And then they furnished it and rented it for $3,000 a month to this nice-looking young bachelor, who was in advertising. They met him often in the hall by the elevator, as he seemed to leave for work the same time as they did every day. This guy had wavy black hair, and looked to be a lady-killer. He told them when he

122

rented the apartment that he would be bringing home different women from time to time, and they had no problem with that. Then when he met them in the morning and they asked him how the action was, he would be give them a bit on his previous night's activity. They started to look forward to their meetings with him each morning as they rode down the elevator.

One day as they came out of their apartment, they could see that their tenant was waiting for them at the elevators. When they arrived, Harry noticed that no one had pressed the call button and he did so promptly. Funny, he thought, but I seem to have scratched my finger someplace. He sucked at it as a small drop of blood formed on his thumb.

Their tenant then excused himself, saying he had forgotten something in his room. The Cotter brothers entered the elevator. Harry Cotter was found dead in his brother's arms by the time the elevator reached the ground floor. It looked like a heart attack.

Just as soon as the elevator doors had closed, THOR ever so carefully removed the almost invisible adhesive strip containing the pinpoint which had been loaded with the venom of the cobra and the rattlesnake mixed together for effectiveness. He had made the pickup from his pharmacist friend yesterday for the usual $3,000 fee. He walked down to the basement level and got into his Jaguar and drove away. Looking back at the apartment building, he could hear the sound of the Emergency Medical Service Ambulance as it pulled to the curb in front of the building.

He didn't have time to even gloat about another of his finely planned conquests when the pain once again became unbearable. He had to hurry home for a fix.

CHAPTER 13

John received a call early the next morning, and it made him seem a bit more satisfied. He told them at breakfast the leak in the Washington office had been plugged. It seems his trusted secretary for the last five years had fallen in love with a lawyer for the Mob. He had bedded her down and drugged her. While she was in a semiconscious state, they took video pictures of her in various sexual positions with two male and one female partner at the same time. When they later showed her the pictures, they threatened to expose her as a sexual pervert. That was unless she provided the Mob with confidential information out of John's office. She had been on the hook to them for the last four years, but when she heard about the death of John's child she had gone to pieces and attempted suicide with an overdose. Her girlfriend found her unconscious and called an ambulance. They pumped out her stomach in time to save her. She told everything, and there was enough evidence in hand to jail the Mob lawyer. The Mob followed up on their threat to expose her and released the pictures of her in those compromised sexual positions to one of the slut magazines. Pictures of her were now all over Washington.

She was aware of what has happened to her good name, and she couldn't wait to testify. She not only gave the Mob information, but when they were sure they had her in their grasp, they started to get careless around her. She used a tape recorder hidden in her bra to document some of the phone conversations the lawyer had with not only Tony, but his son as well. She also taped a conversation of the lawyer to one of Tony's hoods, where he was authorizing a hit on a local politician who was on Tony's payroll and had crossed him. In the conversation, the lawyer actually said, "Tony Calese just called me himself. He wants me to tell you he has authorized a hit on Robert Harris, and he wants it done now."

The body of this Harris character was fished out of the Potomac a month ago.

John approved putting his former secretary into a witness protection plan after she testified. This would give her a new identity and a chance to live, or at least start, another life. She had tried to redeem herself by taking her own life, and John felt that she had paid her debt.

Mike went out to the five locations he had most recently identified, thanks to the tip contained in Dr. Ah Leh's brother's letter. It took him two days to eliminate the two locations in Brooklyn, and he went to New York City's Lower East Side to continue his search. He was in an old factory area and went directly to the office of the company on the list to make his inquiries. The office manager was most pleasant at first, but when he could see where Mike's questions were leading, he started to shut him off from any further information. In fact, he got rather upset and told Mike to leave the premises, and not to come back without a search warrant. Mike felt that by the time he was able to get a search warrant issued, they would have already cleaned up any evidence on the scene. Thus upon leaving, Mike paid a visit to their garbage Dumpster. Looking in the top of it he could see a number of broken bottles. As the garbage men showed up for the pickup of the Dumpster, he paid each of them fifty dollars to put the Dumpster aside at the garbage collection station. Then he asked the men to put a mark on the Dumpster and to certify in writing where they had picked it up. He then called Jesse's number, and he had a man on the scene in fifteen minutes at the garbage collection station to take charge of the find. By the time he reached home base, Jesse was already on the phone. Mike had hit the jackpot. They found broken bottles of three different types of expensive perfumes, and assorted labels for six different types of perfumes. The bottles were not originals made by the manufacturer, nor were traces of the perfume found in the broken ones the real thing. They had them cold, and Jesse expected to have the search warrant issued based on probable cause within the hour. He already had his men at the factory site, and while they reported much activity going on, nothing had been removed from the building as yet. He told Mike that he would fill him in later.

Digging in even further, Mike was able to provide direct links from the purchase of perfume bottles from a French glass factory by one of Nelson Bidder's dummy corporations. It looked as if they had enough evidence to put the President of the Exquisite Aroma company into deep shock with an indictment. But they still did not have any corroborating evidence accumulated that would tie Norm Cotter, the identified crime group leader, directly to the whole damn operation. That is, unless they were able to get this Bidder character to implicate not only Norm Cotter, but tie in some members of the Calese family as well.

Mike received a call from Jennifer telling him that she noticed some rather large indents and splintered wood in the front door of their house. She didn't have any idea where they could have come from. Mike told her not to worry, that he would have it taken care of before she came home from school that day. Then she told him she noticed quite a bit of activity always going on during all hours of the day and night on their street. There was a telephone repair van in the neighborhood. And then there were the oil delivery trucks, yet she knew no one on the block ever used oil, and other strange things. He told her again not to worry. After he hung up the phone he called Jesse. He received confirmation from Jesse as to it being his people covering Mike's house after the shooting two weeks ago. He told Jesse he thought his people were being too obvious, since a novice like Jennifer could sense something was going on.

Jesse told him he would look into it further. But any way you wanted to cut it, he was going to provide the necessary protection cover. Mike told Jesse that he understood, and thanked him.

Then he asked Jesse if he was able to identify THOR from the photographs taken while on stakeout at the apartments of Nancy Preston and that queer gent William Jennings. Jesse told him he had reviewed the pictures of every single person coming and going into the two separate apartment complexes for the entire periods of surveillance. There were 3,756 pictures taken, and they completed doing their visual scan with no positive results. They were now submitting all the pictures to Washington. In the central office, a specially trained clerical task force would assign a number to each picture. Then under a magnified viewer, each photo would have fifteen special characteristics coded and entered into the computer. When all the coding was complete, Bo Denville had created this program to compare for all like characteristics between the different photos, and then produce a list of high probable matches. This was a time-consuming operation. He felt sure that once they had narrowed it down they would have a good picture of what THOR looked like. Next would come the hard part, identifying the picture or pictures with someone they either knew or could find in a mug book. So it was going to be a real long drawn-out ordeal. "Best not to hold your breath waiting," Jesse told Mike.

THOR was having his dream with continued regularity. Each with the same devastating effect on his pain-racked body. He took care of his immediate problem of the extreme bouts with the pain by decreasing the time frame between morphine injections. Somehow after each shot, it allowed him to come back to the world of reality, his reality. He recognized that he had become a sort of Jekyll and Hyde, moving between his character of Tom which in his mind he considered quite rational and reasonable, and his alter ego THOR, who was crazed and got pleasure only by killing. Once again he went to his wall safe and removed his book labeled "RETRIBUTION." Since his attacks had changed direction from mob designated hits to eliminations of mob designees he himself had selected, he created a new section. He closed out the first portion of the book after adding Nancy Preston and the specifics of all he had done to her, not leaving out a single detail. He never was paid for the hit on the Preston woman, because the Mob had found him out when he switched the direction of his terror towards them.

The new section, started two pages after he wrote "Finis" at the bottom, was simply headed "Part 2." At the top of the page, he would list the name or names of the victims. As his plan progressed, he would add the details of the plans he so meticulously created on how he would murder them. He had already documented the mass murder of the four gambling hoods and the men on the tractor trailers. He followed this with the words "extra violence used" scribbled at the end of his description of the events.

He started a new page and seemed to really relish the planning and execution of the toilet-bowl bombing of that stupid creep Howie. Again on another page he wrote the final details of his takeout of Harry Cotter with the poison pinprick.

Now he turned to start another page, and he wrote the name Norm Cotter at the head of the page. This was followed by the words, "One Cotter down, two to go." His planning had to be done while he was in his fully rational state.

He said out loud to himself, "Now I wonder how I can do justice to a man who makes a living out of selling bogus perfume, and who also smuggles the real stuff into the United States without paying any import duties. I know, I know, I'll have him drown in the stuff. But I'll have to time it so that I'm long gone when he actually goes under."

He arrived at the warehouse on the Lower East Side where he knew the bottling process was going on, and let himself in through a back door. He had gained complete access and knowledge of whatever any of Tony Calese's crime groups were doing because he always followed and tracked the crime group head who made the arrangements for a hit on behalf of another crime group. He watched from a vantage point when Norm Cotter spotted, of all people, his father enter the building and start to press the office manager of Exquisite Aroma, Inc., for information. When he first saw Mike Burke, Norm had moved himself into the back room just adjacent to where the large fifty-gallon drums of perfume were stored.

It was a simple matter for THOR to render Norm unconscious without his even letting out a whimper. After all, he was a professional. The drums were stacked in holders, with the top drum set about nine feet off the floor. Each of the drums had spigots used to drain the perfume into a holding tank, which was then used to fill the individual smaller bottles.

THOR stuffed some material into Norm's mouth, and tied another piece of cloth around his head to hold the gag securely. Then he fastened a large plastic bowl around his neck, and used adhesive tape to seal it to his neck so that his head was in an open container. He tied his hands together and fastened a heavy duty rope to the top holding his two hands. Next he hoisted him up toward the ceiling on one of the overhead pipes, and stood him on a small footstool.

Norm was starting to become conscious now. There was terror in his eyes when he saw what was happening to him. A long tube was attached to the end of the spigot, and then taped to the inside of the bowl, which had been fastened and sealed around his neck. THOR then opened the spigot so as to allow a fast drip through the tube. This was sort of like a Chinese water torture, only the drips accumulated in the bowl fastened around his neck. A string was then attached to one end of the footstool and tied to the end of the spigot handle. If Norm moved the footstool in any way, the spigot would open further and the perfume would fill the bowl faster.

Another cord was fastened to the spigot handle, and then carefully attached to the doorknob. Thus anyone entering the room would also turn the spigot on full force. So as not to take any chances, he opened the spigot enough to let the bowl fill to just under Norm's nose. A most horrible way to die, he thought to himself. Well, he deserved it.

He let himself out of the building. He had to get around his father who was in the alley and rummaging around the Dumpster.

Mike took the urgent call from Jesse. He told him that upon obtaining the search warrant and starting a systematic search of the building his men had found a back room. He described the scene his men found with Norm Cotter dead. They were not sure if his men had actually started the final gush of perfume into the bowl, or if he was dead before they forced the door open. Only an autopsy would establish the actual cause of death.

"My God, what sort of a man is this guy THOR? He kills and makes a sport of it. Thank goodness he has focused his attacks on the Mob, and not the rest of the normal world any more. Jesse, do you have any idea why he has changed the direction of his attacks?"

Jesse had no answer, and ended the conversation.

At dinner that night Mike told the other two of the events of his very busy day. It was quite obvious each of them were becoming more hardened to the brutality surrounding them.

Mike picked up his tuxedo on October 15th as planned and had the opportunity to speak with his two boys who were to be the ushers. Nothing much was happening in Sean's life, as he was busy with preparing to take the test to be admitted to the bar exam in New York State on the Monday following Thanksgiving. They would each be doing something different on Thanksgiving Day, so they did not plan to be together. Sean dropped a hint that the gal he had been studying with for the exam was making a move on him, and vice versa. The feeling was mutual, and after the exam they were going off on a weekend to celebrate together.

Tom seemed to be exceptionally tired and didn't get too much into their conversation, only nodding his approval when Sean was telling them about himself. Before they left for the night, Mike thanked Tom for the early warning. He asked Tom how he knew, but he just smiled and told Mike that he had to protect his source of information. Mike let it drop.

The next few weeks went by slowly, and each of them pursued other leads which they felt could lead to more evidence, but they had begun to flounder and were unable to mount any serious new approach. Along with this frustration was another deep-seated fear. Each of them felt it, but each of them never discussed his uneasiness with the others. They knew Tony had been quiet too long. Something was about to happen.

It was Tuesday already and the wedding was scheduled for Saturday. Mike picked up the phone and it was Jennifer sounding very distraught. She had to speak with Martha, now. Mike handed Martha the telephone and heard the conversation that ensued, at least Martha's side of it.

"Oh my, yes that is a shame. You think I'm about the same size? Yes, I'm a size eight. Yes, my bust size is 36C. You really want me now, you're sure? Okay, I'll be delighted. See you at the rehearsal on Friday. Bye, now."

"What was that all about?"

"Your daughter's maid of honor just called from the hospital. It seems she was in a car accident and broke her leg. She is all right otherwise, but she can't walk down the aisle. I'm the same size, so Jennifer asked me to take her place. I'm going out for a fitting of my gown in about an hour."

It was obvious Martha was delighted to be asked, and Mike was pleased also. Before she left they decided to make the trip to drop John off to see his wife and son early on Thursday morning.

Mike and Martha would as usual go on to Greensboro after they dropped John off in Virginia. But this time they would stay the night, and also take out a room for John and they would make it seem as if he slept there. This would give John more time with his wife, as they both thought he was a bit too edgy and talking

130

horny-like back at the house. They agreed both of them would enjoy a night in Greensboro, and they could take in a little dancing after dinner for a change. They all needed something different in their lives. Plans were to pick John back up at noon on Friday, and they would have no trouble getting to the rehearsal by 6:00 P.M.

On the flight back they ran into some strong head winds that not only buffeted the small plane violently, but put off their arrival at the Ramapo Airport by two hours. It was 5:15 when they finally landed. It was somewhat tight on time, but John would come with them to the rehearsal, rather than their dropping him off at home base first as originally planned. As it turns out, fate was again working along its inexorable path.

They arrived at the church at 5:45 P.M. It was just starting to get dark, but it was still reasonably bright yet. Martha was saying how they had made pretty good time getting the plane tied down and all. They had just gotten out of the car and John was the first to be walking up the steps of the church entrance, when all hell broke loose. The staccato rapid firing of a machine pistol—Mike thought it sounded like a Uzi—broke the relative silence of the neighborhood. John was down holding his leg, and at the same time reaching for his .38 revolver tucked into the small of his back. Even though he was hit, he had managed to roll off the steps of the church entrance and out of the direct line of fire. Mike and Martha still were in the safety of being behind the car, as a stream of small caliber bullets tore across the side of the car, shattering the safety glass and peppering the door and the quarter panel.

Both of them immediately dropped to the ground. Mike had already drawn his .45 revolver. He pulled out his .38 and tossed it to Martha, at the same time commanding her to keep down. Another stream of automatic fire emanated from about thirty feet to the left of the first barrage. And then another barrage was sent in their direction from yet another angle. They had weathered the first onslaught of firepower. Mike was already firing in the direction one of the bursts had come from. Out of a storefront directly across the street from the church, two figures came out of the blue, each one approaching a different one of their adversaries from the rear. A flying leap deposited the body of a young man onto the back of one of the assailants, while the other was taking out his opponent with a series of karate blows, chops, and kicks. Firepower from Mike's, Martha's, and John's guns centered on the position of the third attacker. Additional shots came from up the street and the man jerked his body violently. He held the trigger and released all of the shells in his Uzi magazine as he fell to the ground. He was silent, except for the twitching of his body as it fought death. The street fight was over, and Jesse came running into view.

Sean and Tom had gone across the street to a local store for some gum when they heard the noise of the rapid-firing guns. They came out behind the assailants and quickly decided to each head for one of the men that were firing at someone in the direction of the church.

Sean had wrestled his man to the ground and placed a hard right onto his jaw. He had knocked him cold, but it was possible he had dislocated his thumb. He did, and he snapped it back. It would be plenty sore in the morning, but it wasn't the first time he had knocked it out of joint. He remembered the three separate times a wildly thrown baseball had done the same thing to his thumb. Tom had broken the neck of the man he went after and he had killed him. The other guy who was firing at them was also dead. There were at least seven bullet holes in various parts of his body. It looked as if everyone who had fired at him had hit him. He was literally torn to shreds.

John had taken a bullet through the calf of his leg, and had dislocated his shoulder when he rolled off the steps. Martha and Mike were unharmed, but they were dirty from rolling on the ground and disheveled. One of Jesse's guys had taken a bullet which was lodged in his chest. It had somehow gotten around the edge of the lightweight bulletproof vest he was wearing. It apparently wasn't into his body too deeply. He was conscious and more annoyed that the vest had let him down. The rest of the bridal party heard the commotion outside, and had smartly stayed inside the church.

The priest was already giving the last rites to the bodies of the two dead assailants. An ambulance came for John and the injured guy from the Justice Department. John seemed to be okay, and he told Martha and Mike to get on with the rehearsal. And they did just that.

Tony's troops had tried once again to take them out, and again they had failed. They knew they were really getting to him now, and he was in turn reacting in the only way he knew.

"Kill them, kill them all! Why can't anyone get them? Are they living charmed lives or something? I'm going to make them pay. I'll get them, won't I," he was heard to say to Tony Jr., when the news of the messed-up attack reached him.

The rehearsal went off without so much as someone coughing. Everybody who asked what had happened was told that it was a terrorist group who was attacking the church. This was the same story that was fed to the press, only at the time no one thought the number of parishioners to stay away from church the next Sunday would be ninety-five percent of the parish faithful.

At the dinner that followed, everybody was talking about how the Burke family had single-handedly wiped out the terrorist group. Little did they know. Mike noticed how Sean was quiet and withdrawn after their skirmish. On the other hand, Tom was invigorated and seemed to be on a euphoric high. Mike took his boys aside and told them how proud he was of them and the way they handled themselves. Jennifer was very upset, and Martha spent quite a bit of time talking to her and trying to quiet her down. At the end of the evening, she seemed much calmer. Her new in-laws-to-be were upset. Mike overheard them say they wondered what kind of a family their Charlie was marrying into. And Mike thought to himself, "How right they are."

They arrived home at 11:30 P.M. John had already been driven home from the hospital by Jesse. Jesse told them that the Coroner's Office reported the cause of death of Norm Cotter was found to be from the fumes of the perfume. There was no trace of perfume fluid in his lungs at all. John was patched up with a bandage on his left leg that kept him limping from the flesh wound he had received. He wouldn't be going out in the mornings for a power walk with Mike for quite a while. He also had his shoulder in a cast, so he wasn't about to be able to work out on the gym equipment in the basement either.

With a very forlorn look on his face, Jesse cautioned both of them to be extremely careful. This case was drawing to a close, and he did not want to lose any of them. He told them he had made arrangements to have an additional fifteen men added to their security force. They would be available for the wedding on Saturday. It was still scheduled to take place at 11:30 A.M., and the reception was to be held starting at 1:00 P.M. in the ELK's Hall.

CHAPTER 14

On the day of the wedding Mike rose at his usual time for his morning walk. He had no company this morning, and he wanted Martha to catch up on her sleep. After last night's episode with that three-man hit team, he was as wary as could be. As he made his walk, he noticed all the security men at various stages of the trip. Looking up at the sky, it seemed to be a beautiful fall day for his daughter's wedding. At least he had that to be thankful for. When he got home, Martha was already dressed and going out the door. He had almost forgotten that she was the matron of honor, and come to think of it, he also was in the wedding party as a pretty important person. Before he took his shower, the doorbell rang and it was Sean dropping off his tuxedo. While he was in the shower, Sean made a pot of coffee and cooked up some eggs for Mike and John. John was in a lot of pain and had begged off going to the wedding, and Mike understood. There was a quiet ease amongst them all as they sat and had breakfast together. Mike was hoping for a quiet day.

Maybe Tony would need more time before he would be able to mount another attack. Mike was sure of it.

They arrived at the church just a little ahead of Jennifer. She was a gorgeous bride, and her curly red hair contrasted beautifully with her white wedding dress. Charlie was beaming from ear to ear. The wedding went off without a hitch, and Mike was his very best as he gave his daughter away. He winked at Martha as he picked up the veil covering his daughter's face. He kissed the bride good-bye and passed her hand over to Charlie. Nothing happened outside the church either. Everybody just lined up to throw rice at the bride and groom. Mike could see there were Justice Department Marshals stationed all over the place. He was grateful for Jesse's perseverance in this matter. They all left for the reception hall after posing for some pictures in front of the church.

Everything seemed to be going smoothly, and Mike was formally introduced by Martha to her father.

She simply said, "Dad, this is Mike Burke, the man I live with now. And the good Lord willing, we'll be getting married one of these days after a proper mourning period is over. You see, Mike lost his wife more than six months ago, and Steve is gone only a couple of months now. We feel we both have to wait a while."

Mr. Monroe grasped Mike's hand firmly in both of his hands and said to him, "Just treat her always like the lady she is, and if she is anything like her mother, the best is yet to come."

As they moved away, Mike told Martha he thought her father had approved of him. She nodded a yes. It was then that Mike noticed a strange-looking man, rather good-looking, and dressed in a conservative three-piece suit with a vest, staring at him and Martha. He didn't like it at all, and started to ask around if anyone knew who this guy was. He asked Charlie's father. He didn't know who he was. He asked Jennifer and Charlie, and they didn't know him either. Mike was looking around for "Guardian Angel" or one of Jesse's other guys, when this very determined-looking character headed directly toward himself and Martha. Mike pushed Martha aside and readied for an attack. He took one and then another step in this guy's direction. They were headed toward each other in the center of the dance floor.

As Mike drew closer to him the guy stuck out his hand at Mike and said, "Congratulations to the father of the bride. This is a great wedding you have going on here. But don't you have any warm beer around here for a fella to drink? That cold stuff gives me a god-awful case of the runs."

Mike broke into a wide smile. It was Bo Denville. Yes sir, it was a new and different Bo. He had joined the establishment after all. John did say they would find him different, but this took the cake. Mike pulled Martha back and into a conversation with Bo. But it also took her quite a while to realize who he was. When she finally recognized who he was, she threw her arms around him and gave him a big kiss. The Jacobsens and the Withs joined in the group on the center of the dance floor. Bob didn't know who he was talking to until Bo started in with technical gibberish, and it dawned on each of them that it was Bo Denville they were talking with. They all had a good laugh when Bo told them he had changed his ways because he wanted to work for the government. This guy John Smith told him the only way they would take him would be for him to clean up his act. He did, and he got the job. Only the first day on the job, his picture did not match with the picture first taken shortly after the interview. That was because of the shave and haircut he had.

Mike introduced Martha to Kathleen's mother and father. There was a sadness in both of them, but they were indeed glad that Mike was getting on with his life again. Kathleen's father took him aside and told him straight out that he understood his need to love and be loved again. Mike had received their approval as well. This was turning into a pretty good day after all. While he was speaking with Charlie, he remarked how great it was that Martha was able to fill in as the matron of honor. Charlie remarked what a beautiful woman Martha was.

Mike saw his chance and asked Charlie, "Doesn't she look like Marilyn Monroe?"

Charlie looked at him squarely in the eye and said in a questioning manner, "Mr. Burke, I don't even know who Marilyn Monroe is! Am I supposed to know this person?"

Mike said, "Never mind," frowned, shook his head, and walked away.

Mike went looking for Jesse who was notably absent. "Guardian Angel" stopped and told him that Jesse was planning to meet him at home that night. He reported he was still at work in the office, and had just received the list of photographs which the computer had said were high probability for a match. He was bringing those photos over this evening to show to Mike and John, before they tried to match them up with the mug books.

Sean pulled Mike aside to tell him that Tom was acting very strangely. He had started to sweat profusely, and was unable to hold a conversation with anyone in a civil tone. Mom and Pop O'Rourke also thought the same thing and they told Sean, so they went looking for him. When they found him coming out of the men's room, he was calm and looked to be in good shape. He told them not to worry, that he had a case of the flu which was giving him the ups and downs. Mike bought his explanation, but Sean didn't. He told his father he thought that Tom was taking something, which was giving him the wide mood swings. Mike saw Tom heading for the door, but was unable to catch up with him. He saw him leave a trail of dust when he pulled out in his Jaguar.

The wedding was a huge success. The food was just great, and the catering was done with excellent care. A few of the guests got a little into their cups, but no one got obnoxious. Mike waited until Jennifer had left with Charlie, and he grabbed Martha and they said their good-byes to everyone. He paid the caterer by check, and they left for home base.

Jesse had already arrived and was going over the pictures identified by the computer as most probable candidates for being THOR. Mike started looking at them, too, and then his heart started beating very rapidly. In fact he almost passed out. He had just seen at least three pictures of his son Tom. Oh, the hair maybe was colored differently in each picture, and there was a mustache some of the times. But it was Tom all right, no question about it.

His son was THOR. His brain began to pound. His son was THOR. It had finally registered, and so many things that had taken place started to fit. His son was THOR. The blood rushed to his head and he blacked out from the shock.

He awoke in the bedroom with Martha standing over him. Just when he thought what a great day this had been, his whole world was starting to unravel. Jesse had to leave to meet someone in New York City to turn over the pictures. Everyone said they thought Mike had a little too much to drink, and they chalked it up to that. But Martha knew; she knew him better than the others. She knew instinctively that something was drastically wrong to have had that kind of an effect on Mike. She didn't press him, she knew better. At 2:00 A.M. he awoke Martha and asked her to talk with him. He told her what he now knew to be the truth, but he couldn't bring himself to tell Jesse or John. Not just yet, anyway. He needed to talk to Tom first. He had to find out why. Then he would do whatever had to be done, no matter how much it hurt.

Mike spent the next two weeks attempting to contact Tom, but to no avail. He left many messages on his answering machine. The length of the beep started getting longer and longer, indicating no one was taking off the messages.

138

But THOR was a busy person indeed. He was out working the trade he knew best. He was planning the execution of the last of the Cotters. He was now after Phil, a small fry in the organization who had been tapped by Tony to take over for his brother Harry as head of the protection crime group. THOR had come home from his sister's wedding with one thought in his mind. He was going to take out Phil Cotter.

His father and brother almost caught up with him at the wedding, but he was able to give himself the morphine shot before he came out of the bathroom. He was now up to five shots every two days. He knew the end was near, but he had one last good deed to perform. He took out his book of "RETRIBUTION" and made sure he had recorded Norm Cotter's death properly. The newspaper had said he died of asphyxiation, and not drowning in his illegitimate perfume as he had so carefully planned. He asked himself how could he have made that mistake. After all he was a professional, and he wasn't supposed to make mistakes. But in this case it didn't matter, as the target had died anyway. That was all that really mattered. He entered Phil Cotter's name at the top of the next page, and went to bed to sleep on it. He had to figure out a great way to do him in. After all, he was a professional.

He awoke with the same dream and the accompanying pain. He gave himself a fix so he could start to function again. And then it came to him. Phil was now in charge of protection, so he would charge him a protection fee to keep him alive. He called him on the phone and told him flat out that he was THOR. He also told him he was short of cash and demanded $1,000 a day to keep him alive. The first payment was due on Wednesday, and THOR added a threat that Phil had better not cross him up. They agreed to a meeting place where Phil was to turn over the money. Phil called Tony immediately after he hung up the phone with THOR, as THOR knew he would. Tony arranged a trap for THOR. THOR went to Phil's house the night before the scheduled meeting. After gaining entrance using a passkey, he found him asleep in his bed. He drugged him into a state of semiconsciousness. He then dyed Phil's hair red and made it curly-looking with a curling iron. He dressed Phil in his own best clothes, as they were about the same build. He arrived at the site of the meeting two hours early, and locked Phil in the closet. He put a two-way remote speaker phone on Phil's belt, went to a skylight vantage point, and awaited the arrival of Tony's men to spring their trap. When he saw the five heavies enter the room, he spoke into the microphone.

"Is that you, Phil? Did you bring the money like you were supposed to?"

They heard THOR's voice loud and clear through the door. One of them went to the door and pulled it open.

All of them saw the bright red hair and began firing their automatic pistols immediately. They put four hundred bullets into Phil's body. It was a nonrecognizable pulpy mass by the time they finished firing. They gloated to each other about having destroyed THOR for Tony, and said something about collecting the big reward promised by Tony. One guy mentioned that Phil probably chickened out and that was why he wasn't present for the big hit. Well, it was his tough luck. And because he didn't show, he wasn't entitled to any of the reward. They all left together in order to go directly to Tony's house to bring him the good news. They could hardly wait. THOR waited until he was sure all of them were at Tony's house. They were having a party when he called. Tony Jr. was in great spirits when he answered the phone. He turned white when he heard THOR's voice ask him why they had killed Phil Cotter, and then hung up the phone.

Time to take another shot of morphine, as the pain was starting to build to a crescendo in his body again. When he got home he made his entry in the book of "RETRIBUTION." He did not put it into the safe this time, as he now had other plans for the document. He added a new name to the top of the next page. It was Vica Porofundo, head of the illegal alien crime group.

Then he said out loud, "On to the hell you deserve along with me. I'm the devil, and I'm in the driver's seat."

Mike had spent all his available time trying to contact his son.

He went to his penthouse apartment in the Palisades, but couldn't get past the doorman. So he left another message, this time in the form of a written note. It said simply, "Call your dad, I know it all. We have to talk."

Tom had picked up the message when he returned to his apartment the night after he had arranged the death of Phil Cotter. The next morning Tom woke by himself very early and took a fix before the pain started to attack his body. He took five ampoules of morphine with him, a bankbook, his book which he had labeled "RETRIBUTION," and a copy of his last will and testament. He made a special pickup that morning, and as a second thought he made a second pickup. Then he headed for the place his father was living in Spring Valley with Martha. Martha answered the doorbell, and was surprised to see Tom. He looked terrible. He thrust the book and an envelope containing his will and the bankbook into her hands, and said, "Tell Dad that I love him."

With that he jumped into his Jaguar and headed toward the Palisades Interstate Parkway.

Mike had just returned from his walk to see Tom's car pulling out of his driveway. "Guardian Angel" had just come on duty, and Mike told him to get on the phone fast and stop that car. He told him it was THOR who was driving. An immediate phone call was sent to the state police, followed by another call to Jesse. John had hobbled downstairs when he heard the commotion.

Mike painfully told him about THOR's being his son. This was no longer the time to hold anything back.

When he got onto the parkway, THOR really opened up on the Jaguar. The police were only starting to set cars across the road to form a roadblock. When he came upon it, he swerved around them and floored the Jaguar. He was passing all traffic on the road, and kept weaving in and out of the slower-moving traffic at high speed. The police sirens wailed on in the background of the chase.

He came into a clear stretch without any cars in view, and the speed kept increasing: 90, 95, 100. There were tears in his eyes and he screamed out loud, "Oh, God, I'm sorry, I'm so sorry for what I have done."

The speed reached 105. He screamed again, "Grandma, Grandpa, you've got to forgive me. I'm not a Burke, I'm Thomas Henry O'Rourke, I'm THOR. I'm a professional. I'm the best in the business."

The speedometer showed 110. He yelled, "Mother, I hurt so much. Soon we'll be together again."

At 115 miles per hour he said in a most rational voice, "Dad, I tried to make it up to you in the only way I knew. I went after the Mob because of what they made me do to you. I got a lot of them, didn't I? I tried, I made up for some of what I did, I really tried."

The car had reached a speed of 120 when he aimed his car at one of the bridge overpass abutments. It was solid concrete. The car was totally disintegrated in the explosion and ensuing ball of flame.

Thomas Henry Burke was dead, and the assassin THOR was dead and on his way to meet his maker as well. It was all over.

The state police radioed back the news, and Jesse had the sorry job of telling Mike how his son had died. Jesse knew for the past two weeks that THOR was Mike's son. He had arrived at the wedding after all and had caught a good look at Tom before he left the wedding, with Mike just missing him. He put it all together at the time and went to Mike's home rather than show him the pictures at the wedding. He was just giving Mike some extra time to come to grips with it.

It took a day to make arrangements with the funeral home and to notify the other members of the family. Jennifer was already on her way home from her honeymoon vacation. Martha went to the airport to pick up Jennifer and Charlie, and to break the news to them. Sean went to the home of his grandparents, the O'Rourkes, in Ohio personally. They drove back with him.

There was not much left of the burned body to put into the casket, but Mike felt he deserved a decent funeral just like any human being. The Marines sent over an honor guard to stand along the side of his casket at attention all the hours he was being waked.

Jesse came over to give Mike his condolences. He told him they had found another body in the trunk of Tom's car. The autopsy said he was still alive until he died in the explosion upon impact. There was five gallons of gasoline in the trunk of the car with him. The man in the trunk was later identified by dental records as being that of Vica Porofundo.

Jesse also reported the finding of the bloodied body of Phil Cotter in a deserted tenement building.

"He was killed by the Mob. Must have been something that he said or did because word was out on the street he had just been promoted to fill the shoes of his brother Harry. He sure did, didn't he? Do you think this may have been set up by THOR? It has all the markings that he masterminded it."

At the funeral, Tom's former commanding officer asked to speak to Mike alone. He told him about the torture his son had endured at the hands of the terrorists and about the terrible pain always within his body. And then he told Mike about the addiction to morphine. Now at least Mike knew some of the reasons why, but he also knew he would never find out how the product of his love with Kathleen could ever turn out like this. Mike was not ashamed about what Tom had become or what he had done on this earth. He was only deeply saddened by his personal loss, as any father would be. After the funeral, as was the Irish custom, the mourners gathered at the home of the deceased's family for food and drinks. They went to Mike's house, which was now the home of Jennifer and Charlie. There were none of the usual toasts to the dearly departed. After eating foods prepared by the neighbors, only members of the immediate family, John, Jesse, and of course Martha remained. Mike took the envelope containing Tom's last will and testament and his bankbook, and handed it to his father-in-law, Thomas O'Rourke. It had his name on the face of the envelope. When he looked inside of the unsealed envelope, he also found a letter from Tom to his grandparents. It was given to his grandmother as something personal between them.

Tom O'Rourke read the will. He was named the executor. The penthouse condominium apartment and all furnishings were left to his twin brother, Sean, as he was only starting his business life. He stated emphatically that the money used to purchase it was clean and not blood money. He had invested in some small stock venture before he went into the service, and it was only a year ago that the stock had really taken off. Sean would find another $35,000 of clean money in his safe. He was to give this money to his sister. The bankbook contained a balance of $752,150. It was money he had saved from the assassinations he had done for the Mob. If they were able to keep this blood money, he wanted his grandfather to use it in some way to help any and all veterans who had become addicted to any drug because of injuries that were service-related.

To his father he left the book he had labeled "RETRIBU-

TION." He was to use the contents he had so meticulously transcribed to end the reign of the Mob. He stated that he held particular animosity toward Tony Calese and his son Tony Jr. because they pulled so many strings which altered the fate of so many different people.

Mike, Martha, John, and Jesse returned to Martha's home to examine the contents of the book left by Tom before he died. Each of them reviewed the contents and passed it on to the next person. John remarked that Tom had left a legacy which would put Tony and his son into jail for a long time. John kept the book and picked up the phone to call Washington. There were indictments to be prepared.

Martha and Mike flew John down to Washington and returned home alone that night. Mike was brooding something awful. He said out loud to no one in particular, "What the hell is happening in my life? Have I offended God in some way? Am I being punished?"

He then told Martha, "I'm ready to pack it in. What good was all the bodybuilding and training doing for me? Here I am, forty-five years old and behaving in such a way that I've not only exposed myself, but my family, and you, the woman I love, to all of the Mob's worst. Will I really ever be able to bring down the Mob?"

Martha held him in her arms and said to him, "There are two things that I have to tell you. After that you will have a decision to make. First off, don't you realize that you're into it too deeply already? Tony will never let you off until you put him away.

"Secondly, I want to tell you something that I read one time. It makes sense now more than ever. I think it was written by a man by the name of Virgil. I don't remember the exact words but I think it went something like this: Birds fly only because they think they can. If you believe in yourself and what you know you can do, then you must attempt to do it.

"Believe you can, and you will. I'm sure of it, my darling."

144

CHAPTER 15

John called from Washington the next day. He said that the information contained in the book titled "RETRIBUTION" was in fact a deathbed statement, and as such very admissible in court. The fact that THOR implicated himself as well strengthened the government's case all the more. The lawyers were being extra careful while preparing their indictments so as not to allow any of the evidence to be disallowed. If a single piece of evidence substantiated by information found in the "RETRIBUTION" book was successfully challenged in court, even on a technicality, the whole book could be found inadmissible. The government lawyers had waited too long to get their hands on something as good as this. They were not about to foul it up by making a mistake. John told them it was estimated to take at least four more weeks before indictments against Tony, his son Tony Jr., and an assorted bunch of their affiliates would be forthcoming. The target date was set for December 1.

John also told them his wounds were healing nicely, and he thought it would be wise for all of them to cool it for a while. It was John's suggestion that they pick him up in Washington and take him out to where his family was hiding in Virginia for a few weeks. Martha and Mike could then take off to one of their favorite vacation spots. They could pick John back up on the way back, about two days before Thanksgiving. He would spend the holiday with them at Martha's house. Then, God willing, in only a few more weeks this would all be behind them. He would finally be able to go home to Baltimore with his wife and child, and they would bury their daughter properly. How could they refuse him? John further cautioned them that Tony was unaware of the pending indictments, and he was still riding high. He was reported to be planning to hold the meeting with the other top members of the National Crime Family at his house during the Thanksgiving weekend. Martha and Mike were to make their plans in secrecy and not tell anyone where they would be going. Jesse was prepared to provide around-the-clock protection for Mike's two other children, the O'Rourke family in Ohio, and for Martha's father as well. They were not going to take any chances with any of their lives.

That night Mike dictated the update on his activity to Martha for the Insurance Consortium. He had a lot to tell them about the death of the Mob's paid assassin THOR, and the positive effect it should have on the insurance industry as a whole.

He didn't say anything about THOR's being his son. This fact just never came out at all in the newspapers, and Mike was sure that it was Jesse who had a hand in keeping this fact away from the media. He was really taking good care of him, just like Jesse's mother had helped his mother so many years ago. He reported on the closing down of the bogus perfume and smuggling operation. He purposefully did not mention anything about the pending indictments against Tony in his direct reports. He just had this hunch that the less said, the better. For the same reason he never mentioned the book "RETRIBUTION." Besides, he had plenty of other good news to report. However, in order to provide himself with an excuse for the period of time he and Martha were going on a much-needed vacation, he mentioned that he would be meeting with some other Justice Department officials in Albuquerque, New Mexico, in about a week. He was going to be staying at a small motel called the Do Drop Inn on the western outskirts of that town.

If they really needed to reach him, they could leave a message for him when he arrived. Why he did this, he himself didn't know at the time. When Martha questioned his adding this type of information to his report, he told her he was just playing a hunch. He made the three usual copies, and mailed one copy to George With and the other to his boss for the briefing to the members of the Insurance Consortium. He would give the third copy directly to John Smith when they picked him up at the airport in Washington tomorrow.

During their flight to Washington, Martha said to Mike, "I've packed a wide variety of clothes for us to wear on this so-called vacation, but do you realize that the only place you told me about is New Mexico? And, are we really going to go there?"

"You bet, but when we get to Washington the first flight plan you are going to file is for Atlanta, after we drop John off in Virginia of course. I've made reservations for us for three nights at the fabulous Omni Hotel. We've got a set of tickets to see the Atlanta Falcons play the New York Giants. Then we will see an opera and a very distant off-Broadway show. And prepare yourself to have some great food in the best restaurants Atlanta has to offer." Martha tried to get a word in, but Mike continued spelling out their agenda.

"After Atlanta we're off to Las Vegas for five days. We're booked into the Circus Circus Hotel on the Strip. Sure hope you packed your bathing suit, but if not you can buy one there, as I need a new one that fits me anyway. You know my waist is two and a half inches smaller since I went into that bodybuilding routine. I'm not much of a gambler, but I understand the stage shows there are just great.

"Next, we'll do a fly over the Grand Canyon and then we are heading for Alamogordo, New Mexico. We'll rent a car and drive out to see White Sands National Park.

"Then we'll fly to a small airport near Carlsbad and get to tour the biggest hole in the ground in the whole world, the Carlsbad Caverns. I hear it takes more than five hours to tour that place. And then we'll head to Albuquerque. We'll tour that pretty town for about three days, and we will then head back to pick up John in Virginia."

"So, vot you think?" he said with his biggest smile ever. He added, "It's great with you having this plane. We can really get around."

Martha was breathless. A real vacation, and then she thought back to this morning when she was watching him dress, as he put on the three guns and strapped his auto-release knives into place. John had given Mike back his leg knife after he took that bullet through the calf of his leg. Mike was still armed to the teeth, even when he was going on vacation. Martha reached under her left breast to feel the small single-shot derringer that was sewed into her bra. She always wore her little gun, and she too had an uneasy feeling about this so-called vacation.

147

They picked up John at the Washington airport, and during the plane ride to western Virginia John read the report handed to him by Mike. He frowned after he read the part about where they were going to be. Mike then laid it out for them both.

"I don't believe Tony is going to let things stay the same after all the trouble we have caused him. So by letting him lay his trap for us in the motel in New Mexico, we can at least assure ourselves of having some free time beforehand to actually relax. I'm betting that someone in that Insurance Consortium Board who is being briefed on the contents of my reports is directly wired to Tony. If I'm right, then they will make a try for us outside of Albuquerque, and you can bet I'll be looking for them. If I'm wrong, then the whole vacation will have been just great. If they try to get us, it will prove my point about someone from the insurance group using inside information against us."

John reluctantly had to agree with Mike's logic. He wanted to know where else the two of them planned to go, but neither Mike nor Martha would say. John was determined to have them covered and was on the phone to Jesse as soon as he went to the house where his wife and child were staying. When they took off, Martha headed for their first vacation stop, Atlanta.

It was a wonderful three days, and they spent their nights making love as much as their bodies could endure before exhaustion ended the lovemaking in a deep and satisfying sleep. Then they headed to Las Vegas and ran into some very windy weather before they were able to land at the Las Vegas airport. Holding true to form Mike got airsick and had to make a quick trip to the bathroom as soon as they landed. Nothing ever seemed to bother Martha. She was used to anything and everything. Once again they had a great time, and they saw every show they could manage to get into. They got to bed later and later each night, yet Mike was always up at 6:00 A.M. to start his power walk each day.

Mike got a bit of the gambling fever and lost $100 one night. He quit after that and told Martha he was off gambling for life, as he never even made a pass at the craps table. They also spent considerable time working out in the hotel gym wherever they stayed. Mike was not letting up on his bodybuilding regimen at all. And wherever possible, he made sure Martha joined in with him. They spent nine wonderful days and nights together, and it relaxed their minds as well as their bodies. Tomorrow they were leaving Carlsbad and heading to Albuquerque. They both had a restless night. Since they found themselves awake at four in the morning, they made love again. After, they held each other and talked about what may lie ahead. One thing was for sure, whatever happened, they were in this together.

After landing at their destination they rented a car and drove out to the Do Drop Inn. Martha wanted to know why Mike picked out this place. It was nothing fancy, but it had clean sheets and cable TV. Mike teased and said Martha had become spoiled with all that great living over the past week and a half. That's when he told her that he had been here once before. The motel was owned and managed by one of his buddies from when he was in the Army Reserve. This was a guy who Mike could trust, as he was with him all through Ranger training and on that one special assignment they had into enemy territory. Oh yes, and he could be relied on in an emergency. As they checked in, Mike cautioned Martha to take nothing for granted. She nodded that she understood.

Jeff Willup, his friend, was coming on duty at 6:00 P.M., and he left a bottle of champagne in their room to greet them.

They had a sip of the old bubbly when there was a knock on the door. Mike pulled out his .45 and tossed his .38 to Martha. He looked through the peephole; it was Jeff. He let him in and Mike introduced him to Martha. Jeff told them about many subtle inquiries that were being made about them. When they were due to arrive seemed to be important to everyone. He handed Mike a telegram. It was from John. It simply said, "You're covered. Be careful." Jeff had rigged a button in three different locations of their room. When one was pressed, he told them it would take him about twenty seconds to respond and come to their aid. If the button was pressed twice, he had a back way into their room through a false panel behind the bathroom door. He also produced a gift box tied with a ribbon. Mike took it and went into the bathroom and came out a few minutes later smiling. Martha wanted to know what was in the box, but he told her he would let her know later. They went out to dinner that evening to one of the local restaurants recommended by Jeff.

They were both very wary, and neither ate much. Martha kept the .38 revolver in her purse. It didn't take too much prodding by Mike to have her do this. As they arrived at their room, Mike put the key in the doorknob and opened the lock. Martha pushed the door open and stepped inside, reaching for the light switch. It never went on.

Mike heard something like a muffled sound coming from inside the door and went into immediate action. He dove through the entrance and rolled forward. His knees smacked together hard as his hand reached for the knife on his leg. As he rolled to a standing position and made a 180 degree turn, he saw a figure of a man in the doorway. He was bent over, as if he had reached for something entering the room, and had grabbed at nothing but air. Mike quickly threw the knife underhand and heard a thud. The shape of the man in the entrance fell to the floor, and he heard him begin to moan. He reached for his .45 and turned in the direction he heard muffled breathing coming from. The lights came on, momentarily blinding him. There were two more of them. One held Martha with one hand twisted behind her back and his hand over her mouth. The other was holding a machine pistol aimed directly at Mike's stomach. He told Mike to drop the gun and to make sure that he did, he waved his pistol in the direction of Martha. Mike did what he wanted, and sat in the chair being directed to by the gunman. The other guy had taken his hand away from Martha's mouth and had drawn out a pistol. It looked to Mike to be a Baretta.

It was now or never. The man Mike hit with the knife rolled about on the floor squirming in pain, with blood soaking his entire chest all around where the knife still protruded. The assailants looked over at their downed comrade. The one with the machine pistol went over to him. Mike used the distraction opportunity and pressed the button under the seat of the chair twice, and counted slowly to fifteen. In the next motion he reached and brought the 9-millimeter revolver strapped to his leg into firing position.

Martha saw Mike's movement, and stamped hard with the pointed heel of her shoe on the instep of the man who had been holding her. He yelled out in pain, and pushed her away. Mike fired twice at the man's chest. He hit him just above the heart, and his second shot hit him in the neck as he was falling. The guy with the machine pistol stood up and fired at Mike hitting him squarely in the chest with five rapid-fire shots. As the bullets hit his body, he fell backwards onto the bed. The door of the bathroom opened and a single shot rang out. A bullet hole appeared in the middle of the guy's head, and he dropped into a heap on the floor. Martha screamed and leaped to the bed where Mike was lying.

He opened his eyes and said, "Boy, these bulletproof vests are great. But that stream of bullets knocked the air right out of me."

Martha started to cry, and he held her in his arms to console her. Jeff and Mike assessed the damage. Three of them were down and out, but there could be more. He told Martha to stay prone on the floor. Mike picked up his .45, turned out the light, and went to the side of the open door. Two more shots rang out and tore into the framework of the doorway. Then he heard about ten more shots being fired. The only thing he was sure of was that they were not fired in the direction of his room.

He carefully looked out of the doorway and saw "Guardian Angel" standing over the body of the shooter in a lighted area of the motel parking lot. There was a high-powered rifle on the ground next to the fallen gunman. There was another guy about forty feet away who was down on his knees and holding his chest, with yet another one of Jesse's guys, this time Greg Peters, putting handcuffs on him.

So Tony had sent in another hit team, this one with a cast of five, and they had failed again. Two were dead, two wounded, one seriously and another with a few broken ribs. They were lucky once again, but would their luck hold?

Mike thanked Jeff for all his help, and told him to send him the bill for any damage caused to the motel room. His expense account would cover it. Jeff was only too happy to help his old buddy. Mike and Martha spent the night in another room, and next morning left for Albuquerque where they checked into the Hilton at the center of town. They still had yet to see any of the sights in the beautiful city of Albuquerque. After all, they were on vacation, and had two days remaining before they were scheduled to pick up John in Virginia. They were going to make the best of it, and they did.

It was Sunday morning as they checked out of the Hilton. Mike had just finished a telephone conversation with John making arrangements to pick him up on Monday. They would make the return trip East in two days.

They planned to spend overnight in Memphis, Tennessee, and arrive at the pickup point in Virginia at about noon. Martha performed her usual preflight check. The plane had full tanks, and they picked up flying speed as they went down the runway. The takeoff was as smooth as could be, and it looked to be a perfect day for flying. This pleased Mike immensely. He remembered a landing only a few days ago that really bothered him.

About fifteen minutes into the flight the engine coughed and stalled. Martha looked at her gas tank gauges, and they registered full. She switched to her alternate tank and was able to restart the engine. Mike let out a deep sigh of relief. Then the engine coughed and died again. Again she looked at her gauges, and both the main and the alternate registered as being full. Mike tightened up when Martha told him that someone had altered their gas tank gauges. She was sure they were out of gas. She had the plane in a glide pattern and reached for the radio.

"Mayday, Mayday. This is a Cobra 6 single engine with flying time only seventeen minutes out of Albuquerque. I'm showing out-of-gas conditions, yet all gauges are indicating full. Am currently gliding at 6,000 feet, and estimated rate of descent is 1,000 feet every three minutes. Can you advise where to land? Coordinates are not available as I cannot take time to read map. Am currently traveling directly east and running parallel to winding river, with mostly all flat ground in front for the next twenty miles. Over."

"This is the tower in Albuquerque reading you loud and clear. You are in luck. In three more miles you will see railroad tracks crossing below with station on the left. Bank your plane twenty-seven degrees due north and you should see landing field used by farmers to load up crop duster biplanes. You should be able to glide straight in. They can refuel you. Keep in radio contact, and tell us how things are going. Good luck! Over."

"Roger, tower, have railroad in sight. Am entering bank now."

And then Martha was silent for about two minutes. "I see the landing strip right where you said it would be. Will be attempting the dead-stick landing now. Will call you after I'm down. Can't manage radio and my instruments at the same time. Thank you for all your help! I'll make it! Out."

She landed the plane as smoothly as she had done under power so many times before. Mike was white when he climbed out of the door of the cabin. He immediately asked the guy driving the jeep who greeted him to get him to a bathroom, fast. Martha called the tower to let them know she was down safely, and thanked them again for all their help. She was making arrangements to have the first of five gallons of gasoline put into her tank from a container, so that she could restart the plane and taxi it over to where the permanent gas nozzle was located. This time she was sure the tanks were loaded, and disregarded the erroneous gauges which were stuck at full. She had enough gas in her tanks to make Memphis, with about three flying hours to spare.

She had to coax Mike back into the plane. She called him a sissy, and he laughed and strapped himself in. Once again they started on their flight to Memphis. They landed at 4:00 P.M. and grabbed a taxi into town. That night after dinner they spent a quiet evening in their room discussing the events of the day. It seemed that Tony had a sixth man on his hit team. Again the Mob had been thwarted in their attempt to kill Mike and Martha. Once again Mike thought about the cool head and skills of Martha in piloting the plane to a safe landing that had saved their lives. And what a lover this woman was turning out to be. He was a lucky man indeed.

Bright and early on Monday morning Martha had the tanks filled on her plane. She used a dipstick to indicate that gasoline was filled up to the top in both of the tanks. She would have the gauges replaced back at her own airport in Ramapo, where they had a seasoned mechanic on duty that she had complete trust in. They landed at their unrecorded stop in Virginia at the airstrip at 11:30 A.M. thanks to picking up a head wind. John was waiting and quickly seated himself in the cabin. They continued on to the Washington airport in order to keep the Virginia location secret. She filled up her tanks once again, and only one of them could take any gasoline, but after the scare they had on Sunday they were taking no chances. John was shocked to hear about the tanks being emptied and then being manipulated to show they were full. They landed at Ramapo Airport in a gusty wind.

The weather was really feeling like late November, and the leaves had long since been blown off the trees. Back at home base John updated the computer with everything to date and made backups for Mike to take with him to New York City and give to Bob Jacobsen to hold. Mike had called George With in New York and arranged for him to personally brief the members of the Insurance Consortium on Wednesday. His boss Wellington Fernrock III had balked as he wanted to be sure he was able to get off to a head start on the holiday. Mike agreed to start the briefing at 8:30 A.M. sharp, and with George prodding him, Fernrock agreed to set up the meeting and called the other company representatives.

The plan John had devised was simple. Mike would only tell them what he had stated in his last report, and for shock value he would also tell them about the men who were sent by Tony Calese to kill them. After that Jesse would tap all calls being made to Tony's residence and trace the caller back.

Mike finished the briefing in one hour flat, and everyone thanked him and ran out of the conference room to head for their homes. By the time Mike arrived back at home base later that morning, Jesse had already called John. They had their man, or rather they had nailed down their woman. Joyce Benson, Vice President for Amalgamated Assurance of North America had left the meeting and returned to her office on Park Avenue. Immediately she called Tony's home and spoke to Tony Jr.

She told him about the aborted attempt on Mike and Martha, and Tony Jr. said he already had the bad news. He was to meet her that night at their designated hideaway for their usual sexual encounter. She could hardly wait, she told Tony Jr. Little did she know that a warrant was being made out for her at that moment and that she was about to spend many of her next days and nights in a safe house under interrogation, compliments of the Justice Department. John was heard to say, "Another nail in Tony's coffin" as he hung up the phone with Jesse.

Mike went to the supermarket with Martha, where they shopped for a turkey and all the trimmings. They were going to have Thanksgiving dinner together for the first time, and John Smith was their guest. They were all looking forward to a quiet day at home and a chance to watch some of the college football games. Well, so much for the good thoughts!

CHAPTER 16

Late on Wednesday night John received word from Jesse that they had arrested Joyce Benson, and she was scared to death. The interrogators felt she would make an excellent witness, and she was telling all she knew. They would keep her on ice until she could testify in court, and she wanted it that way. He also reported helicopter landings and takeoffs from the back of Tony's estate. No doubt it was the gathering of the clan, and all the kingpins of crime were arriving for the meeting. Only one more of the top guys was due to arrive.

On Thanksgiving morning Mike woke at 5:45 A.M. and was out on his walk by 6:00 A.M. Before he left Martha asked him if he thought she should invite "Guardian Angel," and any others of Jesse's men on duty that day, to partake of their turkey dinner with them. Mike said he thought it was a great idea, since he was wondering who was going to be able to eat an eighteen-pound bird. Certainly not the three of them.

When Mike arrived home, he was shocked when he saw that the front door to Martha's house was left open. His heart skipped a beat as he drew his .45 and cautiously went inside. The place was all torn apart. There had been an obvious struggle, and then Mike heard a groan from behind the sofa in the living room. It was "Guardian Angel." He had been shot in the chest, and then his attacker had put a bullet into each of his four limbs. He was in a great deal of pain, but he was still conscious. He was telling Mike that a big guy, maybe seven-feet tall, had taken Martha and John out of the house unconscious. He was sure that it was Tony Jr. who had shot him. Jesse then arrived on the scene. He said he came quickly when he failed to get an acknowledgement on his two-way radio from anyone assigned to the house. Jesse went to the back of the house and found another of his men. He was

156

dead, his throat had been cut. In the meantime Mike called for an ambulance. Both Mike and Jesse went upstairs with their weapons drawn. The computer room was in a shambles, and the computer had been destroyed with blows from a sledgehammer they found on the scene. Mike dropped into a chair and put his face into his hands. All Jesse could hear him say was, "My God, they have Martha, they have Martha. What am I going to do?"

The ambulance was leaving when the phone rang. Mike picked up while Jesse listened in on an extension. It was Tony Calese.

"Listen up, wise guy! We have your broad and that creep from Justice. We want to invite you, and you alone, to a little party we're having over here at my house. Now you know who this is, don't you? Do I have to give you directions now that you don't have your precious computer to help you out anymore? You had better answer my invitation and get your ass over here by 2:00 P.M., that is, if you ever want to see your sweetie's face with a nose still on it. You get my point real good now, don't you?"

Mike broke in. "If you touch her, it will be the last thing you ever do, you slimy son of a bitch."

"Now there, sonny boy, is that any way to talk to someone who just invited you to Thanksgiving dinner? As I said before, get here by two, and you better be alone, and unarmed."

The phone was slammed down abruptly in the cradle at the other end. Mike went to his room and started to dress himself with all of his armor. Jesse followed him into the room and told him he didn't stand a chance going into that armed camp alone. But Mike was determined and would not listen to any advice Jesse had to offer.

"You know I have to go in there. They have Martha and John, and by my going alone I can at least buy some time while you get a search warrant and can mount an attack on that fortress. If I can't slow them down, then Martha's and John's lives won't be worth a plug nickel. And mine doesn't count at all, not if I can't share it with Martha."

Jesse accepted what was said to him with deep understanding of the situation. He couldn't come up with any alternatives, and he told Mike so.

"Look, Mike, just do whatever you have to do to buy some

time. I'll find some way of getting inside to help you, so help me, I will."

Mike finished dressing and went to get in his car while Jesse was already giving orders on the phone to someone. He was on his way to Tony Calese's house at 16 Winding Way in Fox Hollow, New York. It was a suburb in Westchester, and the drive should normally have taken about forty-five minutes from Spring Valley. He found himself at the front gate of Tony's estate in twenty-eight minutes flat.

As he moved toward the front gate, it opened electrically and slid to the side. He drove inside about a half mile until he came to the house. On this short drive he counted at least fifteen heavily armed men patrolling the inner perimeter of the grounds. It was actually a group of three houses, with a magnificent Georgian Colonial as the central home.

Before he got out of the car, he realized he would never be able to keep his guns and knives concealed. It was as he had thought all along. This would be a physical confrontation. He prayed to God that he had prepared himself properly for whatever lay ahead.

Martha and John were both chloroformed back at the house at the start of the attack. "Guardian Angel" intercepted the first intruder and created enough noise that Martha heard the commotion while she was working in the kitchen preparing their turkey. John had the door closed to the study, and they just hit him over the head and put the chloroform-soaked rag over his face when he stepped into the hall. It took two of them to subdue Martha. She had kicked one of them in the testicles and threw him halfway across the room, when the other guy put the chloroform rag over her face and she quickly collapsed. When they came to, they found themselves in a room that had to be in the basement of a house. It was cold and damp feeling, and there was a musty smell permeating the room they were in.

They were guarded by three of Tony's ugliest-looking henchmen. They were told to strip down by the big one. He looked to be almost seven-feet tall and had to weigh in the neighborhood of about 300 pounds. They took off everything but their underwear. Martha then successfully argued that they were entitled to a little dignity, and they could see that neither of them carried any concealed weapons in their clothing. One of the hoods went through the clothing and verified it was clean of weapons for the big guy. They took their clothes with them when they left the room, locking the door behind them. Martha was dressed only in her bra and panties, and John was in his boxer shorts. They were both very cold and wondered how long they would be left down there. John told Martha that the big character was "Big John" Porter, and that Tony had brought him in from Chicago to replace Mark Russo as the prostitution crime group leader.

Mike was met at the door by two hoods. They led him down a long corridor to a room with double doors. He could hear loud laughter and vulgar comments coming from the people in the room. One of the hoods systematically searched Mike and found each of his three guns and the knives attached to the left arm and the right leg. They pushed open the door and placed all of the weapons taken from Mike on a small table to the left of the door. Mike's shirt and undershirt were then ripped from his back, and he stood there stripped to the waist.

Tony sat in the center of a large curved table. The table contained a large turkey and all the other usual Thanksgiving foods. Hoods dressed in tuxedos were doing the serving. On his right side was Tony Jr.; he looked exactly like a younger version of his father. Tony was really showing his age. He was graying at the temples, and he was a fat slob of a man having let his body go to seed. Mike thought back to his father's description of the man who beat him so badly. The younger Tony fit the description to a "T." Hatred boiled within him at the sight of Tony and Tony Jr. There were two crime bosses sitting on either side of the table. It would seem that the fifth one of these living devils hadn't arrived as yet.

Tony actually presented Mike to his partners. He introduced him to them as the man with nine lives, just like a cat. But then he screamed, "A cat who is about to have his tenth life taken from him today. Before you meet your death at our little party here today, I want you to know that my brothers here have pledged to fill back up the ranks of my boys which you and that THOR bastard have taken out of action. So you see, all your efforts never will stop us. You haven't even been able to slow down our activity one bit."

Mike knew Tony was lying and just showing off to his out-of-town guests. He was still playing out his part in a show he was taking extreme pleasure in orchestrating. Tony nodded to one of his men, and the doors opened behind the big banquet table. Martha and John were dragged into the room. Mike was shocked to see that someone had taken all of their clothes. Tony said he wanted them to be present for the spectacle he was about to put on for his guests.

Tony, relishing what was about to happen, said in his most flamboyant way, "Let the show begin," and clapped his hands to start the action scene which he had planned.

Martha screamed, "Look out behind you." Her warning to Mike came too late.

The giant of a man called "Big John" Porter had come up behind Mike and grabbed him by his hair with both of his hands. Mike did not even see his adversary as he felt himself being picked up by his hair and pulled around and around, until his feet left the floor.

He was then let go, and he sailed about twenty feet into the air before he hit a wall and fell to the floor. He only had moments to clear his brain, as he saw this bulk of a man bearing down with his large hands groping for his throat. Mike rolled to the side, while slipping his legs in between those of the charging giant, sending him off-balance to the floor. Both men were on their feet and circling each other looking for a place to grab the other. Mike lashed out with a vicious kick to the midsection of "Big John," and in the same motion grabbed his arm and pulled him forward into his raised knee. "Big John" dropped to the floor clutching at his groin.

But he was back on the attack in a moment. One of his wild roundhouse rights caught Mike on the back of his head, but he was able to shake its effect and maintain his consciousness while he backed away from his assailant. Mike lunged forward and grabbed both of his hands, and while falling backward planted both of his feet into his stomach and sent him over his head onto his back with a loud thud. There was quiet in the room as it was clear that Mike was beating his attacker. But "Big John" was very resilient and exceptionally strong in his body as well as in the determination in his mind. He said to the gallery of onlookers,

"I'm not about to be beaten by this minuscule redheaded fuck who had arranged to have so many of my friends done in."

In a resurgence of strength, born out of his belief that he was the one being wronged, he rushed at Mike attempting to grab him in a bear hug hold.

Mike hit him with two solid punches squarely on the jaw, but he kept coming. He locked his arms around Mike and started to squeeze him, as cheers came from the mobster audience watching this very real spectacle of life and death. Mike butted him with his head, but was unable to break the monster man's hold on him. He kept squeezing, and Mike was almost ready to pass out. The thought going through his mind was, I'm losing, I'm losing the fight, and I'll be dead in a minute.

With one last effort he banged his head into the bridge of "Big John's" nose, and he dropped him to the floor.

"Big John" grabbed at his bleeding head and nose. He had been hurt. But in less then ten seconds he was back on the attack. While Mike was still trying to catch his breath, "Big John" grabbed him again in the bear hold and started to squeeze the air from his lungs. He had grabbed him higher up on his body, and Mike was unable to butt him in the nose again. "Big John's" nose was bleeding profusely all over Mike, and into his eyes.

Just when Mike was sure he was a goner, a single shot rang out. "Big John" dropped Mike to the floor again, and fell over onto his back dead. There was a bullet hole in the middle of his head. It had entered the front and come out the back, leaving a wide hole and brain tissue on the back of his head and spilling onto the floor. Everyone in the room looked in the direction of where the shot came from. It was Martha.

She had slipped her single-shot derringer out of her brassiere holster while everyone was focusing on the fight going on in the middle of the floor. She had made her one shot count when she needed it most. Martha used the moment of shock she had created when she broke the silence in the room with the gunshot and leaped to the back of Tony. She held the spent revolver muzzle behind the ear of Tony. No one dared to move, because none of them knew she had used her only bullet to save the life of her man.

But Mike was fully aware of what was taking place, and he

ran to the table to get his .45. John Smith also ran over to the table and picked up the .38. The sound of a helicopter arriving was now evident. Mike first thought it may be the last of the crime bosses arriving. Then he heard the sound of automatic weapons firing in rapid staccato bursts, the way they teach them to be fired in the service. Mike knew Jesse was on the move as he had promised. Mike and John started to disarm all the men in the room. It was then they found out that Tony was in a wheelchair and could no longer walk. The syphilis had progressed further in his body than the government report on him had indicated.

In the confusion, Tony Jr. slipped out of the back door as Jesse and his men were coming in the front. Mike took chase after him down another long hallway, and then up a stairway. At the top of the stairway, there was a blind spot that Mike could not see. As Mike cautiously went up the stairs with his gun extended in his hand, a chopping blow to the wrist coming out of the blind spot caused him to drop the gun. It slid off to the side. He now stood face-to-face with Tony Jr., who had a large stiletto knife in his hand. This Tony was twenty years his junior, and he seemed to have good strong reflexes, as most young men do. He looked as if he had used a knife before, and he kept the hand containing the knife moving in a circular motion so that Mike could not focus a hit on it.

"I told my father to let me handle you and not let that big fat stupid shit John Porter try to finish you off bare-handed. This is a job for a professional. I'm going to use some of the tricks of the trade my father taught to me when I was young. I may just finish you up like I did to that jerk agent back at your house."

Mike circled the room with him, keeping his eyes focused on the knife. Tony Jr. became impatient and lunged. Mike grabbed at his knife hand and pulled him forward past him, while he smashed his elbow deep into his back with a crunchlike sound. He was sure that he had broken some ribs with that blow. Tony Jr. dropped the knife, and Mike whirled and hit him with a kick blow to the chest. He reeled, and coughed up some blood as he rushed at Mike again. Mike sidestepped him and grabbed his left arm, pulling it behind his back and then flipping him over. He lay almost unconscious in a pool of his own bloody spittle. His arm was twisted in an abnormal direction. It was obviously broken and was totally unusable by him.

Mike, believing that Tony Jr. was spent of any desire to continue the fight, went over to the corner of the room to pick up his .45. Jesse just came to reach the top of the stairs. Tony Jr. had managed to free a concealed gun with his right hand. He was pointing it directly at Jesse's head. Mike dove for his gun, and in a single fluid action picked up the gun and fired in the same direction where Tony Jr. was lying on the floor. His wild desperation shot tore into Tony Jr.'s right leg, ripping into bone and tissue. The force of the .45 slug entering his leg caused Tony Jr.'s shot to miss its target and only graze across the cheek on Jesse's face.

It was over. Mike found a topcoat to cover Martha and retrieved his jacket taken from him when he was searched. He found a towel and soaked it in water, and attempted to wash his face and hands clean of Big John's blood. He led Martha outside to his car, and stopped back in the house to tell John and Jesse he was going to return to home base.

He and Martha kissed softly when they were in the car, and Mike said, "I'm taking you home now, sweetheart. You were right, this old bird was able to fly after all. We've done it. We've stopped the Mob in its tracks, and we have seen some justice come out of all this. Let's go home!" as he started the car and drove down the long driveway.

Back at the house Martha was shocked to see all of the damage to her home. But it was all superficial, and she knew it could all be cleaned up quickly.

Jesse drove John back to the house and he came in with him to brief Martha and Mike. Jesse told them that he realized one of the top guys in the Mob was late in his arrival because of some severe weather in the Rockies. Jesse knew the private helicopter service who had brought the other top crime bosses in to Tony's armed camp. He just commandeered the service once they had received their Search Warrant. He kept two of his men at La Guardia Airport to delay the guy coming in from the coast and not let him get to a telephone. The helicopter was loaded with six of Jesse's men, and the hoods on the ground thought it was the last of the bosses coming to the meeting. As they hit the ground, another twenty of his men attacked the front gate of Tony's residence. The rest is history.

Jesse continued with his debriefing, taking extreme pleasure in every little item he had to tell them.

"The four of the top bosses are in custody and are being fingerprinted. But they know they will be out on bail just as soon as they can get their fancy lawyers into action. We really have nothing concrete to hold them on, but we are putting them through some grief anyway.

"Now as for Tony and his pack of hoods. They are all under lock and key. What with kidnapping and murder, using weapons against government marshals, and any other number of assorted crimes that they just committed today, we have them solid. Tony Jr. was sent to the hospital. He is listed in critical condition and is undergoing surgery now. The doctors tell me they can patch him up in about a month and that he will be able to stand trial."

It was then that Jesse looked at Mike and said, "If not for your shot at Tony Jr. when I reached the crest of the stairs, I would not be here telling you about our success today. It was I who was supposed to protect you, and you ended up saving my life instead. I owe you one, Mike," and he pointed to the bandage across his cheek.

Martha chimed in, asking if anyone had anything to eat yet today. No one had, so she made a large batch of bacon and eggs. Everybody ate heartily of their belated Thanksgiving meal. "It was the fruit of the desert and nectar of the gods," Jesse was heard to say, and they all laughed with a sigh of relief. Jesse continued his report while they feasted on their eggs.

"Thank God I only lost one man today, the guy I found in the back of your house. I'll have to talk to his wife when I leave here today. Three other guys have slugs in them, one has a badly sprained ankle caused while jumping out of the helicopter before it was on the ground.

"And, of course, there is the agent you call Guardian Angel. I called the hospital and they told me they were able to get all five slugs out of him, but he lost a lot of blood. Only one of the bullets hit a bone, the one in his left arm. You can visit him at General Hospital tomorrow if you like."

After Jesse left, John went into the study to call his wife.

When he came out, he asked Martha if she could fly him back to Washington on Saturday. His wife was driving back to their home in Baltimore on Friday, and he was going to get his life moving in a positive direction again.

On Friday Mike received a letter in the mail from Tom O'Rourke. He told Mike that he had taken the money in young Tom's passbook and used it immediately in such a way that the government would have a hard time trying to lay claim to it. He proudly told Mike about the new wing being built on Children's Hospital in Ohio. It would be used to treat children who are born into this world already addicted by their mothers' being drug users. There was to be a plaque dedicating this wing to the memory of Thomas Henry Burke. The letter also contained a special note to Mike signed by both of the O'Rourkes. It said, "Don't wait too long to be happy again. Kathleen would want it that way."

On Friday afternoon they went over to visit "Guardian Angel" at General Hospital. As they approached the desk to obtain a pass to his room, they realized they didn't even know his real name.

When the clerk asked who they wished to visit, Mike blurted out "Guardian Angel." It was the only name they ever knew him by. The clerk handed them two tickets. They were for a patient by the name of Gerard Angel. They went to the room and looked in. Sure enough, it was him. He never gave them any other name because he was used to being called "Guardian" by his friends instead of "Gerard." The doctor was concerned about the bullet in the left arm, which not only shattered the bone but created some nerve damage. He was still in a great deal of pain.

They thanked him for all of his help. He said he was sorry that he missed the ending after being in on it from the very beginning.

BOOK 2

CHAPTER 17

Mike and Martha flew John Smith back to Washington. They flew back down a week later to attend the funeral of his daughter. It was a very sad occasion. The only bright note was that John's wife told them before they left for home that she was pregnant again. John's little girl was buried the same week that the indictments were handed down on all the members of the Tony Calese Mob.

When they arrived back home Mike immediately signed the house over to Jennifer and Charlie as he had planned.

Sean passed his bar exam and was living in the penthouse apartment left to him by his brother. He was now talking about getting married to the gal that he studied with those long hours. She also passed the bar, and they both were offered positions with a big law office in New York City.

Mike and Martha were married in a quiet church ceremony early in the day on Christmas Eve. It was sort of a Christmas present from each of them to each other.

As Martha and Mike had joked about earlier, they followed through and asked Bo Denville to be the best man. He was surprised, but happily accepted their offer. He came to the wedding with his new girlfriend. She was a knockout, and of course she was a computer fanatic like Bo. Only a few close friends and their family were invited to attend. Jennifer returned the favor and was Martha's matron of honor.

They planned to start their honeymoon on January 1, and had first-class tickets booked to Hawaii. On the Monday between Christmas and New Year's, Mike received a registered letter requesting he meet the next day with the five members representing the Insurance Consortium. The letter was signed by his boss, Wellington Fernrock III.

It was a blustery December day when Mike entered the conference room designated for the meeting. He took the train down to the city that morning, as the car was still stalling and was back in the shop again. "Welly," as he liked to be called by his friends, thanked Mike on behalf of the entire Insurance Consortium for all of his efforts in the past few months. Then he went on to explain that unfortunately without the recurring losses, the insurance companies no longer had use of his services. They would, of course, continue paying him through the terms of his contract, only they were cutting off his expense account. But then they also gave him a check for $50,000.

It was the first of three annual installments on the bonus they were awarding him for all the work he had done for them. And then, too, he was vested in his pension and could start to receive it after he reached age sixty-two. He was pleasantly surprised, to say the least. They suggested to him that he should go private, and as an added inducement, then they offered him a $35,000 contingency fee for his first year of a five-year contract. Another check was produced and given to him. However, this one was conditional. It seems they wanted him around if they needed him in the future. He told them he would give it some serious thought, but he took the check that was offered and asked them to send him a contract to review. He said good-bye to his friends in the office and thanked them for their help.

He left the building and rushed to get to PATH for his trip home. He couldn't wait to get home to tell Martha. The train was on time, and he was again right on time to catch the early train to Spring Valley, and lo and behold it also left the Hoboken station on time. He thought to himself, Things are really getting good for me; when the train hit a car while it was crossing the tracks. No one was hurt, but it delayed his arrival home by four hours. He thought to himself, Nothing ever really changes.

By the time he got home, Martha had left a note that she couldn't wait for him any longer and went out to buy the clothing they needed in Hawaii. She didn't get home until 8:00 P.M. and by then he was bursting to tell her the good news.

Finally they talked, and it was decided that when they came back from their three weeks in Hawaii, he would start up his own company, calling it "Mike Burke Associates, Inc." He was going to be a full-time independent private investigator and president of his own company. This was his dream of a lifetime, one that he had talked about and shared with Kathleen so many times in the past. He was saddened by these thoughts, and Martha sensed this. She then told him she decided that she would attend school to be able to obtain her own Private Investigator License. After all of the recent excitement in their lives, she could never go back to just a teaching career.

The plane to Hawaii was filled with people who were going there on tour. In the airport he noticed two guys pointing at Martha and himself, and whenever he looked in their direction they tried to act nonchalant. This same thing occurred again after they landed in Hawaii. It was their misfortune to be booked into the same hotel as these two guys, and he was sure they were always pointing at them and saying something to each other. One day Martha and Mike were on the beach at their hotel enjoying the sun when Mike left to get them a drink. When he came back, he again saw the two characters pointing to Martha, saying something to each other, and laughing. He had enough. He walked up to these two guys and tapped them on the shoulder. They turned around to face him with a surprised look on their faces. They were wearing name tags indicating that their last names were Fowland and Meehan.

"Okay, you two wiseasses. You better have a good reason to tell me why you birds are ogling my wife."

They were shocked and a bit afraid of the ferocious-looking Mike. "We're real sorry, Mister, but we think your wife looks exactly like Marilyn Monroe. Every time we see her we are just amazed at the resemblance. Didn't you know that?"

"Now isn't that a coincidence? Yes, I've always thought so. But nobody else seemed to agree with me, that is until you two came along. Sorry I bothered you guys, but for Christ's sake, stop staring and pointing at her all the time."

They sheepishly agreed. Mike turned around and headed back to Martha. He couldn't wait to tell her, and he had the widest grin on his face when she looked up at him.

"Guess what?" he said.

They arrived home from their honeymoon late in January, with both of them well tanned and rested. The first thing Mike and Martha did was to contact the New City law firm of Sparrow,

Tweeter, and Vogel, Inc. They were instructed to start the necessary paperwork and forms through the process of incorporation in New York State.

It then dawned on Martha that these guys had names that seemed to be saying they were just a bunch of birds. She became hysterical with laughter every time Mike mentioned their names. She finally let Mike in on her secret, and they both had a good belly laugh about the subject.

They signed all the necessary papers and wrote out checks for all the application fees. Once this was done and the paperwork started to move, Mike and Martha went off to New City in search of an office location to operate from. They had long since decided that their home was not about to be used as a home base anymore. New City had the courthouse close by, and a number of office buildings from which to choose. They found a small building which was formerly used by a dentist on the lower level, and it had living quarters above the office space. With a little bit of refurbishment, the office space could easily be adapted to the needs of a private investigator's office. And then they would keep a small apartment upstairs, just in case. At any rate the price was right, and they signed a one-year lease with an option to buy the place at a prearranged fixed price. So another chore was completed.

In late February, it was reported in the newspapers that Tony Calese would never stand trial. A medical team found him to be a complete invalid and hopelessly insane. It was caused by the syphilis eating away at his brain and his body. He was sent to a mental institution for the criminally insane and would spend the rest of his life there. It was said he had to be kept in a straitjacket at all times. It was the best deal his lawyers could get for him.

As promised by the doctors, Tony Jr. was dismissed from the hospital and stood trial.

He was convicted of five counts of premeditated murder, and other assorted crimes against humanity. He received five ninety-nine-year life sentences, with no chance for parole, as they were assessed to run serially. It was not expected that he would live much beyond his fortieth birthday, as he suffered from severe internal injuries where ribs that were broken pierced his lungs in both the front and the back. His left arm was limited to only twenty percent of normal, and the severity of the leg wound which shattered the bone would cause him to limp and to be in pain for the rest of his life.

Mike remarked to Martha that fate seemed to have played an interesting part in their assault on Tony Calese and his mob empire. The injuries caused to Tony Jr. by Mike in that brief skirmish with him were almost identical to the injuries inflicted on Mike's father by "Mean Tony" almost more than forty-six years ago. They mused that the scales seem to have a way of balancing themselves after all.

Not a single one of Tony's henchmen, down to the lowest level hood that he had working for him, received anything less than seven years in jail. Most of them received sentences ranging between twenty years and life. The crime bosses from other parts of the United States were feeling the heat being put on them by the Justice Department in their parts of the country. The rumor mill had it that they were out for revenge on the guy and his wife that created the big bust at Tony's place. Other indictments were expected to be forthcoming.

One day when they came home from shopping at the supermarket, they saw a state police car parked in their driveway. There were two officers seemingly annoyed that no one was home. Martha got out of the car first and asked, "Can I help you, officer?"

"We're looking for a person by the name of Martha Grant."

"That was my former name. I'm Mrs. Martha Burke now and I live here with my husband. What do you want?"

To their surprise, the officers had a warrant to arrest her. Mike asked to see a copy of the warrant. He read out loud to Martha the supporting details for the arrest contained in the warrant. It seems that one of the crime bosses demanded that the police check to see if she had a permit for the concealed weapon she was carrying in the pocket holster under her breast. This was only one point of the warrant. The second point was that she was being charged with the murder of one John Porter. The officer in charge told them that the district attorney wanted to question her about the man she killed at Tony Calese's house last Thanksgiving. It was he who had requested the warrant, based on a supposed eyewitness account of a man who lived in Chicago and who said she killed him in a cold-blooded manner. They, the

173

police officers, actually put Martha's hands behind her back and applied handcuffs. Martha was in a state of shock and couldn't say a thing. When Mike protested about the handcuffs, the officer was very understanding, but he explained that he was required to follow standard procedure.

Mike was furious, and as they took Martha away in the car, he got on the phone to John Smith. John told him to get a lawyer over to advise Martha immediately, and that he should not worry. John said he would do whatever was necessary to get this cleared up in a hurry. He also suggested that Mike get down to the police station with Martha.

"She is going to need some moral support. Being arrested and booked is a very demoralizing and degrading thing to go through."

Mike called his business law firm of Sparrow, Tweeter, and Vogel, but they told him they did not handle criminal-type cases. They suggested that he call Hubert Fowland, an attorney who was a specialist in handling criminal activity, with offices located in New City. Fowland himself picked up the phone on the second ring, and was quick to understand Mike's chatter and babble about what had just happened. He told Mike to meet him at the court-house, as he would be leaving immediately. He also told him to bring his checkbook. The name of the lawyer he had just spoken to sounded familiar to Mike. At the courthouse he immediately recognized him as one of the two guys he had to speak to about staring at Martha in Hawaii. By the time Mike had gotten there, Fowland had arranged for bail to be set for Martha. Because the charge was murder, the bail was set at $100,000. Mike had to make out a check for $10,000 to the bail bondsman. Martha was released after another thirty minutes. She was as pissed and as irate as Mike had ever seen her. She told Mike that she had been made to strip and was body-searched. Then she was fingerprinted, and they took mug shots of her. It was most humiliating and she started to cry after she got into the car.

The lawyer, who was driving his own car, returned back to the house in Spring Valley to meet and discuss a strategy with Martha and Mike. There was a call waiting on the answering machine when they came in the door. It was from John Smith. Hubert Fowland was asked to pick up on one of the extension phones while John explained the course of action he had set in motion. He had prepared an affidavit to be presented in court at the hearing by the lawyer. It simply stated that he, John Smith, a Special Prosecutor and member of the U.S. Justice Department, and Martha Grant, who was working with the department at the time of the alleged incident, were abducted from the home of the latter and rendered unconscious. During the course of these events it became necessary for her to use deadly force to protect the life of another individual assigned to Justice who was being held captive. He also stated that all three of them were in a life-threatening situation at the time, and that the incident took place while federal agents were storming that particular location.

Within the week the hearing was held in the New City Court-house, and Hubert Fowland offered the affidavit to the magistrate. He immediately dismissed the murder charges against Martha. However, he left open the charge of possessing a firearm without a license.

Bail was eliminated, but there was no refund from the bail bondsman. He explained to Mike that his money could have been tied up for a much longer period of time in the event Martha was held over for trial. After the hearing and the disturbing information that was presented, Mike told Fowland to continue with all the necessary legal efforts to get Martha cleared of this misdemeanor. Unless he was successful, she would be unable to get her Private Investigator License. He gave him the name of Jesse Garrison to contact as an additional government support person to help clear up this problem. It seemed to Mike that Hubert Fowland was a very competent lawyer, and he was pleased to have him working on the case.

Later that night Mike admitted to Martha that the Mob had just scratched them enough to make it hurt. It had cost them $10,000 and some yet undefined amount of legal fees just because they wanted to get even. When would the old adage "enough is enough" prevail?

The phone rang, waking them out of a deep sleep at 6:00 A.M. the following morning. It was Mike's son, Sean.

"Dad, I'd like to see you sometime today if I could. Could you meet me in the lobby of my building at noon, and we'll get some lunch together. I've found something that I'd like to give you. I'll tell you all about it over lunch . . . I'll even buy. See you then, okay." He hung up before Mike even had a chance to tell him yes or no.

Mike told Martha he had a lunch appointment with his son. Martha joined Mike in the drive down to the city, as she had some business to take care of at the school where she used to teach. She was now attending a local college where she was studying to be able to take her Private Investigator License exam. She found out that many of the courses that she had taken for her master's in education would be applicable to the courses needed to be licensed as a PI in New York State. Because of this she would be able to get her license in only one more year. That is if this problem with the concealed weapon could be cleared up. They arrived in the city at 9:45 A.M. and each went their separate way. They were going to meet back at the parking garage at 2:30 P.M. That should give them both enough time to do what they had to do.

Mike went to the office of the insurance company he used to work for and dropped in to say hello to George With. He was not his usual cool self and seemed to be in a frantic state of mind. He told Mike that he was being referred to one of their clients who was having some security problem. Something was wrong, Mike could sense it. George was either not fully versed in what was happening, or he was not allowed to talk to Mike about the problem while in the office. He told Mike to expect to be contacted within the next twenty-four hours, and let it go at that. At least his eyes said that to Mike.

George told Mike that Nina and the kids were doing just fine and that they wanted Martha and Mike to join them for dinner at their house sometime soon. Nina would call Martha and make arrangements. They shook hands when they left, but George was obviously preoccupied with something that was on his mind. Mike knew that whatever it was, it was serious to be having George act this way.

Mike met Sean in the lobby of his office building at exactly noon. They went to a local restaurant for a sandwich and a beer. Once they had ordered, Sean passed a three-by-five-inch index card, with some Scotch tape hanging off the ends, to his father. He told him he found it taped to the top of the safe in the apartment Thomas Henry had left to him in his will. It had printed in the center of the card:

Suisse National Union Bank
500—THOR.

"What do you make of it, Dad? The only thing I can think of is that Tom had a Swiss bank account. But without having a specific number, I hear that you can't get at what he has in the bank. You can't even tell if it is a bank account or a vault storage box."

"I think you're right. Tom's book that he called 'RETRI-BUTION' had a running account of all the money he had made from working for the Mob. It did seem like there was about $500,000 never accounted for, at least it was not with the money he left in his regular account. The '500' could be alluding to the amount."

"I'm sure of it. But I'll be damned if I can think of how to come up with the numbers to allow us to get to the money."

"Thanks, I'm glad you found this. I'll let you know if I come up with anything. Sure wouldn't mind getting some more of this blood money into the hospital wing that Grandfather O'Rourke set up in Tom's name."

"One more thing, Dad, did you see this story in the newspaper? I was lucky to catch it at all, as it was buried on page five. It seems the guy, who was drunk when he crashed the truck into you and killed Mom, is close to death in the prison hospital. Someone put a knife into his side, and twisted up his guts more than just a bit. They got the guy who did it, but he is a dopehead and can't remember why he did it. He says he even liked the guy who he put the knife into. Looks real strange to me. Just thought you would like to know."

Mike took the newspaper that Sean passed to him and read the story himself. It was exactly as Sean had told him. A chill came over Mike, and he shivered.

When Sean asked him if he was okay, he said, "Is it possible that it was not an accident when that drunk broadsided me and your mother? My God, could that terrible thing have been engineered by someone? And if so, then why?"

A visibly shaken Mike left the restaurant. He reminded his son to keep in touch. "And for God's sake, you had better be careful and not take anything for granted."

Mike met Martha at the prescribed time and they started the drive home. It was 3:00 P.M. when they crossed over the George Washington Bridge. Martha's sixth sense came into play, again.

"What's wrong, honey? Something's bothering you."

He told her the whole story about his meeting with Sean. Then he told her about the strange meeting he had with George With. After hearing all this information, this time it was Martha who shuddered.

When they arrived home, the light was flashing indicating a call was on the answering machine. It was his daughter, Jennifer. She had received an urgent call for Mike thinking he still lived there, from a prison hospital in upstate New York, asking that he call them back immediately. He dialed the number Jennifer had given him.

A Dr. Schwartz answered and introduced himself as the person responsible for a patient by the name of Warren Jensen. He reported he was in critical condition caused by a knife wound. He told Mike that he was not expected to live through to the morning. But he did have a lucid moment, and told the doctor that he had to speak to Mike. Dr. Schwartz then told Mike that he knew about the death of Mike's wife as the prisoner had told him all about it. Jensen said he had something very important to say to this guy Mike Burke before he died and that was the only way he could make peace with his God.

"Do you want to come up here and listen to this deathbed statement? If so, I'll make arrangements for you to see him. But you had better hurry. His end is very near."

"It will take me about three and a half hours to drive up there. Please keep him alive, please!"

Mike told Martha to pack an overnight bag for them both as they would probably stay somewhere close to the prison that night. They ran into a snowstorm on the New York Thruway and it was nine in the evening when they finally arrived at the prison gate.

It took them another forty-five minutes to get the necessary clearances to get themselves into the infirmary. Dr. Schwartz was waiting for them at the bedside of his patient. He told Mike he was very weak and that he was to put his ear close to his patient's mouth in order to hear him. He then gave the patient some sort of a shot, and he stirred and became semiconscious. The doctor told the prisoner that Mike Burke was at his bedside as he had requested. Mike strained to hear the words this man was saying.

"Forgive me for causing the accident that took the life of your wife. I was paid to do it and to take the jail sentence. I was paid by . . . " and then his voice became inaudible. Mike pressed his ear even more closely to his mouth and told him to please say it again. "They paid me so much money to do it. So much money. And I needed it to pay for the operation on my own wife, you know. She died anyway."

"Please tell me who paid you."

"Do you forgive me?

"Of course I forgive you." He said it even though he hated him. Mike would say anything to find out who had caused his wife's death. He knew deep down inside of him that he would never forgive this man.

"The Society of the Ark," he said in a subdued voice that Mike could hardly hear. And then with all the strength he could muster, he yelled it out loud, "The Society of the Ark."

These were the last words he ever spoke. The doctor moved to his bedside and held a stethoscope to the man's chest. He shook his head from side to side to Mike, indicating the man was dead, and then pulled the sheet over the man's face. Mike stood in puzzled disbelief. He had no idea who or what this Society of the Ark was. He asked the doctor if he could talk to the man who had put the knife into this guy. The doctor said that he would speak to the warden and see if he could arrange it, but not until tomorrow. The warden did not come into his office until 8:30 A.M. Who could blame him? This was a terrible job for anyone to have.

Martha and Mike took a room at a close-by Knights Inn. The snowstorm had put about twelve inches of wet snow on the thruway, and it was reported closed further upstate west of Utica.

179

They found a place still open at 10:45 P.M. and ate a late dinner. There wasn't too much dialogue between them during their meal, and neither was hungry. It was a restless night for them both, but they were at the warden's office at 8:30 A.M. sharp.

The warden was hesitant to allow them to meet with the prisoner they identified as Peter Flow. It was only through Dr. Schwartz' influence, telling the warden that Mike may be able to find out why Peter stabbed Warren Jensen, that he allowed Mike to meet with him in the warden's office. This guy Peter Flow was as high as a kite one minute, and then completely rational the next. Mike asked the questions.

"Did you stab Warren Jensen?"

"You bet I did, did a really good job on him like they told me to do. I liked him, but they offered me such good stuff if I would just do this little job for them. So I did it, and I'm not sorry, not one little bit."

"Who told you to do it?"

"What do you think I am? I'm not allowed to tell or they will kill me. Worse yet, they could cut off my supply of the good stuff. Then what will I do? I'm not going to tell anybody anything."

In a desperation move Mike said, "Oh, we know already that it is the Society of the Ark who arranged for you to kill Jensen. And we also have the name of the guard who is your supplier."

In a smuglike manner, Peter replied, "So you know about the association, so what? I ain't talking anymore."

The warden had recorded the conversation and ordered that the prisoner be returned to his cell. Mike thanked him and the doctor for all of their help.

All Mike had gotten out of him was a confirmation that this Society or Association of the Ark did really exist. But who were they, and more important yet, why had they singled out his family to attack? There were no answers. There weren't even any questions between Martha and Mike on the ride back home. It took them six and a half hours to drive back home, as the weather really started to get bad. At least they were driving during daytime hours when it was still light out.

The phone was ringing when they entered their house. Mike picked it up. It was Dr. Schwartz. He told Mike that both Peter

180

Flow and a guard were just found with their throats slashed.

So, thought Mike, the Society of the Ark was fast closing off any tracks that could lead back to them. Mike told Martha that they would surely have to deal with these people sometime, whoever they were.

CHAPTER 18

Mike called Sean the next morning to let him know what he found out about the man who killed his mother. They both thought it wise not to say anything to Jennifer, as there was no sense in their alarming the mother-to-be. Then Mike told him about the Society of the Ark. Sean never heard of it either, but he said he would research it and call him if he was able to pick up any leads. Mike ended their conversation with his caution again to his son to be very careful. Then Mike put in a call to his son-in-law, Charlie, at his place of business at Met Life. He had a bugger of a time tracking him down, as many people didn't know who Charlie Russell was. He had yet to make a name for himself in his company. But Mike was sure that he would. He told Charlie to just keep his eye out for anything that didn't look right. And he told him of his concern about this organization The Society of the Ark that had been directly responsible for the death of Jennifer's mother. Charlie got the word loud and clear and told Mike that he would be on guard. He thanked him for the update, and then went on to tell him about how much he liked being married to his daughter.

After he hung up with Charlie, he called Jesse Garrison in Washington. Jesse had been transferred to another office, and when Mike dialed the number he was given, the receptionist answered, "Secret Service, Mr. Garrison's office." When Jesse picked up the phone, he went into a long spiel about getting promoted just in time to be assigned to protect the presidential candidates prior to the election in November. Right now there were fifteen potential candidates from the two main parties who were opting for the job. It would take time, and some unfavorable primary results, to prune the list down to just a few before the conventions. But for now, he really had his hands full at this time.

Before Mike had a chance to ask Jesse any questions, he told him he had arranged to make a deposition to be used to clear Martha from the gun charge. Included in the deposition, he said that he had personally recommended that Martha carry the weapon after she was attacked outside the supermarket. Because of the dangerous situation that existed, no one even thought about transferring the registration of the gun from Mike Burke to Martha Grant. That was good news for Mike, and he thanked Jesse for his help.

Then he asked him if he had ever heard of the Society of the Ark, and to his surprise Jesse said that he had. It was reported to be a relatively new terrorist organization, and supposedly was formed with outcasts from all the other terrorist groups.

Jesse had picked up this tidbit of information from a confidential monthly report that is prepared by Interpol, the International Criminal Police Organization based in a Paris suburb. Jesse had no more information on the subject, but he could recommend someone to Mike in France. This man could, with no doubt in Jesse's mind, give Mike the whole story about them. He was the man that collected and prepared the information, and then wrote the monthly news briefing. Mike was given the name and telephone of Jacques Paisson to contact at Interpol. Jesse made it a point and said emphatically that his name was to be pronounced as "passion," and not to make it sound like he was a friendly Italian. It seemed that someone had misplaced the letter "i" when they recorded his name at birth, and that French law required that he use the name as issued. The cost to change someone's name in France is known to be prohibitive, so he just kept the name and pronounced it as he wanted.

Mike could really empathize with this guy. After all, he was supposed to be named Micah Berke at birth, and it was the foul up at the hospital that gave him the name that he used. He thanked Jesse once again, and said he would keep in touch.

Before Mike hung up, Jesse told him to look up Gerard Angel. He was out of the hospital, but had some recurring problems with the arm that was shattered by the bullet he took at Mike's home. He was no longer working for the government, and had been pensioned out of the Justice Department with a medical release.

Jesse heard that he wouldn't talk to anyone, or even let anybody get close to him. He was reported to be having a drinking problem, and his wife had taken the children and left him for another man.

"This is a good man," Jesse reiterated, "and I hate to see this happening to him."

Jesse said he lost contact with him and did not know how he could be contacted. Mike assured Jesse he would track down Gerard, aka "Guardian Angel." He and Martha both owed this man a debt they never thought they could ever pay.

Martha and Mike made arrangements with a local contractor to have the new offices of Mike Burke Associates, Inc. fixed up to their satisfaction.

There was the creation of a enclosed secretary/receptionist workstation immediately as you entered the office. Some nice leather couches and some end tables and lamps gave a nice touch to the outside waiting room. Because the previous tenant, the dentist, had set up many separate rooms they found it easy to set up the office both for now, as well as for the future. There was an office each for Martha and Mike, a conference room, and another two offices that were empty for the time being. They had two rooms still left over and one of them was made into a computer room. The other was used for storage. Since they had a lot of extra furniture when they combined their two households, they had more than enough extra pieces of furniture and beds, to completely furnish the two-bedroom apartment above the office. All they had to buy for upstairs was a refrigerator.

Martha's father had given them a check for $25,000 for their wedding present and they were using that money. When Mike first looked at the check he thought it was for $250, and then recorded it as such on the bank deposit slip before they went off on their honeymoon. It was more than a month after they returned back home that the bank officer had contacted them, notified them about the mistake he had made, and they then made the correction to their savings account. Fortunately for them, the bank teller who caught the mistake made sure they had been credited for the correct amount. They were receiving interest on the money all along. Martha had been quite surprised to hear that her father had only given them $250 as Mike had told her, but she didn't give it much thought at the time. It was at this recent revelation that Mike asked Martha how much her father was really worth.

She hesitated at first, and then blurted out, "At the last time he told me about his net worth, it was somewhere in the neighborhood of $1.5 billion. He owns thirteen different international companies, and has major interests in two large banks. He had made most of his money in chemicals, and then diversified and bought other companies. It seems to everyone like he has the Midas touch. It's a known fact about all his successes. I can't disagree."

Then she looked at Mike who was standing there shocked as could be with this news that he just heard for the first time. My God, he thought, I am married to a blooming heiress.

"I'm sorry that I never told this to you before, Mike. I'm just a poor little rich girl, and it just never dawned on me. I hope it doesn't shock you too much, and that it doesn't make you sorry you married me. Because I have another shock for you today, but I'm only going to tell you about this one when I get you into bed."

Then she gave him her tricky-looking smile, grabbed him by his tie, and led him up to their bedroom. They made beautiful rhythmic love, and when they both were satiated with the results of their ecstasy, she told him she was pregnant. She had conceived, just like a newlywed, on her honeymoon. They were so happy with the news. Mike wanted to know if Martha was in any danger to be planning to give birth to her first child at the age of thirty-nine. She told him that she had been to the doctor already, and while he did not recommend her having a baby so late in life, he could find nothing wrong with her pregnancy. She would of course have to be extremely careful, and do nothing in a quick or violent way. In other words, she had to take it very easy. Also, the doctor told her that he would probably deliver her child by cesarean section, just to play it safe.

On Wednesday evening, March 30, the Burke clan held a family party in the new office of Mike Burke Associates, Inc. They had so much to celebrate. Mike was now forty-six years old, Sean was twenty-five, and Jennifer was twenty-four. It was the day that the new company was officially incorporated as well.

Jennifer announced to them that she was pregnant and was expecting twins and was due to deliver on Labor Day. Then Mike made the announcement about Martha's pregnancy, and everyone was delighted, as well as shocked. Mike took everybody out to dinner, and the champagne flowed. It was in the bar area when he went to the bathroom, that Mike noticed a forlorn-looking man who seemed to be staring at his happy group. As Mike approached him, he got up and was planning to leave when Mike grabbed him by the arm and turned him to face him. It was Gerard Angel. He was sober, as Mike saw he was only drinking ginger ale. It took quite a bit of effort, but Mike coaxed him to join their party. He did so reluctantly, but once Gerard started talking to Martha, he seemed to brighten up considerably. Martha was able to get out of him the fact that he was both broke and homeless. His pension from his previous work with the government was just enough to support his two children in the custody of his wife. He had hit the bottom of the barrel, recognized the fact that he could not live out of a bottle, and had started on the road to recovery. It was obvious that he needed some help. And as far as Martha and Mike were concerned, he was in the right place to get it.

That night they took Gerard Angel back to the apartment over their office. They had just stocked it with some basic staples such as coffee, sugar, and put a loaf of bread in the freezer along with some frozen sausage and orange juice. Mike left two twenties and a ten on the table in the kitchen. When Gerard balked, Mike told him that he was on their payroll as of March 31.

They would discuss salary in the morning. Gerard had only a small suitcase which contained all of his worldly belongings. They also noticed that he did not have full use of his left arm. It was not a question in either of their minds that they were going to hire Gerard Angel to work for the new company. They would use him first to get the office started up and to help install the new IBM computer system they had ordered to replace the one at the house that had been destroyed. They knew he had a lot of experience with computers. But they both wondered when they would get some business for the new company. They did have the $35,000 a year retainer from the Insurance Consortium to count on to pay all of the office bills. They knew they would survive with the new business, but they were anxious.

They were unaware that many things had already taken place that would not only give them much work to do, but would change

186

their lives in many different ways. They would be put to the test once again, and they couldn't fail. There would be too much at stake.

The next morning Mike was in the shower when he heard the phone ring and Martha answered. He was toweling himself dry when Martha told him to hurry up. With the weather being so inclement, Mike had not been able to get out for his morning power walk. He was able to get down to the basement and work out on the installed gym equipment each day for at least an hour. He also was able to get over to Russ, their martial arts instructor, at least once a week, in order to keep his skill level up in that area.

They were to be meeting with Dr. Ah Leh at their new office at 8:00 A.M. She had been given directions on how to get to their office by Martha. Dr. Leh had told Martha she was very tired after just coming off the twelve-hour night shift at the hospital. It was already 7:00 A.M., and the phone company was due to install their telephones that morning at 7:45 A.M. Dr. Leh was to be their first official client. They got to the building just before the phone man arrived. Gerard had already made a pot of decaffeinated coffee, opened up a can of frozen orange juice, and had made some toast. It was a good thing, since they didn't have time for breakfast back at the house. The money Mike had put there was still on the table. Mike took it, folded it, and stuck it into Gerard's shirt pocket.

Gerard was initially asked to follow the phone guy around to make sure that he got all the phones put in the right places. Mike gave him a floor plan to follow. Dr. Leh came in and they sat around the table in the conference room. Before she started with her detailed explanation, Mike asked Gerard to sit in on the meeting.

He introduced him as "Guardian Angel" to Dr. Leh, and they smiled at each other at their private joke after the introduction. It seems that Dr. Leh had just received another letter from her brother. It was postmarked Sonoma, California, and was dated only six days ago. His situation was reported to be just about the same as it was when she had heard from him last year. He believed he was still working to pay off his expenses of being brought into the country. He was working in a vineyard picking grapes by day, and then working in the factory part of the vineyard at least another four hours each night. He received no wages, but now he received a spending allowance of five dollars a week. He slept in a bunkhouse with fifteen other men, all of whom were also of the belief they were working off their fares. The food was okay, nothing special, but it kept him and the others in reasonably good health.

The problem was that when he had asked about how much longer it would take before he paid off his fare, he was told it would take another three years. When he complained, the foreman, a man twice his size, beat him into a state of unconsciousness. He was out for twenty-four hours, and they had to call a doctor in to treat him. His health had returned to normal since, as the beating had taken place on last New Year's Eve. Once again, he had bribed someone to get this letter out. This time his letter was written to his sister in English, and not done too badly either as near as Mike could tell. He must have spent a considerable amount of whatever free time he had to learn to write in English. He could probably speak the language pretty well by now also. He had signed the letter "Joseph Soo Leh." Mike thought, So he picked up an American first name as well.

Dr. Leh wanted her brother freed from this slavery he was being subjected to. She wrote out a check for $15,000 to Mike, and told him to find him. She understood that her brother was still an illegal alien, and would probably be deported just as soon as they found him. But more than anything, she just wanted him to be a free man. She told them that she would pay more if necessary, but please get him free. She left the office in tears.

Mike looked at Gerard and said, " 'Guardian Angel,' you have a job to do, if you want it. Are you up to it? If it's yes, then go and find her brother. You'll be on expenses, and your starting salary will be $40,000 per year. If we make any money in this business, you'll get a bonus at the end of the year." Again Mike asked him, "Are you up to it?"

"You bet I am. I won't let either of you down. I appreciate all the trust the two of you have put in me. No way will I let you down."

Martha was busy writing out a check for him for $5,000 cash. He could pick up his tickets to San Francisco, and take a good portion of the money with him as Traveler's Cheques. Martha told him she would get him an American Express card. She had a friend there and could get a card in three days just as long as she had co-signed it. Also Guardian—and that's what they were going to call him—had to get himself some new clothes in the meantime. He could use whatever cash he needed out of the expense money, and they would take the money out of his salary to pay for the clothes and any other immediate needs he may have. Yes, it would take at least three days before he would be ready to leave for the West Coast to locate Joseph Soo Leh.

In the meantime, he could set up the new computer system. Martha went along to the bank with him to be sure they would cash the check. He still looked a little bit shabby, but he had a good night's sleep and there was a brightness radiating from his eyes. She also used the opportunity and deposited the check she had received from Dr. Ah Leh. Boy, she thought, we would be in great financial shape if we didn't have to shell out that $10,000 to pay for my bail bond. Oh well, life can't always be fair. She went over to the State Employment Office to review résumés of five potential candidates for the secretary/receptionist position. She had a good group to select from and spent about an hour delving into the details contained on the résumés with the personnel director. She chose two résumés and asked that interviews be set up on the following day, one in the morning and one in the early afternoon.

When she got back to the office about three hours after she left, she was shocked to see her father, none other than George Monroe in person, in Mike's office. He had arrived just a few minutes after she had left to go to the bank. He was writing out a check for Mike when she entered the office.

"Hello, Dad. What brings you around here?"

"Would you believe me if I told you that I just hired Mike? Correction, I just hired the firm of Mike Burke Associates, Inc., to do a very important job for me.

"I know you just started as a private investigation firm, but you came highly recommended by the insurance company that I am a major stockholder in. Incidentally, they will also have to shell out a lot of money to my chemical firm in France, if you're not successful in your endeavors. This is strictly a business arrangement. I would never just select you because we are related. So good luck, you two."

189

And then he kissed Martha twice. One time for the way in, and another kiss on the way out. Martha picked up the check off the desk after he had left the office, and looked at the amount. It was for $150,000. She almost fell into the chair.

"What's that all about? I know my father. What in God's name do we have to do to earn this much money?"

And then he quieted her down, brought her over a cup of coffee, and started in to tell her everything that had just transpired.

"First off, this is only expense money, as we may have to travel around the globe a few times before this case is settled. Your father's firm CHEMFRANCE, located in Paris, France, was asked by a group of European nations to develop a chemical substance that could be used to destroy swarming killer bees. This African strain of bee is now infiltrating commercial beehives in all locations of the world where honey is produced. They have been known to attack so suddenly, and without provocation, as to cause widespread loss of life.

"It is reported that over 300 deaths have been attributed to them this past year alone. Many of the victims were children. Your father's French company was successful in developing a new chemical compound with a useful life of sixty seconds after exposure to the air that we breathe. After that, it dies immediately and leaves no residue. You see, it is a living bacteria and uses a virus to carry and spread it. It is not really a chemical at all. The name of this alleged new compound is Sterilization Straptocin Romule, or better known by its shortened name of Sterile 1.

"There's more, and it gets even worse. A single drop of this bacteria kills everything within five feet of it for 360 degrees, whenever it is exposed to the air. So the bright boys at your father's laboratory went and developed a delivery system to expand the area of coverage to twenty-five feet off the ground, and to fifty feet in any direction. Picture a circle one hundred feet in diameter and twenty-five feet high. This is roughly slightly larger than the area covered by a swarm of these killer bees. The idea was to set off this device when it was judged to be in the center of a moving swarm of these bees.

"They invented a device that explodes more than 5,500 minute ampoules of this compound. It is set off by a distinct radio signal established for each of the prototypes. So each one has their own specific detonator, capable of sending the precise radio signal from as far as one mile away.

"When it receives the signal, first it leaps into the air about ten feet and explodes into fifteen subunits. Each one travels in a controlled lateral direction, and some upward direction, for ten feet. Then it explodes with fifteen more subunits, and this repeats again, and again, until a diameter of one hundred feet is covered. It only lasts for sixty seconds, but everything living, even plant life is killed by that deadly bacteria. There is no antidote to be able to take in advance. It enters the body through the skin, so even the best gas mask made can't protect anybody from it.

"The military, namely some NATO generals, got word of this project and latched onto it. They authorized funding to make six prototypes of this new germ warfare weapon. They rationalized they needed it just in case the Russians would come up with one of these type weapons, too. Thank God they didn't. They set off one of the prototypes for a test, and it proved to be exactly as bad as they thought it would be. But then clearer minds prevailed at NATO, after reviewing the horrible results of this test. They then reported what they had done to the NATO ministers, and they recommended destroying the other five remaining prototypes. The NATO ministers were terrified at what they were told, and quickly agreed. They immediately issued the order to destroy the prototypes as well as the formula for Sterile 1, and even the delivery system that had just been developed."

Martha looked puzzled. "So all's well that ends well. What's the problem?"

"That was the relatively good news I had to tell you. It seems that before they could follow the order to destroy them, the five remaining prototype weapons were stolen. Each one of them is only the size of a softball cut in half, something like a half of a large grapefruit. The transmitting units for each of them are only the size of a pack of cigarettes. Get this now, they were stolen by a group of terrorists calling themselves the Society of the Ark. What's more, our intelligence community seems to think that these weapons will be used against targets in the United States. It should be no problem smuggling weapons as small as this past our Customs Inspectors."

"Oh my God!" Martha exclaimed.

She turned white as a ghost, and Mike went to fetch her a glass of water.

"I'll be leaving on the Concorde for France next Wednesday morning. I'm supposed to meet with members of Interpol when I arrive. Why don't you fly out next week to Switzerland and see what you can find out about that Swiss bank account of Tom's? I should be able to fly over to Switzerland on Friday to meet with you, and we'll play it by ear from there."

"That's a great idea. I'll hire us a secretary/receptionist by next Wednesday, and I'll leave on Wednesday night. I'll fly into Geneva and go to the bank first. After that I'll be staying at the Hilton in Zurich where I've been before. It's just beautiful there. You can call me there on Thursday evening before you leave Paris."

"You have got a deal, lady. Now go home and fetch our passports."

Mike got on the phone and contacted Jacques Paisson at the number he was given by Jesse. He forgot about the time difference, and Paris was six hours later than in the USA. Jacques had already gone home for the day, but someone at his office at INTERPOL was able to patch Mike through to his home number. He spoke pretty good English, which is a good thing, because Mike couldn't speak a word of French. As a matter of fact, this guy spoke two more languages as well. He had already gotten word from George Monroe's security man at CHEMFRANCE to arrange a briefing on the Society of the Ark for Mike and for some other representatives of Interpol.

Next Mike called Air France and booked himself on the 8:00 A.M. flight from Newark Airport to Orly airport in Paris. The flight was only going to take three and a half hours. He booked a limo service to pick him up at his home in Spring Valley and take him to Newark. They would pick him up at 5:30 A.M.

Guardian came back to the office wearing a new suit, and with a few extra boxes. Mike briefed him on the events, and the plans he and Martha had made. He told them not to worry, as he had already been thinking about how he was going to locate Joseph Soo Leh somewhere on the West Coast. He had two leads to follow: First, the postmark on the letter, and then he said in his letter he was treated by a doctor when he was unconscious for twenty-four hours. These were good leads, he told Mike. He would not be able to take a gun with him on the flight, but Mike suggested he take the knife and harness designed for quick release from his right leg with him in his luggage. It had come in handy for Mike once already back in New Mexico, as Guardian remembered. He took it gladly, and told Mike he would practice with it before he left.

On Wednesday morning, Mike woke very early. He lay there with Martha and they spoke softly to each other for fifteen minutes discussing anything and everything, until Mike just had to get to his personal morning chores to be ready for his limo pickup. He gave Martha a long and lingering kiss before he left. He told her to be careful, and that he would be counting the hours until he would meet with her in Switzerland.

He felt a strange sense of foreboding as he left the house that morning. He pulled the collar of his topcoat up around his neck, as he felt the cold chill of the early morning air rush against him when he was getting into the car. He sensed that something was about to go wrong.

CHAPTER 19

The flight to Paris was advertised to take just under three and a half hours. It left Newark Airport at 8:00 A.M. sharp and landed at 5:30 P.M. French time, with a six-hour time difference. It was Mike's first trip on a supersonic aircraft, and if not for the serious nature of his trip, he would have been able to enjoy it. Well, at least this time he didn't get sick as he always seemed to get when he flew in the small plane. But he was missing Martha already. He was met at the airport by a driver supplied by George Monroe's company CHEMFRANCE. However, it took him more than an hour to clear through French Customs. His driver did not speak any English at all, so Mike just blindly got into the car when he opened the door for him when they left the airport. The driver did seem to know where he was taking him, and in fifty minutes flat he found himself getting out of the car in front of a very unimpressive dark stone building.

The streets were very drearily lit, and it was damp and cold. He had only taken one step away from the car when the driver gunned the car away from the curb. Mike was hoping he was not too late for the briefing, but even more so he hoped he was at the right location. He had no way of knowing. A light abruptly went on in the center of the large stone edifice, indicating that there was a set of doors. He stepped through them, and then went through a revolving door. He was met with the outstretched hand of a tall, lean, balding Frenchman, who said, "Welcome to France, Mr. Burke," in almost perfect English. He then introduced himself as Jacques Paisson, with the pronunciation of his last name sounding like "passion," just as Jesse had told Mike.

"Am I too late for the briefing?" Mike said to Jacques, at the same time looking at his watch. It showed five minutes to two. He immediately adjusted his watch by putting it ahead by six hours, thus making it almost 8:00 P.M.

194

"Not at all, Mr. Burke. We are still awaiting the arrival of representatives from two other nations, but most have arrived and are in the briefing room already. You must be tired after your long trip, and we have some food and light refreshments in the rear of the conference room. Please feel free to help yourself when we get upstairs."

Mike was escorted to the elevator, and they got out on the second floor.

Mike was asked to sign the register located on the desk in front of a set of very large mahogany doors. The man sitting behind the desk was also very large. Everything seemed very large for some strange reason. He had pockmarked facial skin, as if he had severe acne when he was younger. He was not wearing a jacket or a uniform, but had a shoulder holster with a .45 stuck in it as evidence of his authority in the matter. He stood up and walked to face Mike at the front of the desk. He indicated that Mike should raise his arms, and after he did so he was searched. After that he made what looked like a superficial search of Mike's travel bag. Having found nothing to raise his alarm, he offered Mike his hand and grasped his and shook it vigorously. At the time he said something to Mike in French, which seemed like a greeting of sorts. Mike replied with a simple "thank you," and the man smiled at him and sat down.

Jacques ushered him through the doors into a large room about 150 feet in length and about 60 feet wide. There was a 5-foot wide aisle down the center, and aisle space on each side of the room. There were rows of tables facing a raised stage at the far end. Two chairs were behind each table, and Mike reckoned that the room could easily handle a briefing for about 250 people. He hung up his topcoat on a rack at the rear, and shoved his single travel suitcase under it. He kept his attaché case, but he didn't know why, as he did not have any more than a pad and some pencils in it, along with a book he had started reading at the start of his flight.

There was an area inset by about 25 feet to the right of the entrance to the room which went in deep behind the larger conference room. It looked as if there already were about fifty people gathered around in small groups talking, while sipping coffee, or whatever, and munching on sandwiches. There were tables at the back with the soft drinks, coffee and hot water urns, as well as large trays of sandwiches. Jacques excused himself without introducing Mike to anyone, saying that he had to make a final preparation before the briefing. Mike was all alone and didn't know a soul. He headed over to the sandwich tray as soon as he realized he was hungry. It had been a long day, not so much in elapsed time, but in other ways he could not really explain. He was dead tired, as he had not been able to even doze off on the airplane. He read the book instead. At least he started reading it, but he could not bring his mind to focus on the subject.

He grabbed a sandwich thinking it contained ham, bit into it heartily, and almost choked once his taste buds recognized it as something like tongue. He hated tongue with a passion, that and liver. Martha had tried to give him liver once, and he tried it and almost threw up after the first bite. She never tried to give him anything in that family of foods again. He remembered they went out for hamburgers that evening, and she dumped the entire meal, vegetables and all, down the disposal. Funny how these little flashbacks occurred at the strangest times. He gagged and discharged the mouthful of food into a napkin.

So much for sandwiches, he said to himself. He had lost his appetite, and went over to draw himself a cup of coffee from the spigoted urn. A man wearing a dark brown double-breasted suit walked over to him and introduced himself as Louis Bar-Levi of the Israeli Secret Police. This guy was barrel-chested although not really heavy. He was much shorter than Mike, and he estimated that he was about five feet eight. Mike shook his hand, told him his name, and looked at him with a little surprise. The man sensed his questioning glare and went on to explain.

"Most people don't realize that the state of Israel has a secret police. But I assure you that we do exist as an official body within the Israeli government. We report directly to the minister of defense, and are called upon often to brief the Knesset. As a matter of fact, let me now introduce you to my associate, Irv Klein."

Irv was walking toward them as they spoke. He was very heavyset and a few inches taller than Louis.

"We're on assignment to Interpol, while the better-known Israeli organization the Mossad is busy with crime in general elsewhere in the world. We are specialists in the arena of the terrorist.

So now you know all about why we are here. What about yourself? What is your involvement with this terrorist group?"

Mike shook hands with the man introduced to him as Irv Klein, and had just started to answer his question and was ready to tell them about being called in by the owner of CHEMFRANCE, when they were all asked to take a seat.

Mike followed the two Israeli secret police agents up the aisle to the first row of tables, after he first grabbed another cup of coffee, and a sandwich that he was sure contained cheese. There were earphones and a dial that allowed them to hear the presentation in simultaneous translation in five possible languages. He wondered if this wasn't the same way they did it at the United Nations. He was about to put them on over his ears, and dial in English, when Jacques Paisson went to the podium and introduced himself. He advised everyone that he would be making his presentation in English. Mike looked back around in the room and only saw about five people putting on the earphones. The room had filled up considerably, and there were at least sixty people seated. Most of them were up in front as far as they could get.

Jacques then announced that his presentation of what was known about the Society of the Ark would take about thirty minutes. After that he would open up the floor to questions. He also told everyone that he would fill them in on what he knew about the theft by these people of a new weapon which was developed by CHEMFRANCE. The room silenced down, and everyone seemed to be very attentive to the presenter. All of these guys were pros, and they didn't want to miss a thing. Jacques started speaking again.

"The Society of the Ark is a new terrorist organization formally brought into being by a Chinese doctor of acupuncture by the name of No Wah, and his brother, also a doctor, but of philosophy not medical, Dr. No Lee. They were both born into riches, having been direct descendants of the old Chinese warlords on the island of Taiwan. Yet both of them were educated on the mainland of China. It is said, but we do not have any proof, that at the time of the Chinese cultural revolution, these two returned to Taiwan and murdered their parents. They force-fed them rat poison. They did this because they wanted their parents to sign over the parents' business to them, and the parents refused. They would have given it to their sons gladly, if they agreed to stay and run the three companies owned by the family.

"The brains of the organization, Dr. No Wah is reported to be blind. Our information is a little hazy on just how this happened to him. There were reports about some prisoner getting loose while he was torturing him, and the prisoner using two of his acupuncture needles to pierce his eyes. He supposedly has never touched an acupuncture needle since this happened to him.

"His brother is the strong man of the two. He personally locates and chooses new members of their so-called Society. It's really a very simple process. He seeks out and recruits members from all of the various terrorist organizations.

"He identifies those members who feel that their own organizations are too tame for them, or they are not satisfied because they are not brutal enough for them. Only two members of the original terrorist organization can be allowed to belong to this exclusive group of terrorists at one time. This is why they call themselves the Society of the Ark. But if one of them dies, they recruit a new member from the same organization to take his place. They always want to keep their ark full.

"I used the word his, but I really mean from either sex, as not just men belong to this organization. And we understand there is a waiting list to get in. By now you may be asking yourselves, why would any terrorist, with a supposed cause he would gladly die for, ever want to join this group? I can tell you in the simplest terms. They do it for money. Surprises you, doesn't it? Everyone seems to think that terrorists are dedicated people. Well some of them may be dedicated, but many are not.

"These are a few of the qualities which we have been able to ascertain that Dr. No Lee looks for in his recruits. Mind you, these are only the basic minimum requirements. The worse they are, as far as being a member of the human race, the better they like it. Usually the world's most wanted list is a good place for them to start searching for candidates. First and foremost they must be greedy.

"They must be obsessed with having all the money they could ever need to satisfy themselves with. They must crave for all worldly things. Ruthlessness and viciousness are the second of the required personality traits. They look for those seemingly ob-

198

sessed with a savage brutality, and they must be able to show evidence beyond any doubt that they have killed at least three people in cold blood. They must have done their heinous crimes in the most vicious possible way. To be considered, they must be hateful of almost anything and everything. Also, they must be both ferocious and fearless, giving no quarter in any situation, and never expecting any.

"Lastly, the most important qualification is obedience. Once they pledge themselves to the Society of the Ark, they are required to follow the lead and instructions of the Master, Dr. No Wah, without question or hesitancy. It is said that to break their oath to the society, or to disobey a direct command of the Master, would lead to a death so horrible that it would take thirty days until you actually died. Oh yes, they have been tested by someone who broke the oath, and they have devised this most painful method by which to kill someone. All the members are aware of it, as most of them were present during at least one of these long drawn-out and painful executions."

Jacques Paisson stopped for a minute to sip at a glass of water on the podium.

It was obvious, as he was relating this tale, that he was becoming more unnerved by what he had to tell them. His voice had started to lose its normal cool delivery, and he was visibly becoming more emotional. He put down the water glass and continued with the briefing.

"To date we believe that there are forty-two members of this organization. There may be more than twenty-one terrorist organizations throughout the world, but this is all they have brought into their fold at the latest count. They have been recruited, by twos, from such organizations as the Iranian-sponsored Islamic Jihad for the Liberation of Palestine and *Hezbollah*—The Party of God. Also included are personnel recruited from the ranks of such organizations as the Japanese Red Army, the Basques, the IRA, the military wing of the Ulster Defense Organization (UDA), Ulster Freedom Fighters (UFF), Palestine Liberation Organization (PLO), Italian Red Brigades, and Latin American Cells. The list goes on and on.

"They all kill for the love of killing, and seem to draw an extreme amount of pleasure from it. As you know, many of these

Islamic-backed terrorists are Shiite militants called Mujaheddin or Holy Warriors. Thus, their original terrorist activity was based upon their religion, and their extreme hatred of the Jews. How anyone can kill so indiscriminately in the name of their God, is beyond me. Yet one only has to look back to the days of the Crusades to find killing taking place in the name of God.

"There is an envelope that will be passed out to each of you before you leave here tonight which lists the names of the men and women we have been able to identify as members of this group, and the organizations they used to belong to. We have been updating the list weekly.

"It was reported to us that two members of the Ku Klux Klan, an anti-Negro terrorist organization from the United States, declined to accept their offer to join because they found out that there were some black men in the group. They said they could accept all other foreigners, but they couldn't bring themselves to be in a brotherhood with anyone from the black race. Shortly afterward they were both found dead. Their faces had been obliterated with acid. The autopsy report said that the acid was put on them a drop at a time, over a period of at least four weeks. This illustrates once again what they are capable of doing to another human being.

"So you see, gentlemen, once someone is chosen and called by this new terrorist society, they dare not decline the offer. By this time they will have already known too much about them to be let off the hook, so to speak.

"Now let us focus in on what holds this ultimate of terrorist organizations together. First of all, they do not require that the participants renounce either their religion, or the cause that made them terrorists in the first place.

"They are allowed, and even encouraged to keep these inner feelings, and along with it their deep-seated hatreds. But, I must impress upon you that they are second to the primary will of the Master. This is a neat little mind trick they have come up with. Since the members are already so far removed from their original causes, why not let them keep their reasons for hatred in their hearts? They recognize their need to hate. It's part of their makeup.

"The second and most important glue that holds this organization together is money. They make an awful lot of it. They get paid quite well for, as the Americans say, putting a hit on someone. But their favorite way of making money is by kidnapping and ransom. To this, they have added a little twist of horror. The kidnapped victim will be put through some sort of mental and physical harm every second day they are held in captivity. Mind you, not enough to kill them, but something terrible is done to them every second day. If the ransom is paid within two weeks of the abduction, the kidnapped person has always been released. In this way the word gets around, and more often then not the ransom is paid. But never before at least three days have elapsed. In that time they will have done their dirty work to that person at least once. If the ransom is not paid within the time limit I just told you about, then the victim has always been killed. And I might add, once located, the body of the victim always showed a great deal of abuse.

"But they really would rather get their money, so once the ransom has been paid, they always have returned their victim. There was the case of the Saudi prince who was held by them for twelve days, while the king decided if he was going to pay or not. By the time they got him back, they had cut off the first joint on both of his thumbs, both small fingers, and one big toe. And then, they circumcised him. They used a bolt cutter to do all of this damage, and he was obviously in pretty bad shape when he was finally released. All this was done without any anesthetic. Does this give you any insight as to what we are up against?

"That is all I can tell you about the Society of the Ark, gentlemen. I think it's enough to make us all sick.

"I'll take questions now about this group and then I'll finish up this briefing with all I know about this weapon they have stolen."

There was a hushed silence in the room, as all of the representatives of the police forces from around the free world just sat back and started to digest and comprehend what they had just been told. Louis Bar-Levi raised his hand, and it was acknowledged by Jacques.

"Could you please tell us when this organization was started, and how much money they have accumulated to date?"

"It was started twenty-five months ago, just as soon as Dr. No

Wah was released from his hospital. Apparently more damage to him was done than just the taking of his sight with those acupuncture needles, but we don't know what it was. He was in the hospital for quite some time after they found him barely alive.

"They have already collected approximately $21 million from ransom alone. We don't know how much they have collected from assassinations. The word on the street is that they charge $1 million per murder, but we have been unable to verify this fact so far. We do know they have made seven political assassinations, and two business-related assassinations. They have killed four kidnapped people when ransom was not paid according to their deadline, and forty-two more people were kidnapped, for whom ransoms were paid. They charge a flat $500,000 as ransom for each victim to be returned. It is always payable in American dollars, and they furnish the attaché case, with instructions, which they want used to have the money passed to them in. Apparently, $500,000 in their specified denominations just fits into an attaché case. You can see by these numbers they have been very active, and want the notoriety to be able to be more effective in their endeavors. As I said before, none of these people were returned without some scar, either physical or mental, and in most cases, both. As part of their modus operandi, they use local criminal talent to assist them whenever they go into an area. They have no trouble finding these types, as they pay quite well. But if there is any possibility they will reveal anything damaging to the organization, these associates are immediately terminated. We have been able to apprehend six of these associates to a crime, and every one of them were found dead in their cells in less than forty-eight hours. We have also captured two of the direct terrorist members. However, before any of them could be interrogated, they had taken a fast-acting poison. It was concealed in a cavity of their tooth. All they had to do was bite down hard, and they were on their way to Allah, or whatever other God they may profess to believe in to carry them to heaven."

"One more question please, Mr. Piasan," asked Louis as he stood up once again. He had pronounced his last name badly. "How did you get so much information, the names and everything about this organization, in such a short time? Also, where do they claim to have their home base?"

A very disturbed Jacques fought off the urge to be sarcastic to him because of the slurring of his name, but he controlled himself and just replied, even with the hint of a slight smile on his face, "The name is pronounced passion, not piasan, Mr. Bar-Levi. I am a Frenchman, not an Italian friend of the family."

A chuckle went through the audience, and it was obvious everyone present needed something to divert their intense thoughts at this particular moment.

Jacques accepted the joke on himself, in order to achieve this small amount of levity. Then he straightened himself up, and said most forcefully, "I tell you this with a secrecy that must be observed by all of you. What I tell you now must be carried in your minds only, and must not leave this room. We have successfully infiltrated this terrorist organization with an undercover man, our own informer. Unfortunately this man must continue to commit these and other heinous acts which are assigned to him, even murder itself, until such time as we can crush the life out of this new and most violent terrorist organization. Believe me when I tell you that this man is a hero, living in his own daily hell. He lives only to keep us informed as to what they are doing. We have already had to stop him from committing suicide, as he only wants to die for all of the crimes against humanity that he has already committed in their name. Please, for all of our sakes, and for the sake of all the decent people of this world—please I beg of you, keep this secret of his very existence."

He was pleading with the audience at this point, and realized he was again letting himself get emotional. He caught himself, and continued, "The Society of the Ark makes its home base somewhere in Libya. They are the paying guests of General Radaffi, just like so many of the other terrorist organizations that he allows to make their home there, and to train and fester on his country's soil. As you know, he took over in Libya and followed in the footsteps of his predecessor.

"Are there any more questions? If not, I will now talk about the weapon these madmen are reported to have stolen."

There were no more questions, as everyone in the room was quite aware that Jacques had to stop talking on this subject. He went on to tell all of the attendees the same information that George Monroe told to Mike back in his office. He added only one more thing to Mike's knowledge on the subject matter. The effect of being touched by the bacteria was an immediate stopping of the heart of any human, animal, or insect. They still were unsure as to why it also killed all plant life which came in contact with it, and were still trying to find this out. It defied known reason.

Mike made a mental note that tomorrow he was going to pay the company known as CHEMFRANCE a visit. He needed all the information he could gather, if he was going to be able to set up some countermeasures to neutralize it. Gad, that's a funny word to use, he thought. Neutralize a weapon called Sterile 1. He picked up his envelope containing the list of the terrorists, and stuffed it into his attaché case. It was at this point that Louis volunteered to take Mike back to his hotel, where he assured him he should be able to get a room for the night, or a few nights if he so wanted. Mike accepted his offer of a ride, as he never even thought about booking himself a place to stay when he made his plans to go to France. He was just a little too preoccupied to worry about those little details. In the car ride to the hotel, Irv Klein started to ask him some questions about his assignment with CHEMFRANCE to locate the missing five prototype weapons. Funny, but Mike didn't remember ever telling them about his assignment. He thought he was interrupted from answering that question by the start of the meeting. Oh well, he must have said something. Or could it be that he was under some sort of surveillance by the Israeli Secret Police? Probably not.

He was tired and all he wanted to do now was check into the hotel, get a call placed to Martha, take a hot bath, and get a good night's sleep, all in that order. He would make arrangements to get over to CHEMFRANCE's plant in the morning.

He did sense one other thing. It seemed to him that Irv Klein and Louis Bar-Levi did not really like each other. They may have been assigned to work together, but he was sure there was some animosity between them. It was the way they talked to each other. He was sure of it.

Looking at his watch as he entered the hotel, his digital indicated fifteen minutes after ten. This means that it was only a little after four in the afternoon. He put a call to Martha at the new office number as soon as he entered his room and dropped his luggage on the bed. While he waited for the call to come through, he looked around the room. Not bad, he thought, not bad at all. It was a larger standard room than you would get in the States, but then the cost per night was $325. The reduced value of the dollar was very evident to him. Martha spoke to him after he picked up the phone on the first ring. Actually it was a double ring as appropriate with all European telephone service.

"Honey, I can't believe that you're gone less than a day. It seems like such a long time."

Then she went on to tell him she had hired a secretary/receptionist, but that she could only start work in another four weeks.

"She is involved with doing a special assignment for her current employer and feels she cannot leave him in the lurch. She is a naturalized citizen, after coming from the Philippines seven years ago with her parents. They are both dead now, and she is alone, except for the large Filipino community which consider everyone of their nationality a brother and sister. She attends the same college where I am taking courses. Her name is Maybelle Divina, and she is a very pretty little young woman, with dark black long hair. She has great secretarial skills, including knowledge of the computer. As an added plus, she not only speaks English and Tagalog, which is the language of the Philippines, but she also speaks French, Spanish, and one of the Vietnamese dialects."

Guardian had already set up the computer, and had loaded some of the accounting programs they would need. But there was nothing else to put into it yet. He was preparing himself for his search for Joseph Soo Leh, and she caught him so deep in thought while he was talking to himself about what he was going to do. She was preparing to catch a regular flight out later on Wednesday night. Her flight was to leave at 9:00 P.M., and with the six-hour difference in time, she was to land in Geneva at 10:00 A.M. their time. Her airtime was to be approximately seven hours, and she planned to sleep on the flight over. She was going immediately over to the Suisse National Union Bank and make her inquiries about Tom's bank account. Then she would grab a limo over to Zurich, and relax for a day. She couldn't wait for Mike to be able to join her at the Hilton on Friday evening. She had to end their conversation rather quickly, as she had to get ready for her flight. Mike told her he would brief her on everything he found out in France, when they met on Friday. They hung up with a kiss. Mike was hungry and tried to order himself a steak. The kitchen was closed, but he was able to get two cold beers and some chips sent up to his room. While waiting for them to be delivered he drew himself a hot bath in a very elaborate and exceptionally large bathroom. After his bath and the two beers, he went right to sleep, even though his body was telling him that it was only 7:00 P.M. where he had come from. Before he went to bed he put in for a wake up call at 7:00 A.M. He dreamed of making love to Martha all night. He had a pleasant night's sleep in a most comfortable bed.

CHAPTER 20

Mike awoke to that strange-sounding double ring of the telephone. His first thoughts were that it was his wake up call, but when he glanced at the big red digital clock next to his bed, he saw that it was only 6:00 A.M. He picked up the receiver. It was his father-in-law George Monroe.

"I just flew in on my private plane. I've been told that you were at the Interpol briefing session last night, and I thought that today you would like to meet with the people over at CHEM-FRANCE. I think they may have some interesting additional information for you, something that could quite possibly give you a one up edge on these buggers that stole the prototypes. I'm at the airport and still have to clear French Customs. Do you think you can be ready to have me pick you up at 7:30 A.M.? Grab yourself some breakfast first, as you can expect a long day."

Mike acknowledged the time for the pickup at his hotel. He should have plenty of time to get ready and shower, and to get some of the cobwebs out of his head. He was now feeling the effects of jet lag, as it was only midnight back where he just came from. He left his room at about ten minutes to seven, and told the front desk he was going into the restaurant to get some breakfast. If anyone came for him, they could find him there. He received a very polite, *"Oui, Monsieur"*; at least it sounded that way to him. He was not very good at French at all. He was seated immediately in the rear of the restaurant at a table which gave him a view of the entrance. He had ordered an American-style breakfast, consisting of bacon and eggs, with toast, jam and coffee. While he was being served, he noticed Louis Bar-Levi come to the entrance and scan the tables. It was quite obvious he was looking for someone. He spotted Mike, and headed toward him. Without being asked, he pulled out the second chair at Mike's table and said, "I'm glad I caught up with you today, Mr. Burke. Do you mind if I breakfast with you while we talk a little?" He volunteered that Irv Klein was already on his way back to their headquarters in Tel-Aviv. And then he added almost under his breath, "Thank goodness for small favors."

Mike picked up on this little slip of the tongue, and thought to himself that he was right, there was some bad blood between them. He didn't let on to Louis at all. Louis asked Mike to call him Lou, and gave him his business card. Mike gave him one of his new business cards. It was the first one he had ever given out to anyone. He never even gave one to George Monroe when he visited with him back in his new office. He told Lou he should call him Mike. Immediately Lou was questioning Mike about what he was going to be doing that day. He had the feeling that Lou knew he was going out to the CHEMFRANCE plant, and he seemed to be wangling himself an invite to join him. It was then that Mike spotted George Monroe at the entrance, and he waved him over. Mike made the introductions, and very abruptly George said they had to hurry up for their appointment.

They left as Mike paid for his breakfast tab by signing his name with the room number, and he quickly shook hands with Lou telling him he may see him later in the day. They walked out of the restaurant leaving a very perturbed looking Louis Bar-Levi at the table. As they were leaving George said, "I've heard about that guy. He is a real pushy SOB individual, and I just don't like that type of character. I know he was trying to get an invite out to the plant, but no way. Not for the likes of him."

Mike didn't understand George's animosity towards Lou, but what the hell? It was George's show and he had every right to limit access to his plant and to the details about Sterile 1. The same driver who had picked Mike up at the airport was holding the door open on a beautiful Mercedes limousine. They both stepped into the rear seat, and the driver entered the front on the driver's side.

He told them it would take about forty-five minutes to drive to the plant, and that there was hot coffee in one of the compartments in the rear. Both men declined, and they rode in silence while George read a copy of the *Wall Street Journal*. So Mike picked up a copy of the *New York Times*. He couldn't find a sports section right away, but then smiled when he came across it.

They ran into some traffic on the way and the trip took closer to an hour. When they came to the gates of the plant, they were stopped while the man in charge of the gate had to get approval to let them enter. Once the call came back that it was Mr. Monroe, the owner, the apologies flew in French, and they proceeded immediately to a large office-type building in the center of the compound. They were surrounded by many other buildings that looked as if they were factory buildings. George put down his paper, excused himself for being so untalkative to Mike on the trip down to the plant. He told him that most of his people at the plant spoke English, as he had hired them from all around the world. He should have no trouble with understanding what they were going to tell them today. As for last night, he wanted to know from Mike if he thought the meeting with the Interpol people was worthwhile. He asked specifically if Mike thought he would be able to deal with this terrorist organization in recovery of the prototypes. He never really wanted Mike to answer the question he had just posed to him, but he had to say it anyway. He was a disturbed person, because of what had happened, to say the least.

They entered the building and took an elevator to the eighth floor. This seemed to Mike to be the top floor of the building. They entered a large room which had a circular solid mahogany table in the center, and enough chairs around to seat thirty people. The room was full of somber-looking people, more men than women by about a two to one ratio; some of them were wearing lab coats, and others were in business suits. There were two open chairs at the far end of the room, and Mike and George went over to them and sat down. All eyes focused on George Monroe.

He told them in the interest of time he would only be introducing the private detective he had hired to recover the missing prototypes. There was a little flutter of activity, and some comments were passed between some of them in French after he introduced Mike. George stared down those people who were being so discourteous. He said further that the format of the meeting would be to present all the information on the subject of Sterile 1 and that as a person was called to tell his part of the story, he or she should introduce themselves, give their position and title, and a short summary of their responsibility here at CHEMFRANCE. He pointed to a gentlemen wearing a white lab coat who was seated at the other end of the room, and asked that he start the briefing. He was emphatic. He wanted to know everything there was to know, and cautioned everyone in the room not to leave out even the slightest detail. All eyes focused on the other end of the room. Mike looked at his watch. It was 10:30 A.M.

"My name is Dr. Franz Killergrove. I am the president and chief scientific officer of this company. It was I who took upon us the assignment to develop a chemical compound which could be used to destroy killer bees while they swarmed, or in their hives for that matter. A consortium of nations, mostly from the third-world countries, but with representation from the United States, Great Britain, the Netherlands, and France, requested that we take on this project to develop something to put nature back on an even basis. It was reported to me and my close staff that colonies of these bees were being formed like stepping stones, from one country to another. It only took a few infiltrating bees to be able to impregnate the queen bee in a hive colony. The reproductive process keeps expanding, until all of the worker bees of the colony become aggressive. They attack anything which moves near them while they are swarming. I accept full responsibility for my actions in this matter, and believe everyone in this room would have acted in a similar manner, had they been asked to help in what looked to be a worthy, and I might add, potentially profitable endeavor. I am finished, at least for now, with my part of the presentation."

Mike took a quick glance at George. He seemed to wince when Dr. Killergrove mentioned the profit motive for his company. The man next to the previous speaker picked up the lead he was given. He was a small man, barely able to have much of his body show over the edge of the conference table.

Mike judged him to be only about four-feet five- or six-inches tall, if he was to stand up. He spoke with a high-pitched voice.

"I am Dr. Pierre Flinch. I am a Frenchman. My father was English. I am the vice president of New Product Development. It is my department that sat in on the original presentation when we were asked to develop the chemical compound to destroy these insects. We were assigned the task of creating direction on just what we would have to do to invent a substance which could meet our goals. We requested, and had delivered to us, a thousand of these bees for experimentation. Our plans were to develop chemical substances, or bacteria, through combinations of other chemicals, and to test each of them against live bees, while recording the hopefully toxic effect on them. We separately tested more than 4,700 chemical and unique bacterial concoctions, all with the same result; no effect on the bees at all.

"They were a very hearty strain of insect and would not even be affected when they were exposed to pure DDT, which as most people are currently aware, is now a restricted chemical. We worked on this effort over a seven-month time frame, with four of our scientists dedicating themselves to this task at least six days a week. We were about to abandon this effort and report to management about our unsuccessful attempts to kill the insects, when Madame Maurice came up with the idea to merge the bacteria with all of the different chemical substances which we had already created.

"I personally discussed this approach with Dr. Killergrove, and he approved our spending only four more weeks on the project."

Dr. Killergrove nodded that he did in fact give the approval to continue with their efforts. Eyes now focused on Madame Maurice. She was a woman in her sixties, who wore her gray hair in a bun at the top of her head.

"My fellow colleagues, Mr. Monroe, and Mr. Burke." She spoke with a French accent which was difficult for Mike to follow. "I am the chief chemist here at CHEMFRANCE. It is my job to develop chemical and bacterial compounds to do specific things. After we create a compound, we test it and report on the results, as well as any negative findings. As you were just told, it was my idea to attempt to mix our chemical compounds with a form of bacteria to test on the bees. Unfortunately, as it turns out, we were all too successful, but not at first. We started to work seven days a week in our quest for this insect-killing compound. We were in the fourth and final week of our extended test period, and I might add, just about ready to give it up, when we made an accidental discovery. One of the test bacterial and chemical compounds, which we had created, had fallen into one of our plastic garbage cans. The can was empty and the technician reached into it to retrieve the formulated compound. Then in a clinical and sterile environment he ran the test with the unclean substance, and it killed the test bee immediately. He tried it with another ten bees, and the results were always the same.

"We still did not know what we had here, but through a process of elimination, we were able to isolate the catalyst bacteria to the chemical substance we had created as bacteria from the plastic from which the garbage can was made. We gradually tested the killing of the bees further and further away from the compound we had created, and found out that the killing range of it was limited to exactly three feet. Once again some happening interfered with our work, and one of our test experiments was started, and then not brought to fruition for approximately 115 seconds. The compound had failed to work in this instance, and the test bee was still alive. Under the microscope, we found out that the bacteria was dead. Further experiments, for which we had to receive additional approval of Dr. Killergrove because we had gone over our four-week extension, proved to us that our newly developed bacteria had a life cycle of only 60 seconds."

Dr. Killergrove cut into her presentation with a statement. "I acknowledge that I had in fact made the authorized approval of the extension time, based on the reports of success to date that were given to me by Dr. Pierre Flinch."

This time Dr. Flinch nodded to the group that he had advised Dr. Killergrove accordingly. It was at this time that George Monroe cut in and called for a break of an hour for lunch. Trays of food and refreshments were being brought into the conference room.

"What do you think about all this?" George bent over to ask Mike. "I'll be damned, but their motivation through this seems to have been profit all the time."

Mike answered him. "George, of course there was a profit motive. Isn't that what large companies, or any company for that matter, are all about? I'd like to hold back my condemnations of anyone until after I have heard the whole story."

George said, "You're right, of course, Mike."

With that comment Mike rose from his seat and headed toward the food, and George followed. The meeting was resumed at exactly 1:00 P.M. by George. Madame was still making her presentation.

"Let me get technical for a moment, and tell you about the loss of life we had here at CHEMFRANCE while in the course of developing this bacteria.

"We did not know about the potency of the bacteria we had developed. Before we started to put in the safeguards of extreme care, the lab technician who accidentally developed the bacteria had died from what we could best describe as a heart attack. After this occurred, we naturally had to work with our experiments in a quarantined environment. Everything we did from that point of time was done with extreme care, and in a completely antiseptic environment. It was unfortunate that we did not take the necessary precautions up front, and that the young man lost his life.

"But let me assure you, we did not know about the toxic effects this bacteria would have on a human being. The chemicals we used to create the basic chemical compound, that is before it was mixed with the bacteria is, and has always been, harmless to humans. After we ascertained what the bacteria could do, we turned the results of our tests over to the engineering department. I am now finished with my presentation, and will be glad to answer any questions which may develop."

"My name is Alphonse Krenn. My last name is spelled with two *n*s. I am the head of the Engineering Department here at CHEMFRANCE. I have only been on the job for nine months, starting to work at about the same time this project was started. Prior to that I was a colonel in the French Army Corps of Engineers."

Mike noted that he was only about fifty years old, and had a full beard along with a thinning and receding hairline. He was extremely fidgety, and kept shaking his head with a ticlike nervous disorder after each sentence he spoke was completed.

"When the project had progressed to a point where they would need a delivery system, it was turned over to my department. I was asked to have my people expand the killing range to twenty-five feet high and one hundred feet in a diameter, or fifty feet from the point of wherever it was set off. To achieve this goal I borrowed a concept used in an American antipersonnel mine. It is called the Claymore mine, and once it is activated it leaps

213

approximately five feet into the air. After this it explodes, sending shrapnel for 360 degrees. It usually kills anyone within fifteen feet of the explosion."

His nervousness was becoming less evident, as he started to explain things which were totally in his element. He knew the subject matter very well, and his explanation started to sound more like a brag about his ability to engineer something so clever.

"It really was a simple matter to be able to have one small explosion distribute the very small size of the ampoules which contained the bacteria fifteen times while expanding the range outward. And then to explode each of them again fifteen times, and then again another fifteen times, until the desired total range of one hundred feet was met. All that was necessary was to be able to package the inner-bursting ampoules of the bacteria in a stronger encasement. This was a simple matter for our computers to provide us with the correct engineering elements.

"The trigger mechanism is a small transmitter, no larger than a pack of cigarettes. It contains a battery which creates a special radio signal, set to coincide with a receiver in the weapon itself. When the transmitted signal is received by the weapon, the series of controlled explosions occur, and another signal is transmitted back to the sending unit. A small light on this unit will turn red, indicating that the explosion to start the chain reaction has taken place. There are two separate pushes of the button allowed before the transmitter is rendered useless because it is out of power.

"Each of the weapons has a corresponding trigger transmitter. They have been simply numbered one through six. We used number one for the demonstration test that was shown to the NATO generals. Remember now, the range of the transmitter is only 5,000 feet, just a little shy of a mile. Oh yes, I almost forgot to mention that the weapon is contained in a thin shield protective carrier that is only the size of a large half grapefruit. Each weapon and transmitter is stored in a small foam-insulated box to shield it from any shock while moving it. This package is only about the size of a half a shoe box. And I wish to add, the explosions generated in the device are almost minute in size. Hardly more than the bang of a small firecracker.

"This is all I have to say. That is, unless there are any questions?"

There was a smile of satisfaction on his face. Mike and George both thought he had said enough. George asked if he could explain how the NATO generals had become aware of this device. He turned red in the face, and as he answered he coughed and sputtered.

"I believe I may have told them about it, when I went to a reunion with my old army comrades in arms. I think I may have said something when they were all telling us about their personal accomplishments."

The nervous tic had returned, and George, with utter contempt in his voice, told him to sit down.

Madame Maurice asked to speak again, and George gave her a nod to continue.

"I wish to tell you two things that you should know about disarming the weapon or making it ineffective. We were asked to test the actual workings of the prototypes immediately after they were put into the release mechanism. You see, there were actually eight prototypes created. My department used two of them to test out our theories about controlling these devices. If the device is placed into a large plastic garbage can, and the lid is fastened down, then the minute series of explosions occurring from within do not allow any of the bacteria to escape. Once again, the bacteria contained on the surface of the plastic seems to smother the bacteria. The small exploding charge is not strong enough to blow open the container. Also, we have found out that submerging a weapon of this type in boiling water causes a twofold reaction. First, the boiling water kills the bacteria, even within the ampoules that contain it. Second, the hot water also negates the charges that have been placed in the weapon."

This was the best news that any of them could have expected .to hear. There were no more presentations. Everything had been told that could be told. George Monroe thanked the staff and dismissed them. It was five minutes to four. They had been listening to the presentations for just about five and a half hours. George suggested to Mike that he make a trip to the bathroom before they attempt the long ride back to the hotel.

George said he would meet him in the lobby, as he had something he had to do first. When they met about fifteen minutes later in the lobby as planned, George told Mike that he had terminated the services of Alphonse Krenn. They got in the car for the ride back. Once again there was not too much talk. When Mike got out at the hotel, George gave him his business card with five separate numbers all over the world where he could be reached. Mike gave him one of his cards as well.

"Good luck, Mike, God be with you. Many people are counting on you. Keep in touch, and keep me advised as to your progress. Give my love to Martha when you see her."

Once again the chauffeur left the area with the tires squealing. Mike went through the revolving doors to the hotel, and found Louis Bar-Levi waiting for him. He had apparently been waiting for him the entire day, based on the anxiety he exhibited when he finally saw Mike emerging from the car.

"How about having some dinner with me tonight, Mike?"

"No thanks, I still have to make some calls to the States and to Switzerland, and I'll have room service send me up something. But tell you what, I'll meet you for breakfast again tomorrow."

"You've got yourself a date in the morning. See you in the restaurant at 7:00 A.M."

Mike went to his room and dialed his number at the office. There was no one there to answer. He then dialed his home number, and by pressing a digit on the push-button phone he was able to activate his answering machine. At least he thought that he could, as he had never tried it from a foreign country before. It worked. Sean had called to tell him that he was unable to come up with any information about the so-called Society of the Ark. Well, he sure had a lot to tell Sean about them. Nina With had called to ask them over for dinner. Martha should call her back to set up a date. That was all there was. He then dialed the hotel operator and asked that he be put through to the Hilton Hotel in Zurich, Switzerland. She was asked to connect him with his wife, Mrs. Martha Burke. While waiting for the call to be placed, he dialed room service and ordered that steak he had wanted last night, and two bottles of beer. He was just coming out of the bathroom, when he heard the now familiar double ring of the phone. The operator reported that she was unable to reach Mrs. Burke as she had not arrived at the hotel as yet. She told him she left a message for her to call him at the hotel in France. He said thanks. As he was hanging up the phone, there was a knock on the door. He let in the attendant with a rolling tray, tipped him with American dollar bills, for which the waiter seemed real pleased. He picked up the lid covering the dish and saw a large steak, and that's all he saw. He had made the mistake of not ordering a potato or anything else. Everything was served à la carte.

He had finished his steak and was in the process of downing his second bottle of beer, when the phone rang again. It was Martha. She told him she had just gotten into her room, and that she was very tired. She had been able to obtain some information about the account belonging to Tom Henry, but she was too tired to even talk about it. She would tell him all about it when she saw him. She wanted to know if he could get out of France any earlier, and he said he would try. He told her to get a good night's sleep, and that he would be with her as soon as he could get a flight out. After he hung up he dialed the operator and she connected him with the reservation clerk at Swissair. The only flight leaving France for Zurich from any airline was 10:15 A.M. tomorrow. It was less than a one-hour flight, and was scheduled to land at 11:00 A.M. He booked a first-class seat, which was all they had available. He took a walk through the lighted streets of Paris for about two hours, while mulling over and over everything that had happened in his mind. He did not sleep very well that night as he kept thinking about Martha. Once again he had that feeling that something was about to go wrong.

CHAPTER 21

Martha had arrived in Geneva on Thursday morning after her all-night flight. She was unable to drop off into a deep sleep on the plane as she had planned. She had been experiencing these cramplike pains all through the flight. The plane was about an hour late in arriving, and it took her more than two hours standing and waiting in line to clear Customs. She felt a little light-headed at one point, and chalked it up to not having any breakfast. After clearing Customs, she went into a little bakery and ordered a cup of tea and a sweet roll. She drank the tea but only took a bite out of her sweet roll, and went out into the street to hail a cab. She directed the driver to take her to the Suisse National Union Bank building. The trip took only about fifteen minutes. As she stepped from the cab, she saw the very stately marble edifice with the name of the bank clearly exhibited by being carved into the stone at the top of the building. It appeared to be a three-story building, but there were steps that led only to the second floor.

She traversed all the way around the one city block that the bank building encompassed, and could not find any other entrance than to climb the steps. So she started up, and was heaving quite a bit by the time she had reached the top. She stopped for a moment to catch her breath, and then entered the revolving door. She went to a uniformed guard and asked him where she could find an officer of the bank. There were no teller windows as in banks she normally went to back in the States. There were only rows and rows of closed office doors. The guard went to a telephone, and in a few short minutes she was introducing herself to Mr. William Heller. He told her he was a senior member of the bank and on the executive board, and he would be most happy if he could help her. He clicked his heels when he shook her hand. A nice touch, she thought. He then asked her to follow him to his office.

He went on to explain to her that the ground floor of the building, and the basement level floor below it, were used exclusively to house numbered safety deposit boxes from clients around the world. The walls were eleven feet thick, and one could only gain access to the vaults while in the company of two armed guards and an officer of the bank. They would not even be able to get that far without first supplying a ten-digit number, which had been assigned to them when they took out the box, and they had to furnish two types of proof as to who they were. In addition, they had to sign the register, and the signature was then checked against the original signature on the application.

The two top floors of the building were all offices. He then asked how he could be of service to Martha. Did she want to open up an account, or was she there to obtain a safety deposit box? He iterated to her that cash accounts were handled in a slightly different manner. They required only an eight digit number.

"Mr. Heller, my husband's son, Mr. Thomas Henry Burke, was very recently killed in an automobile crash."

She had wisely brought a copy of the Death Certificate with her, and passed it over to him. He took only a cursory glance at the document, laid it face up on his desk, and focused his attention on Martha. She felt a little uncomfortable with his hard stare. He told her he was most sorry to hear the news, and offered her his condolences. He then asked her to continue.

"In his papers which he left in my husband's hands for safekeeping, we noticed that he had on deposit with this bank the sum of $500,000 American dollars." And then she decided to make up a little lie. She continued, "From the records he left with us, which we examined after his untimely demise, we believe he converted it into Swiss francs at the time of the deposit."

At this point Martha offered proof to him as to who she was. He asked to excuse himself and left the room for about ten minutes. When he came back, he was smiling.

"My dear Mrs. Burke, I have been able to verify that a Mr. Thomas Henry Burke did in fact make a deposit with us in Swiss francs of approximately $500,000 American dollars.

"As you can see, you are correct about the conversion into our currency before the deposit. It was a good thing that he did this, as approximately a year ago when he made the deposit, the

219

value of the dollar was considerably higher than it is today. The money is placed in an interest-bearing account at a modest three and a half percent per year, not compounded of course, and has increased in value to—excuse me for a moment please while I work this out." He took out his calculator and put in a few numbers. "Let's see, now that works out to be approximately $517,500. Now if you will kindly put the proper eight-digit number on this withdrawal slip, I will have the necessary papers drawn stating that you are withdrawing the money on behalf of the estate of the deceased person."

He waited, and when Martha made no attempt to fill out the form, he said, "You do want to draw out the total amount in the account, do you not, Mrs. Burke?"

Martha then had to tell him that she did not know the number. She asked if there was any way she could get at the money. He told her that in the case of a known deceased, such as in this particular case, that she would have one year from today to come up with the correct account number. After that, by Swiss banking law, the money escheats to the Swiss government. Further, after that time had elapsed there could never be another claim to receive this money from the bank, and all future dealings would have to be made with the Swiss government bureaucracy.

She thanked him for his help, and told him that her husband would be in on Monday to draw out the money. She lied again and told Mr. Heller that he did have the number of the account in his possession. She didn't know why she said this, but she just wanted to keep the door open for Mike. He advised her that Monday was a Swiss bank holiday, and that Mr. Burke should see him on Tuesday. Martha left the building and climbed down the forty-seven steps to the street level. She counted them. She was getting those cramps again and was not able to find a limousine service or cab who could take her to Zurich, so she had a cab take her to a train terminal. It was there she found out she had to wait until 3:00 P.M. to get on a train for the relatively short trip. By the time she finally registered and got to her room in Zurich she was exhausted. She had received Mike's call waiting at the desk for her, and called him back immediately.

Mike was awake long before the wake up call at 6:15. He got ready and packed his small travel bag. He looked out the window of his tenth-floor room, and was able to see most of the Eiffel Tower. Funny, he thought, I never even noticed it during the two nights that I stayed at the hotel. He met Louis Bar-Levi in the restaurant at 7:00 A.M. sharp. He was waiting for him at the same table as yesterday. After the informal greetings of the morning, and after they had placed their orders and had their coffee served, Lou was at him with a barrage of questions.

Mike remembered George's comment of yesterday about him being a pushy SOB individual, and had to agree with his assessment. He wanted to know how everything went yesterday at the plant, and if there was any new information about the stolen weapon that he would care to share with him. Mike told him he had not learned anything new about the weapon yesterday that he had not already known. Then he told him he was leaving France today, and Lou all but asked him directly if he was going back to the States. While he didn't say no, he didn't exactly say that he was flying home either. Lou wanted to drive him out to the airport, but Mike wouldn't have it, telling him he was sure he had other more important things to do. He grabbed a cab outside of the hotel, and a forlorn-looking Louis Bar-Levi waved good-bye to him.

The plane ride to Zurich was about as normal as could be, but he was held up at Swiss Customs for almost three hours, as it was very crowded during the time of day he was traveling. He grabbed a cab to the hotel, and he was delighted that most everyone there spoke English. He arrived at the hotel at 3:00 P.M., and checked at the desk to see which room Martha was in. She had already registered them as a couple, and he was able to get his own key. He let himself into the room, and found Martha asleep on the bed. He shook her gently awake, and as they embraced he seemed to think she looked a bit drawn. However, she soon bounced out of bed with a new vigor and told Mike she was hungry enough to eat a horse. Mike joked about not being able to get any horse in Switzerland, as he heard that they were sacred or something over there. They both joked a little and laughed a lot, as they prepared themselves to go out for dinner. The view of the mountains from the window of their room was just beautiful. They were together again, and as always, time seemed to stand still while they enjoyed it.

After devouring a delicious veal dish that neither of them could pronounce the name of, they returned to their hotel room. Mike first briefed Martha on the Interpol meeting. And then he told her about the additional information he had found out about the weapon at the CHEMFRANCE presentation which her father had arranged for him. It was Martha's turn now, and she explained everything to Mike about what it would take to get the money out which Tom had deposited there just exactly one year ago. She gave him the copy of the Death Certificate for Tom, which she had thoughtfully brought with her, and made Mike put it into his wallet for safekeeping.

They went to bed, and he held her in his arms until they both dozed off. There was no lovemaking even attempted. They had each other, and that was all that mattered to either of them.

Martha was not feeling too great when she awoke on Saturday morning, and Mike suggested she stay in bed for the day. She wouldn't have any of that, and in an hour she had him on the go with her to see the sights of Zurich. But they went back to the hotel room early, as Martha was experiencing those cramps again. She thought she was coming down with the flu or some other strange virus. They had dinner sent up to them in their room on Saturday evening. Martha hardly ate anything at all.

Once again, by the next morning she had perked up again, and they went for a walk in the park. But Martha got a sharp pain in her back, and those pesky cramps persisted. Back in the room while Martha was napping, Mike tried to come up with the possible numbers that Tom had used when he created his bank account. Since he had written the name of the bank and the number 500 on the index card, and Martha had been able to verify that a bank account started with $500,000 existed, then logic dictated that the name of THOR would somehow be used. He started with the basics, and assigned a two-digit number to each letter of the word THOR. He used the number of each letter in the alphabet, and came up with 20-08-15-18. This came out to the eight-digit number Martha was told by Mr. Heller that she had to have. But it was too simple. Tom would have been more devious, so Mike reversed the numbers and came up with 81-51-80-02. It had to be one of those two numbers. What else could you make up from the name THOR? Martha had awakened and wanted to go out for dinner that Sunday evening. She said she was feeling a lot better, and she looked like it to Mike, too. He was dressed, and she was almost ready when he told her he was going out to pick up a newspaper from the States. He would meet her down in the lobby in about ten minutes. He told her to take her time, as the reservations he made would hold for at least an hour.

Martha had just finished dressing and completed putting on her makeup, had grabbed her purse and was about to reach for the doorknob, when she heard a knock. She asked who was there, and was told it was the bellboy with a message from her husband. Without thinking, she opened the door and three men rushed into the room. They grabbed her and one of them was trying to insert a needle into her arm. She struck out with the heel of her hand to just under the bridge of the nose of one of the intruders with all of her might. The man crumpled at her feet, as the bone of his nose was driven back hard into his brain, killing him immediately. By then the needle had already been inserted into her arm, and she felt herself falling into unconsciousness. They pushed a large soiled linen basket into the room, and picked up her unconscious body and dumped it in. They threw her pocketbook into the basket as well. Then they covered it over with a sheet. An attaché case was left in the center of the floor, so that it had to be noticed when entering the room. They headed to the freight elevator and left the body of their fallen comrade lying in a pool of his own blood. He was dead and would no longer be a threat to them. Besides he was only local hired talent.

Mike grew impatient waiting for Martha in the lobby. He didn't really want her to be that late for their dinner reservation. After thirty-five minutes had elapsed, and he had just about finished perusing the paper he had purchased, he went back upstairs to their room. As he got off the elevator and approached the room, he could see that the door was ajar. His heart seemed to skip a beat as he cautiously pushed open the door and saw the fallen thug on the floor. Then he spotted the attaché case. He knew in a moment what that meant. He cried out loud with a shout of sheer anguish, "Oh no, oh no! Those people have kidnapped my Martha."

He carefully opened the attaché case, knowing what he would

find, but still hoping he would not. He picked out the typed message which had been left there for him. It read:

We have taken your wife, but only for a few days if you follow our orders to the letter. You are to get the sum of $500,000 American dollars in the denominations we have listed on the back side of this page. Put the money into the attaché case and have it delivered to the third booth at the **Risky Business Restaurant** at **25 Rue de St. Marie** any evening after 9:00 P.M. Do not make the drop yourself, you must get someone else to make the delivery. The sooner that you make the delivery, the sooner your wife will no longer have the pleasure of our entertainment. Ask around, and you will find out that we put on our entertainment every second day. You can count on it. If your contribution to our cause is not in our hands by fourteen days from the date we took her, she will die in a most horrible way. You can also count on that.

The Society of the Ark

Mike called down to the desk and asked that they call the police. His hands were shaking so hard, he was barely able to use the phone. When the police arrived, they made arrangements for the body of the thug to be removed. The officer in charge recognized him as one of the young punks that hung out in the seedy part of town and would hire himself out for a price to do just about anything. The detective assigned to the case read the letter. He suggested to Mike that he comply with their instructions at the earliest possible moment. He told him he was aware of another kidnapping, which had taken place in Zurich, where the ransom was not paid for nine days. When they got the victim back, all of his fingers and his toes had been broken two and three at a time. The police left the room, but they were unable to convey to Mike that they were even going to try to find Martha. He grabbed the card that was given to him by George Monroe and called each of the five numbers that he was told he could reach him at. In each case no one answered because of the time zone difference, or he was only able to leave a message to have him call him back. George Monroe was not available at any of the locations. They could not say when he would be calling in to their particular office, if at all. Mike just didn't know what else he could possibly do. George Monroe was the only person he knew who would be able to come up with that kind of money on short notice . . . and time was of the essence.

The phone rang. It was Louis Bar-Levi. He told Mike he was in Zurich, and was staying at the same hotel. He seemingly was unaware as to what had just taken place, and wanted to come up and visit with Mike. Mike told him to come on up, but that he would appreciate it if he was to bring along a bottle of scotch. When he arrived at the door to his room about twenty minutes later, Mike was indeed glad to see him. He at least had someone to talk with and to confide in. Mike told him the story of what had happened to Martha, and he was aghast with the news. He was in on that briefing at Interpol, and was well aware of what this kidnapping would do to the victim.

Then Mike looked at him square in the eye and asked him, "How come you are here in Zurich? Are you following me by any chance?"

"Yes, I'm sorry to say that I am. You left me no alternative. I am a detective, you know, and I am also interested in finding out where the new weapon was taken and where they plan to use it. You know that Israel has many terrorist enemies, and most of these members of the Society of the Ark came from their ranks. I'm sorry, Mike, but it is my job. And I am so sorry to hear the news about your wife. What do you plan to do?"

"Pay the ransom as soon as I can get the money. Once I do come up with the money, will you make the drop for me? For some reason, they do not want me to deliver the money. But right now my first order of business is to raise the cash."

Mike went to the phone and dialed each of the five telephone numbers that George had given him again. This time he got through to one of the offices which had been closed earlier. He left a message for George that he desperately needed access to $500,000 at any of the Zurich banks in order to pay money for the release of Martha. He was unaware at the time that the secretary who took the message thought it was some sort of a crank call, and while she wrote it down, she put it under the pile of work that was building on George's desk. He actually came into the office about fifteen minutes after the call was made.

Mike kept calling the numbers every two hours, and in between the calls, both he and Lou polished off the bottle of scotch.

Mike awoke at 10:00 A.M., and found that Lou could take no more scotch and had left him a note at 4:30 A.M. when he left. He said he would see him in the morning. Mike tried to shake off the effects of a hangover with a cold shower, and ordered coffee to be delivered to his room. He tried the telephone numbers again throughout the morning, still to no avail. Lou came back to his room at noon, and insisted he eat something. Mike was even more frantic when Monday drew to a close. He knew that something was about to happen to Martha. Tuesday was the second day of her kidnapping. He asked Lou to stay by the phone while he went out for some fresh air.

While walking the streets of Zurich in no meaningful direction, Mike came across a cathedral. He went inside, genuflected as he had been taught as a child, and made the sign of the cross. He even used the words "Holy Ghost," and not "Holy Spirit" as is used in the modern version of the Catholic religion. He said a small prayer that he would be able to get Martha back soon, and he wanted God to make a miracle and not let her come to any harm while in captivity. As he got up to leave, he thought of the money Tom had stashed away here in Switzerland. He was going to get at it some way. He just knew that he would.

On Tuesday morning he waited until the bank opened their doors at 9:00 A.M. sharp. He had the attaché case they provided with him. He immediately went to Mr. Heller's office, told him he was the father of the deceased Thomas Henry Burke, and that he was going to withdraw all of his son's money. He told Mr. Heller he should prepare any necessary paperwork, but that he was short on time. Mr. Heller asked him to fill out the withdrawal slip indicating the correct eight digits. He also wanted the copy of the Death Certificate in order to start the paperwork, and he excused himself.

When Mr. Heller, returned, Mike had filled out two sets of numbers on each of two separate withdrawal slips. One contained the numbers 20-08-15-18 and the other series of numbers were listed as 81-51-80-02. He explained to Mr. Heller that his son had left him a few combinations of eight digits to try. Mr. Heller balked initially, but Mike persevered and he went off to check the numbers.

Mr. Heller returned somber-looking and told Mike he

thought he was wasting his time. Mike was dejected, and turned to leave the office. He suddenly had another thought as to how Tom may have used the word THOR to set up the numbers. He would reverse the letters in the name THOR, but then he would use the direct representation of the reversed numbers to form the eight-digit number sequence. He grabbed another withdrawal slip from the desk of Mr. Heller and wrote the numbers 18-15-08-20. He growled at Mr. Heller, ordering him to check these new numbers. Mr. Heller wanted to refuse his request, but he was clearly afraid of Mike when he saw that his temper was flaring. He left the office and checked the numbers again. This time he came back with a smile on his face. Mike knew immediately when he saw his face that he had been successful.

Mr. Heller, still trying to hold his austere composure, said to Mike, "Please sign these papers, Mr. Burke. And how do you want the money?"

Mike told him to pay in American money, and to package in denominations as indicated on the page he gave to him. "I'll want the $500,000 in the attaché case, and I'll take the remainder along in my pocket."

Mike was buoyed in spirit when he left the bank and started down the steps leading away from the bank. And then his thoughts went back to Martha. It was already 11:00 A.M. on the second day, and the delivery could not even be made until 9:00 P.M. that evening. He shuddered at the thought. Somehow he knew that Martha would survive this crisis.

He went back to the hotel and told Lou he had obtained the money. As promised, Lou was ready to make the drop for Mike, and Mike was so grateful to have him around at a time like this. Lou reported to Mike that he did not receive any calls. Mike didn't need the money anymore, but he sure wished that George would return his call. He started calling the numbers that George had left with him again.

CHAPTER 22

Martha came out of her drugged state. She found herself in a dingy room without any windows. She was lying on her stomach across an old four-poster bed. Rolling over, she saw a small night table with a lamp without a shade. It was a dim lighted bulb. She saw a desk at one end of the room with a chair in front of it, and a door off to one side. Then she saw a heavier door on the opposite wall. She had no idea what time it was, nor what day it was for that matter. Her watch was missing from her wrist. Staggering to her feet, she began to steady her shaky legs, and made her way over to the door which looked less ominous. She found a toilet bowl without a seat, and a small sink. There was a half a roll of toilet paper sitting on the floor. The bathroom also had no window, and the place smelled accordingly. She was able to relieve her bladder, and got out of the small smelly room as fast as she could. The odors were beginning to make her sick. She went over to the bed and sat down on the edge. Her mind was clearing faster now, and she realized she had been kidnapped. But by whom?

Were they going to hold her for ransom? Then she remembered Mike telling her about the kidnappings which were done by the Society of the Ark. She remembered only too clearly now what Mike had told her about the treatment of their victims. A chill went through her body, and she shuddered. She made a mental note to herself that whatever she was going to be subjected to, she would survive somehow. She knew Mike would be at work that very moment trying to set her free. Yes, she was going to be a survivor, no matter what it took.

She heard a noise which sounded as if a lock was being removed. The large door opened, and a man, who was about six-feet tall and heavily built with dull red hair, entered carrying a tray. He was followed by another man who was much smaller in size and rather dark-skinned, who seemed to be grinning at her. He was carrying an automatic weapon. She recognized the second man as one of the men who had broken into her room. The tray contained a cup of hot tea, a bowl which looked to be filled with something resembling corn flakes, another small glass of milk, an apple, a banana, and a Hershey bar. Also there was a spoon and an already soiled paper napkin. The big redheaded man spoke to her as he placed the tray on the desk.

"You had better eat this, as it's all you're going to get to eat today. For your information, it is now 10:45 on Monday. To-morrow, we have prepared a little entertainment for you, and we have already drawn lots for you. I am delighted to tell you that I am second, so you will just have to wait a little longer before you can have me. Believe me when I tell you that I'm worth waiting for. Oh yes, my blond-haired beauty who can kill a man with her bare hands, I await my chance, with relish."

With that, they both left the room, and she once again heard the sound of the lock on the other side of the door. It didn't take too much thought for Martha to think that beast was going to rape her. But there was nothing she could do about it now. She went over to the food tray which they left for her, and realizing she was hungry, ate everything but the Hershey bar. She put that into the night table drawer. She would use it to give her some quick nourishment at a later time. She tried to put herself in a frame of mind to be able to handle the attack she was sure would come.

Somehow she made it through the rest of that day, and as the night came, she lay awake thinking only of the ordeal she knew would come. In the morning, at least she judged it to be that time of the day, she was able to use the bathroom again. She ate her Hershey bar, and started to feel the cramping in her stomach again. She heard sounds at the door again, and she tensed. It was the same two, only this time the other man was carrying the tray and the redhead was carrying the gun. They were both smiling and leering at her. Again they told her it was 10:45 A.M., but it was Tuesday, and the entertainment was soon to begin. The food tray contained exactly what had been given to her on the previous day.

The two of them left the room grinning from ear to ear. She

heard the now familiar sound of the locking of the door. She ate her meager food allowance, once again saving the Hershey bar.

Time seemed to move so very slowly in her captivity. Once again she heard the sound at the door. The two whom she had seen before entered first, and three other men entered the room. The last man to enter the room was slightly built, had a thinning beard, and wavy hair. He was carrying four pieces of rope in his hand, and a shopping bag.

The redhead announced, "Time for the entertainment to begin."

The first four men who had entered the room grabbed Martha and held her by the arms. They literally tore all the clothes from her body. They also tore off her underclothes. When she was naked, each one took an arm and a leg and spread-eagled her on the bed face up. The fifth man tied her hands and her feet securely to each of the four bedposts. She heard one of the men saying that when it was his turn he wanted her face down, and they all laughed. There was nothing Martha could do. She knew that she would scream and fight, but she felt so helpless just lying there. There was just nothing she could do but endure. One of the men took out a thin kimono-type bathrobe from the shopping bag and threw it over the chair. He then picked up all the remains of Martha's clothes, including her shoes, and stuffed them into the shopping bag. Four of the men left the room, but they kept the door ajar. The fifth man started to disrobe.

While he was going through this act, he started to brag about how he was accepted into the society. He went on to tell her his name was Khaled Fajr. He was recruited from the Palestine Liberation Organization after he was seen carving the hearts out of the two Israeli soldiers he had killed. As he was taking off his shorts, his manhood was already fully extended. Once he was completely naked, he called over to the four of them just outside of the door to close it. He said to them that he was, after all, entitled to some privacy. The door closed shut, and he stood at the base of the bed looking down upon Martha's naked body. She was straining at her bonds, but to no avail. As he crawled on top of her, her skin cringed at the touch of his.

He put his head next to hers and said into her ear, "Scream and yell just as loud and as much as you can, Mrs. Burke. I will not be entering your body, but for both of our sakes it must seem to the others that you are being subjected to a violent rape. Forgive me even for touching you, but I must, as I have been the winner in the drawing for you. I pray that you will be released before another two days come to pass.

"I have already told you my name, and I must tell you many other things for you to report back once you are released."

Martha did as she was told and started to scream and yell and shout obscenities at the man on top of her body.

"I am an undercover agent for the international police force known as Interpol. Believe me when I tell you I mean you no harm. Please keep up the charade. Yell and scream louder. First, you must tell your husband that I have switched the numbers four and six on the markings. He will understand what I mean by this. Also, if it is at all possible, tell him I will send him one of the bacterial weapons, if I can steal one from them. Next, you must tell him to beware of the Israeli agent. He is one of the society. Lastly, tell the Interpol people that they have selected somewhere in southern Italy to attempt to extort money with the threat to use the bacterial weapon. Keep it up, Mrs. Burke, you must let them believe that I really raped you."

With that, he withdrew himself from on top of Martha's body. Martha continued with uncontrollable sobbing. She rolled over on her side after he took a knife from his clothing and cut the ropes. As he was dressing himself, the dark-skinned man who was always smiling came back into the room and asked him in English how he had liked her. Khaled replied to him with something in Arabic, and he started to laugh. Khaled took the thin kimono-type robe from the chair and threw it over Martha's body. He ordered her to get up and clean herself up. She was to be ready for her next entertainment period. They left the room and put the lock back on the door.

Martha was sobbing deeply, but it was from happiness, not despair. She had survived the first ordeal, and was really not too worse for the wear. Now more than ever she had to get out and tell the information which was passed to her during the act of rape. Yes, she thought, it really was an act after all. She sat up on the end of the bed and thought only about being released before the fourth day. Surely Mike will have arranged to pay the ransom by then. She went back to the bed and lay down. It had been a tough day for her, emotionally and not physically as it could have been. There was a smile on her lips as she dozed off.

It was Tuesday evening at 8:30 P.M. and Lou was getting ready to make the drop-off of the money. It had been a terrible day for Mike to endure. He took a walk back to the cathedral he had visited yesterday, and gave thanks for allowing him to get the money. He had a heck of a time stuffing all of the poor boxes in the church with the $17,500 extra American dollars he had taken out of the bank. It was the least he could do. Lou left to pay the ransom, and the wait began. In less than an hour he returned to Mike's room. He told Mike that all went as planned. He was carrying a shopping bag which he said he found in the booth where he had left the money. It contained the remnants of Martha's clothes. Mike filtered through the pieces. None of the clothing contained any traces of blood. That was the only solace he could take as he stuffed the remains of the clothing back into the shopping bag, and deposited it in the large wastebasket in his room. He failed to realize that her pocketbook was at the bottom of the bag with all of her personal papers in it, including her passport. He started the waiting period, and filled himself with pot after pot of coffee. He dozed off from sheer exhaustion very early the following morning. When he awoke he realized that it was now Wednesday, the third day, and Martha was still not returned to him.

He called the police, and they had not heard anything nor had they found Martha. He had paid their blood money ransom. What else did they want? The telephone rang in the room at about 4:00 P.M. It was George Monroe. He had finally come down through the pile of work on his desk, and had come across one of Mike's earlier messages. The secretary who took the message was immediately dismissed, but that had nothing to do with the situation as it now stood. Mike told him the entire story, about how he was able to get the money to pay the ransom. And then he told him they still had not released Martha. George said he was on the other side of the world, and that he expected he could be with Mike in an estimated fourteen hours. But he would call Mike from time to time from his private plane while he was in flight, so that he could be kept up to date with any current news. He tried to assure Mike that Martha would probably be returned soon and that he should take her to the hospital immediately.

The third day had come and gone, and Martha was still held in captivity. When they had come in to bring her the food tray, she had heard one of them say that the ransom had been paid. Neither of them knew why she had not been released yet. They just shrugged, and one said it was the will of the Master, and who would want to go against that.

It was noon on the fourth day of Martha's captivity, and Mike was like a caged tiger. George had called to say that he would be delayed by another ten hours, as the plane had developed trouble which had slowed down their flight and forced them to make an emergency landing for repairs at some small out-of-the-way airport. But that was behind him, the plane had been repaired, and he was once again on his way. He was disheartened when Mike told him that they still had not heard from Martha.

Martha was not feeling very well. The cramps had started to become more severe. Each time before they started, she had a sharp pain in her lower back. She felt as if she was running a fever as well. At about 4:00 P.M. on the fourth day, while she was lying on her back in the bed, five of them came to her again. The redhead said when he saw Martha prostrate on the bed that this was his day and look, the bitch couldn't wait for him. They only had to pull open her robe to display her nakedness. She was unable to put up any sort of a fight, and they once again tied her hands and her feet to the posts at the four corners. It was the same ritual as before, and the redhead said his name was Jocko Mulrooney. He said that he was recruited into the society; and he added they really sought after him because he had slit the throats of two British soldiers, as well as the throats of their girlfriends after he had raped and sodomized them. He was from the Irish Republican Army, that sissy bunch who never wanted to profit monetarily from any of their activities: "I have all the money I ever need now!"

Martha's head began to swim as the man calling himself Jocko started to undress himself. The others left the room. She saw his naked body standing in front of her on the bed. She had a sharp pain in her back, and the cramping became intense. The last thing she felt was a rushing wetness down her legs, as she passed off into sweet unconsciousness. Jocko looked down at her and saw that she was bleeding from the vagina. He cursed and started to dress himself, as his extended penis lost its vitality when he looked at her.

"I'm not going to fuck any woman who has her period. What do they think I am, an animal or something?"

Martha was only semiawake when she heard the door to the room slam. She knew that she was aborting. The life within her was being given up to protect her from the abuse they had planned for her. She had beaten them from doing their very worst to her. For the second time in the four days, she thought. But she was really shouting as loud as she could.

"Oh Mike, please come soon and rescue me."

She fell into a deep state of unconsciousness. It was in someone else's hands now, surely not within her control anymore.

Deep in a desert stronghold in Libya, the two brothers were arguing, and their shouts could be heard all over the compound.

"You must give the order for her release. The husband has paid the ransom, and if we are to continue to be successful with getting money for any future kidnappings, then we must continue the releasing of them as we have in the past. Our credibility depends on this happening. Your petty sense of revenge is putting our whole organization into jeopardy. Don't you realize how this act of pure selfishness on your part will be interpreted by our followers? You are the Master and must, of all people, always put the good of the society before all other wants."

"It was not you who was deprived of his sight, my dear brother. You have never suffered as I have. But all right, all right, you have convinced me. I have at least received some pleasure knowing that we kept her into the fourth day. I will give the order to release her. But I want you to spend the life of one of the hirelings when she is freed. Make it look like she was found by accident. Go, give the order. Tell our men that I now approve of her release. Now that the son who caused me such pain is reported dead, I will find many other ways of obtaining my revenge on the father of the man who did this to me. His whole family will feel my revenge."

Mike had gone to the police again. They still had nothing to report. He went back to his room on Thursday night. He had no other way to move. He was trapped with the thought of the pain that Martha was sure to be suffering. He dropped his head into his hands. Lou came into the room. He told Mike he had received news from one of his spies in the Swiss criminal community. He had a lead as to where they were holding Martha. He wanted Mike to go with him, as he felt unsure of trying a rescue alone. Mike jumped at the chance. Lou gave Mike a gun, and he had another for himself.

They went into the back streets of Zurich, past the restaurant where the money was dropped off, and down two more streets until they came to an alley. They entered a doorway at the end. It had been left open. They drew their guns and moved silently down the corridor, with each of them staying as close to the wall as possible, until they spotted a man with brown skin holding an automatic weapon standing in front of a large doorway. Lou made a motion to Mike to stand far back, and returned his gun to his jacket pocket. Then he made a noise, and the guard came forward to check it out. He passed by Lou who was hiding in the shadows. Lou sprung at the man and threw his arm around his neck in a viselike grip. His gun clanked as it hit the stone floor. Other than that, the guard had made no other sound. Lou squeezed his arm tighter around his neck. There was a sharp snappinglike sound, and the guard slid to the floor, his neck broken.

Mike ran to the door. It was locked with a padlock through a hasp and bolt. Mike hit the door hard with his shoulder. Lou joined him in putting his shoulder to the door, and it finally sprang open.

Martha was still tied to the four corners of the bed, and she was lying in a pool of her own blood. A white kimono of some type was only covering her shoulders. Mike began to unfasten the bindings holding her hands. He shouted to Lou to leave and get an ambulance. He wrapped her freed body in the already blood-soaked blanket that was on the bed. He could see that she was still bleeding as he wrapped the blanket around her. She was very white-skinned. As gently as he could, he picked her up and walked through the doorway and down the long corridor. He heard the screaming sounds of a siren, and an ambulance was already backing into the alley when he arrived at the doorway. The attendants took the unconscious Martha from the arms of Mike, and they took off the bloodstained blanket and transferred her to a stretcher. Mike rode in the back of the ambulance holding her hand, while he listened to the wail of the siren as he felt the ambulance weave its way through the streets.

At the hospital, he was met by George. One of his people had gotten the news to him when his plane had landed that Martha had been found. Mike told him that she didn't look too good to him as he saw them wheeling her away to the emergency room. He had heard them saying they had to clear out the remains of the fetus, and it would be necessary to cauterize her to stop the bleeding. While they were waiting for word from the doctors, Mike told George he wanted to get Martha back home as soon as possible. George went to the telephone, and after a few minutes on the phone came back to where Mike was pacing in the waiting room. The doctor came in and told them that she was now resting comfortably, as they had to give her two transfusions. He thought she would be all right, but had to say that it was too early to really be able to tell. George asked if she could be moved, and the doctor said that he supposed so. George said that his plane was being fueled at this moment and would be standing by for takeoff as soon as they got to the airport. He had made arrangements to have a doctor and a nurse on board for the flight back home. They were to bring along with them any possible medical equipment they thought they would need. They were allowed to see Martha for only a moment before they started to prepare her for the long trip to her home. She was awake, but very groggy.

Mike asked her how she was doing, and she replied, "Quite a bit better than you may imagine. Have I got things to tell you. Don't worry, my darling, I'll make it all right. Right now I've got to get some sleep."

The injection she just received was starting to take effect. She saw her father standing behind Mike. She gave him a big smile before she closed her eyes.

On the way out of the hospital, Mike was met by Lou who wanted to know how his wife was doing.

"Thanks to you, my friend, I feel she will be okay in time. I owe you one. Thanks for all your help, I don't know what I would have done without your help."

Mike grabbed Lou in an embrace, and then turned and

headed toward the doorway where they were wheeling Martha through on a hospital gurney.

They were only an hour into the flight when a grave-looking doctor told them that Martha had started to hemorrhage again. He had plenty of plasma on board, but he really should be giving her whole blood. To do so he told them he must have an exact blood type match. Mike said they could try him, but her father should have a better chance for a match. George then told Mike he was not Martha's natural father. He had married her mother when she was already pregnant by another man. It had been the classic case of the butler who did it, and then the cad ran off. Martha's mother was a maid in George's household at the time, and George had been very fond of her. He related that he was sterile and could never have a child of his own. In his own way he had loved her mother, and he had wanted desperately to have a child. So he married her, and she died in childbirth. George had raised Martha as if she was his own, which by every law on the books, she was. George asked Mike to never tell Martha about this secret of his, and he assured him it was forgotten already. The only other chance for a direct transfusion was from Mike. They tested his blood, and found it was a match to that of Martha's. They were both Type A positive. The transfusion took place, and Martha's color seemed to brighten immediately.

At about one hour short of their arrival time at Westchester County Airport in White Plains, New York, the doctor woke up a dozing Mike with the news that Martha needed another pint of whole blood. The doctor was reluctant to take it from Mike again, but what other choice did they have? So another transfusion took place. This one left Mike feeling a bit fuzzy. The plane landed as scheduled, but they were held up from transferring Martha to the awaiting ambulance. The Customs Official had not yet arrived. Since this was not an international airport, George had pulled some strings to set the plane down at a location nearer to the hospital. The Customs Official had to travel all the way from Kennedy Airport in Queens, and was reportedly held up in traffic. The fact that they did not have a passport for Martha when he finally arrived slowed up the process again. But George used up a few of the IOUs that were owed to him, and after a few phone calls Martha, Mike and George were speeding in the ambulance to General Hospital in Nyack, New York. They were already going over the Tappan Zee Bridge when Martha gained consciousness. She did look a lot better to both of them. When they arrived at the hospital about seven minutes later, it was a very confident Dr. Ah Leh who was taking charge. She sent Mike home to get a good night's sleep. He looked pretty terrible himself, she told him. He left the hospital knowing Martha was in the best possible medical hands.

CHAPTER 23

Mike awoke with a start. He reached for Martha, and her not being there brought him quickly back to reality. He reached for the phone and dialed the hospital. They put him through to her room and he held his breath while he waited with hope that she would answer the phone. Dr. Ah Leh picked up and told Mike she was just about to call him. Martha was doing just fine and was under heavy sedation until about 3:00 P.M. It was then that Mike looked at the digital and read that it was now 9:00 A.M. She told him she had just sent George Monroe home. He had been at the hospital all night. She further divulged that all of Martha's vital signs were fine, and the bleeding had stopped completely. She then told him that Martha would never be able to get pregnant again. She was already late in her childbearing years, and this pregnancy, the subsequent inability to carry and eventually aborting was her body's way of saying so. There were no signs that she had been raped. Dr. Ah Leh had been told by Mike the previous night that he thought this had happened. And therefore, she told him, she felt there would be no emotional scars to heal. Mike was advised that he could visit with her at 3:00 P.M., and that he should busy himself with other things until then. She would meet him back at the hospital then and provide him with an update on Martha's condition. He thanked her for the good news, and hung up the phone. Now he was really puzzled as to what had happened. He remembered Martha's words to him, about having a lot to tell him, back in the hospital in Switzerland. He had to put these questions off until he could hear the answers from Martha herself.

He showered and put in a call to Sean at his office. Then he realized it was Sunday, and dialed his home number. He told him what had happened to Martha, and that he had used the money from the Swiss bank account squirreled away by Tom to pay the

239

ransom. He once again asked his son to be extra careful. He was sure they would try in some way to harm him as well.

He grabbed breakfast at McDonald's, and went to the office at about 11:00 A.M. While browsing in the office at his desk, he heard movement coming from the apartment upstairs. He took his .45 out of the locked drawer where it was stored, and proceeded to cautiously enter the upstairs apartment. He pushed back the door which he could see was left ajar, shoved the gun in front of him, and shouted, "Freeze!" He was face-to-face with a startled but smiling Guardian Angel. Before he was able to say anything, a light brown, Asian-looking, medium-sized young man with black crew cut hair emerged from the bathroom.

"Mike, I'd like you to meet Joseph Soo Leh. Yup, I got him out. It was really like duck soup. All I had to do was follow the leads that I already had in California, and I found him, along with fifteen other guys of various nationalities that were in the same predicament. They now are all in the hands of the West Coast Office of Immigration and Naturalization. Joe, here, is in my custody pending a hearing scheduled back East rather than in the West, at my request."

"So very pleased to meet you, Mr. Burke. Mr. Guardian here has done nothing but say these wonderful things about you. You must be a very special person to him. And you are to me, too."

Mike sat himself down in the nearest chair. He was flabbergasted. This had to be the start of good things happening to him. Guardian then told him the details about his search.

"When I first arrived in California, I went to the post office of the location from where he sent the letter. They gave me the boundaries of the area they covered. Next I went to the local library and was able to get maps of the area. Then I went around to stores in the neighborhood and had people tell me where the wine-producing vineyards were located. Some of them just grow grapes, you know. They don't do any processing, just grow them for other larger vineyards. I came up with sixteen vineyards, and started to visit them. I got lucky and noticed a doctor's license plate parked at one of them; I think it was the tenth one I had gone to. I wrote down the plate number and had it checked out with one of my friends at the California State Police. He gave me the name of the doctor, and I paid him a visit. I must have scared the shit out of him when I flashed my old identification from when I was working for the Justice Department. He remembered being called out on New Year's Day to treat someone, and gave me the name of the place where he treated Joe. He was only a doctor who normally serviced the vineyards doing a house call, and he didn't want any trouble. I believe him. He had no reason to lie about it.

"Then I went over there to get some proof, and I noticed sixteen guys working in a field picking grapes. This was too much of a coincidence for me to pass up, so I went over to the big guy in charge and started asking some questions. He was belligerent and started to shove me around. He knocked me to the ground and pulled a knife on me. I used that gadget knife you had given me, and I got in the first cut. Not so bad for a guy with the use of only one good arm. I had slashed his arm and he gave up. Just like that. Then I called the police and told them what was going on. They in turn called the Immigration and Naturalization people, and the rest is history. So here we are!"

"Well done. I see you haven't lost your touch. Will Dr. Ah Leh be surprised to see what we have for her this afternoon."

Mike then filled Guardian Angel in on all that had transpired with Martha and himself. He wanted to go over to the hospital with Mike, and Mike wouldn't have it any other way. He took the both of them out to eat a hearty lunch. They had much reason to celebrate.

They arrived at the hospital at ten minutes to three. Mike called up to the room to be sure that Dr. Ah Leh was there. He was told she had just returned to the hospital after only a few hours at home. It seemed that she was with a patient that was brought in last night from overseas who was in critical condition when she arrived at the hospital. And then this gabby nurse volunteered that the patient was in real fine shape now. Mike was happy with the news anyway. They went to the third floor of the hospital to Martha's room. Mike suggested to Joe that he wait outside in the hall. He wanted this to be a surprise for his sister.

He went in alone, as Guardian chose to wait out in the hall with Joe until after Mike had a few private moments with his wife. Martha was sitting up in bed. She was beaming radiantly, and Mike handed her a bouquet of a dozen red roses. They kissed, and Dr. Leh had to butt in before Mike jumped into the bed with her.

She gave Mike a good prognosis about Martha's condition. She could leave the hospital in another two days, but had to stay in bed mostly for another week. After that she could start to move around more normally. But she cautioned them both about not having any sex for at least six weeks. Now it was Mike's turn to lay on some good news.

"There is someone waiting to see you outside this room in the hall. Please send my friend in to visit with Martha in about another ten minutes."

Dr. Ah Leh seemed to be a bit taken aback when she was so summarily dismissed by Mike. Mike was already busy quietly telling Martha that Guardian had found Dr. Leh's brother. Dr. Leh was leaving the room sort of dejected. Her dismay turned into a nirvana beyond her wildest expectations when she first saw her brother. There were many tears and sobs of sheer joy, followed by a jabbering in their native Vietnamese tongue. Mike let the door to Martha's room close, and first asked Guardian to give him ten more minutes alone. They hugged again, and then Martha told him about everything that had taken place since she was kidnapped. She was explicit, especially when she told him about the fake rape she had acted out with the man who introduced himself to her as Khaled Fajr. He told Martha that he would relay the information she had given him to France, and directly to the person he knew at Interpol headquarters.

In her excitement to tell Mike everything, especially the conditions under which she learned about the information, she completely forgot the remark about the Israeli agent.

Guardian knocked on the door and Mike asked him to come into the room. Martha put out her arms to embrace Guardian, and he seemed embarrassed by her warmth. But one could tell he appreciated it. After a visit of more than an hour, Mike and Guardian left Martha's room. Mike said he would return to visit with her after dinner, but right now he had to go wake somebody up in France.

After dropping off Guardian and Joe at the apartment, Mike went down to his office and dialed the number of Jacques Paisson. To his surprise he was still at his office. It was 5:50 P.M. here, that put the time at 11:50 P.M. in France. Mike told him everything his agent Khaled Fajr had told to Martha, with the exception of the item she had completely forgotten. Jacques stopped Mike for a moment to tell him that Khaled never killed those Israeli soldiers. He did cut out their hearts, but they were already dead after being hit by a fragmentation grenade someone else had thrown while they were in the Sabra Refugee Camp located in the West Bank. Jacques told Mike he would call a friend of his in southern Italy by the name of Aldo Anestaisa. He was a known arms trader, and had links to the Italian and Swiss Secret Services. If anyone could sniff out something about the threatened use of one of these chemical bombs, he was the man.

The reason Jacques was still so late in the office that night was because one of the ex-army men he had once been stationed with had been reported kidnapped by the Society of the Ark. He had since left the army for a high-paying civilian job at CHEM-FRANCE, but Jacques understood he was no longer with them. His name is Alphonse Krenn. While it was known his family was very wealthy, they nonetheless said flat out they would not pay for his release.

And now his wife was trying to arrange capital from some private sources.

"She has asked me to help." Jacques lamented to Mike, "This, paying ransom, is against the rules for me, you know." They both hung up after Mike had said, "Good luck."

It was Monday afternoon and Martha was due to come out of the hospital on Tuesday. Mike was edgy, and his morning walk, even though it was cold and rainy, did little to put him at ease. He waited until 9:15 and put in a call to Sean at the office.

"Look, son, I can't tell you exactly why, because I don't even know myself, but I want you to get out of that apartment now. Don't go back to it at all."

"Gee, Dad, I just ordered a new king-sized bed. It's due to be delivered and set up for me today. That old one that Tom slept on is as hard as a rock, and I just asked Lois to live with me and she accepted. We plan on getting married in June. I told you that I'd be careful, so stop worrying."

Mike could not get him to change his mind on the subject, and he hung up the phone in a huff.

Sean went into Lois's office at work and told her about the call from his dad. She too thought he was being alarmed about nothing. They were going to dinner and a Broadway show that evening. After, they went to a little bar in the Village where they agreed in advance he would place the engagement ring on Lois's finger. Then they would spend the night together at his place and break in his new bed.

The night had gone exactly as planned, and they got out of the cab in front of his apartment house at two minutes to two in the morning. As they walked to the elevator, the whole building shook with a violent explosion. They ran back out in the street and looked up. The top of the building was on fire. It looked like his apartment in the penthouse had been completely demolished.

Mike's phone rang and he reached for it after he was sure it would not stop ringing. His eyes focused on the digital clock. It was 4:05 A.M. Sean told him the news. Mike told him to head for Jennifer and Charlie's house, and to stay with them until he saw him later that day. Sean said he had Lois with him, and Mike told him to bring her along. As soon as he hung up, he called his daughter, Jennifer. The phone rang at least fifteen times before a groggy Charlie answered. He was finally able to wake Jennifer, and he told her to plan to house both Sean and his girlfriend. Jennifer meekly agreed, after her father told her he would explain everything to her in the morning. After that he had a hell of a time falling back to sleep. He was due to pick up Martha from the hospital at 10:00 A.M.

He set his alarm for 6:30 A.M. He had a heck of a lot of things to accomplish today. The phone rang again at 6:00 A.M. It was George Monroe. He had heard about the plan to bring Martha home from the hospital that day. He insisted they use his limousine, with him in it of course. He wanted desperately to see how his daughter really was doing after her ordeal.

Mike could do little more than agree. Besides, he wanted to brief him on everything Martha had told him, especially the part about the threat to use one of the weapons in Italy. By 6:30 A.M. he was at the apartment talking to both Guardian and Joe. He wanted them to move into his daughter's house in order to provide twenty-four hour coverage for them. He really didn't want to use Joe, but under the circumstances he had no other choice. He was available now, and besides he had to stay close to Guardian as he was responsible for him. They both agreed, packed up their things, and Mike drove them over to Jennifer's.

Charlie had taken the day off, and they all had a long talk while sitting in Jennifer's kitchen. Mike laid it on the line: They were all in danger from this terrorist group, and they surmised it was because of something Tom Henry had done. They were powerless to change what was done. They had to arrange their lives to cope with it, that is, until they were able to do something about the situation. Mike assured them he would. Lois would go to her family's home. She could only see Sean at work and on weekends. There was no sense in exposing her to their wrath as well. She argued like hell, but in the end she had to agree. They called a limo service to drive her back to her family's home in New York City. Mike called George With's office and got him on the line. Yes, it was his company that held the insurance on the condominium in New Jersey that had the roof blown off it late last night. The bomb men had just called to tell him it was definitely plastic explosive, and in a very large quantity. They found remnants of it mixed with the insides of bedding, or mattress stuffing. And they found the remains of the clock-timing mechanism. Mike thanked him for the information, and hung up. Then he told Sean, who acknowledged that it must have been the new bed he had just ordered.

Mike got back to his office to see George Monroe's limousine stopping in front. He was right on time as usual. George commented, as he was getting into the car, that Mike looked somewhat frazzled. So on the ride over to the hospital, Mike brought him up to date. It had been a long day already, and it was only 9:50 A.M. when they arrived.

To say Martha was overanxious to leave the hospital would be an understatement. She had become more perky each day she was there, and having both of her men being there to pick her up, brought a tear to her eye. Mike already decided she would be staying in the apartment over their office during her rehabilitation period, and she agreed. They made her comfortable on a soft couch in front of the TV, and George made his apologies and left. Mike went back up to talk to her, and to tell her about last night, and where his kids were. She told him there was something important she had to tell him, but she could not remember. They shrugged it off.

It was 2:30 A.M. when Jennifer had an urge for some ice cream and coaxed Charlie out of a sound sleep to get it for her. He went downstairs without turning on the lights, and had just passed the door leading to the basement when he heard the tinkling of glass being broken down the basement. They had left a large iron frying pan on the stove after they had heated it to make it dry and not rust after washing. Charlie picked it up and walked over to the basement door. After what seemed like an eternity of waiting, the door slowly opened into the kitchen, and a large redheaded man attempted to step up the final stair into the kitchen. Charlie hit him in the high part of his face just as hard as he could swing that six-pound frying pan. The blow caught the man Martha had known as Jocko Mulrooney, squarely on his nose and forehead simultaneously. He crashed back down the stairs and lay at the bottom unconscious. He never knew what had hit him, and he would be out of it for quite a while.

While this little scene was being played out downstairs, a half-sleeping Joseph Soo Leh heard the window in his room being raised. He remembered he had opened it a crack before retiring, and he had seen then there was a shed portion of the house just outside of the window in the room he was asked to sleep in that evening. Guardian was sound asleep in the other twin bed in the same bedroom. Once the intruder was halfway through the now open window, Joe was at him. He grabbed his head and twisted it violently, causing him to black out. Guardian was, at the same time, leaping out of his bed, as he had only been feigning sleep. Joe beat him to the punch.

The house came alive with the disturbances occurring on both floors. Guardian and Joe were dragging the intruder Joe had immobilized down to the first floor.

In the meantime Sean was helping Charlie drag the heavy and bulky body of the redheaded intruder to the same level. Sean asked Jennifer, who was surprisingly being very cool through all of this, if she had any rope with which to tie their hands. Joe interrupted and asked for her sewing kit. He apparently had a better way. He took out two of her longest sewing needles. First he went to the right ankle of the man he had rendered unconscious, pulled down his sock halfway, and inserted one of the needles while rubbing it between his fingers. The man's left arm seemed to go completely limp. He repeated this with the left ankle, and the right arm also became limp. Then he went over and repeated the same steps with the big redhead, and achieved the same results. He said to the astonished looks of his audience that he had just anesthetized both of their arms. He noted that it should last for approximately twenty-four hours, which he said should be long enough for the police to take them into custody.

They were still looking at him in a quizzical way, when he said to them quite matter-of-factly, "I was training under an Old Master to be an acupuncture specialist in Vietnam before my sister, myself, and other members of my family were able to escape the Communist takeover of the South. I had to give up my studies at this time. Before this I was already an authorized medical doctor. I know I look very young, but I am twenty-eight years old."

By this time both of the men had regained consciousness, and neither one could do anything other than to sit meekly in a chair waiting to be arrested. As the redhead was being put into the squad car, he contorted his jaw and bit down hard. He had managed to break through the capsule containing poison which was carried in one of his teeth. He was dead in less then a minute. It was his choice to die then, rather then to risk the punishment meted out by the society for failure. The police were shocked by this act, and they rushed off to the hospital.

At 6:30 A.M. Guardian called the apartment and woke Mike from the arms of Martha. He congratulated him on his instincts, and told him all that had happened. No, there was no need for Mike to come over. Everything had been nicely put to bed. The entire household was all going back to bed to try and get some sleep. That is, all except Charlie and Sean. They couldn't take another day off. He hung up.

No sooner had Mike's feet hit the floor when the phone rang again. This time it was the overseas operator calling from France. Jacques was on the line shortly and told him that his contact in Italy had put him in touch with the Milan Antiterrorist Police Chief, one Ippolito Searra. He had received word that the Mafia head in Locri, Italy, had been contacted by the Society of the Ark.

"This man, known as Antonio Guardino, has been at large,

247

despite being under sentence for twenty-eight years in jail. The society wants him to pay $10 million, American money, or they threaten to destroy his family and his friends.

"He has until 8:00 P.M. tomorrow night to pay up, or be shown the worst they have to offer. I think the society knows they will never extort this money from this man, and they are using it as an excuse to test the weapon for themselves. They want to give the world an example of their power to destroy human life on a grand scale. My superior, a man you have already met, has given me permission to ask you to join with us in trying to stop this slaughter, wherever it is scheduled to take place. We thought that perhaps you, not being an agent of Interpol, would be able to talk to this Mafia chief and describe to him what can happen."

Mike glanced at his watch. If he hurried, he could catch the same Concorde flight that he had taken last week. He told Jacques to expect him at Interpol headquarters at 6:00 P.M. his time and hung up. He immediately called Guardian and told him to leave Joe at Jennifer's, and to get back to the apartment to cover Martha. He made his plane at Newark by a hair. Things were happening so very fast, and he could not, would not fail his family.

At 6:30 P.M. he was getting out of the cab in front of the Interpol headquarters building outside of Paris, France. He was met at the front door by Jacques and his superior. He did know the man. It was the big guy with the pockmarked face who had frisked him the night of the briefing. He was introduced as Marcel Dubot. Jacques apologized, but they were heading back to the airport to get on a flight for Palermo, Sicily, and from there they were to motor to Locri. It would be a long night for all of them.

During the trip, Jacques told Mike that if Marcel did not have good feelings about him when he was attending the meeting, he would not have let him in the door. Jacques told him that this man had great instincts about people, and he was convinced that Mike was a good man, but more important, an achiever. It was 4:00 A.M. when the car rolled into the small town of Locri on the Island of Sicily.

Mike had been traveling for more than twelve hours and was dead on his feet, yet it was only 10:00 P.M. in the evening back home. He chalked it up to jet lag, but he had to get some sleep. They found a small local hotel to catch a few hours of sleep. A meeting had been arranged between "Mike Burke, American Citizen," and the wanted felon, Antonio Guardino. It was to take place in the vestibule of the Church of the Holy Mother at noon. No police, no hoods, just the two of them. It would be Mike's position to tell the man that he should pay the extortion money if he could. The meeting had been scheduled as a personal favor to Ippolito Searra who had grown up in the same poverty-stricken town as Antonio. Somehow, even though on opposite sides of the law, they had remained friends. Antonio was known to understand English, but did not speak it very well. It was all they had going for them.

At exactly noon Mike walked up the steps leading to this very old church. He went through one of the large stained glass encrusted doors into a dimly lit vestibule with statues of saints lining the walls. Antonio was in the shadows, and Mike was unable to see anymore than a dark figure of a man.

In broken English he said that Mike should give him one good reason why he should give in to the extortionists. Mike told him everything he knew about the Society of the Ark. He told him about the kidnapping of his wife, and all that entailed. He described the biological weapon that was in their hands. And then in a last appeal, he said he was sure they would use it on his people. Antonio said only what sounded to Mike to be a thank you, and then he was gone into the shadows.

Mike went back and briefed Jacques and Marcel. Ippolito had joined them to hear Mike's report. They waited. A courier came to Ippolito and brought news that the word was out that Antonio was raising the cash, but doubted he could get it all before 8:00 P.M. that evening. The hours passed, and it started to get dark. The streets started to fill with people after the dinner hour, as many of the women and old people gathered at the church for the evening novena. Antonio had stationed his men outside of the church, allowing only those they recognized admission. At exactly 8:10 P.M. there were screams coming from people outside of the church. The four of them rushed up the steps of the old church and opened the door and looked inside. Everyone was dead. The body count came to seventy-three men and women and four children. It was a horrible sight, the faces of the victims were twisted and distorted as their hearts had stopped functioning. After the

249

bodies had been removed, Mike, Jacques, Marcel, and Ippolito walked through the church aisles over and over, in an attempt to find the device which had caused so much death. It was Mike who spotted the half-grapefruit size canister. It was attached to a bulb-type backing and set in a row of many. It was made to look like a spotlight that was shining on the altar. It was that simple. Mike carefully picked up the spent canister and turned it over. It had a large number 2 pasted on the back. He handed it to Jacques and asked that he ship it back to the people at CHEMFRANCE.

With that he turned and said to the others that he wanted to go home.

CHAPTER 24

Mike arrived back at Newark Airport at 5:00 P.M. on Thursday evening. Guardian had driven Martha down to pick him up, despite Mike's arguments with her on the telephone from his last stopover in Europe. But he was glad to see her anyway. He told them about the slaughter he was a witness to back in Italy. He had already called George Monroe and gave him the bad news. There were still four more of these "killer things" out there, was the way George had described them. Martha said that two packages had arrived for him while he was gone, and she put them on his desk. He never went to his office that night, settling for an early dinner made in the microwave, a large glass of scotch, and a hot bath. Martha was still bothered by whatever it was she had forgotten to tell Mike.

Next morning he approached the first of the two boxes. One was about half the size of a shoebox, and when he opened it he saw that its contents were encased in foam. He knew what it was immediately and had Guardian take Martha for a ride around the block. In fact, he ordered him to get her out of the building. He went up to the apartment, grabbed the largest pot they had and filled it with hot water. Then he put the pot on the stove to start it boiling, and went back down to his office. He gingerly lifted the top of the foam container, and two separate components were displayed. He picked up the one which he knew contained the weapon and very carefully carried it into the kitchen in the apartment.

By then the water was boiling, and he dropped it into the pot, put the cover on it, and promptly ran like hell out of the building.

After about fifteen minutes Guardian drove up with Martha. He had taken her to a local diner for a cup of coffee, but she was pissed. Then Mike told her what he had just done, and she didn't want him to go back inside the building.

He went back upstairs anyway, and turned off the gas from under the pot. Most of the water had already evaporated, and it took about another two hours before it had cooled sufficiently to be able to take out the canister. Mike placed it back in the foam box, after spotting the number 3 displayed on the back of it. Then he picked up the small transmitter with the button and the light and looked on its back. It also had a 3 displayed. After this was done, he started to wrap the package in the original paper it arrived in and found that it had a letter enclosed.

Dear Mr. Burke,
I am sending you this complete unit which I have stolen from them. They do not even know it is missing. I feel I cannot send it to my contact in Interpol as I am sure the Israeli agent is a member of the society. But you know that already because your wife has already told you. I hope that she is well. I am sorry for having to touch her body in that way, but it was necessary at the time. Please tell her to forgive me. I am sending you another package. This one only contains a trigger mechanism. It says that it is for number 4 unit, but I have switched it with the number 6 unit which is also still in their hands. Their next target is the presidential debate due to take place on April 21. You must be able to stop it.

Khaled - 9 April

He quickly opened the other smaller package and found the transmitter detonator, which was labeled with a 4 on the back. He put it into his desk drawer.

Mike leaped to the doorway and motioned to Martha and Guardian to come back into the building. It was Friday the twenty-first. The debate between the eight remaining presidential candidates of the majority party was due to take place at 8:00 P.M. in Madison, Wisconsin. He tried to call Jesse, but his office said he was on location with the candidates.

He then asked Martha, "Honey, I know you are supposed to be resting, but is there any chance you can fly me to Madison, Wisconsin, today? The lives of so many people may depend on my getting there in time to find the device before it is exploded."

"You bet I can. I'll call them at Ramapo Airport and have them service the plane while we are in transit over there. I'll still need some time to file a flight plan. But let's go."

"Guardian, I want you to send this package to the CHEM-FRANCE company in Paris by Express Mail. Call George Monroe and let him know what we have here. Tell him it has been disarmed in the manner they described to us at the meeting. Then call Jacques Paisson at Interpol and give him the same message. Don't mention anything about the smaller package that I received. Also, tell them both I'm on my way to Madison to prevent another slaughter, that is, if I can find and disarm the damn thing in time. We've got to go. We'll be in touch."

With that, they were out the door. Martha read the letter Mike had received from Khaled in the car. She told Mike she was sorry she had goofed and forgot to tell him about the Israeli agent. Mike made some remark like he was going to skin that bastard Irv Klein alive. He thought back to that night at the Interpol briefing. So that was how he knew who he was, and what he was doing at Interpol that night. He knew for sure now that he never told either of them about himself before they were interrupted to be seated.

The plane was ready, and Martha made sure the tanks were full. She had calculated they could make Madison by 4:00 P.M. with two stops for fuel on the way. Mike told her he felt that should give him enough time to get to Jesse, and to be able to have the whole area cleared. Soon after they were airborne, Martha told Mike she was thinking about adopting an older child since she would never be able to have any children of her own. Mike seemed to think that would be a great idea, but he made Martha promise not to do anything until after they could put this whole mess behind them. She agreed, and he could see the happiness in her eyes.

They ran into some severe thunderstorms and Martha was forced to fly almost 300 miles out of their way to get around them. Then they were grounded at one of the airports where they had to stop for fuel while an oil spill had to be scrubbed off the tarmac. It was already 7:30 P.M. on Mike's watch when they set down in Madison. Mike was able to rent a car, but he told Martha to stay at the airport and rest. He now had the feeling he would be too late as he started driving toward Madison. His heart sank when he saw that the road signs indicated it was thirty miles away. He pushed the pedal to the floor. He knew he was going to be too late. He thought if nothing had happened yet by the time he arrived he could maybe get Jesse to clear the room where the debate was being held. Then he looked at the digital clock on the dash of the rented car. It was showing only 6:45 P.M. They had picked up an hour with the time zone change.

It was 7:25 P.M. when he screeched to a stop just outside the auditorium. A screaming police siren had wailed behind him for the last three miles of his journey. The policeman had gotten out of his car and was about to arrest him, when Jesse pushed his way through the crowd that was gathering in front of the auditorium. Martha had called from the airport and gotten a message through to him. She told him Mike was on his way. Jesse showed his Secret Service badge and vouched for Mike, and was able to defuse the situation.

Mike told him to clear the entire area, as they would be subjected to a terrorist biological attack. Jesse told him that the League of Women Voters, who were sponsoring the debates, had received an extortion letter demanding $10 million. They chalked it up as a crank letter, and only turned it over to Jesse this morning. Jesse asked Mike for more information on these guys that called themselves the Society of the Ark. Mike assured Jesse that this was no idle threat and that these terrorists were for real. They both spent the next fifteen minutes arguing with the people who were responsible for the debate, trying to get them to put it off and to vacate the auditorium. It was to no avail. They tried talking to the candidates themselves, but they were trying to show how brave they were and would not use their heads. It was now two minutes to eight, and the candidates were positioning themselves on the stage, where the television cameras would carry the debate live across the entire country.

In a desperation move Mike ran onto the stage looking for the device. He spotted a spotlight that was not working. Looking around the stage, he saw a covered plastic garbage can. He ran over to it and dumped its contents on the floor. He dragged it over to the row of spotlights, and started to unscrew the one that was not lit. When he had it out, he saw the number 5 displayed on the back of it. He threw it into the garbage can, and snapped the two handles over the lid. Leaping off the stage with the garbage can in his hands, he started running down the aisle of the auditorium. By now Jesse was running in front of him trying to clear the way. He could hear the introductions of the candidates being made in the background. He leaped through the doorway and continued running toward the parking lot, which was full of cars but was now vacant of people. He stumbled and dropped the can, and he saw one of the handles come loose. He fastened it into place again and continued running away from the auditorium.

It was then he felt and heard the sound of a firecracker going off in the container he was carrying. It was followed by a series of pops, each one growing less in intensity. He stopped, put the garbage can down, and then stood there both still and silent. He was still alive. His watch showed two minutes after nine. He had never reset it to the correct time in Madison.

They had been right all along about how to neutralize this thing back at the CHEMFRANCE briefing. Jesse came running up behind him. He told Jesse that the bacteria in the garbage can had only about fifteen seconds more of life.

Jesse was asked to send the closed garbage can back to the CHEMFRANCE company in Paris. Mike got into his rental car for the drive back to the airport and into the arms of a grateful and relieved Martha. They stayed in the Madison Hotel that night, and ordered from room service the two biggest filet mignons that any two people had ordered and never ate. They had no appetite. He made a call to George Monroe to tell him there were only two more of those weapons he had labeled "killer things" out there, and he had in his possession the detonator for one of them. He called the Interpol office in Paris and left the message for Jacques when he came in the next morning. Then he called Guardian, to let him know they were safe and would be home tomorrow. After 11:00 P.M. that night, the two of them went out to get themselves a Wendy's Doubleburger, and it tasted like steak to them.

They flew back to Ramapo Airport the next day. They made it in record time as this time they had a tail wind.

It was Sunday morning when Martha heard Mike on the phone making reservations for himself to fly to Israel on Monday morning. He had a score to settle with a certain Israeli secret policeman, one that couldn't wait any longer.

When the plane landed in Tel Aviv, he quickly cleared through Customs. When he was asked why he was visiting Israel, he replied that he was there to visit an old friend. He took a cab to the office address on the business cards he had been given by Irv Klein, and his friend Louis Bar-Levi that night in Paris. He was directed to a basement office, which was way out of the mainstream corridors of the building. So much the better, thought Mike. He came to an office which had the name Irving Klein on a small plate next to the door. He knocked and entered the office without waiting for an answer. Irv was sitting at his desk and was surprised when he saw Mike enter his office. He recognized him and offered him his hand to shake. Mike reached over the desk and grabbed his hand, and pulled him toward him. He swung his left hard and caught Irv square on the chin, and Irv immediately dropped to the floor behind the desk. Mike saw that he was not out yet, and sprang around to the back of the desk with the intent to land a karate chop to the back of his neck to render him unconscious. But Irv was only shaken up by Mike's blow, and deflected the downward motion of the chop and grabbed Mike's arm. He came up from the position he was in on the floor, and had Mike's arm twisted behind his back. Mike struggled, but was unable to break the hold, as Irv fastened his other arm around his neck in a stranglelike hold.

Irv yelled, "Listen to me, Mike. I know what you think, but you have the wrong man. I am an agent of the Mossad, and was assigned to the Secret Police with the special assignment to watch Louis Bar-Levi."

"I don't believe you. You gave yourself away when you started asking all those questions back in Paris that night. How did you know who I was or what I was doing there? I never had a chance to tell you before we were interrupted."

"That's so simple, my dear Mike. Louis told me when we were sitting down. I just thought you had already told him about yourself, and so I just naturally engaged you in the conversation at the time."

Irv loosened his hold on Mike. He turned around to face him. It started to make sense to him. Irv continued.

"The Mossad became interested in finding out more about Louis when he started living far beyond his means. It was then I was assigned. That was after his previous partner was found with his throat cut. Last night we raided Lou's apartment and found evidence of his betrayal. He was found in his bed in a stupor, after having taken a large dosage of cocaine. We took him first to the hospital and extracted the poison cap on his tooth. I am due to see him today, and to start the interrogation. Do you wish to accompany me?"

Mike nodded that he would. He was hardly able to look Irv directly in the eyes. He had attacked him without thinking and without having any evidence. He was ashamed of his action and annoyed at himself for not seeing through Lou's manipulation of him. It all became very clear to him now, Lou's being around to deliver the ransom and his coming up with the location of where Martha was being held. And then he also killed the guard, quite obviously now he knew it was because he had recognized him as one of the society who were holding Martha. He could have kicked himself, as the truth flashed through his mind.

And to think, he thought he was his friend, when at all times he was his hated enemy. Irv took him to a room below the base-ment level they were already on. Mike asked him to find out from Lou the location of the terrorist stronghold in Libya. Mike watched through a small window in the door, as Irv prepared an injection of Pentothal, and skillfully injected it into the arm of Lou who had been strapped into a chair. He saw his lips moving and an-swering every question being put to him by Irv. Lou was seen to write something down, and Irv interrupted the interrogation to go to the door. He gave Mike a piece of paper. He told him it was the coordinates of the location of the terrorist camp. Mike asked him what was to be done with Lou.

"Once we have drained all possible information from his now open mind, we will take him to a zone near Lebanon. He will be executed there, and it will be made to look like he was killed while an attack by the Shiite Moslem group Al Fatar took place. You see, we cannot allow him to stand trial, as we have too many do-gooders around here as well, who will want to give him freedom because of his previous war record. We cannot allow this travesty of justice to happen. He will be officially listed as killed while in the service of his country, and we will give him a military hero's funeral, of course."

Mike told Irv he would brief the people back at Interpol, and he was sure they would maintain their silence in this matter. They would be glad to have the traitor out of their midst.

Mike thanked Irv, shook his hand gratefully, and returned to the street. He grabbed a cab back to the airport. While waiting for his plane he placed a call to George Monroe, and he was surprised to get him on the line. After Mike's update of the situation, they agreed on a plan of action. Mike's plane landed at Newark, and Martha and Guardian met him at the airport. It was only a stopover for Mike, and Martha passed to him the trigger mechanism he had received from Khaled and had placed in his desk drawer. George Monroe's private plane was waiting for him. It had as its destination the British Isles.

At the terrorist camp in Libya all the members of the society had gathered with the exception of only a few who were away on an assignment. They were meeting in the large tent located at the center of their complex. The Master had just told them of his plan to use one of the devices as rent for their next year's use of the Libyan base camp. It was costing them $5 million a year, and General Radaffi had agreed to take one of these weapons as payment. They had just realized that one of them had been stolen, and that another, number 4, was missing its detonator. He had decided that since the theft of the five prototype weapons had not brought them any monetary advantage to date, this would be a good way to cut their losses and to still get something for it. No one would dare disagree with the Master's decision. He went on to say that they had caught the traitor from their group and they were all to be present for the start of his execution.

It was then that General Radaffi arrived to pick up his alternative to the rent of their base. They fussed about him and gave him the box containing number 4. They left the box containing the number 6 weapon open. It did not have the trigger mechanism, and they thought that somehow it was never packaged in the first place. He did not check the detonator in the box that he was given to make sure that the numbers matched. In fact he was afraid to take it out of the box. But he was so happy to have this weapon to use against his enemies.

It was then that they brought in a badly beaten Khaled Fajr. He was identified to all of them as the traitor, and he was to receive the traitor's death. The Master had spoken. They stripped him of all his clothes and tied his hands and legs to a large table which had been brought into the tent. The Master's brother approached the squirming Khaled and withdrew a dropper filled with acid from a large decanter. He placed a drop on each of his cheeks, then one on his chin, and continued putting additional drops of the acid on different parts of his entire body. Khaled started to scream in agony as the first drop was applied and started burning through his skin. The smell of burning flesh was in the air, and General Radaffi reeled and became sick and his men ushered him out of the large tent and over to his awaiting jeep. He clutched onto his package, not knowing that it would not work with the detonator he was given.

Back in the tent, Khaled's body went limp as he passed out from the excruciating pain to which he was being subjected. They were attempting to revive him so that he once again could feel the pain.

Outside General Radaffi and his troops heard a faint sound as if an aircraft was approaching. They looked up and saw a strange aberration of an aircraft coming over the trees in the distance, the noise of its engine still not loud at all. They dove to the ground, and tried to bury themselves into the sand as this thing passed overhead.

Mike was in the backseat of the newest stealth-type airplane that was being developed by one of George Monroe's companies. It was made of a new lightweight material, which not only gave it a vast round-trip flying range, but it absorbed rather then deflected radar signals better then ever before. The design of the aircraft was different from anything flying today, and it must look to someone on the ground like it came from a different planet. Mike was aware that this plane had no weaponry at all. It was him and the test pilot, who was a personal friend of George, coming in under the protective screen of the Libyan Missile Defense System.

They had made it so far undetected, and now it was all up to Mike. He held the detonator in his hand and pressed the button as soon as the plane came near the edge of the desert compound. He noticed that it had failed to glow which would indicate detonation had taken place. He pressed it again as the plane flew directly over a large tent, holding his finger on the button. He knew it was the last chance.

The indicator light flickered and then started to glow. The glow remained for only five seconds, as the plane continued its flight path and was soon out of range of the camp. He gave the thumbs-up signal to the pilot, and he banked the plane to set the direction to home. Mission accomplished, thought Mike, now if we only got them all.

It took about three minutes before General Radaffi and his men realized that no bombs were dropped and that no strafing had occurred. They got up from the ground and brushed themselves off. General Radaffi thought he should say good-bye to the men of the Society of the Ark who had done this great favor for him in getting him this new biological weapon. He went back to the large tent and pulled open the flap covering the entrance. He was aghast to see all the faces of the men twisted in death. He failed to see the shallow smile on the lips of the man who was tied to the table. General Radaffi immediately ordered that the entire camp was to be razed and everything, including the thirty-seven bodies in the tent, were to be buried under the sand. When he returned to his office, he issued a report to the news services that a peaceful group of nomads he had allowed to live on Libyan territory were attacked and killed by another American wave of air strikes. He further reported that his antiaircraft had destroyed more than half of the attacking force.

Mike took a call from Jacques about two days after he had returned back home. He confirmed to him that the Society of the Ark was no more. The few terrorists still at large would be tracked down and disposed of by members of the various police forces from around the world. They no longer had an organization or a leader. They were already outcasts from their original terrorist groups.

It was time for Martha and Mike to live like normal human beings again, and to pursue those things that were dear to them. His family was free from the threats on their lives.

EPILOGUE

So many things, both good and bad, had already taken place in their lives. And then, some of the nicest things started to happen.

Joseph Soo Leh applied for and was given permanent residence in the United States under the Alien Amnesty Law, which even though it had expired he was still allowed to qualify under because he had been held a prisoner. He was taking an internship at General Hospital. This was at the same hospital where his sister had become Chief of Surgery. He lived in the apartment while not at the hospital, and met and fell in love with the Filipino secretary Martha had hired by the name of Maybelle Divina. They hit it off immediately after they met at the office, and they were already talking about getting married as soon as he was licensed in the United States to work as a doctor. He was going to specialize in acupuncture.

Dr. Ah Leh had operated on Guardian Angel's left arm and had been able to give him back almost ninety percent of the use of his arm. They had started dating, and it was looking as if they were becoming an item.

Sean used the money he got from the insurance on the penthouse apartment to put a down payment on a three-bedroom house in Tarrytown, New York. He married Lois in one of the most lavish ceremonies Mike had ever been to, compliments of Lois's fine Jewish family.

Jennifer and Charlie had a pair of twins on Labor Day as projected. They both had red hair at birth, but it was starting to darken up and look more like Charlie's color of hair every day.

The lawyer came to visit Martha and Mike at the office one day and told them he was able to have the arrest of Martha on the gun charge dismissed, and that it was wiped completely from the record. That meant that Martha would be able to get licensed in the State of New York as a Private Investigator whenever she passed the exam. He submitted a bill for $6,000. While Mike was writing out a check, he confessed that he had sent a picture of Martha in a bathing suit, which was taken by his friend Jack Meehan when they were in Hawaii, to a contest for Marilyn Monroe look-alikes. When Mike asked him how they judged it, he told them they sent it back to him as not even being close. He gave the picture to Mike, and he looked at it and put it in his wallet. He mentioned something like the fact that those guys must be blind, and Hubert Fowland agreed. Martha laughed at it all. She had been too busy concocting her own little surprise for Mike, one that she was sure would make him happy.

It was September 26, and they had just come back from a visit with Jennifer, Charlie, and the twins when she broke the news to him that they were flying out the next day on her father's private plane. No, it was not a vacation, and he did not have to even pack a bag, but he had to bring his passport. She said that it had to do with something she had been working on for quite some time now. He had to not ask any questions, and she told him it was the culmination of all those long-distance calls that she had been placing to all parts of the globe. He went along good-naturedly, and was surprised to see that George Monroe was taking the trip with them.

The private plane took off from Westchester County Airport on a beautiful fall morning. The flight took eight hours, and they landed in Ireland. They stayed at a local inn that night, and Mike was still not getting any answers as to why they were there at all. Martha just kept telling him to trust her.

They drove out the next morning to someplace in the beautiful Irish countryside, and walked to a large old building which looked like a school. A nun greeted them and ushered them into a small but comfortable waiting room. In a few minutes the door to the room opened, and two young children entered the room holding on to each other's hands. They both had beautiful red hair. Martha hugged them both and introduced Mike to them as their new father.

The boy was aged nine and his name was Tom. The little girl was six years old and her name was Kathleen. Martha went on to explain to Mike that the mother and the father of these two young children were visiting their relatives in Ireland. They were from Boston. The children were with the relatives when the parents were both killed instantly, when the automobile they were driving in went out of control after the gas pedal had stuck, and the car had hit a large stone embankment. They had no relatives in the States, and the few relatives they had over in Ireland were too poor to be able to support two more children. They were theirs if he wanted them.

Mike looked at the two miniatures of what was once so much a very important part of his life. The little girl reminded him of Kathleen when they were growing up back in Ohio. The little boy looked exactly like a young Tom Henry when he was his age. He grabbed the two children in his arms, and then embraced them both. He stood up, and took each one of them by the hand. He said to Martha and her father, who were both standing there with tears rolling down their faces, "Let's all go home now. This has to be more than just a coincidence."